OUT OF THE DARK

Also by Caro Ramsay

DCI Christine Caplan thrillers

THE DEVIL STONE *
IN HER BLOOD *

The Anderson and Costello series

ABSOLUTION
SINGING TO THE DEAD
DARK WATER
THE BLOOD OF CROWS
THE NIGHT HUNTER *
THE TEARS OF ANGELS *
RAT RUN *
STANDING STILL *
THE SUFFERING OF STRANGERS *
THE SIDEMAN *
THE RED, RED SNOW *
ON AN OUTGOING TIDE *
THE SILENT CONVERSATION *

Novels

MOSAIC *
THE CURSED GIRLS

* *available from Severn House*

OUT OF THE DARK

Caro Ramsay

SEVERN
HOUSE

First world edition published in Great Britain and the USA in 2024
by Severn House, an imprint of Canongate Books Ltd,
14 High Street, Edinburgh EH1 1TE.

severnhouse.com

Copyright © Caro Ramsay, 2024

All rights reserved including the right of
reproduction in whole or in part in any form.
The right of Caro Ramsay to be identified
as the author of this work has been asserted
in accordance with the Copyright,
Designs & Patents Act 1988.

British Library Cataloguing-in-Publication Data
A CIP catalogue record for this title is available from the British Library.

ISBN-13: 978-1-4483-1411-9 (cased)
ISBN-13: 978-1-4483-1412-6 (e-book)

This is a work of fiction. Names, characters, places and incidents are either the product of the author's imagination or are used fictitiously. Except where actual historical events and characters are being described for the storyline of this novel, all situations in this publication are fictitious and any resemblance to actual persons, living or dead, business establishments, events or locales is purely coincidental.

All Severn House titles are printed on acid-free paper.

Typeset by Palimpsest Book Production Ltd., Falkirk,
Stirlingshire, Scotland.
Printed and bound in Great Britain by TJ Books,
Padstow, Cornwall.

Praise for the DCI Christine Caplan novels

"A breathtaking combination of police procedural and twisted psychological thriller"
Kirkus Reviews on *In Her Blood*

"A taut, suspenseful police procedural with plenty of dark twists to keep fans riveted"
Booklist on *In Her Blood*

"Gripping . . . Ramsay has created a fascinating character in Caplan"
Publishers Weekly on *In Her Blood*

"Dark, suspenseful and atmospheric"
Booklist Starred Review of *The Devil Stone*

"Intriguing characters people a challenging mystery fraught with peril"
Kirkus Reviews on *The Devil Stone*

"Caro Ramsay fully deserves a place in the upper echelons of Scottish crime writing . . . top-notch"
Financial Times on *The Devil Stone*

About the author

Caro Ramsay was born and brought up in Glasgow, and now lives in a village on the west coast of Scotland. She is an osteopath, acupuncturist and former marathon runner, who devotes much of her time to the complementary treatment of injured wildlife at a local rescue centre. She is the author of thirteen Anderson & Costello thrillers, two standalone novels of psychological suspense and the DCI Christine Caplan thriller series.

www.caroramsay.co.uk

PROLOGUE

The Grim Reaper never shouts.

He whispers as he taps you on the shoulder.

I still smile at the irony of thinking that I'd been blessed with time; time to think, time to plan. It's something not given to many of us, a few moments of reflection, to put right a few wrongs, to say some goodbyes.

The dying is definitely for the present.

And it is for me.

It's all going, slowly slipping, and I am focusing on one thing: the clock. Don't wait too long as you never know how long you have.

There's more to life than life.

There's always love.

Or maybe revenge.

My one wish? My only wish is that someone will be holding my hand.

A kind and gentle hand, soft fingers folding into mine.

Instead of lying on the kitchen floor, kicking and screaming. Powerful fingers, gripping my neck.

Ever tightening.

ONE

The man lay in bed, the duvet pulled neatly across his chest, the crisp collar of his navy-blue pyjamas tucked under his chin. A few strands of grey hair wandered over his balding head and the glow from the bedside lamp highlighted patches of dried sweat. His face was angled towards the window, and there was a slight curve on his lips, as if he had seen something fly past and it had amused him. He would, it appeared, have been extremely comfortable if the deep chill to his skin had not been due to the failure of his heart to beat. The lower half of his body, as the duvet was lifted, revealed the heels of his feet and the backs of his lower legs to be a deep cerulean blue.

DCI Christine Caplan looked again at the man's face, thinking how quiet this house was – a modern house in a cul de sac of seven four- or five-bedroom properties on the Old Luss Road. Not far from the main road north, two streets away from the loch, a busy wee village with a pub at the corner of the street and a twenty-four-hour shop. Yet in this room, as the sun set on an autumnal day, nobody had heard a thing and two men had died.

Her team, a local PC plus the crime scene techs, were moving with the minimum of disruption. Nobody was talking. The officers working in the cramped upstairs landing, kneeling at the base of the banister where the other body had been found swinging by the neck, were also quiet.

Caplan made her way back down the stairs, switching her phone off when it buzzed in her pocket, the drone echoing round the stairwell of the house. The nurse from the hospital had an unerring instinct to call at exactly the wrong time. The body from the banister had been cut down and was being laid, in an unzipped body bag, for more photographs.

'The neighbour's in the front room, a Mrs Lorna Gains. She's very shaken. She found them. Well, she found this one. She didn't go upstairs.' The young constable on duty, Karl Pordini, was not looking too firm himself.

'How many fatals have you attended?' Caplan asked him quietly, keeping her eyes on the body, now having his arms folded as the zip closed.

'Oh, a few,' he said, nodding.

Caplan looked at him. Raised an inquisitive eyebrow.

'Well, they're normally spread over the road, needing cut out of a vehicle, or lying with a needle still in their arm. Never seen one like this; just hanging there. *Countdown* was on the telly when I came in, his phone was on the arm of his chair. It looked like he'd got up to put the kettle on.' He shook his head slightly. 'I never thought suicide would be like that. Dictionary Corner with Susie Dent and then you hang yourself. It's not right.'

Caplan gently patted his upper arm. 'Don't worry, it's not something that you should ever get used to. It's good you're picking out the anomalies. We don't judge it as suicide until somebody tells us it is. Who's your DCI?'

'Ted McCormack. Clydebank.' Pordini's gaze floated up to the cut ends of the rope tied round the upper banister. 'Why was he there? Why was his partner upstairs?'

'We don't know the chain of events yet. Keep an open mind. I'll have a word with Mrs Gains now. Get some fresh air if you need to, and if you find DS Craigo wandering around, send him in here.'

'I don't know him.'

'Wee guy. He'll look confused, like he's forgotten where he's parked his car.'

The constable nodded, smiling. 'Oh, I know who you mean.'

The house was testament to two art lovers, with warring tastes. For a modern house, the living room was huge, but dominated by three Chesterfields placed round a fine Persian rug. Heavy brocade curtains the colour of aged Barolo hung in neatly ordered swathes, with no telltale dust marks on the leading edge. The walls were painted a rich bottle green, covered in ornately framed oil paintings of naked ladies, God and thoroughbred horses. But the eyes were drawn to the fifty-inch TV screen placed neck-achingly high on the wall, still paused on the *Countdown* conundrum. Underneath was a single geometric bookcase, the top shelf full of leather-bound classics, the middle of popular paperbacks, the bottom shelf stacked with art and photographic magazines, three holiday brochures piled on top, one lying open at Santorini, and ruffled as if it had been thrown there from across the room.

Thornton, the female constable, was perched at the far end of one of the sofas, close to an older lady sitting on the corner of the next one. The neighbour, Mrs Gains, had her sweatshirt sleeves pulled over her wrists, hands fisted around a damp tissue; a woman who had popped out to see a neighbour and walked into a nightmare.

Neither heard Caplan come in. Thornton was waving her pen about, figuring out who lived where in the cul de sac, who might have seen what, who gossiped about whom.

Mrs Gains noticed Caplan first, as the words 'it was a terrible situation for them both' left her lips.

The constable stood up. 'This is Lorna Gains who lives next door. DCI Caplan.'

'A DCI for a suicide,' said Mrs Gains, regarding Caplan with eyes still bright and full of intelligence.

'Oh, modern policing. All forensics and computer searches,' Caplan said as if that was an answer to the question.

Mrs Gains nodded in the same way the late Queen used to; polite but not convinced.

'Lorna knew the couple well. She lives next door to the right, has done so for twenty years. Roderick Taylor and his partner Peter Todd have lived here for fifteen. She wasn't aware of any noises during the night, nothing out of the ordinary. It's a very quiet cul de sac. But she had a note put through her door at some point last night. She found it this morning. It asked her to pop round, said she might need her key.' Thornton paused for the significance of that to sink in. 'She came over at five this afternoon, knocked, nobody answered, so she used her key and saw Peter Todd hanging there. She called us.'

'Did you go upstairs, Lorna?' asked Caplan.

The old lady shook her head. 'Thankfully, no.'

'Still, what a terrible shock for you.' The constable nodded sympathetically.

'When did you last speak to them?' Caplan asked.

'Monday evening. I'd taken an Amazon parcel in for them and Todd collected it. I asked him how Rod was, and he said things had taken a bad turn. I asked him in for a gin, but he refused. Looking back, he didn't seem himself.' She dabbed with the tissue again.

'And when was the last time you spoke to Rod?'

'Rod? Not for a long time.'

'Days? Months?'

'Months. He wasn't about much.'

Caplan asked, her voice kind and encouraging, 'Even with you living next door?'

Mrs Gains tried to think. 'You know, I haven't seen him for ages, not out and about, but he was in the house. He had visitors.' She sighed. 'Poor Todd, coming home to that.'

'Was it usual for Todd to put a note through your door?'

'Oh yes. Todd was a note leaver. Beautiful handwriting, italic nib, brown ink but that last note was . . . untidy. I should have known something was up.'

Thornton leaned forward slightly. 'She was telling me that Rod was living with a terminal diagnosis.'

'Todd told me, in case of emergency. But I was to keep it to myself.' Gains dabbed her mouth with her tissue.

'They'd talked about how it would end.' Thornton nodded towards the hall.

'They'd talked about suicide? Can you recall what he said?' Caplan asked Mrs Gains softly.

'Just that if it got to the stage where Rod was in pain, or it started affecting his behaviour, then that was something that neither of them wanted.' She paused, taking a deep breath to steady herself, fingers clawing at her chest. 'I guess it had got to that point. It's terrible.'

'Why don't you take Mrs Gains home for a cup of tea?' Caplan said, the police shorthand for a further conversation to take place, in less stressful circumstances. Just as she spoke she heard the door open behind her, followed by a dull thud and a sharp intake of breath as her sergeant stubbed his toe on the side of a Chesterfield.

Pordini had found Craigo then.

Her sergeant leaned over and whispered to her. 'Control are asking you to switch your phone on. They want MIT at an incident in Glen Douglas, it's on your way home.'

Caplan got up and said goodbye with the usual 'we'll be in touch'. She added to Thornton, 'Make sure you get the note bagged up.'

Caplan looked at her watch. It was already quarter to eight, a Friday night. She was near Balloch and the caravan where she lived was ninety miles away. She wondered what 'on your way home' meant.

She walked towards Craigo who was now standing at the door, his beige jerkin jacket looking more crushed than usual, reminding her of a few arrests she'd made outside the public toilets in Glasgow in her youth.

He was looking past her, staring up at either the curtains or the TV screen. Then he sniffed and followed her out of the room.

'DS Craigo, you're in charge here. It's pointing to either double suicide or one suicide and one natural causes, but you never know. And get that Amazon delivery.'

'Deceitful?' he asked.

'What? What's deceitful?' She realised he was staring her down, those pale-brown eyes regarding her as a hawk regards a mouse.

'Deceitful is the answer to the conundrum.'

Caplan pressed the accelerator on the Duster. Glen Douglas. It sounded vaguely like a bad country and western singer. It was twenty-eight miles to the north, twenty-eight miles closer to home. Funny that the house in Glasgow, where Emma and Kenny had grown up, had so quickly been replaced in her heart by a caravan, a roofless cottage, and Pavlova, a stray cat with a bad hip and four kittens.

The Duster left the dual carriageway, swept round the wide bend towards the twists of the loch road, and came to a sudden halt behind a long queue of traffic.

Lowering her window, she looked out. All she could see out the front windscreen was the panting face of the yellow lab in the back of the car in front.

She closed the window and sighed, letting the Rod and Todd situation drift into her mind. Rod and Todd. Off pat. Something about that scene had disturbed her. Maybe the same thing that had sparked the solution to the *Countdown* conundrum in Craigo's brain. Even the inexperienced Pordini had picked up on the fact something was 'off'. The perfection of it. Maybe they were very well organised, logical people. If they were, then why think about a holiday when one of them was so ill?

The suicide or natural causes dilemma would be answered by the post-mortem exam. Something seemingly benign – she winced at the choice of word – may have tipped the balance. Or it could have been discussed, planned, a date put in the calendar. It was a gift not given to many, to decide when and how a person spends their final hours on earth. Maybe Rod didn't want to spend his last few days in a hospice. No matter how comforting they were, they weren't home. Craigo would be tracking how they had spent their last hours. There'd be a meeting between McCormack and the Fiscal and it would move forward from there.

Moving forward was certainly not what her car was doing. Her phone rang. She pressed to accept the call.

'Christine Caplan?' The voice didn't wait for a reply. 'It's Sadie Watson from the Lorn Hospice.'

'Oh sorry, yes, been meaning to get back to you.' Caplan winced a little as she asked, 'Are you sure it's us she wants to talk to? It is Rachel Bellshaw we're talking about?'

Watson was quick. 'Rachel Ghillies as she is now. Just wants to see you and Sarah and Lizzie, the girls she was at college with?' The voice drifted up to a whisper; Caplan's uncertainty was catching.

'Oh, yes,' Caplan confirmed. 'We graduated together from police training college.' She couldn't say they'd been friends. They hadn't.

There was a short silence on the phone, then Watson said, 'She's in palliative care. Maybe sooner rather than later?' Another silence that Caplan couldn't fill. 'It seems important to her.'

'We'll try for tomorrow. Thank you for letting us know.' She swiped the phone off and sighed, feeling guilty for suspecting that Rachel might have some ulterior motive. Turning up the radio she started drumming her hands on the arc of the steering wheel to 'Dancing in the Dark', Springsteen's gravelly vocals filling the Duster. She didn't look at the stillness, at the rock wall to her left, the black, oily water or at the darkening sky.

Rachel Bellshaw? As far as Caplan could recall she had married some top brass, stalling her own career to support his. Rory Ghillies? The name and face floated in front of her: tall bloke, handsome, moustached in the image of a Hollywood Golden Age star.

She picked up her phone and messaged Linden and Fergusson on their group chat to say the nurse was hinting Rachel might not have long. Then she typed: *Tomorrow morning, 11 a.m. Lorn Hospice?*

Fergusson came back immediately with a thumbs-up emoji which gave Caplan some confidence in the shape of their friendship. They'd had a blazing row last time they'd met but they were both grown-ups – they could put their personal feelings to the side for a dying colleague.

Her phone beeped. Linden. *Who's Rachel again?*

Rachel Bellshaw? Beat me at the hundred metres on sports day. Tennis champion. Small, glasses, brown bob? messaged Caplan.

Iain McLean took a photo of us at that twenty-first party. The

one where Bobby McDade climbed into a field and punched a llama, Fergusson replied.
Caplan couldn't help message back. *Alpaca. Four broken ribs. The alpaca or McDade? Moany wee cow. I burned that photo.*
Fergusson then posted the photograph. Caplan looked at it. They had changed. They had stayed the same.
Ha ha. Chris hasn't changed her hair at ALL. Still looks like an opera singer with worms. Did Lizzie join the polis when she was twelve?
Lizzie did look absurdly young, a riot of curly fair hair tumbling over her chubby cheeks.
Ahh, look at the state of you Sarah! How come you look younger now than you did twenty-one years ago?
Surgery. I pouted before it was trendy. Note my fashionable scarlet hair. Is that wee Bellshaw peeking round the corner? Neb.
Rachel was in the picture but slightly apart from the other three. Her broad face was serious through her smile, her sharp bob cut shining, not a hair out of place.
Married Rory Ghillies.
Oh aye, that selfish arse. What does she want? Oh, I know, she has a list of colleagues she wants to say 'Fuck You' to. And we are top of the list. Wee cow.
A text came through, direct from Fergusson to Caplan. *How much has she had to drink?*
Another text from Fergusson. *We'd better stop this before she gets so pished she sends it to the wrong person, like Rory Ghillies.*
Does she know him?
Knew him as in shagged him? Yeah, probably!

Caplan looked up as headlights flared on the loch road ahead of her, figures walked around and blue lights flashed on her side of the road. Some vehicles were doing U-turns and driving back the way they came. She rolled down her window again, the night scents rushing into the car as Caplan looked for any sign of the obstruction. A boat being relocated? A static caravan? Transportations of that size were usually in the small hours of the morning to minimise disruption.
Then she saw the beam of a torch bounce on the tarmac, sparkling the white lines. A man in a high-vis jacket was waving the Volvo

in front of her through, but indicated that she was to stay put. Then he walked away, leaving her sitting in the dark, her fingers resuming their impatient dance on the steering wheel before another man came back, noted her registration number and took a slow walk round the Duster. After confirming with him that she was the DCI who'd been requested at an incident in Glen Douglas, she was told politely to follow his vehicle and he'd escort her up the glen. She opened her mouth to ask what was going on, but he'd already walked away.

It was an order, spoken with clear authority. Few people spoke to senior police officers like that. Those that did tended to have very short hair. The little nagging idea in the back of her mind stretched to a fully formed thought. Sure enough, within a minute, a black Land Rover appeared. It was almost half past eight, it was dark, but even so, Caplan thought it had blacked-out windows. It was also exceptionally clean.

She followed them as they turned up a narrow strip of tarmac with two immediate hairpin bends set into the steep incline. The Land Rover ground its way through the gears. The Duster, much lighter, made easy progress to the top of the hill where they continued along the road, wider now, the surroundings flattening out to farmland she could barely see, a blackened world on either side, only the lights of the cars giving sense to the landscape.

Caplan realised they were heading to the far side of the glen. The Duster twisted and turned for six miles along the road, to where a body had been left in the deep and absolute night. Somewhere near the military base?

She swore as the road took a ninety-degree turn. Like she was the only DCI around; this was only twenty-odd miles from Clydebank. Where was McCormack? This was his patch. She'd heard the name Glen Douglas recently, but couldn't think where. Something her husband had said to her. She made a mental note to ask Aklen when she got home. The car in front of her slowed and she looked out and up, trying to see where the ben stopped and the sky began, but it was now black upon black.

After fifteen minutes of slow progress an arm appeared out the driver's window of the car in front, pointing repeatedly to the right. She drove on, seeing lights in the distance, along a further track which opened out to a car park, the sign forbidding wild camping and cooking over an open flame.

As she approached, a young cop, high-vis vest over his jumper, pointed to a space that had been left vacant. He followed the car as she parked, waiting at the driver's door for her, not allowing her time to ask any questions or pull her boots on.

They must be right at the opposite side of the glen, near Loch Long. But all she could see in any direction was darkness, apart from the dancing group of lights in the distance, hidden then revealed by her companion as his torso swayed with his gait.

She followed him, coming across her colleagues sooner than she had expected, disorientated by the landscape and the consuming darkness.

Three of the men present stepped back as she approached, retreating into the night.

'Hey, Caplan? Over here.'

Caplan looked up the slope towards a large rocky outgrowth on the steep grassy slope of the mountain, then saw a flash of a torch glint from a large mass of ferns.

'Will you manage through there? You should have brought your wellies,' commented her young companion.

Caplan looked at the mire and stayed put. The torch bearer moved towards her, two stick-thin legs poked out the bottom of a bulky jacket, a phone in her hand and a green pointy hat that made her face more elfin than usual.

'Leonora? Hello!' Then Caplan saw the bump under the anorak. 'Bloody hell, when are you due?'

Leonora Spyck looked down at her swollen abdomen. 'Not as soon as it might appear. Hope it's not twins, and one hides behind the other at scan time. Him indoors has a cold, snorting and sniffing all over the place. You'd think he was dying. I was bloody happy when I got the call.' The pathologist turned her head towards the white tent being erected, presumably around the body that was still hidden from view. 'What do you think of the MoD plods eh? They're really something else.' She nodded subtly towards the four men standing in the shadows, silent, watching. 'I thought the CID was bad, but Jesus.'

'Present company excepted.'

'Sometimes,' conceded Spyck. 'At least you get on with it. We've no power-crazed form-filling timewasters in our department. Ryce and I are hyper efficient.'

'You deal with dead people who don't argue,' said Caplan. 'Are you spinning this out for overtime, or do you really not want to go home?'

Her companion was serious now, not responding for a moment while the figures up the slope were highlighted by the torch beams and repeated flashes of the camera. Caplan could hear indistinct chatter over the sound of squelching boots caught in the mud as the light blue of the Tyvek suits was swallowed by the tent. A figure left the group and started making its way towards them.

'Here's Brady, the Fiscal. The MoD plods called him out, nothing to do with me,' said Spyck, turning away slightly. Such was the internecine power struggle between the Fiscal's office, the crime scene technicians, the police, the pathologist and the crime scene manager and, in this case, the Ministry of Defence. Caplan always agreed with everyone, so everyone thought she was on their side; as far as she was concerned, she was in charge.

'DCI Caplan.' She introduced herself as Spyck wasn't going to.

'Yes, I know.' The figure pulled his mask down with a gloved hand. 'John Brady.'

'Oh, I didn't recognise you. Sorry.'

Brady dropped his voice so that they would not be overheard, although nobody was nearby. 'Had a bit of a to-do regarding the arc lights with our friends over there. The military. The base isn't close, but they're very sensitive. We've the body of a young man, been dead for about a week, but had been lying there for less than four hours when he was discovered.'

Caplan ignored the eye-roll from Spyck. Brady had quoted her verbatim. 'You're good, wasted as a Fiscal. Ryce should recruit you.'

It was Brady's turn to eye-roll. He was semi-retired and desperate to be completely so. 'Our friends in the military'll give you a report, but simply? They drove past, no body. Four hours later? Body.'

'Really?' asked Caplan, looking at the ferns, the landscape, the ground cover.

'Please don't ask the obvious,' said Spyck through the side of her mouth. 'That's all they're saying. Nothing there at 14.15. Body there at 18.14. Very precise with their times.' She looked up at the infinite sky. 'Maybe the circling vultures alerted them?'

'The timings are precise and reliable?' asked Caplan, quietly. 'Them being who they are?'

Spyck smiled. 'I'm not brave enough to question it.'

'They want us out ASAP,' warned Brady.

'We'll go when we're ready,' said Caplan, knowing the same words were on Spyck's lips. 'Be nice to see it in daylight.'

'Because of the depth of the glen, there's little light down here as soon as the sun drops. There's a high outcrop up there . . .' said Spyck.

'Couldn't be as simple as a hillwalker getting too close to the edge and falling to his death?' asked Caplan, searching for some logic.

'Could be. If he was walking around nude. There's a vegan place on the lochside, so he might have come from there,' joked Brady.

'Walking around nude after he'd been dead for a week,' added Spyck, dryly. 'It might be that the military are wrong, and he's been lying there for ages, and nobody noticed.'

'Three words,' said Brady. 'TikTok challenge. Cheers.' He doffed his hat at them. 'You'll be hearing from me. I'm finished for now. I'm going back to my bed with a hot chocolate and *Love Island*.'

The two women said goodbye as he walked down the path, one of the MoD plods slipping out from the shadows to accompany him, though how a semi-retired Fiscal with a bad back would pose a threat to the defence of the country was slightly puzzling.

'So, suspicious and unexplained death?' asked Caplan. 'TikTok?'

'Or yet another weird drug that makes folk think they can fly?' said Spyck, then perhaps remembering that Caplan's son had nearly died from such a drug, said, 'Sorry.'

'No need, it happens.'

'We suspect an internet challenge of some sort. We've had planking on top of high places. We've had see how many days you get to stay in hospital from the paracetamol overdose, and that's kids as young as eight. We've had the choking game: see how long you last before you pass out. And recently, three dead from shoving marshmallows in their mouth. Here the guys get naked and try to climb down rock faces.'

'Yes, we caught one at the Falls of Falloch before he jumped in the water, and another one over at an old quarry at Neilston who was stopped before he could do anything reckless.'

'Is it illegal?' asked Spyck.

'Only if being stupid is now illegal, but the NHS is stressed enough. Have you something for me?'

'Well, I *was* thinking that him and his mad mates have been out.

This poor bloke has fallen, sustained fatal head injuries, and his mates have scarpered. But the grass looks recently broken. I tend to agree that he's not been lying here for very long. His bare feet don't look like they have walked anywhere.' Spyck leaned forward, acting like a spy. 'And he's been dead for a while, so died after a prank then brought here for deposition. Somebody not wanting a corpse complicating their lives.'

'Interesting,' said Caplan.

Spyck held up her phone. 'Want to see the body without getting your feet wet?'

Caplan peered at the images, their colours intense and dramatic against the total darkness of the ebony night. The deceased was lying surrounded by ferns, naked, on his side as if he had tumbled from a height, spinning as he landed. His blackened, battered head was partially hidden by his right forearm as he nestled in his bed of green. His skin was darkened to blue in places, like Rod Taylor, the Balloch man, found dead, snug under his duvet. But this young man had not died in peace.

She looked at Spyck. 'You really think this is a social media challenge?'

'I'm hoping so. Or one of those dark web things.' She looked at the phone, regarding the body. 'Good God, we don't want it to be anything else. Do we trust their story?' She nodded over at the men still in the shadows. 'I mean, imagine the paperwork if those buggers moved him. Or even worse, undressed him and moved him.' She rolled her eyes. 'Or killed him, then undressed him, then moved him. Or even worse, undressed him, then . . .'

Caplan smiled. 'Maybe just stick to cause of death for now.'

'You're no bloody fun at all.'

TWO

William Robertson listened to his daughter moving around in the bedroom overhead. Bethany's usual Saturday morning routine; the slamming of the bathroom door, running water, door opening and ricocheting off the stopper, then rummaging in the cupboard for matching trainers.

Now, there was dancing footfall on the stairs.

He scooped the poached eggs onto the toast, slipping the spoon into the sink. Bethany was down, on time for once, humming something to herself while she wound up her headphones and stuffed them into her blue rucksack. As usual, Tufty the owl, a small soft-toy mascot she'd had since she started uni, was hanging from the back. She'd been obsessed with birds of prey since she was a little girl. The big black bag was dumped on the floor.

'Where're you heading off to today? Somewhere exciting?'

'Usual Saturday.' Bethany sat at the table. 'Going to the Revolve. Shiv has an interview. I said I'd go through some questions with her.'

'When'll you be back?'

Bethany stuck a forkful of poached egg in her mouth and swung her knife around. 'I'll tell you what, Dad, why don't you get one of those ankle tags so you'll know where I am, then you could sit here at the kitchen table and look at your phone all day? You'd still worry.'

He didn't answer. He handed her a cup of tea – a splash of milk and two sugars.

She placed her hand over his. 'I'm not Mum, you know.'

He sat down, always rather intimidated by his bright, sparky daughter, his only child. That certainty of youth that shone out her eyes, her black-and-white world.

'I don't like you working with these people.'

'Define *these* people, Dad.' Her voice mocked him. 'These people who have tattoos and piercings? Shiv had a terrible time as a kid, her mum died when she was two, she never knew her dad. You wouldn't believe the way she had to grow up. She's twenty and can't read. But you know, we get on okay.'

'What could you possibly have in common with somebody like that?' The idea repulsed Robertson.

'Well.' Bethany started to tick off the list on her fingers as she spoke with slow deliberate sarcasm. 'Human DNA, a dislike of arsehole boyfriends, Adele, dogs. She has ambitions, Dad. Maybe not mine but she has them. More than most. She's okay is Shiv.'

'Well, you watch yourself,' Robertson said. Every day that Bethany volunteered at the Revolve, he felt he was losing her to a bunch of drug-taking jakeys who'd neither work nor want. He was a bit annoyed at his friend Rory Ghillies for getting her the volunteer post in the first place. Ghillies had called it a terrific opportunity. Bethany had agreed. It would be good for her after everything that had happened, he'd said, not needing to add 'with her mum'.

Robertson's heart sank when Bethany started to refer to the Revolve residents as 'friends'. He didn't want her making friends like that. She should have been at the gym, at the tennis club or at the student union in St Andrews clawing back the social ground that she'd lost over the last couple of years. They hadn't spent a fortune on her education for her to help the homeless, addicts, alcoholics and God knew who else. There was plenty of support for them out there, they didn't need his daughter's help as well.

He stirred his tea, watching her ramming the toast into her mouth, mashing the rest of the poached egg up like she'd done when a tiny tot, while she scrolled through her phone, her feet tapping on the carpet tiles. She always had been a ball of restless energy.

He felt he should express his disquiet about her volunteering but every time he mentioned it, Bethany either laughed it off and explained that it would look good on her CV or rolled her eyes and stormed out. Both the women in Robertson's life spent their time doing exactly what they wanted to do and to hell with what he thought.

'And,' Bethany said, as if she'd been reading his mind, 'Shiv grew up without you for a dad. Where would I be if I'd done that, eh?' She kissed her fingers then tapped him on the head. 'That's me away.' She sprang from the chair, scooping her bags up, and was out the door in a whirlwind of auburn hair and pomegranate perfume.

A pause at the front door. He could see her in his mind's eye, plucking her jacket from the rack, tumbling a cascade of hats and scarfs on the tiles. Then a shout, 'Bye.'

'Bye.'

Such an insignificant little word.

The front door opening, slamming shut.

The instant, unsufferable silence.

His daughter never looked back. She trotted down the garden path, rucksack on her back, bag over one arm, her jacket dangling from the other.

She paused at the gate, hefting her bag up onto her left shoulder properly as she walked away. The early morning sun glinted off the copper tones in her hair, worn up, screwed into a yellow scarf that was wound round her head. She'd taken to wearing it like that, like the girl from the Revolve – a trend he remembered seeing in photos of his grandmother.

He had his phone ready, the screen primed for a close-up shot of her. As always, she paused before she crossed the road and headed down the hill to the park. For a fleeting moment she'd turn her head to look up the street and he always thought she'd catch him, behind the curtains with his phone up, ready.

But no. There she was. Her pretty face looking past the garden, her eyes slightly closed against the sun, shouting 'Hi' to Sean from over the road. In the image on his camera, he could see the amber flecks in her eyes, the dusting of freckles that covered the bridge of her nose, the few tendrils of auburn hair that flickered across her forehead.

He took a few pictures on rapid shoot, capturing her forever.

Just in case.

Christine Caplan closed the door of the caravan and turned to look at Challie cottage. It appeared rather forlorn, tumbledown and unwanted in the sunshine of the September morning. The builders had started stripping the roof. The cottage resembled a small child with their front teeth missing.

She put her anorak onto the passenger seat, smoothing her navy-blue jacket underneath her as she slipped into the Duster. Was there a dress code for visiting the terminally ill? She'd done it often enough with parents and in-laws. But this was different. This was her day off and she had a list of things to do with the caravan, then some shopping. Emma was coming round tonight. But first she was embarking on a two-hour round trip for no good reason other than emotional blackmail from a woman she hardly knew.

She'd left Aklen in the caravan sleeping a natural sleep, long and deep. He was slowly returning to her after eight years of being lost in a tunnel of depression and anxiety, dark moods and fatigue. He had, under his doctor's supervision, come off all his medication so now, when he woke up, he'd be refreshed rather than exhausted with the effort of sleeping. He had slept through Caplan making her breakfast, having a shower, getting dressed, feeding their two cats, Pas and Pavlova and counting the kittens (named unimaginatively Eeny, Meeny, Miny and Moe) who lived underneath the caravan, keeping safe from the birds of prey perched nearby, waiting. None of these were quiet activities in and around a four-berth touring caravan that had seen better days.

But Aklen was here. With her. The Glasgow house had been sold and they had money in the bank to complete the work on Challie cottage. She hoped.

It would all take time.

Instead of being overwhelmed by it and retreating into his depression, Aklen seemed stimulated by the situation, using his design skills to oversee the project. He was able to do a few hours physical work when labour was required, rather than skill, helping Pavel the Ukrainian builder. They had become friends, Aklen's ear for languages and Pavel's need to learn English being of mutual benefit.

He now had a reason to get out of his bed. He had even mentioned, in passing, his idea to make one of the rooms into a design office for him, the first words he had uttered about going back to work in some form.

Pulling down the visor, Caplan drove into the autumnal sun, averting her eyes from the lay-by with the dead deer in it, glimpsing a falcon flying up to a nearby tree, and she thought about Aklen. Cause or effect? Did it matter? She was getting her husband back by increments. Aklen wasn't yet able to face going into Cronchie, or into Oban, but he was talking about it.

Now he could walk the acre of land they owned, from the beach to the lower slopes of the ben behind the cottage, getting fresh air, and, if they were around, enjoying the masculine chitchat of the builders. His appetite was better, he was putting on weight. His sense of purpose had returned.

They had agreed that they would make the property windproof and waterproof, then take stock and think how the cottage might work best for them.

Aklen was trying to get some rest today. Pavel was coming round with his wife and his children to see the kittens. Emma was visiting from Skone. After visiting Rachel, Caplan would make a quick trip to the supermarket then she'd be back to enjoy some family life.

She could see this journey to Lorn far enough. If she was honest, she couldn't really care less about Rachel Bellshaw, but she'd promised to visit, and a promise was a promise, especially to the dying.

It took her over an hour to get to Lorn due to some Highland cattle wandering along the road, followed by a traffic control system for some non-visible roadworks. Caplan spent the time listening to the music from *Coppélia* on repeat, trying to recall memories of Rachel. As she hit the turn-off her phone rang.

'Hi ma'am. The Rod and Todd situation? DCI McCormack's busy.' Craigo's lilting accent was always exaggerated on the phone.

'Is he now?'

'Yes. You've to do it. Because you have nothing else to do.'

Caplan ignored the jibe that she knew had come from McCormack. 'So you've to tidy it up and send it to the Fiscal? Surely you can do that, DS Craigo.'

'Fiscal's not happy.'

'Useful if that bit of information had been at the start of the conversation.'

'And Dr Spyck's busy but will get to the body from Glen Douglas ASAP. And we've found no match in the misper database. So that's good.'

'Doesn't make him less dead,' muttered Caplan, cutting the call.

Caplan arrived at the hospice five minutes late after hunting for a parking space and looking at the directions to the Wallace Wing where Rachel was being treated. She found the lift and wished she'd had time for a coffee and a sandwich as her stomach growled. She was waiting in the short queue that had gathered when she heard a familiar voice.

'DCI Christine Caplan, if I'm not mistaken.'

She turned to see her old friend. 'Lizzie! How are you?'

'I'm good.'

'And the boys?'

'Oh you know, wee angels one minute, little sods the next. Mum has them today. You got any idea what this is about with Rachel?' asked her friend, her eyes narrowing.

'No.'

'Not like you not to know what's going on, you're normally good at spying on people.'

And there it was.

The lift arrived and Caplan sidestepped, forcing Fergusson to move with her as four people emerged through the open doors, to be replaced by those who had been waiting. The two of them stood back, Caplan saying that they'd get the next one.

Once they were alone Caplan turned on her colleague. 'Lizzie, I didn't spy on you. I was coming to visit you and I saw Grace Brindley leave your house. End of. What you do with your life is nothing to do with me. I couldn't care less.'

Fergusson pouted, tilting her head, the corkscrew fair hair bouncing lightly as she moved, like a child considering an apology when they'd been hoping for a good argument.

'And before you accuse me of anything, I've told nobody. But Sarah, who is, don't forget, ACC Crime, suspects something's going on. She damn near asked me outright, and knew I was being less than complete in my response, but she won't hear anything from me.' Caplan shoved her small leather rucksack higher on her shoulder. 'Right, do you know what's wrong with Rachel?'

'Well, the grapevine said she's gravely ill, from Covid a couple of years back, then lung issues, then pneumonia, then lung cancer. Might be easier saying what she doesn't have.'

'Jesus Christ,' said Caplan, working out in her head that Rachel Bellshaw had been a couple of years younger than her. 'I only heard about the cancer.'

'Yeah, but whatever it is, it's end-stage now, palliative care.'

'Maybe she wants to get something off her chest. Maybe she'll confess to being the lesbian lover of the wife of Glasgow's chief gangster,' said Caplan out the corner of her mouth.

'Shut the fuck up,' Fergusson responded sweetly with a smile as the lift doors opened.

The hospice corridor was quiet. The walls were decorated with a mural of daisies growing up from the skirting board, the pastel colours no doubt intended to soothe troubled souls. Caplan asked at the nurses' station. The young woman on the desk confirmed that Rachel was awake, was in room ten, but made them aware that the patient was very weak.

The room was overly warm and lit only by two sidelights, the curtains closed tightly. A radio played quietly in the corner, Caplan recognised the heart-rending melody of 'The Dying Swan' and steeled herself; too many memories for her, few of them good. Rachel was unrecognisable, the woman they knew was shrouded by the thin old lady on the bed, covered by a single light-blue sheet, oxygen tube attached to her upper lips, a smaller tube snaking up each nostril. Three bags hung from a stand, one of them dropping a clear fluid into a cannula on the back of her left hand. The cannula on her right hand was closed. Each limb had some sensor attached. A small silent screen jerked with green and red lines, numbers flashing up every now and again.

The figure on the bed showed no recognition that she had company.

Caplan and Fergusson looked at each other and pulled the two chairs in the room over to the side of the bed and sat.

And waited.

They chatted quietly to each other about the weather, the kids, Caplan's husband, Lizzie's ex-husband, the cottage. Caplan's daughter Emma and her recovery. The tour de force that was Kenny, Caplan's son, twenty now and still useless.

'When did that ever stop any man, they've a bloody license to be useless, I mean what the . . .'

Then Rachel made a noise that may have been 'hello'.

'Did we wake you up? Sorry,' said Caplan.

There was a slight shake of the head. Wild eyes looked from one to the other, narrowing, then relaxing as recognition flooded in. The eyes fluttered closed in relief, the lips pursed. 'Nico . . .?'

'Nico?' Caplan asked, looking at Fergusson, who shrugged as if she had no idea. 'It's us, Chris and Lizzie. You asked us to pop in . . .'

'How're you doing?' asked Fergusson, then pulled a face. Not the right thing to say in the circumstances.

'Fffff . . .'

'Fergusson? Yes me. Lizzie?'

The patient shook her head infinitesimally. 'Nico . . . las,' said Rachel, her voice weak and raspy. Her eyes looked from Caplan, who was directly in her line of sight, then wandered over to Fergusson. Thin, bony fingers crept across the top of the sheet towards her, the cannula waggling like a reptilian tail, the thin wedding band dangling on the twig of a finger.

Fergusson placed her hand under Rachel's, wincing slightly at the surprising power left in her grip. 'Nicholas?'

Rachel nodded, her head rolling a little, her lips working to try and gather the energy to form a word. 'Hardman. And straight man.' She nodded. Paper-thin skin stretched and folded round her eyes. The hand that once held a tennis racket so powerfully now lost its grasp.

'Hardman and Straightman?' repeated Caplan.

'Nicholas? Fin emmmm.' Rachel coughed, the pain racking through her body. A small bubble of blood appeared at the side of her mouth, her head lolled slightly, but she was fighting to get the words out.

'Here, here,' said Caplan soothingly while patting Rachel's cheek with a tissue. The blood had formed a crimson rose on the parchment skin. 'Was that Finan?' asked Caplan, quietly. 'Does she mean Finan Craigo?'

They waited until the coughing was over and Rachel's breathing had returned to normal. Caplan poured some orange liquid from a covered plastic jug into a small tumbler and held it to Rachel's lips, as Fergusson plumped up the pillows.

Once Rachel had settled, her eyes once again open and focused on her visitors, Fergusson asked, 'Did you say Finan? Or find him?'

With eyes that were more dead than alive, Rachel stared at Caplan. A tiny shake of the head, the side of her mouth cracked, a perfect sphere of blood appeared then grew. 'No.' A deep breath, a huge effort. 'Them. Find . . . them.'

A nurse bustled past, then stopped and retraced her steps as they made their way back to the lift.

'Who the hell was Nicholas Straightman?' Lizzie was already trying to google the name on her phone. 'So are we thinking he's a criminal whose name is stuck in Rachel's drug-addled head?'

They heard the nurse's footsteps behind them.

'Excuse me? Have you been visiting Rachel Ghillies, room ten?'

'Yes.'

'Are you the friends from her police days? I thought three were coming?'

'One couldn't make it,' said Caplan politely.

'I'm Sadie. We've spoken on the phone. Rachel was keen to speak to you.'

'Yes,' said Caplan vaguely, noticing the nurse's slight sidestep,

the furtive glance back to the nursing station to see if anybody was watching.
'You'll be Christine and . . .'
'Lizzie.'
'Is Sarah going to make it? Only Rachel's not got much longer left, and . . .' Sadie flicked her hair back. 'And to say that you've not to let on to Rory, about Nicholas. He knows she wanted to speak to you, but thinks it was just a goodbye.'
Caplan nodded. 'We'll keep that to ourselves.'
Fergusson said sweetly, 'We will.'
They strolled back to the lift doors.
Fergusson asked, 'So, you do know who Rachel was going on about?'
'No bloody idea,' said Caplan.
'But it was important to Rachel for some reason. Maybe the one big case of her career that got away? But if so, why don't I remember it? If it was a big case, it would have worked its way up the wire to us.'
'And I'd have recalled the name at least. But I don't.'
'That'll be because you are too busy being a high-flying arse-licker to do any real police work.'
'Oh, is that what it is,' said Caplan airily. 'I was wondering.'
She dropped her voice, aware of a couple walking past: a man in his early fifties in a very good suit, holding a leather laptop case, and a taller blonde woman in a grey shift dress, a jacket swung over her shoulders. It was the noise of the thin, four-inch heels on the lino floor that had caught Caplan's ear. He had the appearance of a senior surgeon. She was more difficult to place; a well-groomed PA rather than a medic.
Caplan heard the heels stop.
'Christine?'
Caplan turned.
'Christine Caplan?' asked the man, walking back towards her, his hand outstretched in greeting, a slight roll to his walk. 'I knew it was you. It took a moment to place you. How's Aklen?'
Caplan raised an eyebrow, shaking the proffered hand. 'He's good.' Keep it vague.
'I don't think you've met my better half, Wilma. Wilma, this is Christine Caplan, Aklen's wife. You remember him? Opening of the quiet space at Glasgow University, The Radlan Room?'

'How could I forget such a handsome man.' Wilma smiled, showing uneven teeth, which added some character to a bland but pretty face.

'That was a while ago,' agreed Caplan, working out that it was a few years before lockdown, before Aklen's mental health crumbled. 'This is my colleague, Lizzie.'

The man shook hands with Fergusson then looked at them both, making a judgement. 'Sorry, I've just realised, you two are at work? Are you based up here now, Christine?'

'Yes.'

'Great, get Aklen to give me a call. We are over at Benderloch, be good to catch up.' He looked serious for a moment as if another cog in his brain was turning. 'You haven't been to visit Rachel, have you?'

'Yes, we have.'

'I'm sorry, I've only made that connection. Police.' He snapped his fingers again. 'You must know Rachel well. How is she today?'

'Tired,' answered Caplan.

'Too tired for more visitors then?' asked Wilma, her voice high and melodic. 'Maybe we should leave it for today?'

The man nodded. 'We'll come back another time.' He put his hand round his wife's upper arm, giving her a comforting rub while turning back towards the lift, decision made.

They got in the lift. Caplan avoided Lizzie's eyes.

'Don't know how Rory's bearing up,' said Wilma. 'We invited him round for dinner. Men don't eat properly when they're on their own.'

'Difficult times like this . . . you want to help but there's nothing you can do,' said the man.

'It's very hard,' agreed Caplan, not finding this conversation easy either.

'Tell Aklen to call me. It'd be good to catch up. We could drag Rory out for a bite to eat or something more fluid. If not, why don't you and Aklen come round for a meal?'

Wilma said that would be lovely as the man took a business card out of his pocket and handed it to Caplan, who resisted the temptation to look at it.

'In fact, tell him I'm after him to take some tickets for the Tinmen's Ball. Yes, it's a dance, not a raffle. I'm expecting him to buy a table. And this time, you've not to be too busy at work.' He laughed and shook both women warmly by the hand. The lift doors opened. The two cops waited while the couple walked out to the left, then they went to the right.

'Who was that then?' asked Fergusson.

'No bloody idea.' Caplan looked at the card. 'Felix Vance.'

'And who's Felix Vance?'

'Like I said, no bloody idea.'

The Advice Works team had been in at the Revolve. Bethany had taken Shiv through some interview etiquette then had ended up in the kitchen, doing basic cooking.

They had spent the late morning in Shiv's room as Shiv tried on Bethany's plain, grey dress, with her own selection of trainers, spiking her hair and putting on a mock Californian accent as she talked about 'the authentic fucking me' while moaning about Bethany's advice to tone down the goth, remove at least two of her ear piercings and maybe hide the tattoo. Shiv turned sideways, displaying the words 'Angel of Death' scrawled on her shoulder blade.

Bethany switched to her American accent. 'Or do you feel that you are repressing the authenticity of your chosen belief system?'

Shiv jumped on the bed with her, plonked a beanie hat on Bethany's head, and lined her phone up for a selfie. Mo, one of the older volunteers, a kaleidoscope of colour in red and blue dungarees, came in to tell them they'd break the bed if they carried on like that, then offered to take their picture. Shiv spread her fingers behind Bethany's head; Bethany reacted with some bunny paws.

Later, Bethany happily mopped the kitchen floor, while Mo complained about being the only one who emptied the bins, and Shiv sat on the worktop using the calculator on her iPhone to work out how much the pasta with ragu sauce and garlic bread had cost per head. Mo told her how much it would cost through Just Eat and think what she could do with the money saved.

Shiv thought for a moment and said, 'Buy more fags.'

Bethany laughed. She envied Shiv her freedom. Shiv could swan off whenever she wanted without anybody watching her. God, Bethany's dad would be mortified if he ever found out about her boyfriend and their secret trysts. There was one thing Shiv had taught her; it was boring being the good girl.

THREE

They stood in the midday morning sun when they got out of the hospice. Fergusson was due at her mum's to pick the boys up. Caplan should get on with her shopping for their visitors before driving home. For a moment, they lingered in the car park, neither of them voicing any of their thoughts, both feeling the weight of their mortality.

Caplan felt a slap on her back, smelling the cigarette smoke before she turned.

'Hello, girls. I've escaped the budgeting meeting from hell so popped along. How was she, the lovely Ruby?' asked Sarah Linden, falling into step between them, somehow guiding them towards a wine bar that neither of them had noticed.

'Her name's Rachel,' corrected Caplan.

'Do we have time for something to eat? Of course we do. Chris has no kitchen and you, Liz, have spent far too long eating cheesy Wotsits.'

'A quick bite then,' agreed Caplan, realising how hungry she was. 'But I need to get home. Emma's coming over tonight and I need to buy nibbles for both green-conscious vegans and rampant carnivores.'

'I'll have to call my mum first. And I'm on the mineral water,' said Fergusson. Both Caplan and Fergusson knew from experience that there never was only one drink with Linden, there was always a second, a third, a tenth.

'You two have got nothing to rush home for.' Linden pointed at them in turn. 'Your mum loves your little rodents, and you,' she turned to Caplan, 'have your wee monkey to deal with the double suicide. Let him do it in case you lose any evidence.' Linden paused, waiting for a reaction.

Caplan didn't dare look at Fergusson who turned away, leaving her to take Linden by the elbow and tell her the essence of what Rachel had said, the names she had mumbled.

'Nicholas Straightman? Hardman? Find them?' Caplan asked. 'What do you think?'

Linden shrugged. 'Doesn't ring a bell. It must be preying on her mind though. You'd think she'd better things to think about, like meeting her maker. But she was a shit cop at Tulliallan . . .'

'Sarah!' Caplan cautioned.

'Oh, you know what I mean. And why the hell tell you? Me, I could understand, but you, Chris? You police cows on a single-track road and Liz does the filing. Why you two?'

'You were asked, you didn't show. Why didn't you come in? Where were you?'

'Better things to do, and let's face it, if it was important, she'd have contacted me.'

Caplan didn't rise to the bait. She knew that Linden, at times, felt genuinely uncomfortable at their differing career paths. Linden's career had involved a meteoric rise through the ranks. They were different people – why should their working lives resemble each other at all?

'Good point,' Caplan said. 'I've been thinking *Why us*? I was never friends with her. The two times I worked with her I thought she was always hung up on detail. Sneaky, a compulsive note-taker, as though if you said anything, she'd use it against you.'

'She thought that you were a stuck-up cow, with your wee bun and the fact you walk like the queen.' Lizzie Fergusson pursed her lips, enjoying her little moment.

'Don't hold that against Raquel . . . Rachel . . . whatever,' said Linden. 'Loads of folk think Chris is a stuck-up cow.'

'Try not to say that with so much relish.'

'Did she not have a nickname for you?' Fergusson asked.

'Aye, she did.' Linden frowned.

'What was it now? I wonder?'

'Bond Girl,' said Caplan quietly.

'Oh yes. Bond Girl. Your take downs were balletic. She'd never seen anything like it.'

'That was her problem, not mine.' Caplan could recall how the comment had stung. It was long ago, best forgotten. She looked around her. The sky was clouding over. No doubt it would be raining soon, and the wind was rising. Were all her visitors expecting to fit into the caravan? And she was wanting to stop and see what the team were doing, now that they had inherited the suicide case. DS Callum McPhee either wasn't well or he was up to something. DS Toni Mackie was clucking around him, concerned. Her team. She didn't like to think of them coping without her.

'It wasn't her big case that got away, her great unsolved. I'd recognise the name if it was. There's no media traction that accompanies an unsolved case,' said Linden, adjusting the collar of her sharp suit. 'If Rachel's that ill, she might be talking complete shite.'

'Quite consistent complete shite, though. The nurse and us, we got the same story.'

'Name, you got a name,' corrected Linden. 'Do you think Rory might know? He and I go way back. I could have a chat.'

Caplan and Fergusson exchanged a quick look, a question passing between them.

It was Fergusson who said, 'The nurse was very clear that Rachel didn't want Rory to know what Rachel said.'

'Now that *is* interesting,' said Linden, opening the door of the wine bar.

They sat at a corner booth. Caplan said, 'Rachel Ghillies wasn't a stupid woman, and it's bothered her enough that it's still on her mind as she's dying. People don't use the last piece of energy they have for something that doesn't bother them.'

'If it was me, I'd like somebody to look into it. But why not somebody that she's worked alongside and really trusts?' asked Fergusson.

'Maybe she knows that all cops are arseholes deep down,' said Linden, looking at the wine list with interest.

'Do you know anything about the Tinmen's Ball?' asked Caplan.

'I know it can be treated nowadays,' Linden snorted. 'Trade Union from the Land of Oz? Why?'

Caplan put the business card in front of her colleague.

'Oh my God, you ran into the lovely Felix Vance. Did he have his arm-candy wife with him? Blonde, well dressed, silicone implants and two brain cells?'

'He did.'

Linden put down the wine list, serious for a moment. 'Of course, he'd be there to see Raquel . . .'

'Rachel.'

'The four of them were very friendly back in the day. Vance, his missus and Rory are all rather glamorous and there was wee what's-her-face trying to keep up.'

'Rachel,' said Caplan automatically.

Linden handed the card back. 'But now he has you in his little black book for his do-gooding, he'll relieve your bank account of cash in aid of the helpless.'

'My kids have been doing that for years.' Caplan picked up the menu, choosing a green salad. 'How does Vance know my husband?'

'Business. Rotary. Everything with Vance is business and money, money and business.'

'If we're thinking of tracking "Straightman", where do we start?' Fergusson said. 'I've easy access to the system. I'll clear it with my Sarge then dig around and let you know if I find anything.'

'Who's drinking what?' asked Linden.

'Mineral waters for us.'

'Fucking lightweights. Get a bottle of Chardonnay for me. With a large glass. I'm going for a pee. Have a look at the menu. My treat – I'm feeding the poor of today.'

Linden slid out of the booth, her phone at her ear before she got to the toilet door.

'How does she do a day in those heels?' muttered Caplan, browsing the menu.

A-ha's 'Take On Me' floated through the air. There was a burst of laughter from a small hen party near the bar.

Fergusson stopped smiling. 'When I saw your number on my phone, I thought you were going to give me a talking to. Sarah'll be finished in five minutes. If you want to have a go, you need to do it now. I've been scared that you'll tell her.' She bit her lip. 'She could end my career, what there is of it.'

'It's none of my business what you do in your private life,' said Caplan curtly. 'But Police Scotland is a gossip machine. Your ex-husband is not daft. I worry what he'd do if he found out. And it could've been him sitting in that car park, he could've seen what I saw.' Caplan smiled at her old friend. 'But don't worry.' Then gave her a hug.

Sarah Linden crashed in next to them. 'Bloody hell, I'm away for a pee and you two get touchy-feely. Where's my wine?'

Bethany left the Revolve after three o'clock, heading home along the promenade, having given Shiv a hug and wished her all the best for her interview for a job as a housekeeper/cleaner in a local hotel, morning shifts only. But Shiv was going to the pub, promising not to get totally rat-arsed. Shiv was a little scary at times, irresponsible, but she was always fun.

Fun wasn't a word that Bethany'd had much use for in the last few years.

As she walked on along the promenade, she looked for the lad at the ferry terminal and, seeing him, she stopped and waved. He was cute, but not her type, and she was involved with somebody – that was a good word, 'involved'. She was stressing that her dad would find out. She needed to keep her freedom; her car breaking down had been a total bummer. At least now it was getting fixed. Sean had taken money for parts and said she could catch up on paying for the labour.

Her heart was light as she went through the gate of Pulpit Hill Park, emerging on the other side of the path, making her way across the grass, still under the shade of the trees, letting her eyes adjust to the dull light. She was sure many of the service users at the Revolve had spent evenings here, on the swings drinking Red Bull and Thunderbird. Bethany heard her name being whispered. She looked around. She heard her name again and crouched down, looking into the bushes. Two women were kneeling, hidden by the leaves of the large rhododendron, looking rather ridiculous. Then Bethany saw the green van behind them, the familiar logo on the side door.

'Oh, hi Beth, can you give me a hand, my knee's about to give out!'

Bethany sidestepped onto the grass as one of the women crouched precariously behind a bush with a large dirty towel and a cat basket, gloved fingertips to her lips, beckoning that Beth should come closer, her face partially covered by the peak of her baseball cap.

'What the hell are you doing?' Bethany whispered, laughing.

'Come here. I'll show you.' The movement of the fingers quickened.

It was only when the woman turned round, moving a few leaves, letting a glimmer of sunlight through, giving her a better view, that despite the familiarity, despite the humour, Bethany realised she didn't know her at all.

It was on the tip of her tongue to say, 'Do I know you?' but it was too late.

Caplan was sitting in the Duster in the car park behind Cronchie police station, checking her phone messages; her head was still reeling, as it always did after being in Sarah Linden's company. And Rachel's request troubled her. It sounded to her that there was somebody called Nicholas, first or second name, who was a straight man or a hardman. Somebody who had been an enforcer but had now gone straight? Maybe in Witness Protection with Rachel as his handler? But she'd never operated at that rank; it was way above her paygrade. Something was troubling Rachel, level-headed and detail-obsessed Rachel. From her hospice bed, their colleague had recognised them, she'd used every ounce of the energy she had to say the name, but had been too weak to make herself understood clearly.

The word Nicholas they were sure of. Straighter or Straightman? Hardman? Who knew?

In the solitude and the gentle heat of an autumn sun, Caplan's mind drifted to Rod and Todd. She made a mental note to check if the post-mortems had been scheduled yet. The fact that one of the deceased had not been seen in person for some time was a red flag.

A car, exhaust roaring, raced into the long, narrow car park, far too fast for safety. The small white Mercedes jarred to a halt, the brakes screeching. The passenger door opened and the tall figure of DC Callum McPhee clambered out, followed by the driver's door flying open, missing Toni Mackie's wee Citroen by an inch.

This must be the new girlfriend that McPhee was so taken with, leaving the others in the team to question what a girl like her saw in a quiet, weedy guy like their constable. He was punching well above his weight with the lovely, petite brunette who only came up to his armpits. She flung her arms round her boyfriend's neck, stretching up on her tiptoes.

He stepped back, laughing, a red flush colouring his cheeks, with a quick look up to the windows of the incident room on the second floor to ensure that Mackie was not spying on them from her favourite position, the desk by the large middle window. McPhee reached over and pulled his girlfriend's hood from behind her, up over her head, then rammed it down over her eyes. He kissed her on the top of the hood, and walked away, smiling at her over his shoulder, giving Caplan full view of the bruising on his face as his girlfriend waved back, both hands in the air, fingers wide like a two-year-old. She got back in the car and reversed into the space beside the Duster, zero to sixty in three milliseconds, missing the front wing by inches. She saw Caplan sitting in the driver's seat and gave her a wide smile of beautifully even teeth, then roared away, leaving the car park to its studied silence. The silence was broken immediately by an angry blare on the horn from a car on the main road, no doubt the vehicle the Mercedes had pulled out in front of.

An expensive car. He was a DC and she was a nursery nurse. She wondered how much debt they were in.

Caplan looked at the clock. She should be going home now. As there had been no talk of Emma needing to be picked up from the ferry, she must have transport. Caplan deduced that Magus would be bringing her over in his wee green electric van with the tiny flatbed at the back. Caplan doubted she'd get any time on her own with her daughter. Why couldn't Emma meet somebody like McPhee? Okay, he was a bit boring, a bit thick, but he did have a police pension going for him if nothing else. The Magus was twenty years older than Emma, a millionaire who dedicated his land to the breeding of rare butterflies. The cliffs on the island had long been a sanctuary for puffins. The life made Emma happy, but it wasn't the life Caplan had wanted for her daughter.

Caplan, the cynic that she was, wondered when it would all come crashing down and who would be left in pieces. Her phone pinged, a text from Emma. Her daughter had already picked up some vegan food for the barbeque and some craft beer for the boys.

The boys?

Emma was being her usual organised self, but Caplan felt the slight to her own catering. How many times during her teenage years had Emma opened the door to an empty fridge? She climbed out of the car. She may as well make good use of the time if they were all getting on so well without her.

Bethany's eyes were open wide now. Open and sticky. Her brain was rallying, trying to make sense of the light, the blackness and the pain. She'd been asleep and in the dream – she'd known that it had been a dream – she'd been sitting in the back of the funeral car. Her dad in his black suit, hair neatly combed, on her right. Rory on her left. She was trapped in the middle as the car slowly followed the hearses along a narrow country road. Her mum and aunt Rachel lay in the coffins. Except they didn't know which was which, they didn't know who to follow. Bethany was crying. She looked down. She was wearing a grey dress, not the black one she'd put on that morning. Her dad was sobbing. Rory reassured them that they'd do both funerals at the same time. The ladies wouldn't mind as they were dead. Then Rory told Bethany that she was too pale for grey.

Then they got fed up. Her mum got out the coffin and walked away with her dad. Rachel and Rory did the same. Bethany was left, locked in the mourning car, kicking and screaming to get out. When she woke up, she was lying in blackness. Beneath her, the vibration of movement. Around her, the thrum of an engine. On her lips, the tension of tape.

William Robertson glanced at his watch for the twelfth time in the last half hour, walking up to the bay window, pulling back the curtains, looking up and down the street.

Nothing.

A glance at the clouds. It was beginning to rain; darts of water splattered the pane. Bethany knew the rules about being late, she was supposed to call back as soon as she could. Robertson sat down at the table, fixing the curtain so he could keep an eye on the street. It was gone five o'clock.

Another look at his watch. He waited. He picked up his mobile, called her again. This time the phone was off. He tried the location app, there was no blue dot flashing at him.

Nothing.

He'd called the Revolve. Somebody called Mo answered, not a resident from the way she spoke. She said that Bethany had left at her usual time, and yes, she was fine, hadn't complained of a headache, she hadn't said anything about going anywhere else, then added that she'd walked out the door with Shiv McDougall.

Bethany had gone somewhere, and she was not alone. That was good, but not letting him know was against the rules.

FOUR

Bethany woke up. Unable to lift her head from the pillow, she stared at the ceiling, high above. The single light bulb swung in a draught she couldn't feel. Her arms were too heavy to ease her off the thin mattress, her skull throbbed, and her thoughts were swimming. This wasn't her bedroom.

Where was Dad? Now she was wide awake, unable to ignore this alien world.

She was only able to look at the ceiling that she didn't recognise. This ceiling. A hospital? She shivered. She was naked under a thin blanket, lying on a hard mattress on a concrete floor. Using every bit of energy she had, she tried to lift one hand. The other hand came up too. A thin rope bound her wrists. Another, tighter, bound her ankles.

She wasn't going anywhere any time soon.

That confused her. She tried to think back to a solid memory. Waving at Paul. Walking through the park. Then what happened?

A voice in the bushes. Faces she thought she knew.

The pale, emotionless face of the young desk constable greeted Caplan as she walked in the door of the station. He had more than a fleeting semblance to Christopher Lee's Dracula, and his android approach to the job made her yearn for the laid-back efficiency of Jackson, a man who either knew everybody, or would know somebody who knew somebody.

Constable Stewart shouted from behind his screen. He didn't shout to her or at her, he simply shouted. There were two messages. One was a number, with the name Irene Kennedy in brackets after it. She read the other as she buzzed herself through the door. *Call Rory Ghillies as soon as possible.* It was *very important*. Was he already aware of the conversation they'd had with Rachel? She sent off a message to Linden and Fergusson on the group chat: had Ghillies been trying to get in touch with them?

No, he hadn't.

That piqued her curiosity.

Walking through the incident room to her office, she punched out the mobile number. She saw Toni Mackie sitting in the opposite corner by the window, her hand on the side of her face, which might have been her fixing her hair, or cupping her ear in an attempt to hear McPhee's private conversation. It was getting on for four o'clock. Her phone call went straight to voicemail. He might be at the hospice for afternoon visiting. She left a message that was interrupted by her desk phone ringing. Ghillies calling back already?

It was Ryce, the pathologist. After a few sarcastic comments about how Caplan's day was going, she complained about how busy the DCI was keeping the post-mortem suite at the hospital, and would it be easier if she too moved lock, stock and barrel up to Loch Lomond. Anyway, her voice dropped, becoming serious, she was holding back on the Rod and Todd deaths, scheduling them in for later in the week as she wasn't sure that all the medical history was intact.

Caplan asked, 'Do you suspect something?'

'First rule of the forensic pathologist; make sure you have the right guy on the slab. The body on the slab is Roderick Taylor. He looks well nourished, he has no sign of any long-term medical intervention so I'm keen to see what malignancy he was suffering from. Or it is my subconscious bias of years of seeing patients who have been through the treadmill of chemo and radio, showing evidence of surgeries. The usual stuff. I know you have anecdotal evidence of terminal cancer, but, apart from being dead, the subject on the slab tells me a different story. Also, there's no record of any cancer on his medical file, but that could be a record-keeping error. I'll collate all his notes before we look inside. But, more interestingly? Your naked man at the bottom of the hill? Glen Douglas?'

'No, we don't have an ID. Do you?' asked Caplan.

'Is he not called Glen Douglas? That's what it says here.'

'No, that's where he was found.'

'It's typed in here under "name of deceased".'

'Okay, we are understaffed and overtired. We'll keep that little error to ourselves. Are we any closer to finding his real name?'

'Nope, we thought we had his real name. Brady put a rush on his DNA, no doubt leaned on by the MoD, and he's not on the database on any interim search. Which means he's never been convicted of a crime in Scotland, or maybe his details have been logged incorrectly.'

'I'm sure it does happen,' said Caplan guardedly, suspecting there was more to come, and it wouldn't be good.

'His blood chemistry is off the scale. "Dead-in-Bed Syndrome", which is a vague term for any person with diabetes who is presumed dead from hypoglycaemia. His vitreous humour's also abnormal. We've asked for microscopy on kidney tissue samples . . .'

'And?'

'A young healthy male with type 1 diabetes has a fatal hypoglycaemic attack? I'm not buying it. I think he was a well-controlled diabetic for a while and then it looks like he stopped eating, or there was an issue with his insulin.'

'And?' repeated Caplan.

'If the latter, he'd get to his GP, the hospital, whatever. If the former, then it might be some innocent malarky, maybe out with folk who didn't realise. They were partying. He'd be behaving like he was drunk. That'd be what you'd think if you didn't know. Then he'd fall asleep and not wake up. Given the distance, and the clean feet, my conclusion is that he was dumped here. And, this is kicker number one, he has a nasty injury to his left leg that was cooking up a nice infection. Kicker number two are the signs of him having something round his wrist, and something tighter on his ankles, on both sides. Bound in some way, kept against his will? And his stomach was totally empty. That's not normal for a careful diabetic. Like I said, I'd suspect his feet to bear some lesions from walking up a hill like that, but the skin on his feet is clean. Either he took his shoes off when he finally lay down and we've not found them, or somebody carried him up there. But, mainly, and most importantly, he does have his head and face caved in. And I suspect that was post-mortem, no vital response.'

'Okay,' Caplan said slowly.

'For belt and braces you could send somebody up there to look at the rocks he might have fallen from, looking for tissue from head trauma. But I doubt you'll find anything – it was the blunt instrument that did the damage. And . . .'

'God, is there more?'

'He's not clean. By that I mean he's dirty, not that he's had a drug problem. He has dirty fingernails and feet, natal clef – bum crack to you – and dirty armpits etc. He's been a stranger to personal hygiene for a while, maybe a recently homeless diabetic man in his early twenties. No tattoos, no identifiable marks. Homeless very recently though. He has had some pretty impressive and expensive dental work done. Veneers like that cost a fortune. They are understated, no Turkey teeth for him, but the upper canine left is missing, not extracted by somebody with a dental degree. But recently, he's had no access to soap and water. Mental health issue? Was dead but somebody clubbed him over the head anyway? I'm confused. We need more to go on.' She heard Ryce sigh. 'And the lack of ID is in itself unusual in today's electronic world. Everybody is somewhere except for this young man who has been . . .' she paused, '. . . elsewhere?'

'Spyck was saying something about a TikTok challenge?'

Ryce shook her head. 'I can see why she thought that, but no. We've had a spate of death by stupidity. Beating the train on the level crossing tends to go spectacularly badly. Two fatal cases of eating chilli peppers without drinking. I might have been bored as a teenager, but I'd bop about the bedroom listening to Pulp, rather than play Russian roulette with the 5.20 to Glasgow Central. Mr Glen Douglas: summary so far? Wrist marks suggest held against his will. Fractured fibula on left, canine tooth extracted on left. Starved, died. Then some attempt to smash his facial features to delay ID.' There was a respectful pause while they both reflected on what hell this young man had gone through. Then Ryce's voice moved into sarcastic mode. 'Do you have a roof yet?'

After hanging up, Caplan sat behind her desk, knowing that she was looking for a reason to delay joining Aklen, Emma and anybody else who was there. Maybe have a quick chat with Craigo before she went, make sure he was up to speed on Rod Taylor and the body from Glen Douglas.

Her phone went. Ghillies, his voice echoing around as if he was calling from a barn as he greeted her like a long-lost friend, explaining that he was sorry he had missed her call. He'd been at the golf club and was about to head out to the hospice. She asked how Rachel was doing.

There was a pause. The voice became sombre. Caplan knew what that was like, taking a bright spot in the day and then somebody bangs you back down to earth.

'Well at this point, the only turns in the road are going to be downward, but we take the positives where we can. She had a good night, and that's the best that can be expected. She was excited at the thought of you and the girls coming in to see her.'

The girls? Not condescending, not flattering, merely friendly. The voice was rather attractive, well-spoken and engaging. Ghillies had moved in circles one level higher than Linden. The thought crossed Caplan's mind again about why Linden had been close to the hospice yesterday, but had, in effect, waited outside.

Guilt?

'We had a good chat.'

'Oh yes, she was very pleased you'd taken the time to visit.'

'It was nothing,' lied Caplan.

'But you're here now, aren't you, up near Cronchie? You're a very busy police officer. I know what your workload's like in Major Incident. You took time out to see an old friend, and I'm very grateful that you did.'

'It was nice to see her, despite the circumstances.' Caplan wondered what Ghillies was actually getting at, and how long it was going to take him to get to the point. As he himself had said, she was busy.

'No doubt she was talking about her obsession, the Nicholson bloke. She's been going on about that for years.'

'Really?' Caplan hoped she sounded as if she had no interest, but with Ghillies she was dealing with a retired cop and there would be no fooling him.

'I'm really phoning to ask a favour. It's a bit awkward as I'm ex-job but a friend of mine, a good friend of mine, has been in touch; his daughter, Bethany Robertson, has gone missing. Nice kid, twenty-one, something like that, not vulnerable.' She was aware of his police speak. 'But it's not like her. I feel responsible as she was last seen at the Revolve Centre. It was me who got her a position volunteering there.'

'In Oban?'

'Yes, you know it?'

'It's a halfway house for those coming out of care. The last of the big houses on the promenade. The police in Oban know it well.'

'Oh, God, aye! The council are always trying to close it down because they see it as a public nuisance. I'm on the board there and got Beth a volunteer post when she was off uni last year. She didn't come home this afternoon. Her dad is very worried. I was round at their house last night and everything was fine, she was her usual self.'

Caplan knew where this was going. 'And you want me to do a

phone round? She's an adult and a few hours isn't a "missing person".'

'I know that, Christine. Bill's a lovely bloke. His wife walked out the front door and died very suddenly, a year ago, maybe two years ago. I think he's called every hospital twice now.' The line went quiet with some reflection. 'You can understand why he's twitchy. I was thinking maybe DC Fergusson, she's on the wire but I don't have her contact details. Bill's called Oban, but there's nothing they can do. I thought I'd try you.'

Caplan kept her voice light. 'I'm sure she won't like it if she's stayed out for a cuppa with her hunky new boyfriend and her dad has the cops circulating her description. I know teenagers, I know what they get up to.'

'Beth doesn't have a boyfriend, but you'll appreciate that there's not a student on this earth that has their phone off for four hours. I'm worried about her.'

'Okay. I'm presuming that there are no red flags, no issues at home that might have made her run?'

A pause. 'No.'

'I need to know the facts please, Mr Ghillies.'

'Call me Rory. It's just that Beth's got friendly with a girl called Shivonne McDougall.' He spelled the name out. 'She's a service user, not a volunteer. The staff don't know where she is either.'

'So, they are together, having a good time?'

'No, I doubt it. The manager said they left together, but Beth was heading home and the other girl was going to the pub. The Shivonne girl is trouble.'

'Why?'

'She has a record. I got an old colleague to check when she befriended Bethany. They don't end up at the Revolve for being citizen of the year.'

'Okay, I'll bear that in mind. Lizzie's off duty but I'll get somebody to do a welfare check on Bethany. Can you send me her details, her dad's contact details and a reasonable photograph? I'll text you my email address. Is this a good number to get you on?'

'Yes. Really can't thank you enough, Christine.'

She swiped her phone closed and texted her email address then waited for the information to come through. It was odd but it made sense, she supposed. Ghillies might be aware that Bethany was living a life she didn't want her dad to know about, and after this afternoon he had elevated Caplan to 'friend'. She was still on the job, a useful contact. Her phone pinged: *Bethany Elspeth Robertson, date of birth 09 01 2002.* Then a photograph arrived, a slightly odd picture, a side view of the subject. It looked like a surveillance photograph. It showed a young, slightly built woman. Pale-faced, maybe with a few freckles on the exposed cheek, with an explosion of auburn corkscrew hair held back from her face with a yellow headband. Her outfit was typical student: a denim jacket, a blue rucksack over her shoulder with a furry brown and white toy hanging from it. The lower half of her legs were obscured by the garden wall. Caplan tilted the phone screen, noticing little flashes of light.

The picture had been taken through glass.

She looked at her watch, then texted Aklen to see if the visitors had arrived. He replied straight away that yes, they had, but the wee black and white kitten, Moe, had gone missing and they were looking for it. She replied saying that she'd be back ASAP, hoping that they wouldn't find wee Moe's entrails discarded after the falcon had feasted.

From the sound of it Mackie was back, talking to McPhee, who still had his jacket on, still holding a file. She was interrogating the poor bloke on his new girlie. Caplan thought that Mackie had never had much of a love life. She was one of the lads, had plenty of male friends, and most of the men wanted to keep it that way.

As Caplan walked into the incident room, she heard McPhee trying to get off the phone without being the last to say 'I love you'.

Mackie drew her finger across her throat, telling him to quit it.

McPhee ended the call, threw his mobile in his drawer and slammed it shut, glaring at Mackie.

'God, you've become a right cheery wee bastard since you met Carrycot,' she muttered, loud enough for all to hear.

'Her name is Carrie-Louise,' McPhee retorted, devoid of his usual good humour.

'Was she actually christened that? Or did she win the name in a cracker?'

'Better than bloody Toni with an I.'

'I use less ink.'

'Okay, if we can step out the playpen for a moment and have a look at the board, please,' instructed Caplan.

Craigo had elevated the Rod and Todd house to a crime scene, with a printout of a picture of two cartoon characters at the top.

She decided that question could wait, and updated them in a minute flat before calling Mackie through to the office. Her colleague sat opposite her, chubby legs crossed, a wire-bound pad on her knee, a pen ready, her jumper hanging off one shoulder. Caplan instructed her, or McPhee, to do another trawl for the Glen Douglas body on the misper list, and if there was nothing there to start the laborious searching for a diabetic who wasn't picking up their medication.

'That might take time to come to light if they had just picked up a scrip. I could check with his GP.'

'If we knew who his GP was, then we'd know who he was.' Caplan gave her constable a comedy eye roll.

'Sorry, getting carried away with Callum and his latest squeeze, Carrie-Louise. That rhymes, you know. Have you seen her?'

'She almost bumped into me, literally. I wonder how well the guys in traffic know her – she drives like a maniac.'

Mackie, unusually, wasn't keen to offer an opinion. 'How was your visit to the hospital? Your friend? Did she pass away? Hubby was on the blower bloody quick.'

'Rachel is comfortable, and Rory Ghillies was asking a favour. In fact, if the Glen Douglas search gets stalled then can you do a trawl on Rachel Ghillies's career? DC in Glasgow. Any deceased, unsolved, first or last name Nicholas or Nicholson. Any unsolved deaths that sound like that. Words "hardman" or "straight man".'

'Do you know what division she was with?'

'No idea.'

'You could ask her man. He asked a favour of you?'

'I'd rather not,' said Caplan. 'Not yet.'

'Was this her fancy man, this Nick?'

Caplan closed her eyes and sighed. 'More likely a case that she was involved with.'

'Okay, I'd get McPhee to act on Glen Douglas but I think he's too knackered to do anything, ma'am. He's been at the shagging all night, I can tell.' Mackie took one look at Caplan's stone face. 'And he's steering a couple of constables through some housebreaking, then preparing something for court. He's checking something out for Craigo, about those two dead men. But mostly he's staring at his phone, looking at her selfies of her pout, well I hope it's her pout and nothing more gynaecological. He's love-struck. Have you seen his black eye?'

'I did notice it, yes.'

'It must be love if she can put up with that daft article. He slipped getting out of the shower this morning. Being half asleep and having a slippery floor is more than he can cope with, and his face hit the wall at great speed.'

'It looks bloody sore.'

'I hope it is, might teach him some sense. Anyway, should you not be at home, ma'am? I thought Emma was coming over.'

'Yes, she is.'

'She bringing that gangly, veggie freak with her?'

'Yes, she is.'

'Well, if you are going to fall for a gangly, veggie freak, she's right to fall for a millionaire gangly, veggie freak.' Mackie went to stand up, then changed her mind. 'Ma'am. Are you a bit concerned about McPhee?'

'No, I'm concerned about your interest in his love life. Are you his mother?'

'No.' Mackie paused as if to calculate something. 'No.'

'Don't be concerned. He's in love, he'll get over it.'

'Not that, ma'am. I know I've been taking the piss, but he doesn't really seem himself. He's had a headache for about a fortnight. I know he'll be getting no sleep with all the pumping, too many nights out and going out for nice meals and all that . . . stuff . . .' She sounded very jealous.

'That's nice that you care,' said Caplan, with only a hint of sarcasm.

'But he's getting on ma tits with his bloody moaning.'

'Have you said anything to him?'

'Kind of. He said something about seeing the doctor. He felt like throwing up earlier. He's in the bloody toilet more than he's at his desk.'

'Toni, I can't say anything to him unless he says it to me first. Do you think it is affecting his work?'

'Not any more than usual, ma'am, he's always a bit slow.'

'Well, off you hop. Back to work. And can you have a phone round, see if you can find Bethany Elspeth Robertson, age twenty-one? All the usual haunts, last seen about three p.m. this afternoon at the Revolve. You're not writing any of this down. I'll check a list of contacts from the dad. It's not a full on official missing person . . . yet.'

Mackie let out a long sigh and burped quietly, then looked at the ceiling. 'Would that be Rosemary Robertson's daughter? She'd a weird name like Bryony or Beverly. Could have been Bethany.'

'Yes, you know her?'

'Know of her. From Pulpit Hill? Her mum's funeral was the talk of the steamie, ma'am, every bigwig of the parish was there. My aunt went, for the purvey like, said that poor Bryony was like a wee lamb in the headlights. It's early days for a misper but I'll track her down.' Mackie picked up her notepad.

'Rabbits are in headlights, lambs to slaughter, Mackie. And it's Bethany. Not Bryony.'

'Aye, ma'am, but what good did pedantism do anybody?'

'Pedantry,' said Caplan, quietly, to the closing door.

Caplan checked her watch. It was after six, time for her to go.

Driving back to the caravan, Caplan listened to *The Nutcracker Suite*, thinking that it might be a good name for the incident room at Cronchie. She popped into Tesco on the way, bought some dips and crisps, vegan dips and vegetable crisps, some beer and wine. Mineral water for herself and for the joyless Magus.

Turning the final corner onto the coast road, she could see the small, green van parked on the drive opposite to the caravan. There was also a taxi, a blue Skoda Octavia, pulled up alongside.

Caplan parked the Duster and fished the keys to the caravan from the bottom of her rucksack. She got out the car, enjoying the quiet air, the gentle hiss and rush of the waves, the birds in the trees and the noisier seabirds making their presence felt.

Pas was asleep at the caravan window. Pavlova, still a little feral, was in a basket behind the wheel and Caplan checked to see all the kittens were there. The small black and white face, wee Moe, looked out at her. The missing one had been found and returned to his mother. She looked up, landward, into the thick trees that spread across the lower slopes of the ben. The falcons in there would think nothing of taking a tiny kitten. Horrible to think about but it was a fact of life. Death was inevitable and up here it was accepted as such.

The caravan was unlocked. Aklen couldn't be far away, maybe at the house but round the back. Quickly, she got changed into jeans and a thin jumper. The autumn evening was still warm, even the constant breeze coming in from the sea loch had not yet gained its chilling edge.

She unpacked the car, stacking the groceries into two bags, leaving them near the steps of the caravan. A quick look round the house. The back door was closed and locked. The area behind the house where the grass had been cut had an old kitchen table for picnics. The swing seat was still, protected from the wind by the house, but the yellow cushions were out. Somebody had been sitting there recently.

Caplan considered herself the most rational of people, yet she started thinking about the *Marie Celeste* and the house where Rod and Todd had lived and died, the house that had remained quiet despite the manpower who were present, trying to tease evidence from the silence.

That whole thing was bloody odd.

A falcon took that moment to start screeching, making Caplan jump. There was a flutter of feathers and the downdraught of air ran over her left cheek as the bird took flight from the house off to the trees. Had it been sitting up in the eaves somewhere, waiting for twilight, waiting for the kittens?

She walked back round the house to the drive then onto the road that swept round this part of the sea loch; one car every two hours was rush hour and the peace was much more likely to be disrupted by the noise of a logging truck or a motor home that had taken a wrong turn. Then there was a scream, followed by a yelling cry, a child in pain.

Instinctively, she ran across the road, swiftly picking her away across the stones that separated the road from the sand. The noise had come to her from her left. She started along the beach to the jagged rocks that formed the north edge of their private bay.

She clambered up, not looking over the top until she got there, ready to rescue whoever needed rescued.

There was a crying child, one she didn't recognise. A young woman, the mother she presumed, was bending over the girl, making a play of looking at the scraped knee, saying something in a language Caplan didn't recognise but the body language was uniform. *I told you not to climb on that!*

She looked over to the rocks that huddled the road, causing a nasty turn that had been the site of more than one accident. Her visitors were sitting there, laughing, eating, drinking, chatting. It crossed Caplan's mind to reverse back down the rocks and retreat into hiding until she saw her daughter's face. Emma was watching her dad, concern evident on her face. It appeared she wasn't convinced he was as well as he wanted her to think. Caplan had suspected that Aklen coming off his medication was wishful thinking.

Caplan turned to look at Aklen. His smile was a little too fixed, the conversation too forced. If she didn't know him, it would seem all was well.

'Mum!' Emma slithered off the rock she was sitting on, the Magus helping her to her feet. She crossed the soft sand, limping slightly as she rushed to greet her mother, still protecting the injury that Caplan herself felt responsible for. Aklen also stood up, as did the two men, one of whom was the Ukrainian builder, with a young boy of three or four in his arms. The other she didn't know but she deduced was the taxi driver.

Emma gave her a big hug and the rest of them, kids included, stood almost to attention at her arrival. Caplan felt self-conscious in her trousers and jumper, amongst the baseball caps, shirts and T-shirts of everybody else.

Emma led her by the hand up the beach to where the others were. Caplan got the feeling that her mere presence had ruined the party. She wished her phone would ring.

Her phone stayed quiet.

Caplan, because of Aklen, had lived a very quiet life for the last seven years. She'd had the stimulus of some challenging cases but always had 'home' to go to, to decompress. As Emma introduced her to her own guests, she wondered if she was experiencing social anxiety; this invasion of her quiet idyll was challenging.

Caplan was polite to them all, and gracious. It was lovely to see her daughter. The Magus, who looked after Emma so well, was engaging Aklen in conversation. She knew Pavel in the way that most women know builders, and his wife and his two children with their reluctant smiles were enchanting. Nobody could know what they had been through to get here, to the wet, windy coast of a dark little country, but it was safe and quiet, a place for their children to grow. Caplan acknowledged all that as Aklen, Pavel and Bob the taxi driver started a skimming stones competition.

She wished Emma had given her more notice of the visit. If she'd known, she wouldn't have gone near work. But she *had* known and still made that choice. The day had been long, a lot had happened, and now the evening looked like it was going to stretch into the small hours.

There was nowhere for Caplan to slip away, but she tried, saying she was going back to the caravan for something. Then realised she wasn't on her own.

'Christine?' It was Christopher Allanach, the Magus, wanting a quiet word with her. She braced herself. She owed him so much, her daughter's health for one thing, yet she couldn't bring herself to like him.

'Yes?'

He was a very handsome man, quiet and thoughtful, with the air of a preacher. Or a cult leader, which Caplan thought he was, at heart. The murder of the McGregor family, the incident of their devil stone, had proved it to Caplan beyond doubt. A manipulator is still a manipulator. A charismatic one is the same but much, much more dangerous.

'I want to reassure you that I'm trying to persuade Emma to go back to university and finish her masters, but I can't make her do anything that she doesn't want to do.'

'Nobody can.'

'But I'm keen for her to go back. In case you think that I'm trying to prevent it.'

'Like you say, you'll never make her do something that she doesn't want to do.'

'And to say also that if it wasn't for you, I'd probably not be here. Those who wanted to inherit my estate weren't going to wait until I got to a ripe old age.'

In Caplan's mind the case had closed, other innocent people had died. 'It was a team effort, it wasn't only me.' Caplan knew she was being unfair, her voice was curt, her tone bored.

'But I'm not a poor man.'

'Oh, I know that, Mr Allanach.'

And there was that smile, a smile that could force a confidence from the unwary. 'You don't trust me?'

'Being a cynic goes with my job, I'm afraid.'

'Aklen's thinking about getting back to driving.'

'Is he?' She was so surprised at the news, she forgot to be annoyed. 'I didn't know that.'

And that smile again. He knew more about her family than she did. Her dislike of him ramped up a notch. 'Sorry if I've spoken out of turn.'

Caplan doubted it but forced a smile.

'You need a car. We've vehicles on Skone that we don't use. Not after all that . . . Anyway, I know Aklen would jump at it, but, well, you know how he's doing better than I do.'

'Yes. How much does Emma know about this?'

'I discussed it with her. She was in agreement. We could give you a van?' He looked over to where Emma was holding a vegan sausage over the flames of the barbeque.

Caplan caught his profile; his aristocratic cheekbones, the perfect jaw. He had excellent breeding.

He didn't turn back when he spoke again. 'I don't need you to like me, but I do owe you a lot. Probably my life. That's all.' And he slowly walked away, limping on his sore knee.

She waited until he was nearly out of earshot before she said, 'Thank you.' She'd said it very quietly, but even with the noise of the waves and the chatter, he heard it and turned slightly to raise his hand in acknowledgement.

She stood away from the sounds of their happy conversation which involved translation both ways. They were thinking of adding more wood to the fire. Caplan looked at her watch. She was dog tired and wanted to sleep. Aklen, after years of hiding away from the human race, was suddenly Mr Gregarious and encouraged Bob the taxi man from Cronchie to have another beer. Caplan found herself volunteered to run him back to Cronchie as he was too intoxicated to drive.

In the end the Magus, who they called Mags, with his totally charming and quiet manner, said that was ridiculous and he'd run Bob home. He ran the Ukrainians home as well as they were too tired to walk the length of themselves. As the van was a two-seater, with a small flatbed, the kids and one adult piled on the back to run the gauntlet of a faceful of midges on the way home.

Caplan gave up trying to speak to Emma on her own, thwarted by Aklen, making up for lost time, then by Mags on his return.

In the end, she escaped to her bed. Aklen, Emma and Mags stayed up late, long into the small hours of the morning.

Aklen climbed into bed, still talking nineteen to the dozen about what a nice lad Pavel was, how well Mags looked after Emma, shame that Kenny couldn't be there but maybe next time they could plan it in advance, maybe Caplan could take the day off . . . maybe even have a party to help clear up some of the rubble from the house, make it a social occasion. Once they had the roof finished. 'What do you think?'

Caplan banged her head into the pillow. 'By the time you get the roof finished, Emma will be a mother of five, Kenny will be in jail, and I'll be pushing up the daisies.'

'After suffering from what?' asked Aklen, playfully tapping the end of her nose with his finger.

'Lack of sleep.'

FIVE

*S*he was still here, in the cold, small room with no windows. There were two buckets now, one empty and one with water. A clean flannel, folded up, sat on the rim. A piece of black cloth lay beside it.

The sight of the water brought on a desperate thirst. Her lips were dry, the side of her mouth was cracked open. She managed to roll onto her knees, making her way over to the bucket like a hobbled donkey, where she kneeled, dipping her lips to the surface and drinking, trying to ignore the dizziness in her head. Closing her eyes, she dipped her face in, regaining some clarity.

It did clear her head. She fell onto her side, her body cradling the bucket and then she decided to panic. She couldn't think of anything else to do.

In that panic was the persistent but dull memory of the figures who'd been crouching in the bushes, a falcon with a broken wing lying nearby. Bethany had known them but the more she tried to see them, the more elusive their faces became.

She'd thought the jab in her hip was accidental. They'd apologised, laughed, the three of them. She'd actually laughed when they'd pulled on the protective gloves.

Then, it all got very hazy.

Sunday breakfast had been interesting; Aklen acting as mein host, but Caplan could see the strain on his face. In the caravan, he was at the three-ring burner in the small kitchen area passing rolls with sausage and vegan sausage out the window, careful not to mix them up. With mugs of coffee, Aklen, Mags and Emma sat and munched their way through most of the shopping. Caplan, collar up against the early chill, listened to the conversation, adding very little, looking at her daughter, thinking about Bethany. The girl hadn't returned overnight, and she'd texted Bethany's father to prepare a full list of his daughter's friends and contacts, mobile phone numbers and her email address. He'd called her back, clinging onto any comfort after a sleepless night. William Robertson was like a lamb in a storm.

How awful must it be not to know where your child was, helpless to know what to do for the best.

Looking at her own family in daylight, she thought that Emma had lost weight. Emma told her she looked tired. Both agreed that Aklen was better – he had his enthusiasm for life back, but he still needed to be careful.

Listening to their casual chatter, she doubted they noticed that she was going in to work that day, all of which meant that Caplan couldn't use the tiny shower in the caravan because there was no room for her to dress. Even when she put her laptop in her case and hung her ID round her neck it was a bit of a surprise to them. On a Sunday. As if the other three had a working week.

Her work phone had been beeping most of the night with updates. Lizzie Fergusson had been on the nightshift, sending the odd text re her thoughts on 'Nicholas' that had ended with an optimistic *I think I'm onto something*. Sarah Linden's texts were progressively rambling, about how did Rachel stay married to That Tosser for that length of time. And if she, Linden, didn't know about Nicholas, then there was nothing to know. Rachel's comments could be the ramblings of a drug-induced stupor and Rachel wasn't to be trusted. She'd been a bitch at training college and after all, look who she married. Her texts had continued on a similar vein for the rest of the evening.

Caplan had a thumping headache from lack of sleep so she pulled the Duster over in the first lay-by, scaring the birds who were feasting on the dead deer, and phoned April Farm B&B.

Betty said she was welcome to use the shower in room four; the guests had left but the cleaner hadn't got round to cleaning it yet. But by the time Caplan got there, it was spotless and she took a long time to shower, to do her stretches, ease off the tension in her neck. After a change of clothes, pulling her dark hair up to its chignon, she took a good look at herself in the full-length mirror, checking that she was smart. Then she paid Betty and left to stop at the Shore cafe where she had toast and green tea, out in the fresh air, where there was peace and quiet with only the low rumble of the early ferry approaching from across the water for company. She never knew when she might get to eat again. It was nine o'clock when she got up from the table, leaving a tip, and drove the five minutes round to the station. She called Fergusson. Her call was answered immediately.

'Are you sitting down?'

'Yes, I'm in the car. Do you have something?'

She heard Lizzie Fergusson pause, take a deep breath. 'Well, I know my way round a search engine.'

'I've never doubted that.'

'Well, I've found the fatal incident of Nikolas Kane Ardman. Nik with a K. Body found on the 23rd November 2016, deep in a forest near Beauly to the west of Inverness. Why was Rachel Ghillies looking at that?'

'Good question.'

'I've checked. She had nothing to do with the case. Neither did Rory. But,' Fergusson added, 'his injuries bear similarities to your dead body at Glen Douglas. They were on the wire overnight.'

'Pardon?'

'Glen Douglas and Nikolas Kane Ardman. Same injuries. I thought my screen hadn't refreshed or something but it's true.'

'Okay.' Caplan thought for a moment. 'Fractured fibula and left canine tooth missing?'

'Yes. But Ardman's remains were skeletal, really, so nobody knows what else.' A long silence. 'Are you still there?'

'Yes. Keep digging. Bye for now.' Caplan rang off, recalling Ryce's words about the diabetic man, dirty, found in a remote Glen with an injury to his left leg. She was calculating the timeline when Mackie came in and plumped her fifteen stone on the seat, making Caplan wince.

'Right, ma'am, I think I found him.'

'A Nikolas-with-a-k Kane Ardman, perhaps?'

'Oh, you know.' She looked disappointed. 'Did you get the other one?'

'The body in Glen Douglas?'

Mackie shook her head. 'No. But another one that's a bit of the same. Andrew Pottie?'

'Go on.' Something was niggling at Caplan now.

'Body found in remote place, injury to the leg. I've printed out this.' She handed an A4 sheet of paper to Caplan and kept talking as her boss regarded the image of a man, little more than a spotty wee boy.

'Brief history. Andrew Pottie, date of birth 12th October 1999. Suffered from alcoholism and mental health issues. Both warranted periods of hospitalisation at Gartnavel Hospital. Then discharged via the Loch Lomond Drop-in Centre to a supervised bedsit in a unit in Alexandria. Then he got a job, unspecified in the report, and left around 28th December 2019 and wasn't seen again until his body was discovered near Clatteringshaws Loch on 14th May 2020. Cause of death, unascertained.'

'Where?'

Mackie shrugged. 'Galloway? Down there somewhere.'

Caplan frowned. 'There's no crime there, Mackie. He found a job, left, and probably returned to his drinking habit.'

'Cause of death, unascertained.' Mackie wasn't going to let it go.

Caplan thought for a moment. Mackie had a good brain behind the eccentricity. 'Any pre or post-mortem injuries reported?'

'Fractured fibula, left leg. Left canine tooth is missing. The skull had a few fractures. A few other minor fractures to long bones and ribs.'

'And cause of death was unascertained?'

'Been dead for too long. Predation. Couldn't say exactly what killed him. Rumours were he'd pissed off somebody, they took him out there and beat him up.' Mackie pursed her lips. 'I'm thinking Rachel gave you the names for you to find out whoever "they" are. If it was all totally unconnected cases, then us trying to find commonality would get us nowhere. But it's taken me and PC Fergusson five minutes flat to find similarities in location and age, plus broken fibulas. See what I mean?'

Caplan tried to follow Mackie's logic. 'Maybe.'

'Do you think this could be big?' Mackie was keen.

Caplan paused.

'Do you not agree with me?'

'Let's find out more. Good work. We're busy with Glen Douglas and the Rod-Todd situation. We're short-staffed. I don't have a DI. And we'd need to apply for funding to look into this further. We need evidence to show there's a case here. What do we have? Three bodies, in the middle of nowhere, young people, similar injuries, over what? Seven years? It could be folk being daft. Is it common to break a fibula? I don't know. But I do know I have other priorities on my desk right now.' Caplan glanced at the clock. 'I'll look at it when I have time.'

'Well, don't leave it too long, or they'll be pulling some other poor bugger out the woods in a body bag.' Mackie stood up, hesitantly. 'If you are sure . . .?'

'Sure, for now.' Caplan followed Mackie out.

Craigo's desk was covered with its usual chaotic pile of papers, which on closer inspection were applications for medical reports, more scene photographs of the Roderick Taylor and Peter Todd locus, plus a printout of the spreadsheet of the house-to-house enquiries that had been ongoing in the quiet cul de sac. She couldn't help but notice what different lives the two deceased had led. She pulled a Post-it note from the edge of the monitor. *Rod and Todd anniversary, 2nd Sept, see La Fiorentina.* She googled it to see it was an Italian restaurant in Balloch. Was Rod out or did they do takeaway? Whatever, she was sure Craigo was on it. Scattered amongst the scene photographs were unfolded maps and dirty mugs, but Craigo himself was absent. Caplan reached over to pick up a photograph of an oblong box, nothing else but the box. It could contain a box of expensive chocolates, a small picture perhaps. She consulted the log to see that this was the Amazon delivery to the house of the deceased. The contents had yet to be located but a note from Karl Pordini said he was happy to go back and have another look.

Caplan felt a little stab of disappointment, empathising with Mackie, keen to work on a case that wasn't a case.

There was a single update on Craigo's desk. Nobody had been traced who had spoken to or seen Bethany Robertson after she left the Revolve. Bethany's phone remained off, non-trackable.

She went back into her office, knowing that, in McPhee's absence, Mackie was watching her every move. Caplan made herself comfortable and checked her messages sent through the secure system. More had been added to the Rod and Todd log; no history of depression, no red flags reported except, in hindsight, it had been a year, maybe more, since somebody had set eyes on Roderick Taylor.

Logging on to the case file of Ardman, Caplan checked who had been working on it when the body was discovered. The name Ghillies was absent. As she read on, bits of the case came back to her, more because of the remote location where the body had been found. It was a bit of a mystery, but there was little suspicion of foul play. Had Fergusson stumbled on the right one? Certainly no major investigation team had been set up to look at the disappearance of Nikolas-with-a-k Kane Ardman. Nobody had noticed he was missing until his body turned up in 2016 and it was thought that the body had been lying there for two years or so, in a natural shelter formed by the root system of four trees that had fallen in a single incident. The lifted earth had formed a clam-shaped roof, and a matching basin on the ground. He had crawled in there at some point and died, his body slowly decomposing and subject to predation. He was deep into the forest, there was little chance of somebody stumbling across his body.

Nikolas, aged eighteen in 2014, had dropped out of the little bit of society that he had ever connected with. He had been brought up in the care system and had gradually moved north aged about sixteen. The only way of tracking him was through his DWP payments. He had stayed in a few Glasgow hostels before going to a unit in Edinburgh, the Ashdown Community, before dropping off the radar altogether; he had packed the few personal possessions he had and left. His 'friends', well, the few that could recall him, presumed that he had drifted away. Nobody knew where he had gone or why. Nobody cared. Caplan had a quick flick back through to the records of the Ashdown Community staff. Paul Norman, Mo Maitland, Sean Connell, Robbie Fraser and Karen Mullan. One full-time, two-part timers and two volunteers. And that, from what she could read, was the story of this man's young life.

She requested sight of any more detailed files from deep storage while she kept reading. Ardman was found two years later. That was an estimated date calculated from when he had last picked up a DWP payment and from the estimation of time of death by the forensic pathologist. He was found lying in his natural shelter by a walker who had got totally lost and was himself in need of medical attention when he finally stumbled onto a road. Probably, like Ardman, the walker had taken shelter in the shallow roof of the uprooted trees then realised he was sitting beside skeletonised remains.

It was reckoned that even before death, Ardman had been emaciated. He had a few teeth historically missing, but the left canine looked as if it had been knocked out, perimortem. He could have been involved in an accident at some point as he had a fracture in his lower left leg that had not healed. The pathologist remarked that he wouldn't have been able to walk very well with an injury like that. How he managed to get to where he was found was a bit of a mystery but nothing that couldn't be explained by him running into the forest while under the influence of God knew what then hurting his leg. The body was too decomposed to test for metabolites of drugs, but a hair sample told a story of a long history of substance abuse, though he had been clean for a few weeks before his death.

There had been enquiries of course and there, eventually, she found Rachel's name, attached to the case tangentially, as part of a wider missing person's enquiry that had been looking for a woman called Rhona Welsh, whose body had later been found in an isolated part of a forest near Tain. That was all it said. She'd been listed as a missing person, vulnerable status, four days before she was found. She was identified by her parents.

It had taken much longer to identify Ardman's body. People with such challenges as he had faced in life tended to slip and slide through life without getting their DNA on record if they were careful enough not to be found guilty of any crime.

There was a small note on the file saying there was nothing to recognise facially due to passage of time and scavenger activity. The post-mortem examination had suggested that he may have been alive when he crawled under the roots seeking shelter but he had passed away exactly where he had been found.

It was odd.

But was it suspicious?

The remoteness of the location had given rise to speculation that somebody else had been involved. Certainly, somebody had taken him 150 miles from Edinburgh to Inverness. His last known official address was the Ashdown Community, his single person's apartment within the supervised unit in Edinburgh. There was a link to a website in the references. It was a website full of conspiracy theorists. Even then, there was a favoured scenario; one guy hitching a ride, the driver gets fed up with him, punts him out the car saying that a bus will be along in a couple of hours. The hitcher stands in front of the car hoping it won't drive on. It does and clips the left leg, causing the injury. He decides to take a short cut through the forest not realising how vast it is, how disorientating it can be. Maybe Ardman fell and he crawled into the shelter of the giant tree roots for cover. He may have fallen from the top of the exposed root plate, as if he had been walking through the long ferns and the moss, not really paying attention, maybe drugged, or stoned. Nobody had come forward, nobody had seen him since he walked out of the apartment. Nobody had noticed he had gone, nobody had reported him missing. The website reported that somebody had said Ardman had been happy to leave – he had said that life was going to get better. Impossible though it seemed, it did appear that his short life had got worse.

But what had happened to him in those intervening months?

He had travelled a fair way.

Where had he been?

It was noted that his 'last seen' and his last DWP payment was March 2014. Then his body was found in 2016 with too many variables to give an exact date of death.

Rhona Welsh had gone missing, been found dead in the woods and identified. To Caplan's mind they were not the same 'fit'. Welsh had a history of severe depression; she had been sectioned a few times to safeguard her own health. Her brother and sister had raised concerns. She had been missed and been loved.

And Rachel had said, clearly, find 'them'. Not him. 'Them'.

What did she know? Ardman found in a rural area, with an injury to his lower left leg, just like the diabetic in Glen Douglas. Many more similarities with Ardman than with Welsh.

How neat would it have been if the local radio news story of the body in Glen Douglas had come to the ears of Rachel and it had fired some synapse in her brain? Caplan knew that wasn't true; Rachel had asked to see them before the body in Glen Douglas had been discovered. The timeline didn't fit with Rachel's diagnosis or the terminal prognosis either. Something in early September had prompted her to get in touch with her old colleagues.

Caplan lowered her head to the cradle of her hands, elbows on her desk, and tried to think. She had Bethany and Shivonne to find, she shouldn't be sidetracked by Rachel's deathbed mutterings, yet instinct told her that Mackie and Lizzie were onto something.

She heard the door to the incident room open and somebody walk across the floor. Craigo was sitting at his desk, still in his jacket with the collar turned inward. He had a file in front of him and his little eyes were screwed up as the podgy forefinger of his right hand ran down a list on his computer screen. The forefinger of the left hand did the same on an A4 piece of paper covered in small, dense font. Caplan tapped the glass of her office, indicating that he should join her. DC McPhee had arrived, lingering near the whiteboard with the box of wipes in his hand. Mackie was now sitting at her desk, her head dipped behind her screen, spying on him.

Her phone pinged. Ghillies wanted a progress report about Bethany. She texted back that she had moved the investigation up a notch and it was now an official enquiry. She'd listed Bethany as vulnerable due to mental health. She had no idea if it was true, but she had to work the system.

She then found the number for the Revolve Centre and spoke to Karen Beattie, the day manager; Shivonne hadn't returned, her bed hadn't been slept in, but that wasn't unusual. Mo had called in sick so she was busy. Down the phone Caplan heard a buzzer, and Beattie said she'd need to go. Caplan hung up and was still looking at the handset when Craigo came in, pausing at the door as if he had forgotten something, or got a stabbing pain in his gut.

'Do I close the door?' he asked, needing clarification.

'You usually do,' replied Caplan. 'Have a seat. What's up with Mackie?'

'She's trying to find out what's going on with DC McPhee and that young lady that he's courting. It's very important. To DC McPhee. And no doubt to the young lady concerned.'

Caplan sat back in her chair, moving her phone and the paper pad to one side, her laptop to the other. 'Bethany? Shivonne? We're going out to see Robertson when we are through here.'

'Can I be back by lunchtime, ma'am? Vet's coming to the farm.'

'On a Sunday?'

'The cows don't know that.'

She nodded at him, acknowledging he did far more hours than he claimed for in overtime. 'I need a recent image of Shivonne from somewhere. Instagram, I'd imagine.'

Craigo said, 'Oh, and CCTV has been requested. We've timed the route home. We've traced Shivonne to the Ship Inn. They were not together. Shiv was very drunk going back to the Revolve.'

'But never got there?'

'No. I've two locals finding how she'd get home, only three or four ways and it's less than a mile. And she's well known in the pub. She left at closing time, last seen walking away on her own. Bethany's last seen would be back of three, Shiv's was half past eleven. She was the same as she ever was. Bethany was known to walk past the ferry terminals. There's a timetable and routine there – something might come up.'

'Can you get me some background on Shivonne? MacDougall, isn't it? Good. Peter Todd and Roderick Taylor? What happened to them? Are they related to the Simpsons?' She pointed in the direction of the action wall in the incident room, the cartoon picture clearly visible through the glass panel.

'Oh, they're Rod and Todd Flanders. From the Simpsons. They're religious. They eat cucumber and cottage cheese.' Craigo nodded.

Caplan swung a little in her chair. 'You've no idea what you're talking about, have you?'

'Well. No.'

'What do you have?'

Craigo opened the file and licked his lips in concentration. This was part of his little routine; he could recall this information off the top of his head and would still recall it if she met him in an old folks' care facility in forty years' time. 'Peter Todd was a forty-eight-year-old financial adviser, took over his dad's business, and very successfully from the look of his bank accounts. Office in Glasgow, going back in after three years of hybrid working. He went into Edinburgh one day a fortnight. He got on well with his colleagues. Like I say, his financials look good, but we'll keep digging. There's a fourth account we've found at a different bank where money's going into a premium bond account, under Rod's name only. Todd doesn't have any bonds. Todd and Rod have been together over twenty years. Rod was fifty-two, worked as a chiropodist purely doing home visits until he hurt his shoulder and found the job too uncomfortable. That would be over four years ago now. As far as we can ascertain, he's been a quiet, stay-at-home kind of guy. It could be two years since he's been over the door.'

'Mental health issue?'

'Waiting on GP notes. Todd was the one who went out with pals. The neighbours thought Rod was too poorly to leave the house. It was their anniversary on the second of September. It's in Todd's diary, starred and underlined. It was important. He bought champagne, Jacquart Mosaique. He ordered a meal from a good Italian in Balloch. They don't do take out, but they made it up for Todd to cook at home. There were few visitors to the house, one regular who might be a health worker of some kind?' Craigo rattled his pencil on the desk, thinking.

'Macmillan maybe? Or a mental health nurse if he had been openly talking about suicide?'

'My thoughts exactly, ma'am. As Todd said to Mrs Gains, this was the way they'd bow out.'

'Any other regular callers to the house apart from her? Him?'

'A her, ma'am. No other regular callers. This lady only visited Rod when Todd was out. Todd has a life, and Rod doesn't. Nobody ever looked in on him, apart from the lady. I'm trying to trace her. Easier tomorrow when things are open. The IT guys have Rod's laptop on their list but they say as it's probable suicide there's no rush. There's also a tablet somewhere so I've sent Pordini back to the house for that. Mrs Gains is positive that the visitor was related to the cancer.'

'It's all so bloody sad.' Caplan blew out a long breath through pursed lips. 'Ryce has scheduled the PM for tomorrow morning, after she's checked the medical records. It's true what she said. I've known those with terminal malignancy. Rachel. My dad. You see it in them. Ryce saw nothing in Rod when the body was admitted. He looked healthy.'

'Apart from being dead, ma'am.' Craigo handed her a photograph of them both, standing on a beach, arms round each other.

Caplan wouldn't have recognised them from the inert waxy figure in the bed, or the puffy blue-faced man swinging from the banister. She noticed that Craigo was quiet. He was watching her as she looked at the photographs. Todd had been a handsome man, fair haired, big generous features and a wide smile.

'Pordini found a few pictures of them from round the house. That one came from the bedside table.'

'The one Rod looked at every night? It was important to him.'

'Yes.'

'Hmm. Wider financials? Had they insured each other? Other money? Other family? Ryce will be on to the GP first thing tomorrow. Let's make sure that we have it all mapped out correctly.'

'It's all very sad.'

Caplan placed the picture down in front of her, looking at Rod with his Buddy Holly glasses and the wide grin that had etched deep lines in his face; evidence that he smiled often. It made her wonder what Todd had been like. 'If I'd planned to take my own life, with my loved one coming with me, I think I'd like them to be beside me. Why would I not take whatever they had taken? Especially if we had the drugs? Why not take the same thing, lie down in bed beside them, hold them, then let the waves take you, drift away.'

'I can see you've been giving this some thought, ma'am.'

'And you? What would you do?' Caplan looked at her colleague. 'Nobody could've attended that scene without it crossing their mind.'

'Me, ma'am? I'd climb to the top of Ben Lora, sit and watch the sunset, then slip away. Or as the sun rises, one or the other, everything comes and everything goes in its own time. That's always been the way of it.'

'What about your cousin out there?'

'Oh, her, well.' Craigo shook his head. 'Well, she'd eat the biggest takeaway and then get totally rat-arsed, pardon my French, ma'am. Then she'd pass out on the big comfy sofa. In fact, she's done that many a time when perfectly happy.'

Caplan looked out to where Mackie's gaze was following McPhee around, like a hunter after her prey, like the falcon after the kitten. As McPhee went to sit at his desk, Mackie's head darted from one side of her monitor to the other. It's what made her such a good police officer in a small village like this; she was extremely nosey.

'It's the hanging that doesn't seem right to me. Find out more about Peter Todd, the kind of person he was. Something drove them to take their own lives. They seem happy on their anniversary on the 2nd of September. A week later they are both dead.' Caplan wrinkled her nose, thinking.

'Does that explain the holiday brochures?'

'Who knows? You thinking they were planning a nice romantic getaway? Well, I have holiday brochures, Craigo. I never bloody get to go on one, do I?'

SIX

Another day, Bethany thought, but wasn't sure. She'd no way of marking time.

She was having visitors, they came, they went. Sometimes two of them, sometimes more. Never fewer than two. One of them had a soft voice, friendly even.

She was trying to gain their trust by being obedient, hoping that they would make a mistake or that she might be left alone with Soft Voice. If she had the chance, she might be able to talk her round, gain some traction with her friendship, but so far her captors had worked like a well-drilled team.

The first time, they called out the instructions before they opened the door. She had to kneel down and slip the hood over her head. She'd panicked, not able to see a hood. They told her it was the black fabric beside the bucket. She had to fold herself up and put her covered face on the concrete.

The door opened. There was a rush of movement. She felt a foot on the back of her neck, jamming her chin to the floor.

Then they left.

Shaking the pain and the hood from her head, she saw a bucket of fresh water, an empty one with a sponge for her to clean herself, and a small packet of antibiotic wipes.

And an apple, the end of a wholegrain loaf, a carton of juice.

The rope on her wrists had been loosened.

Not by much, but it was a start.

William Robertson took his time coming to the front door. His appearance and movements were those of an older man, late sixties, early seventies, older than Caplan would have presumed to have a daughter Bethany's age. The possibilities of a second marriage crossed her mind; a more complex family situation than might have been noted in the brief report she'd read. Within two hours of her not returning home, this man had reported his twenty-one-year-old daughter missing.

Caplan and Craigo followed him through the hall of the sandstone

Victorian terrace on the highest tier of Pulpit Hill with spectacular views over the bay, Kerrera and Mull. The décor was the usual mishmash of a lived-in home. Robertson showed them into the traditional front room, complete with heavy mahogany table at the window. The notepaper, pen, landline handset, mobile phone and a half-drunk cup of coffee showed that this was where he'd been most of the night.

On the wall over the settee hung a selection of family photographs. William. Rosemary, the younger-looking wife who had passed away two or three years previously. And Bethany, an auburn-haired girl, the feminine version of her father. At the opposite end of the room was a set of open double doors showing a modern extension beyond, pale wooden floor, cream rugs, low-slung sofas and a large TV up on the wall. Here, in the front room, thick olive-coloured curtains hung round the double-glazed bay window. The curtains framed the incredible view.

Caplan had read that Robertson, like Aklen, was a retired architect. Unlike Aklen, Robertson bothered about his own house as well as everybody else's.

They waited until their host settled himself, pulling one of the dining chairs towards him, resting his hands on the back of it, needing the support. In his light-blue shirt and tie and his matching woollen V-neck pullover, he looked like a golfer about to explain why his round had gone badly.

He cleared his throat, looking at the two detectives, as if their presence here in his home had reminded him of the reality of his daughter's absence. A man trying to keep himself under control. Caplan could sense Craigo not so subtly trying to peer out the window. One of Bethany's 'last seens' was the evidence of one Sean Mathie, the neighbour, as he was leaving his own house for work and had seen Bethany cross the road on her way to her volunteering. From the layout of the street, that hadn't been a casual glance out the front window.

'Do you have any news?' Robertson asked.

'No. Why were you anxious about her? So soon?'

'Why are *you* so anxious about her?' he retorted.

Caplan looked at him, finding him difficult to read. He looked nervous, his eyes darting over her face, looking for clues. He seemed impatient to get on with whatever it was they were here for.

'Have you made a list of her friends and acquaintances? Her routine? Where she drank coffee, her gym, the library.'

'I did that.' He handed over a single sheet of A4 paper and Caplan hesitated before taking it from him. 'It's not much.' He slumped onto the chair. 'She didn't live a busy life, not now.'

Caplan took the single sheet with its scant contents. 'The more friends and contacts a person has, the more eyes are on them, and on their world. The more people'll notice anything odd,' Caplan continued, keeping her voice quiet. 'Did she say anything that made you think she could be in jeopardy? An ex-boyfriend causing trouble? Somebody harassing her or bullying her?'

He shook his head, a little too readily for Caplan's liking. 'Oh no, nothing like that.' Quick, full of denial. Out the corner of her eye, Caplan saw Craigo shuffle slightly, as if noting the slight discord. He opened his mouth to say something then seemed to decide against it. Had there been a boyfriend and Daddy had not approved?

Caplan's eyes skimmed across the books in the alcoves that bordered the fireplace. Architecture and design. She recognised them and the pile of magazines, including the *Architectural Digest*; the same ones that Aklen had collected, though her husband's books were now wrapped up and secured in a storage facility.

Robertson's bookshelves were completed with back copies of the *National Geographic*, *Astronomers World*, *Night Photography* and *Scottish Field*, which all looked well read.

Robertson asked, 'What did you say your name was?'

'DCI Christine Caplan.'

'Any relation to Aklen Caplan? Architect? It's not a very common name and I heard that he'd moved out to the west coast.'

'My husband.'

Robertson's expression relaxed. He gave a little nod. 'Well, tell him I was asking for him. I hope he's on the mend.'

'He's fine. Got a thing about roofs now.' She smiled back then let her smile harden. 'What about names Bethany mentioned? Anybody making her feel uncomfortable?'

He shook his head. 'If there were she would have said. And to be honest, she wasn't the type to suffer fools. If she was having trouble, she'd sort it out herself. Nicely, but it would be sorted.'

'And she helps out with advocacy? Good communication skills, an empathetic listener? No issues there? Nobody latching onto her, mistaking her advice for friendship?'

'She did enjoy helping those less fortunate navigate the world.

She was very kind like that, knew that it would look good on her CV. She was intending to do human rights law at university, but she changed her mind.' He was on firm ground now. 'Social work. There's nothing that she said that caused me any alarm. I haven't been happy about the Revolve place since day one. When she was late, I contacted Rory Ghillies, asking what I should do. I'm scared.' He blinked slowly, a deep breath. 'Never been this scared in my life.'

Caplan responded. 'You're a dad, of course you are scared. Do you know what she was wearing when she set off for the Revolve on Saturday morning? The local branch has confirmed that she was at the Revolve and left after three o'clock.'

'Yes, I've a picture of her. Wait a moment.' He picked his phone up and started to scroll through. 'She was wearing jeans, her usual trainers. She'd taken to swirling her hair up and round in that scarf thing.'

Caplan creased her forehead. 'You took a picture of your daughter as she left the house? On exactly the day that she disappeared? That sounds a little . . . odd.'

Robertson nodded, looking uneasy. 'I photograph her every day. When she leaves.'

Caplan sat down beside him.

'I know how bad that sounds but her mother, Rosemary,' his eyes drifted up to the photograph on the sideboard, 'went out that door and didn't come back in. She died suddenly. Once that happens, you live in fear of it happening again.'

'What happened to your wife?' asked Caplan, softly.

'She left to go to work, went to the gym first as she always did. She collapsed on the running machine. Aneurysm. She died immediately. No warning, no nothing.' His eyes welled up. 'I can't let that happen to Bethany. She was scanned to make sure she won't go the same way. It's hereditary.' His eyes drifted over to the middle distance, looking for a place to rest. 'Sometimes I can't remember what the woman I was married to for thirty years actually looked like. Except at three o'clock in the morning – then I see her all the time.'

Caplan gave him a moment. 'Was Bethany suffering from any other condition? We've an alert out in all hospitals. She's not been admitted anywhere. She walked out of the Revolve into a busy little town. If she had collapsed, somebody would have noticed.'

'But something has happened to her. She wouldn't walk away of her own free will, not without letting me know. Has she been abducted?'

Caplan didn't feel she could agree or disagree, she simply didn't know. 'Not that we can say.'

'Rory was saying something about teenagers going missing. I've been thinking about all those children that disappear and never make it back home. Has she been trafficked somewhere? Is that possible?'

Caplan said, 'Intelligent, middle-class girls like Bethany are not the target group for traffickers. Did Rory say there was a connection with Bethany and teenagers going missing?'

Robertson shook his head. 'No, sorry, it was something he said ages ago. I was going over it in my mind, that's all. You think all sorts at a time like this.' He rubbed his face, exhausted.

'Mr Robertson?'

'Bill, it's Bill, please. Has Shiv turned up?'

Caplan shook her head.

'You have had no sleep. I think Craigo here should put the kettle on. Might give both of us some energy.'

Robertson responded with a weak smile. 'I'm not sure Bethany's right to do this volunteering. It was all because she lost her mum. But then she was ill herself. She's a determined wee lassie. Takes after her mother,' he added wistfully.

'I'm going to the Revolve Centre later. Do you know what she was doing there yesterday, specifically I mean?'

'Well, she helps out with applications for benefits, though Christ knows that type know their way around the system pretty well. And lifestyle skills, whatever that is. She was talking Shivonne through a job interview, like turning up and being on time.'

'How long had she been volunteering there?'

'Since June last summer, nearly full time. But her hours vary. Always a Wednesday morning and Saturday though.'

'But she'd have been at uni, surely?'

'She had an operation, on her back, had to take some time out. That's why her list of friends is so short. She was neither here nor there.'

'An operation?' She heard Craigo clattering around in the kitchen. A rush of warm air wafted into the room from the heat of the glass wall at the back. 'Nothing serious, I hope?'

'She's fine now. It was a pilonidal sinus. Takes ages to heal. She was out of circulation for a while. It's not like the city where her uni friends would pop in.' Robertson sniffed. 'No, Bethany never goes out with friends without saying. She always lets me know where she is.'

'I've a twenty-year-old son and I'm not sure what he does day to day. I'm not sure that I want to know. They live in a different space from us, different generation. It's natural.'

'Not Bethany.'

'You last saw her at breakfast yesterday.'

'Yes.'

Caplan looked at the picture on his phone. The way the auburn curls were rolled tight under her yellow headscarf made her look like Rosie the Riveter on her way to Tesco. Caplan opened up the image as far as it would go. 'It's time-stamped at eight-fifty? Is that the normal bag she carries with her? Or was she going to the gym?'

Robertson looked at the picture, seeing the large bag swung over Bethany's left arm, mostly hidden by her body as she walked from the house, and the smaller strap of her rucksack across her shoulder.

He shook his head, appeared to rethink, and then shook his head again. 'Sorry, I don't think so. She normally has her rucksack, with her wee owl mascot hanging from it. Her mum bought her that.' He took the phone back and swiped once. 'That was Friday's picture. She'd the rucksack then. And Thursday.' Another swipe. 'Or the day before, and she was going out to Revolve each time, covering for somebody's holidays.'

He took a photograph of Bethany every day and it appeared that she had no idea. Caplan decided it could wait. 'Can I have a look in her bedroom?'

'Is that necessary? It's private.'

'Your daughter's missing, of course it's necessary,' said Caplan blankly. 'Helps us get a sense of the young woman as she is, not as she is filtered through the eyes of her dad. There'll be things in her life that she'll have kept to herself, things that could help us find her.'

For a moment they stood in silence as Craigo came back with a tray with three cups and a teapot. They all jumped when Robertson's phone rang. He looked down at it, and gave Caplan a meaningful look.

'Rory.'

'Don't worry, he'll only be making sure that I'm doing as I was told,' reassured Caplan.

As he took the call, Caplan gestured that she was going to go upstairs and have a look round. Robertson looked like he was going to protest, but if he mentioned it to his friend on the phone, all Ghillies would say was, 'What do you expect her to do, she's only doing her job.'

Craigo subtly moved himself in front of the door as Caplan left the room to make her way upstairs. The dark-blue carpet in the hall needed a good vacuum. On the stairs as she went up she looked at the watercolours. They had matching frames and the subject matter was similar. All Scottish mountain landscapes. There were four in all, two painted in daylight and two painted against the backdrop of a starry night sky. What Constable would have painted if he had been born in the Western Isles. At the top of the stairs, the square wall was adorned with an arranged group of four framed photographs showing the moon in certain phases; deep tones of blue contrasted with the lunar bright grey and whites. They were breathtakingly beautiful images, much more appealing than the standard vase of flowers or the cottage garden prints that hung on the walls downstairs. Two conflicting styles, one bumped upstairs out of the way. Who had been the dominant one in the marriage, Mr or Mrs Robertson?

Who did Bethany take after?

And how badly did she feel the need to escape her father's benevolent but watchful eye, because Caplan had no doubt that Bethany did.

Four doors led off the upper landing, one obviously the toilet, positioned at the front of the house. On passing the door straight ahead of her, she tried the handle. It was locked. From the open doors of the other two, she could see the main room had a double bed, which put Bethany in the back room with the beige and yellow carpet, perfectly hoovered.

Caplan walked into the room, slowly, resisting the temptation to knock. The smell of a pomegranate perfume lingered in the air, even though the hopper on the main window was open.

Bethany hadn't had the easiest of times. Her years of early adulthood had been difficult. Materially comfortable, but she had lost her mother, had been ill and off university for nearly a year. She left her school friends, made new allegiances at university, then left them behind as she took a year out, before starting again in the year below. Both Bill and his wife had been only children. Bethany, here in this house, on the outskirts of town, was a little out of step with everybody else, slightly isolated. In the investigation, there had been nobody mentioned as a best friend, nobody's name cropping up again and again as the one who would know, the one she was always on the phone to, the Instagram friend. Nobody.

Aklen had been a hermit for seven years and he had more friends than Bethany Robertson. She looked round the room, incredibly neat and tidy, her eyes drawn to the framed photographs, telling her story. Bethany with her parents, no best friend here. The photographs were arranged chronologically. There was no mum in the most recent ones. Caplan's similar story showed her husband being missing from their kids' life for six or seven years, give or take.

Maybe that's why, from what her dad had said, Bethany had fitted in at the Revolve Centre, with the rest of society's misfits, finding new and unlikely friends, keeping them away from her father, who would not approve. Her eye caught a small series of photobooth snaps; Bethany and a peroxide blonde who she recognised as Shivonne. They were pulling faces and messing around; besties as the youngsters would say nowadays. Was Shiv the confidante Bethany had been looking for? A girl who had grown up with so little, making a friend of one that had grown up with so much.

The single window looked out onto the glass roof of the extension and the back garden beyond that. It was the room of a tidy student with a well-ordered mind; everything was in its place. Caplan had already suspected that Bethany was a methodical young woman. Her dad was right, she wouldn't do anything unless it was planned.

Which begged the question, was her disappearance deliberate? Caplan took another look back at Shiv's mischievous eyes, a survivor because she had to be. Were they somewhere together, drinking shots and having the time of their life? Caplan doubted Bethany would be that cruel to her father. She might have gone, but she'd have left a message.

The design of the room suggested it had been remodelled when she went to university. A bespoke bookcase bridged across the top of the bed. Each little dookit had the right number of books, photographs or ornaments. Nothing looked overcrowded. Caplan spotted some trophies for Irish dancing. The photographs here were from her early life; mum, dad, the same pony eating carrots and getting rosettes, then eating the rosettes. The books went way back to her childhood; some very old editions of Enid Blyton, the *Children's Pictorial Bible*, more modern children's classics. Bethany had a wide taste in books, and they all looked well read. Her desk had a laptop on it and a phone charger with no phone. The single bed was neatly made with a yellow duvet cover with a crumpled area, no doubt where Bill had sat, wondering where she had gone. On the pillow rested a plush, fluffy owl, peering back at her with huge eyes. The bedside table nearest the door had a photo of her mum and dad taken a few years ago and a bottle of eyedrops for nighttime use. Beside that was an ornate wooden box. Caplan opened the lid. It was a typical young woman's jewellery collection; a few precious items still in boxes, the rest lying in little compartments. Mostly silver, good quality, ethnic pieces, nothing vulgar as Caplan's mum would say. And there were no gaps, she'd taken nothing with her. There was a half empty bottle of Jo Malone, Pomegranate Noir, and on top of the other bedside table was a stack of books by Lucinda Riley, then a porcelain hand with a pair of glasses resting on the arch between thumb and finger. Caplan bent over to look through the lens, spreading her fingers behind them. It appeared Bethany needed her glasses to read her book at bedtime.

On the opposite wall hung a mirror with a narrow shelf underneath, and two large prints, both of birds of prey. A hawk, a falcon, hooks of claws. Caplan thought of the threat the falcons were to the kittens and shuddered. Was there a side to Bethany that wasn't obvious in her gentle character?

Caplan pulled drawers open. The bottom drawer in the chest had a small jewellery box, tucked under a pile of gloves and scarfs. Caplan opened it. Medication tucked away where her dad would not see. The contraceptive pill, taken up to date, but she hadn't taken it with her. The other was Trazodone. Caplan pulled out her phone and photographed the labels, suspecting the latter was either an antidepressant or an anti-anxiety medication. God knows, Aklen had been on them all over the last seven years.

The contents of the drawers suggested that some items of clothing were missing; they could be in the wash, or they could be away with her in the bag she had slung over her shoulder.

Could they look at her laptop? Another question for her dad.

Caplan's eyes drifted back to the mother, Rosemary. Always smiling, happy, she looked full of life and cheer. Each picture of her face glowed with an inner happiness and peace, no sign of the abnormality in her brain that would end that life so suddenly.

No wonder Bethany was struggling with anxiety, or maybe sleeplessness. Did her dad have any idea? Was he the same, each keeping their fear to themselves so as not to worry the other?

Caplan looked over onto the roof at the high gable end, a dormer window put in, the flat roof of it slightly risky in a country with a high rainfall. That was the roof over the room with the locked door. Might be something or nothing.

Caplan slid open the mirrored door of the wardrobe, looking for a gap, anything that Bethany might have packed to take with her, wherever she had planned to go. The wardrobe, like everything else, was well-organised with shoes at the bottom on double row racks, from boots through to training shoes through to sandals. There were two pairs missing, if usually every part of the rack was taken. Given the range, it looked like one pair from the trainer end and one from the shoe end. More than that she couldn't tell. Up on the clothes rail there was a gap where the hangers had been parted; maybe something missing there.

Caplan looked at what was before and after the gap. A missing dress? Something formal?

It didn't seem right, and she didn't think that asking Robertson would be of any use.

She closed the wardrobe door, her fingertips touching the mirrored glass as it floated past, smooth, expensive.

Looking at her reflection as the image floated into sight, she saw how tired she looked. The black marks under her eyes had darker marks under them. Still, she wouldn't be doing her job right if she could sleep well during this. It was hard work; long hours and hard work, the daily grind. And she suspected that there was something with Bethany, or her situation, that was very concerning. But as yet, she couldn't put her finger on it.

It was the small things that would solve the case. The devil was in the detail.

Which begged the question, who was Bethany sleeping with, and where was she going with good shoes and a dress?

Caplan listened at the top of the stairs to the chatter below, trying the handle of the first door again, definitely locked. Craigo was doing his disarming idiot act no doubt. She crept into the bathroom – very white, very clean. The window was open and the draught of the brisk autumn day was enough to chill the top floor of the house.

She opened the door of the bathroom cupboard then poked around in the chrome shelving underneath the sink. Nothing much but bleach and toilet rolls. The cabinet above the sink showed that somebody had piles, somebody wore contact lenses, they had good dental hygiene, and somebody was taking Gaviscon by the mouthful.

But the pills? The glasses? These were things that Bethany would have taken if she'd gone voluntarily.

Which led to the conclusion that she had not.

SEVEN

They didn't say what they wanted from her. They kept her fed and watered, kept her relatively clean. Soft Voice would almost caress her with the sponge, running it over her naked body. Soft Voice let her stand up. Soft Voice never hurt her.

And there were more in the corner, she knew that. Watching.

Somewhere in her memory, in her past, she had known that voice.

Then Soft Voice would leave with a goodbye pat on the shoulder and the door would close again.

Suddenly, one leg was pulled from her. She thought her hip was going to dislocate. Then pain, and noise, and a crack she felt in her head. Something hit her hard on the side of the face, so hard it would have floored her. But somebody was keeping her upright. Another blow, then another.

Her mouth was full of blood. She couldn't breathe. She choked, and her ribs rattled off the concrete floor. She went into a coughing fit; spasms in her rib cage as something lodged in her throat. She spat out a tooth.

Then she lay down. Waiting for the next blow. It never came.

They'd left without her knowing.

It was a twenty-minute drive and the roads were quiet, unlike DC Mackie who talked non-stop. From the moment she fastened her seat belt, she had her notebook open.

Caplan couldn't fault her enthusiasm, but the volume could be problematic.

'I might have another one. Stratton. A Lisa Stratton. Her body was found in Chern Wood near Tyndrum. Could that be Rachel's Straightman?'

'Go on,' said Caplan, interested despite herself.

'Another body, found in a remote place, injury to the leg? Do you think this could be big?'

Caplan paused. 'Scotland's full of remote places and hill walkers do get leg injuries. We need to find Bethany. We have to find Shivonne.'

'I know, but this came up as I was doing the search. I didn't waste time. Lisa Stratton was thirty-one years old when she was found dead in Chern Wood, Tyndrum. Naked but no sex crime. She was found with an injury to her left leg and two to her right. She was a PA, deep in debt, a pretty woman and, due to the financial issues, the original investigation was thinking organised crime.'

'Bit odd. We don't normally find victims of organised crime, they tend to disappear.'

'We have wild woods, injury to left leg.' Mackie counted them off on her fingers. 'Nikolas Ardman, Lisa Stratton, Andrew Pottie, Glen Douglas man, and Rhona Welsh. That's five.'

'Yes,' said Caplan. 'I can count. But we need five of the same. Are they the same? At the moment, it's circumstantial.'

'They are similar, ma'am.'

'And those similarities are degrees of circumstance. The nakedness, I agree, is the compelling link between them. Keep digging. But for now, it's all about Bethany.'

Mackie was silent for all of three milliseconds, looking out the window. 'Did you hear McPhee slam the door? That was a smoochy phone call from that wee lassie of his. She's some kind of sex bomb, you know.' Mackie pulled a bit of a face, turning to roll her eyes at Caplan.

'Pardon?'

'That's what it says in the men's toilets,' said Mackie. 'You need to take a left here, ma'am.'

The Revolve was the last in a line of large Victorian houses along the promenade. It had been many things over the years and was about to change again if the local residents had any choice. The building had suffered an undignified decline from a rather grand hotel with beautiful sea views, to a hotel for those of more modest financial means, then a boarding house. Then it had lain empty for a couple of years before being bought over by the Revolve charity. The logo was a hand, palm up, with a circle above, fitting for a charitable organisation involved in turning lives around. It had a good reputation for getting those who had fallen through the holes in society back on their feet. But then the economy had gone into flux, the staycation became popular, and Oban, as the Gateway to the Highlands, was a thriving hub of coaches, ferries, cars, trains and motor homes.

The Revolve Centre was a thorn in the rose.

Everybody thought it was a great idea. But not on their doorstep.

Inside the front door, the smell of bleach and carpet cleaner was overwhelming. There was a hall with two bikes leaning against a chipped radiator. A small reception desk stood to one side at the bottom of the stairs. A framed photomontage of smiling faces was prominently displayed. A corkboard pinned to a door was full of messages, written in many hands, with varying legibility and assorted proficiency of spelling. Shiv was wanted in the kitchen, and there were four Post-it notes for Beth; she was to phone home immediately.

Caplan already had a note of the six people who lived here. Stan, John, Rab, Shiv, Petra and Sux. She knew that Stan was a long-term resident. Not the type of person that the Revolve was supposed to cater for. Stan was in his early forties. He'd got this far and was doing well, according to his social worker who had talked to Toni Mackie that morning. Stan was in hospital having an ulcer on his foot treated, a complication of the circulatory damage of an ex-alcoholic. He'd been drinking paraffin and lighter fluid for most of his life. His eyesight was very poor. The social worker commented that Stan would harm nobody but himself; he was scared of his own shadow.

John had been 'home' on a visit when Bethany had gone missing. Toni Mackie had tracked that down and found it to be true. He'd got drunk in Campbeltown, been arrested and was still in the nick drying off.

Sux had been in town most of the morning but been back for lunch, explained Karen Beattie, the day manager, as she guided them into a small room that was as close to an office as they could get. Caplan's first impression was that there was a child sitting on the desk in Winnie-the-Pooh pyjamas, her hair up in a scrunchy, fiddling with her cuff as she looked at the two women with her huge suspicious eyes.

'This is Petra,' said Beattie, 'who isn't supposed to be in here, are you Petra? You're not allowed in the office.'

Petra looked as if she hadn't heard, or if she had she didn't seem to care. 'Who's them?'

'Cops,' said Beattie, brutally. 'Do you not have somewhere to be, something to do? Like get dressed?'

'I'm okay.'

Beattie squeezed past and sat on her chair. The two cops remained standing, neither of them fancying moving the clothes perched on top of the small two-seater sofa, the plastic decorated by cigarette burns.

'Petra, what did you do yesterday?'

Petra shrugged.

'Did you see Bethany? You know her? Did you have spaghetti?'

'Aye.'

'And then?'

'I dunno.' Another shrug.

'Did Beth say if she was going anywhere?'

'I dunno.'

'Don't know if she said, or don't know if she was going somewhere?'

Another shrug.

'Did she take her jacket when she left?' asked Caplan.

That made Petra think.

'Nice jacket. Aye.'

'And who else was there – Bethany, you, Shiv?'

'Aye.'

'And who else?'

Petra pursed her mouth, then counted something on her hands, using her fingers, as if mentally going through everyone who'd been there the previous day.

She held up her hand. All five fingers. Beattie held up her own, counting them off: 'One, Shiv. Two, Bethany. Three . . .'

Petra looked lost.

'You were there, that's three. There were six sitting at the table to eat spaghetti? Who else?'

'Brian, Brian was there. And Mo. And . . . dunno . . .'

Beattie lifted her phone and got Brian on the other end. After a brief conversation, she swiped the phone off and reported back. 'Bethany was fine. Brian says that he ate the pasta and then went into the lounge to watch the football. Sux was there too. She said it was all very normal.' It was her turn to shrug.

'Petra, where's Shiv?'

'I dunno.'

'When did you last see her? Were you tidying the kitchen with her yesterday?'

'Yeah, yesterday with the spaghetti.'

'Not last night?'

'Nope.'

Beattie was on the phone again, another quick conversation. 'She didn't come back last night.' She raised her eyes to the two cops. 'It's not an unusual thing for Shiv to be out all night. She tends to have a lot of men friends. I checked her room earlier, but all her stuff seems there. I've plenty of experience of them doing a runner, believe me. Her room's along here if you want to have a look.' Beattie indicated that she was happy for the two detectives to follow her.

'And Mo?' asked Caplan as she walked after Beattie, stepping over a pile of dirty laundry that was stacked against the wall.

'Another volunteer, nice lady, in her forties. You'd know her if you saw her. Very colourful. Was a psych nurse, I think. I'll get you her number if you need it, she's not in today.'

'Thanks. And does Shiv have a designated support worker?'

Mackie was ready with her notebook.

'Oh yes, Zoe. Zoe McCulloch. I'll get you her number as well.'

The room was small, just a bed and the few possessions of Shivonne McDougall. The large dressing table had a mirror with a rail of small lights hanging round it, stuck on the wall with some clear tape. The surface of the dressing table was swamped with cheap make-up, but it was ordered; there was method in the mess.

Caplan asked the obvious question. 'Were they close? Bethany and Shiv?'

Beattie sighed. 'They were pally. From different worlds, obviously. I think Shiv looked up to Beth. And there was something going the other way. Bethany was a little reticent, Shiv was far too bold. They cancelled each other out.' She pulled a printed picture from its pin on the wall and handed it to Caplan. Shiv and Bethany. Two young women. Shiv's short hair was bleached peroxide blonde; a pretty face, impish, but there was bitterness in those eyes. Bethany, by comparison, looked . . . 'sweet' was the word that drifted into Caplan's mind.

'Was that the way they looked yesterday?'

'No, Bethany had her hair up and Shiv had dyed hers a deep, rich red. The exact same colour as Bethany's. Nothing like flattery.'

Caplan looked around, seeing the bin. She bent over and picked it up, rattling the contents about hankies, two cans of Red Bull and a pile of empty crisp packets. Then she got a pen from her pocket and carefully lifted a crushed cardboard box from the bottom. Hair dye. Permanent intense colour, deep auburn red.

'I presume this was the colour she used?'

'Yes. Changed her hair colour every week.'

'Do you think Shivonne and Bethany have gone missing?' asked Caplan.

Beattie almost laughed. 'I doubt it. They'll be somewhere else, hanging around. Honestly. We have had this situation many times. People like Shiv have no sense of responsibility and no sense of time. I'd have thought Bethany would have known better.'

Caplan opened the narrow wardrobe door. It stuck, and she had to put her foot against it to jerk it open. Beattie was talking about how she'd never trusted Shiv as Caplan looked at the suit carrier hooked onto the rail. It was facing outward, one of those that folded up. It looked like the black bag she'd seen over Bethany's arm.

'Was this Shiv's kind of thing?'

Beattie shook her head as Caplan unzipped the front. Inside was a simple, grey shift dress. Hanging round the hanger of the suit carrier was an Asda bag, and in it a pair of grey leather loafers with a small gold buckle at the front. Around the shoulders of the hanger was a dark grey jacket. An anonymous outfit for an interview.

'You knew nothing of this?'

Beattie shook her head. She seemed curious now.

'Did you know Shiv was going to an interview?'

Again, a shake of the head.

As the three of them went to walk out the door, Caplan said, 'Karen, when was the last time you saw her?'

'Yesterday at some point. Wasn't really paying any attention.' Another shrug, but Caplan kept up her eye contact. 'She was here making pasta with Bethany.'

'That was yesterday early afternoon. Not seen since then? Do you have her mobile number?'

Beattie got out her own mobile.

'Can you give her a ring?'

'Already have. No answer.'

'No answer, or turned off?'

'Turned off.'

They waited as she called again.

The recorded message told them that the number was unavailable at the moment.

'Is that like her?' asked Mackie.

Beattie shook her head. 'It's normally clamped to her hand. Honestly, it's nothing. She'll be away pissed with some bloke. It's not worth the taxpayer's money.'

Caplan handed over her card, asking her to get in touch the minute anyone heard from Shiv.

On the way out, down the badly carpeted hall, Caplan stopped at the little reception desk and took a close look at the photomontage, taking a picture of it with her phone. Mackie was holding the front door open to let the smell of damp and fried onions dissipate.

'You allowed to do that?' asked a tall, shifty woman, who was leaning on the top of the steps, smoking, and directing the smoke into the hallway for no good reason Caplan could make out other than devilment.

'Yes,' answered Caplan.

'You the cop?'

'Yes.'

'Who's the fat fuck of a friend?'

'That's you she's talking about.' Caplan nudged Mackie.

'Well, my dad's called me much worse than that many a time,' mused Mackie, looking out to sea, the breeze lifting her fringe, taking years off her. 'At least I knew who my dad wiz. There wiz a bloody sweepstake for hers,' Mackie said to Caplan. 'I've arrested most of them.' She reconsidered, 'All of them, actually. Her mum was a popular lass.'

Caplan smiled her sweetest smile at the woman who was blocking the door.

'Youse want to know about the dress?'

'You going to tell us?'

'It'll cost you.'

'No, it won't,' said Caplan. 'Mackie, do you want to explain?'

Mackie rolled her eyes. 'Well, you know she's from Glasgow?'

A look of something flickered across the smoker's eyes but all she said was, 'Whit of it?'

'Let me help you,' said Mackie. 'Tell us what you know or she'll arrest you for obstruction. Once she does that, she'll keep you on a whole host of charges, most of which I can't even begin to spell. So, no, she's not paying you a penny.'

'Fuck you.'

'Mackie, arrest her, will you? I'm getting cold standing here.'

'Youse couldn't arrest a fart.'

The handcuffs came out.

The woman tried to take a step back, realising she was against the wall. 'Are youse fucking serious?'

'Told you. From Glasgow. They arrest you for swearing down there. Inflammatory, you see, could lead to problems. What's it to be?'

'Shiv had an interview. Beth set it up. Morning housekeeping but then some waitressing, nice hotel, evening shifts wi' loads of golfers, men with money. And Ah bet you think that's a great idea. But that's Shiv's con all along. She chats them up, arranges to meet them up in the room. Goes up, has a shag, gets him drunk, he falls asleep and she relieves his wallet of a few quid. Never a lot. Not enough for him to make a fuss, not enough for him to say anything to the wife. She makes sure they are married. That's her trick.' She took a long hard drag on the cigarette. 'Don't think Bethany clocked that.'

'Have you seen Shiv since yesterday lunchtime?'

'Nope.' A long insolent draw on the cigarette.

'Well, if you recall anything else, let us know. And stop smoking and eat something.'

'Least Ah'm no a fat arse like you.'

They walked out to the sea wall, having a seat and a much-needed breath of fresh air. Mackie swung her legs up and round so she was looking out to the Sound, watching the ferry slowly making its way over to Mull. Caplan sat, straight-backed and square, looking at the Revolve.

'Well, what do you make of that?'

'Shiv and Beth have disappeared off to Glasgow. They are both blind drunk lying in a heap somewhere?' offered Mackie.

'I hope you're right. Feels a little odd that we're looking for two young women and there's two entitled old guys trying to help out. I've no idea what that means.'

'That one has lost his wife and the other is about to? We are used to mothers picking up the phone.'

'You've made a good point.' Caplan nodded.

'When Kenny had that fall and Emma was hit by the car, the first thing you did was involve your friends in the force,' said Mackie, surprising her boss with a depth of detail Caplan didn't think she would possess.

Something caught Caplan's eye. 'Why is there a young man on the corner trying to attract our attention?'

'That's Tiggerdean. Looks about fifteen, he's more like a hundred and eight. Foetal alcohol syndrome. I'll see what he wants because he'll be wanting something,' said Mackie, getting off the wall and walking towards the slight figure who had disappeared off round the corner before Mackie had got onto her feet.

Caplan watched her go, content to be left to enjoy the sun. The incessant noise of the waves made them seem more confident here than they were round the bay where she lived. She was enjoying the quiet point in her day, taking some deep breaths when her phone pinged. It was Mackie, asking her to go to the chippy. They'd meet her back on the corner. Fish supper, salt and vinegar, Irn-Bru and a pickled egg.

Caplan returned about ten minutes later, her stomach growling with hunger, angry at being tempted with the smell of deep-fried carbs. Mackie came round the corner, took the hot parcel and dashed back across the road, leaving Caplan with vinegar fingers.

She sat on the wall, waiting for Mackie who soon came hurrying over. 'Can we walk back to the car, ma'am? Mr Tiggerdean has a reputation to keep up.'

'Do you know the price of a fish supper these days?'

'It was an investment. Wee Rab sees a silver Skoda Octavia 19 plate last Wednesday morning beside a red Corsa 05 plate. He says Bethany hangs around the back of the Revolve until about ten a.m. then the car appears and she gets in it. And get this, it happens every Wednesday morning. Bethany is not volunteering at the Revolve as often as she tells her dad.'

'The man in the car? The boyfriend? We need to get her phone records. McPhee has registered her as a misper, hasn't he? Is Mr Tiggerdean good with cars?'

'He should be, he was good at nicking them back in the day. He says there's always an older guy in the car. And he has once seen the older guy in the company of a skinny blonde woman with big tits, who is, quote, "older than you".'

'Okay, I'll go and get the car, you nip in and see Karen and ask vaguely about Bethany's hours at the Revolve. Could, would, Mr Tiggerdean identify the mystery man if he saw him again?'

'I think he's more likely to ID the old skinny blonde with the big tits.'

Caplan got out her car keys. 'I'm not writing that down, Mackie.'

Once they were both back in the car, Caplan drove slowly, starting off at the lane to the side of the Revolve, looking to see where any private security cameras might be. Mackie had spoken with Karen about Bethany's hours on a Wednesday. Apparently, Bethany always popped into the Centre but tended not to stay. She waited for a text or a message. Then she came back at lunchtime and hung about for a couple of hours.

They drove along the seafront to the opposite end of the bay, to the park at the bottom of Pulpit Hill. Her dad was very clear that her preferred way home was to walk along the prom, through the park, and up to the house. It was much steeper but quicker.

Caplan pulled the Duster to a halt outside the railings. 'Do you fancy it, DC Mackie, a wee bit of exercise?'

'Not really my kind of thing, ma'am, to be honest. Craigo was staking it out and drawing a diagram.'

'Lord help us. I'll have a look at the place, take a few photographs. There's nowhere else along here that looks appropriate for an abduction, if that's what we're thinking.'

Pulpit Hill Park was an old park with a few groups of large trees and a pond. Well-maintained concrete paths snaked from gate to gate – only one climbed the steep hill that led up Pulpit Hill. The old bandstand had evolved into a floral display. A van selling ice cream was busy at the bottom. The top side of the park was planted with rhododendrons. Caplan looked carefully around her. She couldn't see how to get somebody out of here against their will. Bethany had gone of her own accord, maybe, with the man with the silver car. Caplan watched as a younger woman sorted the blanket of her older relative in her wheelchair, then continued the slow push towards the ice-cream van; a duty of love and care but it was hard work. Caplan and the young woman exchanged a smile of understanding. If Rosemary Robertson's stroke hadn't been fatal, that could have been Bethany's life. But it had been fatal. What was Bethany running from? And who was she running with?

EIGHT

Bethany sat on the floor, her back against the wall, her mouth open, jaw hanging, letting the blood drip from her lips, looking at the pool of dried blood on the concrete. There was pain everywhere, swimming around before deciding where to settle.

She thought of her boyfriend. He'd raise the alarm. So would her dad. Why was nobody coming?

She'd tell them that her dad had money, not that much, but he had some. He'd give them every penny he had if that's what they wanted. But she got the feeling this was not about money.

They were careful. They were practised. She was sure two of them were women. One was a horrible, vicious cow: Psycho Cow. She liked to pull the ropes tightly, she liked to do the tying. The other, Soft Voice, was quiet, almost loving in her touch.

Which was more unsettling. Soft Voice washed her down as she stood naked, covered in her own urine and faeces, bleeding and crying.

After a beating, it was Soft Voice who helped her back to the mattress, almost carrying her.

How long had she been here? She had no idea. Did it matter? It didn't look like anybody was coming to rescue her.

Once she had dropped Mackie at the front door of the station, Caplan drove the Duster round to the car park. As she was walking away from her car, she put her arm out, pressing the key fob to lock it.

'Excuse me, Mrs Caplan, isn't it?'

Caplan didn't agree or disagree. 'Carrie-Louise?'

'Yes, Callum's girlfriend. Pleased to meet you!' She pumped Caplan's hand in a gesture of warmth, her sleek ponytail bobbing up and down. 'Can I ask you something? Like, it's not anything to do with you but you're the one person I can ask.' The smile beamed. Caplan could see the charm. Nobody could resist that smile.

'Ask away.' Caplan turned so they could talk and walk at the same time.

'I'm a bit worried about Callum. He's been having headaches. Has he always suffered from them?'

'I really don't know. He's never said.'

'He's tired. I don't think he's eating properly. I was going to ask you, like, is he really stressed at work?'

'Not any more than the rest of us are, but I'm going to have a word with him, ask him to see his GP. Unless it's affecting his work, I can't really refer him by force, if you see what I mean.'

Carrie-Louise nodded. The ponytail bounced again. She beamed her smile then stepped in front of Caplan and gave her a hug. 'Thank you so much for looking out for him. You hear all about stress in the workplace these days, and with the stress of the job, the things you deal with, I'm really worried about him.'

As she jogged back to her small Merc, Caplan saw Mackie looking down on them from her observation point on the second floor. She was shaking her head with either amusement or sorrow. From her position, Caplan couldn't really tell.

As she walked past the reception desk, the ever-helpful Stewart handed Caplan another note. One glance told her that Irene Kennedy had called again.

'Who is this woman?' she asked Stewart, as she swiped her lanyard on the electronic lock. 'If I don't know what it is about, I don't call back. They could be trying to get me compensation for an accident I haven't had yet.'

'That's all she'll say. She refuses to talk to anybody but you. And she refuses to say what it's about. Doesn't sound a nutter. But you can never tell, can you?'

Caplan went up the stairs, clipping the note to the front of her folder. As she entered the investigation room, she said to Mackie, 'Toni, did you see that incident in the car park?'

'She's a bit full on.' Mackie rolled her eyes, dropped her voice. 'Shit, here's lover boy . . .'

'Can I have a word, ma'am?' asked McPhee.

'Oh, for God's sake, I've already been accosted by your young lady. Is this a pincer movement?' She looked at his desk. A pen lay abandoned on the open file he was supposed to be working on.

McPhee saw her looking, rubbing his right hand where some swelling round the wrist was visible at the edge of his cuff. 'I'm sorry I'm so slow with things. I'm not good at typing with my left, ma'am.'

'Come into the office, you have three minutes.' She sat down.

'Callum, are you okay? You're not concentrating on your work. Mackie has heard through the Cronchie gossip that Carrie-Louise's last boyfriend didn't have much to say in her favour. Is he giving you any hassle?'

'No, no.' McPhee was emphatic. 'Not that at all, ma'am. He was very controlling, I mean ultra controlling. It didn't end well. I'm thinking of asking Carrie-Louise to move in with me. She's been sleeping on a friend's floor after her sister needed her spare room back. Carrie-Louise's saving for a deposit to rent a place and that seems daft when I'm rattling around in my flat.'

'These things are easier to get into than they are to get out of, so be careful.'

'God, you sound like my mum.'

'Then your mum is right. You do look tired.' Caplan was about to ask if he had been up all night but as the answer to that would probably be 'yes' she stopped herself in time.

'It's that with Carrie-Louise only being a nursery nurse, and, well, we could really do with earning a bit more money, I was wondering if you'd support my application for promotion.'

'First things first.' Caplan pulled a face. 'Carrie-Louise drives an expensive car, she dresses well. Maybe she should rein the spending in a bit.'

McPhee gave her a comedy horror face, more like his old self. 'She's skint and credit-carded up to her neck. Her ex made her feel she had to keep up with him. But with regard to our future, well, that's why I was thinking promotion.'

'You're a bit young, in both years and experience. In the police these days you need to be a manager, you need to be able to direct a team. You need to show your competency in all areas and, to be honest, that might be difficult here in Cronchie. In big-city policing we do have the chance to show our ability to work with different racial groups for example. Not easy to do that here. To get that experience you might need to move.'

'Would you help me, though?'

Caplan thought she sensed desperation. 'Callum, I don't want to lose you off the team, but you'll need to think about going elsewhere. Get experience, gain your competencies and then you can apply to come back – if that's what you want. But first you need to show you can perform on MIT consistently.'

'And you don't think that I have.'

She didn't answer. 'Concentrate on the areas where you think you could perform better.'

A look of annoyance flashed across his face.

'I didn't want to come up here. I couldn't wait to get back to Glasgow,' Caplan said. 'That was the golden carrot dangled in front of me. Do well with the McGregor murders and I'd get my old job back. The sideways demotion to Cronchie could turn out to be one of the best things that has ever happened to me. So maybe you should do some self-reflection? Are you coping okay? Are you putting too much pressure on yourself? You do seem off colour, not on the ball the way you used to be . . .' She let her voice drift up to a question.

'I want to move on, well, move up. Need to make more money and get a house, you know. I'm fed up of being at the bottom of the pile.'

'Have a think about it. Take a bit of time. Let's chat again once we get Bethany home.'

Craigo knocked on the glass, telling her that he had returned.

'Sorry ma'am, keeping you back,' said McPhee.

'But while you're here, track down a silver Skoda Octavia 19 plate. The red Corsa is Bethany's. The Skoda has been seen picking up Bethany behind the Revolve, usually Wednesday morning. Try CCTV for last Wednesday. You know, dig about.'

Rory Ghillies's house was exactly what Caplan thought it would be; a large architect-designed bungalow, on the steep slope of Cruitten Glen Heights. The front of the house was up on stilts and a double garage underneath looked out over the bay to Mull and beyond. The house also looked down on the neighbours, which was fitting. The red-tiled roof sparkled but the house had no personality at all. The same width of curtain was visible at the downstairs windows, pulled and pinched into perfect pleats. The late afternoon sun cast shadows on the immaculate lawn which resembled the green of a championship golf course. The view was worth a fortune. High up on Glen Cruitten, each bungalow was stepped and staggered as the road climbed higher.

Caplan pulled into the front driveway, hearing Craigo mutter something about bad weather and snow chains, and wondered how Ghillies's Lexus got up the hill in winter.

'You nervous?'

'Well, unlike you, ma'am, I don't often meet these top brass types.' Craigo pulled a face. 'We're all the same under the skin.' His eyes, the colour of dry sand on a west coast beach, were full of suspicion – the suspicion of a rural cop for a high-ranking officer who'd rarely move from his office. And who knew nothing about sheep. 'Why did he stop work? It's expensive to live up here,' he grumped, looking at the sunlight glinting off the gleaming windows.

'Done his thirty, got his pension, moved on to golf and charity work. I wonder what window cleaner he uses.'

'Bad for the crows, ma'am. They see that brightness and fly into the glass. No good to nobody ma'am, all that blood smeared on the pane.'

'Well, he retired at fifty-four, he's plenty of time to clean his windows. Rachel kept working. What does that tell you about the state of their marriage?'

'He plays golf and she doesn't?' guessed Craigo, with a fair degree of accuracy.

'He was DCC. If there's anything in what Rachel suspects then he'd know about it. Remember that he has no idea who you are. And he's keen to help with Bethany's disappearance. He contacted us about her, not vice versa.'

Craigo glanced over his shoulder at the view, looking shifty. 'Ghillies is Bethany's godfather. Did he volunteer that information?'

'No, he didn't.'

'Rachel's her godmother,' muttered Craigo, giving Caplan one of his nasty little sideways looks, reminding her again that he was sometimes a few steps ahead of her.

The doorbell chimed all over the house. 'We'll keep that to ourselves, for now.' The door was opened quickly. Ghillies must have seen them pull up outside the house. He was pleased to see them. Caplan recognised him from photographs but had never met him and she was struck by the warmth of his welcome, the grip of his hand, the sincerity of his smile. Like Robertson, he could have just walked off the golf course, but after a more successful round.

Equally, there was a fatigued air about him. He was keen to have company, and company that could talk about his wife was even more welcome. He introduced himself to Craigo, nodding as he walked down the hall, saying it was good that Police Scotland was starting to realise the value of the rural crime squads, after so much being lost with the centralisation of the service over the years. It was good to see the more integrated approach working. He stood in front of the living room door, his arm out to welcome them in.

'After all, at the end of the day, effective policing should always be about people.'

Caplan knew bullshit when she heard it. How many times had he used that line at the end of speeches announcing budget cuts and a diminution in resources?

He offered them tea, putting on the kettle with the constant motion of those that don't wish their grief to catch up with them. The mantlepiece was full of cards. Mostly 'get wells'. That would change soon to those with a black border.

Five minutes later Ghillies sat down in a large floral print chair, with a coffee. Craigo had a milky tea, Caplan a black tea. A chocolate digestive biscuit was perched on the side of Ghillies's plate, the heat melting the chocolate, leaving a brown smear on the side of the cup.

Ghillies looked his age and was as tall as Caplan had expected, being recruited when there was a minimum height. His hair was greying but his eyes were a startling blue. His teeth, slightly uneven, gave him an avuncular appearance.

He asked after Sarah Linden, knowing that Caplan and she were friends. And then he showed some knowledge of her character, saying that she was a woman he'd never like to get on the wrong side of. Caplan wondered if the rumours of Linden and Ghillies were true. What had Fergusson said? *Knew him as in shagged him? Yeah, probably!*

'How is Rachel doing today?' asked Caplan.

'As well as expected. A little better if anything, one of her good days. Are you any further with Bethany? Do you have any positive lines of enquiry?'

'I think we do. One in particular,' Caplan answered. 'And it's an active enquiry. It's up to me to work within the budget restrictions agreed by those that don't do the job.' She smiled her tight smile that confused people.

'So glad I closed the door on that when I retired.' He nodded a little. 'I believe you ran into Felix and Wilma. Sorry, I never put the names together that the DCI Caplan who's doing so much for the morale of the rural police service was the wife of Aklen, the lecturer in architecture and member of the Glasgow South Rotary. It never clicked.'

'Well, she's still a detective and you're now a golfer,' said Craigo cheerfully.

'To be fair, I think he was only a Rotarian for a year or two.'

Ghillies nodded, opened his mouth to say something, then closed it, perhaps remembering that he was no longer a serving officer. 'It's been a long time since I used my brain in criminal detection. I'd be well out of my depth now.' He sighed. 'How's Bill doing?'

'We have an FLO with him.'

Ghillies said, 'Have you questioned him? I know he must be a person of interest but take it from me, he'd never do anything to harm Beth. There was nothing on Friday night to suggest any tension between them. I took in fish and chips. It was a normal evening for us.'

'Family are always of interest. She was twenty-five minutes, maybe twenty, from her front door when she was last seen.'

'As close as that?"

'Ninety-three per cent of women murdered are killed by somebody they know. Can you shed any light on who might be present in her life, somebody that her dad might not know about?'

Ghillies looked troubled. 'I'm afraid I can't. Beth and Bill are close. A bit too close really. I had advised her, maybe that's too strong a word, to get back to university and live her own life. They were always worried about each other.'

'No boyfriend?'

'Nothing like that.' He gave a little laugh. 'Nothing that she told us.' He sat back in the chair then looked at Caplan. 'Rachel often talked about you three, friends from her days at Tulliallen. Your paths have crossed a few times, surely. Rachel went straight into the CID. She enjoyed working at constable level. She didn't want to be promoted so far that she'd be stuck behind a desk reading reports all day, all those weekend seminars.'

'Must be a nightmare,' muttered Caplan.

She tried not to smirk as Craigo, keen to be in the conversation, asked, 'But you do get to stay overnight at the weekend conferences?' He beamed a look of total innocence. 'And you do know ACC Linden from those days? Don't you? Her being in a promoted rank like yourself.'

Again, Caplan reminded herself never to underestimate him. She changed the subject before Ghillies had a heart attack. 'We're following a few leads that DS Craigo has come up with in regard to Bethany's disappearance. We've been told Bethany did have a boyfriend.'

Ghillies raised his eyebrows. 'Like I said, not something that I'd be privy to. Bill has never mentioned anything like that. Is he a line of enquiry?'

'We've a situation to follow up,' said Caplan, knowing that as an ex-cop, he'd know better than to ask her to speculate. 'But as we're here, we wanted to ask if you had any of your wife's notebooks? In my memory, she was always scribbling . . .'

'Purple Moleskin notebooks? I wish I had shares in them.' Ghillies leaned forward and put his cup down on the coffee table. 'Was she talking about the Nikolas enquiry? An obsession, nothing else.' He looked away.

'If something was so important to me that I was thinking about it on my deathbed, I'd like to think that my wife would take it seriously,' said Craigo. 'Except I'm not married.'

'Is that why you are really here? I thought it was about Beth.'

'We're looking for Rachel's notebooks. Do you have any?'

'Oh. She went through loads. All her own thoughts, not her official notebooks. She's been on about one particular notebook since she went into hospital. I've not seen it. I've not read it but it was her cancer journey – something she started during Covid. It's nothing to do with Nikolas Ardman.'

The name tripped easily from his tongue. 'Do you know the case?' Caplan said.

'Of course, for a while she never stopped talking about it. There was no crime, the Fiscal was satisfied. Trust me, I checked.'

'Why is it so important to her? That's why we made time in a busy day,' said Craigo rather pointedly. 'All you did was report a friend's daughter missing.' Ghillies looked offended then Craigo added, as if realising he'd sounded cheeky, 'You know, you must be feeling raw with your wife being ill. When my dog was ill, I could hardly go out the house for a week.'

Caplan felt herself sink into the seat. She studied her tea.

Ghillies nodded. 'I've known for a while that the end was coming. I've been losing her by increments for quite a time now and she'd been suffering terribly. I'm sure you wouldn't have let your dog suffer as Rachel's suffering.'

'No, I shot it,' said Craigo.

Ghillies frowned slightly, as if he hadn't quite heard properly, but ignored the comment. 'I'm sorry but I have no idea where that particular notebook would be.' He placed his open palms over his face, then looked up as if he'd remembered something. 'Did Bill tell you about the location tile, the TRACKX?'

'No.'

Ghillies let out a long slow breath. 'I told him to. A while ago, after Rosemary had died and Beth was thinking of going back to uni, he asked me about devices to keep her safe. I put him in touch with a company that advises on such equipment. I know now that Bethany had a location tile in her bag. A TRACKX. He told me today that it stopped working on her way home yesterday, mid-afternoon.'

Caplan frowned. 'To be clear, Mr Ghillies, are you telling us that Bill Robertson had his daughter, an intelligent adult, under covert surveillance?'

Ghillies put his hand out in protest. 'I wouldn't put it like that.'

'Did she know?'

He shrugged. 'You'd have to ask him. It was just that he'd said about it to me, I thought you'd know. I mean, God knows, this is exactly the situation he got it for.'

'But if it stopped transmitting then either she found it and destroyed it, or her bag has been destroyed and the tile with it. Mr Ghillies,' Caplan said.

'Rory, please.'

'Do you think Bill's relationship with his daughter is normal?'

'I'm not the right person to ask. I don't have children, but he loves her very much. He's been overtaken by grief since Rosemary died. Now there's only Beth. The Ardman enquiry took my wife over. It gave me an insight into how obsession works. It ate away at Rachel. You know, I think that case actually killed her. Well, it distracted her from getting better. I don't understand it. You must've had some train of thought about the Brindley case. I mean, that derailed your career.'

'Did it?' Caplan looked open-eyed and innocent. 'There must be something behind her obsession with Ardman? If you can't help us, then we'll dig deeper. She was a serving police officer, a detective for many years who never worked directly on that case.'

'Why don't you visit her again and ask her?'

Caplan thought she detected a tone of sarcasm. 'I might do that. And I'll ask her about Bethany's boyfriend. She might have confided in her godmother.'

Ghillies looked a little wary. 'Well, don't upset her.' He was slow to rise from his chair, suddenly an old man shuffling through the doorway, making his way down the hall.

At she stepped out into the sun, Caplan turned to him. 'Ardman? She thinks the enquiry didn't dig deep enough. We're going to.'

Ghillies shrugged and closed the door.

'Sometimes you hit and don't miss,' whispered Craigo, impressed. 'Did you hear him say you had derailed your career?'

'Funnily enough, I did hear that.'

The gentle grey of dusk was rolling over the islands in the harbour as Caplan drove down to the seafront to get some peace and quiet. She was nervous that Carrie-Louise or McPhee, or both, would corner her again. Cronchie was a ghost town compared to Oban. People passed through heading further north or further west to the islands.

Caplan felt a little unsure of what her next, or her best move, might be. Why did Robertson not mention that the tracking tile had gone silent? Why had he been tracking Bethany at all? Did he suspect something? She sat in the car, watching the clouds, sipping from her bottle of water and trying to think. She got nowhere, so she phoned Linden.

'What kind of person photographs their own daughter every single fucking day? A bloody control freak, that's who. Covert location devices? But doesn't tell you that?' Linden paused for a moment. 'Seriously Chris, check his alibi, then check it again. Is the creep playing mind games?'

'He's a semi-retired architect who works from home. He was working at the time. He made a few phone calls, from his landline, which would make it difficult for him to get to the park. But however creepy it is, that photo gave us a great image that's already being circulated.'

'And apart from the normal crazies, nutters and those with a vendetta, there's nothing that looks solid enough to follow up?'

'It was after three o'clock. She's on the CCTV at three-fourteen. She left the Revolve, gave no impression that she was doing anything else other than walking home along the bay. We've asked for any transport CCTV. We're the most watched country in the whole world so we'll pick her up at every stage of her way home. We've a team working on it. McPhee is finding the boyfriend with the silver car.'

'Good for the budget. You working this with no DI?'

'Yip, small team, we're okay.' Her phone pinged. 'Craigo.'

'What's he doing? Sending you a picture of some poor villager they are going to burn on a pyre?'

'I'll forward it on.'

'Don't think you have to.' There was a long pause as the pictures went through. It sounded as if Linden was putting a glass on the table. 'Bloody hell, is that Beth and Shiv? Who's who?'

'That's the point Craigo's making.'

'God, I was only joking when I said they all look the same up there,' Linden said. 'If there was an abduction, do you think they abducted the wrong one? Did they abduct both of them hours apart? If they took Bethany by mistake she might be disposed of quickly. Are you tracking Shiv, waste of time that might be?'

Caplan ignored her. 'What would be the chances of getting a genealogy DNA search for the man in Glen Douglas? He's not been on the street for long, if at all. Somebody will be missing him, they just haven't realised it yet.'

'Can you not use a photo?'

'Nope.'

'Artist's impression?'

'Nope.'

'So, you want us to log his DNA with an ancestral site? Your chances of that are slightly less than bugger all.'

'There's legal precedent. Think about his very expensive veneers. A family with money is missing their son. And there's a commonality about those injuries. His family don't know he's gone.'

'In the interest of humanity I'll chat with the Fiscal's office. Say nothing.'

Until it makes somebody's career for thinking outside the box, then everybody will know, thought Caplan as she pulled out of the car park.

When she got back to the caravan Aklen was sitting in the swing chair, a mug of coffee in his hand, looking at some drawings of their house, making notes and using his phone as a calculator. There was a book on the stars of the night sky lying open, face down.

Aklen finding his place in the universe.

Caplan saw the book and looked up. Sure enough, the black velvet and the diamonds were back. The universe was looking after her.

Aklen got up and gave her a hug, asking her if she wanted a cup of tea. She sat down, the seat moving back and forth under her weight, and she looked up at the bright stars and the ebony sky. The heavens were crystal clear out to an uncertain horizon over the water.

'Look at all that universe up there. Somewhere in there is the answer to what is going on with Bethany, with Shivonne. It's like they have all got lost amongst the stars. All we can see is the brightness.'

'Have you been listening to Don McLean or something?'

'No. But the skies have been very clear recently.'

'Or you've never looked up before.'

'Could be. It was very dark in Glen Douglas. The sky that night was like this. You know, this dense dark. No moonlight, but somehow the stars light up the landscape. It's very clear, the air. I hope we made a move today to get him identified.'

'You will, I'm sure. You're like a Jack Russell when you get going.' Aklen sat down beside her, both of them holding their cups out to prevent the tea spilling as the seat moved under them.

'Have you worked in Glen Douglas?' Caplan asked. 'It's in my head somehow.'

'No, but Glen Douglas is a good Dark Sky site. It was on the news. The authorities don't want to make it official because every bugger will go and cause light pollution. There's a clear sky there more often than you might think.' Aklen took a mouthful of tea. 'Maybe when you have a few days off we might think about visiting some dark skies.'

Caplan pretended to choke on her tea. 'What? You? Go out into the world? Out there?' She waved her hand out over the water. Eight years and Aklen was thinking about challenging his comfort zone. 'Are you sure? Maybe you shouldn't push yourself at the moment.'

'Maybe next year. They'd be good places for me to go. The reason they are Dark Sky sites is because there's nobody there. Until word gets out.' He put his arm round her. Caplan enjoyed the silence, the tea, the peace.

'What about Beauly Forest, up near Inverness? Is that a Dark Sky site?'

'Oh, your mind's back at work again.' He withdrew his arm.

'Aklen, is Beauly Forest one?'

He got out his phone. 'Yes. Any more for any more?'

'Can you give me a list?'

'Why don't I email you the link.' Aklen didn't wait for an answer. He placed his hand on Caplan's shoulder and gave it a gentle squeeze. 'After.'

Caplan couldn't sleep. Thoughts raced through her brain that finally there might be a link – and it was the deposition sites. Earlier she had sent a statement in response to a request from Media Liaison, only the bare facts, but even as she was typing it out she could see the direction of the investigation. Now she was lying awake in the caravan, looking at the ceiling panel, listening to Aklen snoring as a vision of Aklen's office floated in her mind. She pictured his books on architecture and then another shelf of similar books rolled in. She closed her eyes and tried to recall where she had seen that. There'd been a load of books at Todd and Rod's. The hospital? Ghillies? The Revolve Centre? Before that she had been into Bill Robertson's house . . . and the architecture books had caught her attention. There was a book on night photography underneath. And then the pictures of the moon on the upstairs landing.

She pulled her mobile phone from under her pillow and texted Craigo, asking him if he was awake. He was. She slipped out of bed, put on her jacket and went out the caravan door to sit on the little step outside as she dialled.

Almost whispering, she told him of the Dark Sky link.

'If the killer is using Dark Sky sites then they've used most of them. If they want a new site, it could be in Dumfries and Galloway,' he said.

She could hear him take a sip of something. 'There already has been one down there. I asked McPhee to look into the background of Bill and Bethany Robertson. I'm checking that he's found nothing? No psycho boyfriend he has forgotten to tell me about?'

'No red flags. He seems to be the innocent father of a missing young woman.'

'Craigo, let's bring him in for interview tomorrow. Can you arrange that? Can you ask him to come up to Cronchie?'

'I'll get that sorted. How're you doing?'

It was an odd question for Craigo to ask. She was momentarily nonplussed. 'I'm fine, DS Craigo, how are you?'

'Callum McPhee? How's he doing?'

'No comment, ma'am.'

NINE

They had been away for some time. They had left her a carton of custard, something she could eat without chewing. It seemed that her mouth was full of blood from the crater where her tooth had been.

The one good thing, the thought that she held on to, was that they were very careful that she had never seen their faces. There was no way she could identify them, except for that voice and the scent that she caught sometimes, over the smell of her own body excretions that stank from the bucket in the corner.

The bleeding from her gum had been bad today. She choked twice, retching up so much blood she wondered how she had any left.

Somebody had tied her ankles tighter this time, maybe because she was being left for a while. Somebody. Not Psycho Cow, not Soft Voice but the one she called The Other. The Other was often there. The Other was silent. They rarely moved from their place in the corner but something told Bethany The Other was in charge.

They never got their hands dirty. They never came near her, except the last time when warm smooth hands caressed her left leg before yanking the rope tighter.

Then they had left. Three sets of footsteps out the door, but not Soft Voice's shuffle.

She thought about Shiv dying her hair red. Both of them tying their hair with a yellow headscarf. Bethany shouldn't have done that. They had laughed, they had pouted for a selfie. They'd had fun, her and Shiv. Good friends.

So she thought. Or had she been manipulated?

She'd walked out the Revolve front door with Shiv.

Secretive little Shiv. Her dad had warned her.

Monday morning brought out the headlines in the local newspaper: 'Oban Girl Missing. Concerns grow'. The article was along the lines of 'popular girl disappeared without her essential medication'. There was the usual quote from the widower father. *If anybody has any information, please come forward*. Caplan's warning not to give the impression that the pretty, middle-class girl was getting preferential treatment by mentioning that Shivonne McDougall was also missing, had been ignored. All that had appeared in the paper was a picture and three columns about Bethany and a small picture of Caplan, while Shiv was mentioned as also missing in the second-last paragraph. Her criminal record was detailed in the last.

Waddell, the family liaison officer looking after Robertson, had called in to say that Bethany's dad was upset that she was on medication that he knew nothing about. Caplan wasn't sure how to answer that. Waddell was wanting to know if it was true or if it was purely for the appeal. Caplan picked her words very carefully. Bethany had the right to her privacy so she said that Bethany was a sensible woman and would take medical advice and preventative treatment, given her mother's medical history.

'He didn't know that,' said Waddell.

'It's really none of his business,' said Caplan. 'Anything else?'

Sitting at her desk, arranging her laptop and her phone, a cup of tea and a croissant next to her, Caplan noted a new email in her inbox. It was from one of the social work departments in Argyll, from Shiv's support worker, Zoe McCulloch. The first paragraph read like a standard copy-and-paste statement informing the recipient that this was an interim statement and a confirmation that all the official documentation had been requested, all the correct mandates had been signed.

The last line sounded more personal, saying that in light of the current events, she thought that speed was of the essence, and she gave a phone number if Caplan wanted to talk.

It was a different mobile number from the one that Karen Beattie had given her.

Here's the basic information. Shiv's mum died when she was two. They lived in Craigmillar in Edinburgh. Her mum's boyfriend, not her father, had really tried to look after her. I mean he went above and beyond. He cleaned himself up, he took Shiv to nursery and to school. The teacher thought he did a great job. I got to know him as well, a little, as I was on placement in those days and I thought he got a new lease of life, being responsible for her. They were closely monitored, of course, and it was regarded as a genuine, father/daughter type of relationship. Shiv really liked him. He's the one that she never talks about. He died of sepsis. After years of heroin abuse, he gets clean then dies of something that appeared simple like a sore throat or a cough. Shiv was not prepared in any way for his death. She was seven at the time and after that it was – well, not good. She hated most of her foster parents, one with good reason. Then she was back in a local authority home. At age thirteen, she went off the radar completely and got very involved with some bad people. You'll have a few files on that. With her being pretty, she got passed around as these vulnerable young girls do. Their con was to set her up with some guy, then while his attention was distracted, by her, they'd mug him. And sometimes beat him up as well. She was under age so nobody was going to say anything about being a victim, were they? Then she was sent up here to get some space, to a residential youth facility up near Oban to get her out the city, and she's been on my radar ever since. Her birth name is Heather, by the way. Heather Alice. She likes to reinvent herself, but who can blame her? I know she liked Bethany. She thought Bethany was all right. I doubt very much that she'd hurt her. I hope you are looking into her disappearance as much as you are into Bethany's. Give me a call if you think I can help.

Cheers, Zoe.

Caplan read the email again, and then looked at Shiv's full name. Heather Alice MacDougall. And her date of birth? December 16th, 2002.

Shiv and her son Kenny had been born on the same day.

After finishing her tea, Caplan's reading of a staffing report was interrupted by Craigo, his beady little eyes burning bright. He was holding a file, almost waving it around with excitement. She was tempted to say she was busy just to annoy him.

'Have the PMs on Rod and Todd been completed?' she asked, second-guessing his news.

He sat down. 'Yes and no. First thing from Dr Ryce. The GP they were both registered with knew nothing of any terminal illness or depressive illness of either party. Neither of them had been anywhere near a healthcare professional for nearly two years, and the last consultation had been about food poisoning.'

'That's both odd and interesting. Has Ryce checked with the hospitals?'

'Quote, *I've checked the entire NHS. Do you think I don't know . . .*'

'Yes, okay.' Caplan leaned back in her seat thinking. 'The second thing from Dr Ryce?'

'They did a CT scan on Rod's body. No malignancy visible. Nothing at all.'

'Okay.' Caplan sat up. 'Obviously she's sure about that?'

'She is. Full PM to follow now.'

'I can tell you have more, DS Craigo.'

'Oh yes, ma'am. Ryce thinks Rod died on Monday at some point.'

'Pardon?'

'Monday. Which means Todd went to work for another few days as if nothing had happened. He concluded business with a few clients. Then hung himself, just as the *Countdown* conundrum appeared.'

Caplan put her hand out, stopping Craigo. 'So after having a cup of tea and some ginger nuts? A suicide by a man who likes leaving notes but didn't leave a suicide note. You've seen the note he put through Gains's door. It's his handwriting, if a bit messy, but no mention of what he's contemplating. What was going on with those two?'

Craigo was quiet. He sniffed and pulled at his nose but didn't move from the seat. 'Do you have any ideas, ma'am? Because Rod Taylor was £15,000 in debt on different credit cards. He was thinking of going to Santorini if we look at the search activity that Pordini found on the tablet. His email, not theirs. A private Gmail account that Todd didn't know about. Nicksrumours39@gmail.com.'

'You mean that he doesn't appear to have access to? Any interesting emails?' asked Caplan.

'The emails are odd, they're all about Fleetwood Mac. We've emailed them. No answer yet. Do you want us to get the tech boys to track the URL?'

'If it's going to cost money, no.' Caplan bit her lip. 'The phones? Was somebody talking to somebody they shouldn't? Who is Nicksrumours? Did Todd want us to believe that he killed Rod just before he killed himself, when forensically it's obvious Rod was killed days before? No. Peter Todd was not a stupid man.'

'The holiday in Santorini?'

'Yes, but who for? Maybe not the two we should have been expecting. Rod was based somewhere when he was a chiropodist. Go back over his colleagues and friends then. I know it was four years ago but friendships can last.'

'And there's no close family he'd reach out to. All Rod had was Todd. And vice versa.'

'Okay.' Caplan gave that a little thought. 'No close family? Who inherits? Keep digging. What was the delivery that Mrs Gains took in on the Monday night? That could be a crucial incident on the timeline.'

'It was a framed photograph of Smoo Cave. The frame is silver, expensive. Maybe it was the frame being delivered. Just so happened the picture was of Smoo Cave.'

'Any message with it?'

'It said "From Stevie".'

'Who is Stevie?'

'No idea.'

'Do we have the frame? Can you get me it? Are we suspecting a love triangle here: Rod, Todd and Stevie? Tell Ryce to keep me updated.' Caplan looked out the window, her eyes resting on McPhee. 'Why do people fall in love with arseholes?'

'Well, ma'am . . .'

'It was rhetorical, Craigo.'

As Craigo left her office, Caplan started reading the log, trying to concentrate on the main case.

Neither Bethany nor Shiv had returned. Bill Robertson and the Revolve staff had heard nothing. Shiv was seen on CCTV leaving the pub in Oban on her own and walking slowly back towards the Revolve. They had sight of her at the car park near the ferry terminal. She didn't come out the other side.

Caplan read the quick summary of twenty-year-old Shivonne McDougall that Mackie had prepared from the documentation the police had. She had a long history of nuisance with the police, and escalating violence with her temper. The words 'anger management' and 'issues' appeared a lot in her documentation. She had a nasty habit of biting and clawing; small situations escalated quickly when Shiv was around. And she'd been offered classes to help manage her anger but she either didn't bother to attend, or caused so much disruption when she got there that they banned her from any future involvement. Shiv was bright but had no structure, nothing to invest in. Caplan allowed herself a moment of reflection on that. Society failed youngsters like Shiv; how different her life would have been if she'd been born in Pulpit Hill rather than a sink estate in Craigmillar. Or grown up in a semi-detached like Kenny, with two parents taking turns to drop her off at school and making sure the homework was done. She might not have changed the world, but it would have been nice for her to have the chance, for her to have any chance in fact.

Caplan sat back and thought about Shiv as the young woman in the Revolve. Feisty, but getting there, forming friendships, thinking of employment, improving her reading and writing skills. Or was that all part of a bigger plan to improve her criminality?

She pulled up the picture of Shivonne McDougall from her record. It was a recent picture; stick thin, hard looking. The stare from those eyes could cut concrete. There was an intense energy about her. Checking the date, she realised that this picture would have been taken when she was seventeen; an angry teenager before she became an angry adult. Had the intervening years mellowed her at all? There was a note attached at the side. The arrest warrant was for assaulting a police officer. The bite wound in the constable's arm had needed six stitches and a month on antibiotics.

Shiv and Bethany? Caplan had seen more unusual friendships. Shiv could focus Bethany's eyes away from the safe world she lived in, show Bethany what life was really like.

McPhee knocked at her door, looking like death warmed over, a look she'd seen on Aklen's face more often than she cared to recall; the young constable was so pale yet the bruise on his face, by contrast, was deep purple. Not for the first time she pondered how McPhee's mental health was doing. He said he was okay, but they often did. 'Someone to see you, ma'am, interesting, could be Bethany's last seen.'

'Bring them in. If you want to come in too, get a coffee. It might help you look slightly less awful.'

'Just tired, ma'am.'

'If you need time off, take it.'

'We are short-staffed as it is, but thanks.' He paused, then went out the door. Caplan shuffled the papers on her desk around, placing the cover copy on the top of more sensitive documents.

McPhee showed in a handsome young man who needed a shave

and brought with him a strong aroma of engine oil. 'This is Paul Lochran. He works on the Coll ferry. He went into work this morning and his boss sent him here.' McPhee nodded, finishing the intro.

Caplan pointed to the chair. 'Please, Mr Lochran, have a seat.'

'Ta.' He looked nervous, and young. His voice had the lilt of the Western Highlands, and he spoke incredibly fast, a trait of the locals.

Once he had repeated his story, Caplan thought that she had it all and that McPhee had written it down. Lochran had gone to work that morning and his boss had sent him here to report his story. He had waved at Bethany on Saturday afternoon at 3.40 or thereabouts. The rest of the crew teased him about the way he'd hang around, waiting for the striking redhead to walk past. Once they had docked, Lochran would stand at the port-side ramps for the foot passengers, to assist those with mobility issues. He was young and strong and he had a good back, he explained. During the previous summer he'd noticed Bethany leaving the south end of the bay, heading for Pulpit Hill. He now knew she was going home. He'd taken to waving at her. She'd wave back. Now there was a smile, sometimes a shout of 'hello'. Once, when Lochran was busy, she'd waited until he'd finished with his passenger before they had their little exchange.

Caplan took him over what he had seen again.

Lochran could recall the passenger he'd been helping disembark, lamenting that if he'd been quicker, he'd have been on the land and might have spoken to Bethany. He hadn't known that was her name, but she did have a yellow scarf wrapped around her head and a small bag slung across her chest. It was definitely her. It was about 3.40 and the ferry had been in port for fifteen minutes. They had not started the boarding process yet. Bethany was well within her usual schedule.

That was the only time he ever saw her at Oban. And then, only some days of the week, but always on a Saturday.

'Was she carrying anything? A bag you said?'

He nodded. 'Her usual rucksack. Wee bird dangles off the back of it. She waved at me and shouted, asking me if I was having a good day.'

Everything was normal. He stayed on his chair, a young man with something on his conscience.

'You never met her at any other time?'

'No.'

'What were you doing that night?'

'Work, five-a-sides with the guys, the pub, then home. I was up at five the next morning so I wasn't out on the piss.' He seemed to remember who he was talking to and apologised.

'Who is at home?'

'Mum, Dad, my three sisters.'

'Well, that is useful for our timeline. Thank you for coming in.' Caplan pushed back her chair.

Lochran didn't move. 'What's happened to her? They're saying she might have fallen in the water somewhere. You do know that's rubbish. She'd need to have walked off the top of the sea wall. Somebody would have seen that. Stopped her. It's busy all along there.'

McPhee showed him out and, on Caplan's instructions, left him in Stewart's hands. When he returned Caplan said, 'Can you check that alibi? Make sure that he didn't make plans to meet up with her after the next crossing.'

'We kind of know him, nice bloke. He aw . . .' Caplan stared at him.

'So you need to check that alibi twice. Lochran being a nice bloke does not stand up in court. Crippen was a nice bloke, even Jack the Ripper probably had an adoring auntie. If Lochran is accurate, then we are really narrowing down her timeline. It confirms how close Bethany got to home. And get it up on that map. Where did she have time to get to? And send in Craigo.'

Craigo came in, looking confused. 'I was getting it all set up for the Dark Sky briefing. Nice bloke that Lochran,' he said, nodding into the engine oil vapour trail.

'Not you as well.'

The incident room was busy. Mackie had been on the phone to Lizzie since Caplan had arrived, and she felt a stab of jealousy as her colleagues had a good laugh and a chatter while getting on with their work. Mackie was writing on the wall, playing a macabre game of bingo of whose death made it onto both lists that had been independently collated with a Dark Sky deposition site. Ardman, Pottie, Welsh, Stratton, Glen Douglas with his inverted commas. With reference to Jack the Ripper, they had become known as the Canonical Five, with McPhee and Mackie almost coming to blows about what canonical meant, and if it should include Welsh. That had sparked a serious chat over Rhona Welsh, the thirty-four-year-old female, found dead in a forest in Tain.

Then they had a further argument that they might be better numbering the victims, with Mackie weighing in that they were human beings and McPhee arguing that it would make the spreadsheet neater.

Caplan's instruction was to concentrate on Ardman, Pottie and Glen Douglas. The other two would naturally follow, if their avenue of investigation was correct.

The list was being collated with the ad-hoc help of Lizzie Fergusson down in Glasgow. Caplan was doing this data gathering, something that would be passed up the chain. She wished she could get her hands on Rachel's purple Moleskin notebooks right now. She'd love to know what Rachel had been thinking. Rachel didn't trust Rory, for no specific reason she could identify, but she didn't. Then there was the timing. And the chances of Caplan meeting three men who knew Aklen, with a connection to Bethany, within a day or two.

Mackie hung up, and gasped, 'Oh, she's a case that one, your wee pal, Bizzy Lizzie.' She twiddled her pen in the air, regarding her new expanded list. 'Do you know how many people go missing in Scotland every day?'

'Well, I know the annual total of how many we have to investigate and that's 22,000 plus. Do you want me to divide that by 365?'

'How many of them are actually missing? Fewer than fifteen per cent. Some run away, some go away. Some simply refuse to be boxed in like normal people. Others are not where their loved ones think they should be. Some float away to become as free as the stars,' said Mackie, fluttering her podgy fingers to the ceiling.

'Others are going into hiding to escape domestic violence. Not everybody wants to be found,' snapped McPhee.

'I was only joking. What the hell is the matter with you, Callum? Jesus Christ on a bike.' Mackie adjusted the position of her keyboard, banging it on the desk a couple of inches to the left of where it had been.

McPhee got up and walked out, nearly slamming the door.

A bad-tempered silence cloaked the room.

Craigo spoke. 'Incidents like abductions are rare. They really stand out. If these people are being abducted by strangers then these actions are executed to a precise plan. And for five, maybe six or more to be taken for the same reason, we need to know what that reason is – murder?'

'Well, it looks to me like they are taken and they escape. They just don't get very far before they die,' Caplan said.

'Somebody killed Glen Douglas,' said Mackie.

'No, no they didn't. He died of a diabetic issue. His head was battered with a blunt instrument after he died.'

'He ended up dead though. Somebody has it in for these people. *If* that's what's happening,' Mackie added. 'And how many? They're repeating a pattern here.'

'And if it was their intention to only pick up vulnerable people, those who'll not be missed, they've made a mistake with Bethany. That should give us an advantage but I'm failing to see it,' admitted Caplan.

'And we're working on the premise that Shiv is missing as well, though she could walk in the door at any moment as she has previous for this kind of thing. Are they connected? Where're we on the CCTV from the park on the screen, ma'am?' asked Mackie. 'The street views and the private stuff will take a bit longer to track down but as far as Shiv's concerned, she walked across a car park and didn't come out the other side. Patrol have checked, she's not there anywhere.'

'That car park has overnight parking. Campervans waiting for the ferry?' said Craigo.

'And guests at the MacIntosh hotel, they use it,' Mackie said. 'Again. No Shiv.'

'Can you ask the boys to log every car that left the car park on the Sunday? Every car. That lassie is somewhere and finding Shiv might lead us to Bethany. She has the right to be missing on her own behalf, but bear in mind that if it wasn't for Bethany nobody would have reported Shiv missing. She's the same vulnerable victim profile as the male victims. Shivonne's the one that might break the case. She's the one who might have come into contact with the perps because she's vulnerable. She'd have piqued their interest, not Bethany.' Caplan pointed to the picture they'd printed from Instagram, of Bethany and Shivonne; one doing bunny ears, the other doing bunny paws, happy.

Caplan regarded the board. Loads of information going nowhere. 'It's obvious, but there needs to be physical proximity between two people when one gets abducted. Bethany did not disappear into thin air, somebody took her, and that person got close enough to take her. Ditto for Shiv. We look at where Bethany went after seeing

Lochran, we look at everybody who went near her. She walked past him but didn't make it home.' She pointed at the two areas on the map for her own reference, as everybody in that room knew the area much better than she did. 'So for most of that walk, along the seafront on the promenade, she's visible. Mackie, are you tracking her on CCTV? Are you sure she's going straight home?'

'From what we have, the only time she leaves open view is when she goes into the park and then the smaller streets up near her house.'

'I'm still concerned that Bethany had started to wear her hair like Shiv and Shiv had dyed her hair like Bethany's. Shiv might have been hiding from a guy she'd nicked money from. It was her wee con according to her record. Had she messed with the wrong guy? Has he taken the wrong woman? Have they swapped in some way? It's not something that I'd have thought Bethany would do. It's easy to look at the situation from the outside and think of Bethany acting as a steadying influence on Shiv, whereas Shiv might have been having a bad influence on Bethany. You never know. Bethany has had her struggles, she might be a bit more fragile than we think.

'Shiv's as tough as nails but how happy was Bethany at home? With the best will in the world the father's controlling. Bethany's on meds to keep her mood stable.'

'Lochran's sure it was Bethany, not Shiv,' said Mackie.

'If he was onboard and she's on the pavement? Relatively, how good was his view?'

Craigo thought for a moment. 'It's close, ma'am, he'd know if it wasn't Bethany.'

'Damn. Who was looking at the location tile?'

'It stopped transmitting when she was at the park, 3.51 according to her dad, but we are getting that checked with the provider. McPhee's on it but he's in the loo. Again.'

Caplan glanced around to confirm that his desk was empty. 'Okay, why would it stop transmitting? If they removed it, then they knew it was there and that narrows it down to very few people.'

'If she wanted to put us off the scent, she'd have stuck it on the back of a logging truck headed for the border,' offered Mackie. 'She might have wanted her freedom to hit the road with the Wednesday morning boyfriend.'

'McPhee's tracking the car. The silver Skoda Octavia 19 plate. Do we know who it belongs to yet?'

'No, he'd got as far as confirming the Corsa as Bethany's but that wasn't hard, was it?' Mackie shrugged. 'Who was the man in Bethany's life?'

'I have no idea, Mackie, there's no men around her. She goes home, she volunteers. The only man we can place her with is Mr Skoda. How long has McPhee been in the loo?'

'He's moaning about his headache.'

'Craigo, when McPhee appears tell him to get palsie with Robertson. Lots of lovely chit-chat. Get the dad to open up,' added Caplan. 'Tell McPhee to fill in the blanks about Bethany and where she could have been meeting this guy. Who was calling her doctor?'

The room fell silent. Caplan's phoned buzzed, sounding like an angry little bee. She looked round, trying to remember who she had actioned that with.

'Oh, shit, it was me.' Mackie jumped, licked her fat thumb, and starting flicking through her notepad. 'Obviously they don't tell you anything that is covered by patient confidentiality.'

'Yes, I told you that,' said Caplan.

'Right, there was no medical condition that would warrant her to be on the pill. That means that she's been at the shagging right enough.' Mackie wiggled her head from side to side. 'But who with, that's the big question. Well, that's ma question. And for me that'll be that nice wee sailor boy that was in here two minutes ago, I'd be at it with him, so aye.' She closed her mouth. 'That's the question for McPhee to ask. Sorry, ma'am.'

TEN

They had not let her sleep. They had made her stand all night. If it had been night.

None of it made sense, except that they were enjoying her torment. Bethany stood with a bag over her head, unable to see anything. Something had been looped round her head then dropped onto her upper arms, pinning them to her sides, and then The Other had come very close, standing beside her. She had felt them breathing into her left ear as they had stood in perfect silence. Bethany could sense slow movement, and she could smell minty toothpaste, and an aftershave or a cologne that held a vague memory for her.

She knew The Other.

She concentrated on the scent, images flicking through her mind. University? No. Something at Revolve? No. Where did she know that person from? The hospital when she had her operation? That image stayed for a wee while. Her dad at the side of her bed, holding an Asda bag and pulling out things she had asked for, although he had, in the main, always brought her nearly the right thing but not quite; green grapes not black, milk chocolate Maltesers not white, original Lucozade not orange. She'd been annoyed that he hadn't bothered to get her exactly what she'd asked for.

She closed her eyes, tears burning the memory.

The smell was an association with her dad. But who was it?

Somewhere he'd be looking for her, not sleeping. He'd be frantic, the police would be searching. Rory would have pulled strings for us surely.

Caplan got up, walked down the short corridor and stood outside the toilet, waiting, then knocked and asked if McPhee was on his own. Instead of letting him come out, she went in. The constable was splashing cold water on his face. Caplan checked that the three cubicle doors were empty.

'What's up?' he asked but wouldn't meet her eyes.

'I was about to ask you the same question. Is everything okay?'

'Yeah. Everything's fine.' He paused. 'Just dandy.'

She saw that he was close to tears.

'Are you okay?'

'Only this bloody cough, ma'am. I need to get back to work. I think Mackie's monitoring my movements.' His hand reached out to his mobile phone.

'Callum, we are quite a close unit here. I'd like to think that if you are unhappy or stressed, you would say, and I will do my damnedest to help sort it out. Sometimes talking to somebody not involved makes a difference.'

He smiled at her. 'Thank you.'

'Have you been to the doctor? You seem to be getting very clumsy, a little forgetful at times.'

'Sorry, ma'am.'

'The only thing to be sorry about would be if you were ignoring something simple, like a vitamin deficiency, a malabsorption, that kind of thing. I'm telling you, go to see the doc and let me know. Let me know that you have been.'

She let him leave. He was desperate to get away. Walking over to where he'd been, she looked down at the five short brown hairs on the back of the sink. Not Craigo's, not Stewart's. McPhee was losing his hair.

Caplan returned to her office, leaving them to their work. She'd been half-listening to them turning ideas over. Chatting away, their conversation had turned to something seen on the dark web, something they didn't have the funding to pursue. Something about gangs of teens, young teens, chasing others, catching the last one. It depended on who they caught, what happened to them. Whatever, it wasn't nice. But, sitting at her desk and studying the map, Caplan thought about the remoteness of the areas and the uniformity of the societal status of those who were missing. They would not be missed, these vulnerable, perfect victims . . . except Bethany and Lisa. They were another little subset; two women with a tangible connection to those organisations that looked after the welfare of . . . the words crept into her mind . . . the other victims. And there was Glen Douglas with his lovely teeth and untraceable DNA. Caplan wondered how Linden was getting on with that. Everybody and their donkey were signed up to some ancestral website these days. And Glen Douglas, in the recent past, had lived a life that had left footprints. All they needed to do was follow and they'd get to where they needed to be, and to the perpetrators of these crimes. Glen

Douglas, whoever he was, could be the key to what happened to the rest. A creeping suspicion was suggesting itself in her mind, a bigger picture, something that Rachel, from her wider viewpoint, had seen. A pattern of young, vulnerable people being taken out to a remote place and killed. Or left to die. What was the point?

Sometimes there wasn't a point.

In the quiet of her office, her mobile rang. As expected, it was from Linden.

Caplan asked, 'Did you ever study that short story at school, what was it called, "The Lottery"? Where a wee village in the back end of nowhere has a lottery and the "winner" basically becomes the prey. I can't recall how it goes but somebody gets chased and stoned or something. It's about many things but mainly man's inhumanity to man, mob rule, the persecution of the weak or of those not worthy.'

'I did pay attention because our English teacher had a great arse. I'd have chased him down had I been a couple of years older. I know the story, 1940s wasn't it? What brought that to mind?' Linden's voice slowed. 'What are you thinking?'

'Is that what's going on here? Is it a game for them?' She heard Linden tap her pen off something softly.

Then Linden was businesslike again. 'Is there any chance, any chance at all, that this Bethany and the one with the stupid spelling have gone off together? Two young women finding some solace in each other?' Linden's voice slipped into that slightly crisp tone that Caplan knew well. 'Wouldn't be the first time that a fine upstanding woman had been led astray by somebody on the wrong side of the law, would it, DCI Caplan?'

Caplan knew her friend was digging for information on Lizzie Fergusson, and ignored it. 'It wouldn't be the first time, no, but I doubt they're together. Bethany's phone has been off. So has Shiv's. Something has happened to those two young women. And I doubt that it's good.'

'Bethany might have turned her phone off so that her creeping Jesus of a dad doesn't know where she is. Who the hell wants to know what company their twenty-one-year-old daughter is keeping?'

'Their parents want to know. He had a location tile in her bag.'

'Fuck's sake. She's not six. Who the hell cares who she's with and where she goes? She's an adult, she can do what the hell she wants. Let's get one mess cleared up at a time. Where's Shivonne?

Where's Bethany? It's too much for both of them to have gone missing. Maybe it's young love. Dad too disapproving. Did they have a shared history of abuse? Maybe Bethany's trust fund for uni has gone. Look into it. Something about it feels off to me. Ghillies is not long retired and still has friends in places high enough to scald my ass from on high so please don't fuck this up. Find her quick. Off you trot.'

'Beth's twenty-one, Shiv's twenty. Ghillies is a bit, I don't know, a bit too defensive, a bit too interested in her whereabouts.'

Linden went very quiet. 'Tread carefully. You could be getting into something deep here. You might be digging into something that'll embarrass your colleagues. Don't expect to get many Christmas cards as your career goes on.' She sniffed. 'Let me know if there's anything else you need. The request for the DNA on Glen Douglas has been escalated. I quoted you on the flash teeth and rich relatives. I had to be nice to people.'

'It won't kill you.'

'As soon as I know, you will. Zoom call later? Anything else I can do for you? No? Good.' The phone went down.

Caplan looked out at the lengthening list of names, then at her team, scrabbling around. They had even titled the board Operation Dark Sky. It was fitting. What they needed was more personnel, more foot soldiers.

And some funding.

Yes, some funding might be good. Might be better to wait until Linden was a bit more receptive.

Caplan went back to first principles. The identity of the boyfriend. Whoever he was, he wasn't coming forward. Even if he was unknown to Robertson, even if he'd been out of the country, he'd now know of his girlfriend's disappearance. So, he was keeping quiet for a reason. Because he was married?

Who was he? And the older skinny blonde with big tits? Caplan recalled how Linden had described Wilma Vance: *Blonde, well dressed, silicone implants and two brain cells.* She would fit Tiggerdean's description. Did that mean it was Vance in the car? Or Rory? Rory'd been concerned when Bethany went missing, but given his relationship with her dad, he could hardly be nonchalant.

She looked at the image on her computer. The grey Skoda had been slowing to join a traffic queue and the image of the driver, blurred by the pixelation of the camera footage, was only visible through the passenger window. It was picked up again at the traffic lights at the roundabout on the A85. That image was even worse.

But there was one more image of the car rolling to a halt at the traffic lights where a partial plate was clearly picked up by Automatic Number-Plate Recognition. Caplan waited for the system to come up with something. All it came up with was 19 AC and a message that there wasn't enough of a number-plate there to recognise.

Craigo was looking very pleased with himself, Google Maps open on his laptop, as he knocked then walked into Caplan's office without waiting to be asked.

'Do you know Pulpit Hill Park? It's on her way home.'

'I know of it but I'm not overly familiar. Have you found Bethany?'

'I've found where she wasn't,' said Craigo confidently. 'But we've had the prelim report from the tech boys in Glasgow about her email correspondence, Facebook messages and a month of phone log.'

'Did we get a warrant?'

'Played the mental health card; the dad and the Fiscal agreed.'

'Good for you.'

'There's wee bit of to and fro but by far and away, the main contact is with someone called Angela.'

'Angela?' Caplan sat up. 'Was there an Angela on her contact list.'

Craigo shook his head. 'But there're lots of calls and texts to Angela. On further investigation, Angela has a number on a pay as you go. Maybe something to ask her dad about this afternoon. And in the meantime, I've narrowed down where Bethany went after she left the Revolve Centre. It's not ideal . . .'

Caplan knew it would take a team of six officers more than a month to look at all the CCTV that covered Pulpit Hill Park. But Craigo was a good deductive thinker.

'Well, you see . . .'

'Talk me through it in one minute or less. We've a very busy day today.'

'It wasn't raining when she left the Revolve. She walked along the prom, passed Lochran at the ferry point. She's seen in the corner of the frame from the camera at the top of the park, she goes into the park then takes the path up the hill.'

'Is that her?' Caplan looked closely at the image on the laptop. It was her. Something about her build made it obvious to Caplan that this was the same woman that William Robertson had photographed on his phone as she had left their house. 'Yes, definitely her, not Shiv.'

'She doesn't come out the park. Something happened to her in there. And this was handed in by Neesa who runs the newsagents on the corner. She walks her dog in the park and found this blue rucksack.' He held up the evidence bag. The fluffy owl inside was crushed against the plastic. 'The strap was cut on the rucksack. It contains all her personal belongings, except her phone. If the location tile was in the rucksack, it has gone. If I'd known we had the rucksack as evidence sooner, I'd have got a bit further with the tile.'

'So, it's not just been handed in?'

'It came in yesterday,' said Craigo, looking out of the window.

'Why are we only hearing about it now?'

Craigo shrugged and looked very innocent.

Caplan placed her head in her hands. 'Did Stewart bring it up here?'

'He did.'

'Who signed for it?'

Craigo ignored her. 'I checked the log. There's another evidence bag. They came in within an hour of each other. This bag had two feathers in it, big feathers, a bit stripey. They were handed in by the park-keeper. He found them in the rhododendron bushes, after seeing the birdy people there. It's gone missing though.' He hummed a little. 'So I had another look at this wee toy here, a real close look, and there are two, maybe three small feathers stuck on the fabric. I'm thinking forensics will take time and too much money?'

'Can you photograph them without touching them? Send an image to . . . whoever knows about feathers? That's your type of thing.'

'Raptor Rescue, ma'am.'

'Was it McPhee who signed for it?' She checked the log on the label and sighed. 'So, the tile?'

'Well, I called Mr Robertson, her father.'

'Yes, I know who he is.'

Craigo ignored her; he was on a roll. 'And asked him how he attached the tile to the leather.' His wee beady eyes looked around the office. 'Normal tags have a clip whereas tiles are much less conspicuous, more covert if you like. They go on with a patch. The patch isn't there, and you'd need to know to look. There's a small square of adhesive residue right in the side at the bottom of the bag, in the fold in the leather.'

'And we don't know where the tile is now because it's been destroyed or turned off?'

'One or the other.'

'The person who took Bethany knew it was there.'

'Or she did it?' Craigo didn't move.

'Where does the tile go on a Wednesday morning?'

'It stays at the Revolve from about nine to one or two p.m., then it goes home. I checked.'

'Good work. So she knew the tile was there. Do we have anything on the boyfriend?'

'Not as yet. Robertson's due in for a chat in the next half hour. McPhee's out the toilet, looking at the Octavia. We need to know how she got out of the park.'

'A way you've not looked at. Would she climb the fence? How many exits are there?'

Craigo pursed his lips, undaunted. 'Four. One that she'd use if she was going up the hill home. It's an old-fashioned park. The main gates allow vehicles through. The Park and Recreation department had no vehicles scheduled to drive through the park that day. But I've seen three on the CCTV. One wheelchair taxi that was picking somebody up, Mum and daughter, Rita Lyle from Westerae gardens. Her daughter is twelve with cerebal palsy. Checks out. Another was an idiot who thought that the park was a short cut. Timing them, they didn't even stop. Lyle saw a green van back up into some bushes. She thought it was the park-keeper's.'

'At the weekend?'

Craigo shrugged.

'And?'

'Here's the van driving out. No windows. I'm trying to get a blow up of that logo on the side. The number plate is unreadable. Bethany would have walked right past it if she was heading home. She did not come out that park, well, not on her own two feet.'

'Good work. Get that van traced. It went somewhere when it left the park. What about the feathers? The big feathers, I mean? Bethany has pictures of raptors on her wall.'

'From a falcon, I'd guess from the description. Maybe a pinion feather. So it was not flying but sheltering in the bushes, otherwise it wouldn't be in the park.'

'So an injured bird. A broken rucksack strap? Keep the guys going on the cars seen coming out of Shiv's car park. Go through McPhee's desk and find out what else he's keeping in there.'

Craigo left as Caplan's mobile went, asking her to join her in a zoom meeting. When she did, Linden sounded and looked happy.

'Glad you could join us. Good news, they granted the search and the expense of Mr Glen Douglas. I'm sending you through paperwork from the legal team, so if this goes wrong it's your fault. All on the need to know, confidentiality etc. Don't go telling everybody or they'll all want one.'

'I know that this is a legal minefield. I'll be careful.'

'And you need to be very careful how you approach the family when you find them.'

'I'll let you know when I do.'

'Bethany?'

'Yes, we've some movement. All the good work of the wee monkey as you call him. And the dad is coming in now to answer a few questions about the covert surveillance of his daughter.'

Linden listened in silence. 'Weirdo. So, she was last seen heading home, then her location tile stopped transmitting? Well, even if she's not alive her body must be somewhere. I'll get back to you ASAP.'

Caplan was about to cut the zoom call when Linden said, 'Wait, while you're on, can I email you a document? Let me know what you think. My DS has a bee in her bonnet. I'd like to see what Lizzie thinks.' On the monitor ACC Sarah Linden typed then peered at a list that had opened as a window on her screen. She didn't look so happy now. As she was reading, Fergusson's fair curls appeared at the corner of the screen, followed by her face, a smile and a small wave. Linden invited her to join her at the big desk, like a 'grown-up' she added.

Caplan hoped that the sound of her stomach rumbling wasn't picked up by the microphone.

'Lizzie, tell us about the woman. Stratton. The first two, Ardman and Glen Douglas, I agree have some degree of similarity. I can see why Rhona Welsh is in the mix unless her mental health is considered. Once you take that into account, and a family that noticed she was missing, she's excluded. Pottie fits the pattern, I agree. But this other woman, Stratton, is way, way too different. And then we have degrees of difference between Stratton, Shivonne and Bethany. Run it by us again.'

Caplan suspected that Linden was looking for a reason to shoot the idea of Stratton being involved down in flames. Rachel had mentioned her. Mackie had picked it up and Fergusson had run with it. Linden was not convinced.

On screen, behind Linden's desk, Lizzie Fergusson looked like a young, nervous DC on her first day in the job. The office, the braiding, the highly polished glass and Linden's uniform ironed to an inch of its life seemed to intimidate Fergusson's bobbled jumper that was almost worn through at the elbows. But she spoke with clarity and confidence.

'Stratton had sold her house and was living in a rented flat in a less salubrious part of town, yet she drove a new Beamer and ate out in good restaurants.'

'Sex worker, or was somebody funding that lifestyle? Something going on that made her need to be a little more financially flexible? Freeing up immobile assets? Or was she not very good with money?' Linden looked at the photograph then held it up for Caplan to see. A pretty woman, dark hair, pale faced, slim, wide eyed and innocent looking.

'And at the time it was thought that she'd been taking money from somebody she shouldn't have been taking money from. A month before she died, she was staying overnight in the Balmoral in Edinburgh with a mystery man,' said Fergusson. 'He's never been identified, didn't come forward.'

'And that led the original team to think organised crime. She owed money to the wrong person and she paid for that,' suggested Linden.

'Too visible for them, I'd have thought,' said Caplan.

Fergusson nodded. 'But I've read Mackie's notes; the way Pottie and Ardman said they were moving on to better things. Stratton said exactly the same. Moving on and moving up. She was working out her notice for the building firm, Fayer Construction. They didn't want her to leave, they were taking their time about replacing her. She was earning good money yet she insisted she was moving on to something bigger and better.'

'Same bait the others were lured with,' agreed Caplan. 'But Stratton hadn't been missing for a period of time, she was well nourished, she hadn't been starved and while she did have that injury to her left leg, she also had two to her right. The pathologist, Leonora Spyck, not Ryce, proposed that Stratton had run into something on the terrain she was found in. Like a fallen tree.'

'Maybe she ran away almost as soon as they abducted her? I agree the victims are very different but the circumstances have too much in common to be ignored.' Fergusson looked at Linden. 'Can you ask for us, lobby them to get some money to look at all this a bit closer?'

'Do you think money'll help?' Linden flipped over the page she'd been scribbling on, then flipped it back. 'The names with ticks are those who have been investigated and an explanation reached as to their cause of death that would stand up in a court of law.'

'Yes.'

'They have been dealt with already. And the others?'

'Questionable,' said Fergusson.

'On the opinion of whom?'

'Me,' said Caplan.

'Seriously? What do I say? Oh, by the way, my mates don't think that these cases, which have all been through the Major Investigation computer systems, have been investigated properly. Come on, Christine, these guys know what they are looking for. The guys who programme these machines and input the data aren't daft.'

'Shit in and shit out,' argued Fergusson. 'I see it every day.'

'Rachel was on to something.'

'No offence to the terminally ill but she was a DC and never got any further,' snapped Linden.

'Nothing wrong with that. When she got ill, she was reassigned to inputting data,' said Fergusson testily. 'She'd have been recognising patterns, plus keeping a pocketbook, not a digital one. Being her age, she'd have had a handwritten hard copy stashed away somewhere, that was how we were taught. Where is Rachel's?'

'Her purple Moleskin notebooks?' Caplan said.

'Anybody want to ask Ghillies?'

'Already have. I refer to my previous answer about Shit Out.'

Linden let out a long sigh and blinked slowly. 'Do you think that somebody somewhere is missing something?'

Fergusson said, 'Sometimes you don't know what you are looking for until you know what you are looking for . . .'

'Rachel knew about Ardman and she knew Stratton. That's about it,' argued Linden. 'The expense of going back through all this will be huge. These crimes have no start point, no end point, no witnesses, no CCTV, nothing much in the way of forensics. We've no idea when these incidents actually happened. People went away. They turned up dead.'

'Wait a minute, wait a minute.' Fergusson was on her feet. 'Why are you talking about getting somebody to put these cases through HOLMES3 with different search engines and its dynamic reasoning engine? What do you think Rachel has been doing for the last six, seven years? Her list? How did she arrive at that? She didn't pull these names out of the air, you know. These names are there for a reason. She was an intelligent police officer, doing her job. She may not have a fancy uniform like you Sarah, or a bunch of backwater acolytes like you, Christine, but she was an on-the-ground, doing-her-job cop. You two need to do what you need to do, talk to whoever you need to talk to, but you'll save yourself a whole load of money and heartache if we work from the names that are on Rachel's mind as she's dying. I've no idea what more you two need, except to get your heads out of your arses and admit that a lowly DC might have connections that you both cannot see.'

Caplan watched Fergusson exit the perimeters of the monitor and heard a door slam.

Linden's face, the crisp whiteness of her blouse, filled the screen.

'That would have been impressive if she hadn't left her handbag,' she said dryly.

'She's right, though, there's more going on here. Rachel knew that. That's why she put us onto it. While we need an area of focus on this, our priority is to find Bethany and Shiv while they're still alive. We don't get a second bite at that. The clock is ticking and I have minimal manpower.'

'Okay, I'll send this upstairs.' Linden nodded at the screen. 'And that's why you're a DCI and Lizzie still makes the tea. You make it sound good.'

Caplan slipped on her jacket and went downstairs to the interview room with the two-way mirror. She stood looking in on Robertson. Mackie and a uniform were interviewing him.

'How's he doing?' she asked Craigo.

'He's been shown the pictures. He recognised Lochran, the lad from the ferry, but none of the others, apart from Shiv. But he did hesitate over Lisa Stratton.'

'Three females gone, and he seems to know them all?'

'Toni pushed him on Stratton. He said he knew her face from somewhere but didn't know where.'

'That's handy.'

'He's upset about Bethany, keeps asking if we know anything.'

'What did he say about him not mentioning the location tile?'

'Just that it had stopped working. He thought she would be in hospital with a brain bleed, like her mum. He was upset, not thinking straight.'

'Again, handy.'

'I think if we don't tell him something, he's going to walk out of here and tell Rory Ghillies that Paul Lochran has got something to do with Bethany's disappearance.'

'Does he know about a boyfriend?'

'Nope. Doesn't know an Angela either.' Craigo switched the speaker on.

Robertson voice was weedy. 'Not that I knew of, she never brought anybody home. There was a nice lad when she was at uni in St Andrews but that fizzled out. He hasn't seen her. I called him.'

'Yes, so did we.' The familiar lilt of Toni Mackie.

William Robertson's pain was etched deep in his face. The man was terrified but Caplan wasn't sure of what.

'You admit you put a location tile in her bag, a tag you tracked on your phone?'

'Yes, I told you that. But I didn't track her, I wasn't really interested in where she went. It was more if anything happened to her.'

'And the minute something happened to her, the tile was disabled. Either she removed it because she didn't want you following her . . .'

'She didn't know it was there.'

'The fact that it's silent means that somebody did know. Who might that be? Who might not want her found?' Mackie was baby-faced innocence. 'You?'

If Robertson was guilty, he was a good actor. His face changed colour.

'Or who else knew about the tag? Who told you about it?'

'Well, it was Rory that advised me about them. Rachel had been working a case where the kid, and it was a wee kid, had a location tile in their school bag. A lot less visible than the tag ones. But for me, I kept thinking about what would happen if she went the same way as her mother. If she was alone. If there was nobody there. I asked Rory and he asked Felix Vance. He'd been to some seminar and began to use them to track his building materials on site. They are a lot more common than you might think.' He thought for a moment, seemingly calmer now that he was on solid ground. 'But she'd go out running and leave her bag at home. What use is it now?'

Caplan waited, seeing what Mackie would do.

'Can I trust you with some information, Mr Robertson?'

'Bill, please. Yes, of course you can.'

'This might be nothing, and I'd appreciate it if it goes no further than this room, but we've noticed a few young people going missing. We're trying to establish the pattern. Bethany doesn't fit into that pattern but . . .'

'Going missing? What do you mean by that? Did Rory not say that right at the start? Why? I mean why don't you get things moving?' Robertson sat up, a hint of aggression in his voice.

Caplan, on the other side of the wall, thought that Mackie should back off now.

She didn't.

'Well, we're trying to figure out why you thought she was missing after a matter of hours. You were the one that brought her to our attention. Why did you do that? Why? You don't know where she is, do you?'

Robertson's mouth closed. Then he said quietly, 'Am I free to go? I'll be in touch with your superior.' Then he looked straight at the mirror before walking out the door.

Mackie had left a tuna roll on Caplan's desk, on top of the printouts about the Octavia. She'd wait until Robertson calmed down, then ask him. They had a partial plate, not enough to identify. A partial plate on an Octavia, the second most popular car for a taxi, in a busy tourist hot spot. Maybe the boyfriend was a taxi driver. She scoured the image of the car. As she expected, there was no taxi plate; that would have been easy. But there was something on the rear window, a strangely shaped sticker. She drew the outline on a bit of paper and looked at it, trying to make some sense of it.

Craigo came into her office. 'I found the feathers, ma'am, and another ten witness statements from the park that haven't been logged.'

'I'll pretend I didn't hear that.'

'I said that I found the feathers . . .'

'Yes, I know.' She showed him the drawing. 'Here, if I put that in front of you, what would you say it was?'

'Drawing of a tractor by a two-year-old?'

She regarded him for a moment. 'If that was a sticker on the back of a car?'

He shrugged. 'From around here?'

'Let's go with "from around here".'

He thought for a moment then got out his phone and scrolled. 'What about that? Henderson's, on the road to Ballachulish.'

'And who are they?'

'Big garage, ma'am, do tractors, vans, that kind of thing.'

'Do they sell private cars?'

'Yes, a few. They mostly do taxis, taxi safety checks and maintenance. Why?'

'Just a thought. What do you have there? Something important in that file?'

'Ryce has done the physical PM on Rod Taylor.' Craigo sat down on the end of the chair, perching there like a schoolboy handing over his homework as Caplan took the file of printouts from Dr Ryce. He bit his lip, then looked at the ceiling as if this was a report card that might be ill received.

'Have we got some idea of what happened to Rod?'

'Ryce can find no pathology at all, nothing. No ongoing disease process apart from those mild ailments that people your age get, ma'am.'

'Thank you, Craigo,' muttered Caplan. 'But to get this straight, Rod had been dead for days, since Monday night. Todd is still alive on Thursday night. Did Todd come home from being away and find him on the bed and decide he couldn't live without him? Do we have a cause of death for Rod?'

'Well, Ryce thinks that it might not have been a suicide pact after all, Todd and Rod, Rod and Todd.' He bobbed his head as he said it, like a child rehearsing a nursery rhyme. 'You might want to read that, ma'am. Ryce has highlighted the bits we need to pay attention to. That was her opinion. Which might not be your opinion. Or even mine. I haven't read it yet. So I wouldn't know. Except the highlighted bits, I did read them.'

Caplan ignored him, scanning down the report, looking for the key words. Then she muttered, 'bloody hell.'

'Yip. There are signs, ma'am, that he was held down while somebody poured a mixture of drugs down his throat. And they held him there until the drugs took effect.'

Caplan sat in silence for a moment, digesting that. 'He was murdered? And Todd? Suicide or murder?'

'Suicide, Ryce thinks. We need to look at his state of mind at the time. Who knows what was going on between them? Ryce thinks that somebody, one person, maybe Todd, kneeled over Rod, a knee on either side of his head, pinning his shoulders to the bed, sitting on his chest. That'd leave both hands free to administer the deadly potion.' Craigo handed over a small pencil drawing. 'Ryce thinks that Rod was held by Todd like that, ma'am.'

She took the single sheet of paper. 'Deadly potion?' asked Caplan, wondering if they'd stumbled into a Brothers Grimm fairy tale.

'Yes ma'am, a mixture of tablets, mashed up, mixed in with neat whisky. He'd pass out quite quickly after that. There's bruising around the shoulders, all round the anterior aspect of the joint, above the joint and in the anterior fold of the armpit. Rod had bruising on the inside of his mouth, caused by pressure of the teeth as Todd held his mouth open, then held his mouth closed. Ryce found skin cells under Rod's fingernails. Todd's skin. And faint scratch marks on his neck.' Craigo tapped the drawing Caplan was holding with his biro.

'Rod was conscious in some form. He knew. He fought.'

They both turned round as the door to the main incident room opened.

Caplan got up and left the office, ready to intercept the couple that Stewart accompanied into the room, taking them to McPhee's desk without saying a single word. The female, harsh-faced, had a quiet word with the young constable whose pale face went even paler.

'Who, me?' McPhee stood up, then misjudged the distance to walk round his desk and bumped into a tower of files, spreading blue and white paper all over the floor.

'Sorry.' He bent over to pick them up.

'Leave them.'

The office fell silent. Only Mackie's barely muttered 'Oh Jesus Christ' floated from her lips, into the air.

McPhee stood up automatically and walked out the door without looking anybody in the eye.

The man, slightly older than Caplan, asked for a quiet word.

'Of course.' She went into her office and closed the door before pulling the blind down, not trusting Mackie not to lip read.

'DCI Caplan. What's happened?'

'DS Davidson. There's been an allegation of domestic violence against your constable.'

'And the evidence is?'

'A black eye and a fractured cheekbone. He belted her across the face. Does he have any history of that, between you and I?'

'Never seen a bit of temper in him. Will you detain him?'

'With no history, he'll be out with a restraining order. The wee lassie is a mess . . .'

'Yeah, but take your time processing him, please. Can you request a report from his GP and a tox screen? Be very thorough.'

'Of course. Do you think he has issues?'

'We all have issues, DS Davidson.'

ELEVEN

She thought she was asleep. Her mind was rolling through a field of marshmallows, pastel colours everywhere. Her body floated to the left and to the right, somersaulting in the air before it came to a soft landing, bouncing. Then it took off again, floating towards the light.

She thought she was dead. Dead again.

Bethany was hungry. Could you be dead and hungry? If there was something that she could hold onto, then she'd be able to anchor herself, stay down here and get herself grounded. Then she might be able to think straight. Then when she got to think straight, she'd be able to make sense of it.

But there was no point if she was dead. Was there a solution to being dead? She thought about that for a moment and her aerial self had a laugh at her, a real giggle. Bethany herself was finding it hard to see the funny side.

But if she could think it, then surely she was not dead. Not dead at all.

It was very tiring, staying awake, so she went back to sleep when she could do all her acrobatics without interruption. If she was dead, she'd be bouncing her way to heaven.

Or more likely to hell.

Her unconscious brain was looking for refuge in a safe place because her intellect told her that there was no safe place. They were going to kill her.

Caplan stood in the middle of the room, having stepped over the scattered papers McPhee had knocked on the floor and pulled on her jacket. Her mind was buzzing but she tried to appear calm for the sake of the team, what there was of them. Mackie was doing what most Scottish people do in an emergency. She had put the kettle on.

'Right, I think we all need to take a moment after that.' She rubbed her forehead in circling movements with her fingers. They were one man down now. Okay, he hadn't been paying much attention but at least he had been here. 'As to the allegations made against him, it appears that Carrie-Louise had a broken cheekbone. I have brought the Domestic Abuse Investigation Unit's attention to Callum's recent medical history and requested a full tox screen on him. We've all been cops long enough to know that none of us knows what goes on behind closed doors. But all my instincts tell me that the DAIU have the situation wrong. They'll interview us, hopefully sooner rather than later. We'll respond professionally. I feel like some fresh air.' She sighed. 'I'll be back in a mo.'

'But can we do anything to help?' asked Mackie.

'We can't interfere. I'll be back in five minutes.'

She zipped up her jacket and went out to sit in the car, the wind tugging the door from her grasp. Then she called Henderson's Garage, introducing herself and asking to speak to somebody in charge. The phone was put down and the sound of their radio playing Taylor Swift reached her ears. The call was transferred, quiet, then a voice said, 'Wo?'

She introduced herself, said it was off the record but did they know if they'd sold a silver Octavia, 19 plate, partial number was . . .

'Grey.'

'Pardon?'

'Grey, not silver. Hang on a mo.' She heard typing.

'Yeah, I can tell you exactly who I sold that to. Not a problem, is there?'

There was something in the way he said it, his tone; a pride that had sold a car to a very respectable member of the community, a fear that something had gone wrong with it. By the time he said the name it was no surprise to her at all. 'What do you have, Craigo? Please make it good.' Caplan took the green tea proffered by Mackie and walked into her office, lifting something from the printer. She looked at it and nodded to herself. Craigo trotted in behind the others.

'I've the history here of Andrew John Deayton Pottie.'

'Yes, his body was found in Clatteringshaws, Dumfries and Galloway? May 2020?'

'Yes. He has a friend called Spudboy, sorry, Spudbam. Here's a photo, ma'am.'

'I'm familiar with that. It's the one on the wall.'

'Spudbam tells us the recent history. Andy had started with the same talk we've read in the other reports, hitting the big time, leaving all this shite, sorry ma'am, behind. He'd packed his worldly goods into the patient clothing bag he'd brought home from the hospital. And left. He didn't say where he was going.'

'They never do, do they?'

'He wouldn't say in case the others wanted a bit of it too, without saying what "it" was. When asked what sort of thing might attract Pottie, Spudbam had answered cash and girls, that was about it.'

'And his meds?'

'He took them wi' him.' Craigo nodded.

'He lived in a bedsit, though?'

'Loch Lomond Centre. It's supervised bedsits and near the Heatherbank Raptor Rescue.' The beady eyes twinkled.

'Really, so birds of prey? Do we have a list of who else was there? I know residents will be hard to track down but ask the local nick first. It's not so long ago. These victims have a scattered life. The only constant is their residential environment, and somebody dangerous is common to these sites.'

'PUPS.'

'PUPS?' Caplan's headache got worse.

'Pickup points. The place where we think they came into contact with their abductor.'

'Is there a common link?'

'Not yet, but we haven't started looking.'

'Yes, I know. Go through them one by one. The Lomond? Get Pordini to do that. You can do the Revolve. Ask the local stations about the Blueberry Centre, the Gretal Rooms and the Ashtown Community Unit. In particular we're looking for anyone who volunteered there before our victim went missing and – and this is the important bit – left shortly afterwards. Never to return. I don't expect the list to be comprehensive but it's a move in the right direction. I have a photo from the Revolve that might help.

'Find out who owned the place, who cleaned it. Who the odd-job man was. The window cleaner. The addiction counsellor. I'm hoping to hear about more funding today, so the workload was going to drop, but with Callum missing . . .' She noticed Craigo was still waiting. 'What else do you have?'

'Mackie's got the same for Ardman.' Craigo went to open his next file. 'Let's do that next door.'

They walked back into the incident room. The few members of

the team present shuffled round to face the big board. The floor was still a sea of white and blue paper.

'I'll get somebody to pick it up,' said Caplan.

'Well, I'm not bloody doing it,' said Mackie.

Craigo's eye met Caplan's. He gave a gentle shrug and looked away.

Mackie took the floor. 'I've been on the trail of Nikolas Kane Ardman. He was last known at the Fairmount Hotel, called Castle Grayskull by locals because the residents are mostly heroin addicts. Kylie Innes worked there in those days. She wears a black hoodie and smokes like a wood-burner. Can't say that she was interested in talking to me. She knew Nik was dead and that was the end of that. He went missing nearly seven years ago and stayed at Grayskull for two years before that, on and off. Nobody was surprised when he went off again. This time, obviously, he never came back.'

'And she remembered him well, amongst so many others?' clarified Caplan.

'He's the only one found dead in a Dark Sky forest.' Mackie's eyes twinkled. Then she continued. 'Anyway, Kylie was saying that there are some at Fairmount who have lost their job, can't pay the rent, their family breaks up and they can't negotiate their way through the system. So, eviction, homeless, then they get to Grayskull, gather themselves, get sorted, move to a flat, get back on their feet; a passing nightmare in an otherwise normal life. They've known normality so they know how to get back there. Ardman was, quote, "born into shit and will die in shit". His only ambition was self-destruction. Kylie concluded that Ardman was an unpleasant little shit, a smart-arsed, thieving little monkey, a taker and a waste of oxygen.'

'Not on her Christmas card list then?'

'Like Revolve, volunteers run courses to help residents read and write and help them with documentation. She then said that the university students are the worst volunteers as they know they are going back to uni, in pursuit of their six-figure salary ambitions . . .'

'No bitterness there.'

'She then mentioned Bethany, by name, as an example of exactly that, which I thought was interesting.'

'Did she now?'

'Yeah, she's been following the story. Nik manipulated the newbie volunteers, the ones who thought they could not only show the vulnerable the right road but could force them to go down it. Nik was heading for a bottle of vodka a day. Had been since he was thirteen.'

'He left at what, nineteen?'

'Stole somebody's rucksack and he was away. It sounded like he had somewhere to go. Again, Ardman didn't say anything outright, it was a big secret and they were supposed to be jealous. Sound familiar?'

'Good bait, offering a way out of the mess.'

'There was a scam going, ma'am, where youngsters, ten years old or thereabouts, start running drugs round town. They'll be attacked and their drugs stolen. Then their superiors accuse them of stealing the drugs or selling them on themselves, and, after much consideration, the wee guy, or girl, is offered the opportunity to earn it back rather than getting a brick over the genitals. That often takes them into the sex industry.'

'What, getting a brick over the genitals?' asked Craigo.

'Instead of, not as well as. And Nik was a handsome lad who looked younger. Kylie couldn't explain why he ended up dead, but she guessed organised crime.'

'Was he close to anybody?'

'He was too much of a user to make friends. The staff saw it as their job to protect the other residents from him. He was predatory. But here's the interesting bit. He did get close to one female volunteer, older, kind of a mother figure. She could tell him to fuck off and he did. I asked Kylie for a name but she couldn't remember. But she said it was a short name.'

'Okay.' Caplan nodded as they all looked at the board. 'That's another mention of a female they got close to. Can you get a description?'

Craigo scratched his chin. 'Do you know that vampire bats will feed those they are not related to?'

'No, I didn't know that, Craigo,' said Caplan, wearily.

'Well, ma'am, it's a concept of friendship, isn't it? Who did Nik here share his voddy with? We all have a degree of friendship.'

'He was an obnoxious shit,' shrugged Mackie.

'Thank you for that insight. Is that all?'

'One more thing. There was somebody else interviewing Kylie recently about Ardman. That might be a good lead for me to follow. About two, maybe three, months ago.'

'Get a description, then show her a picture of Rachel Ghillies, before she was ill. I bet it was her.'

Mackie looked rather crestfallen. 'Kylie did say she was plain clothes, female, short dark hair with a face like a bag of spanners.'

Craigo took a quick call on his mobile as all eyes turned to look at the photograph of Rachel Ghillies that was up on the wall. She was smiling but there was no warmth there.

'Was she asking anything in particular?'

'Nothing much, just general, same as I was.'

'Ardman's life trajectory was only going in one direction. DS Craigo, I see you've been very busy with . . . bits of paper?'

They all looked towards the two sheets of A1 paper the sergeant had sellotaped together and stuck on the wall. And for a moment Caplan was back in Glasgow, in a huge incident room with tablets, smartboards and laser pointers, colleagues in good suits and a wall full of screens and monitors. Here she was with McPhee, arrested, and Craigo with his creased trousers, flicking his fringe over his bald spot and holding a drumstick to use as a pointer, waiting for her to say it was his turn to speak, like she was the class teacher.

'So, we are in Pulpit Hill Park, the last seen of Bethany. Thirty-five minutes walk, a bit less as she's fit and young. The paths are designated by the blue lines.' He pointed to them as if his small attentive audience was afflicted by colour blindness. 'The swing park, the bike park, the small pond.' He pointed at each in turn.

'I fell on my bum there when I was wee, gave my brains a right rattle,' said Mackie, then she pointed at several matchstick shapes, looking puzzled.

Caplan realised they represented dogs, complete with directional arrows. They covered the paper, giants out of scale. In the middle of the drawing was a stick girl, looking like she was about to be crushed by a bunch of celery.

'This is Bethany, seen at around half three. I've plotted the movement of the dogs, not the people, as people notice dogs more. Come and look at the footage we have so far, and remember that we've no phone-camera footage as yet, only that from the two security cameras that cover this bit of the park.'

They stood round the monitor and Craigo guided them with outstretched arms, like a maiden aunt shepherding young children to sit round the fire after being out in the cold.

'It's interesting, ma'am.'

Caplan was tired, she had a lot to do. She sighed inwardly, trying to keep her focus on Craigo and whatever had piqued his interest, ignoring her concerns about McPhee. She'd asked Craigo to do it, the least she could do was look interested.

'We've spent most of the night looking over the film again, ma'am, trying to see where she was going, where we see her for the last time. She never left the park, ma'am. This is Bethany Robertson going home, we're looking at 3.23 here. We've seen her going in, she's strolling through, her normal routine.

'You see a Border collie run for that frisbee. A jogger goes past. This old guy has been sitting on that bench.'

'That's Stan that is. He's just out the pub, I bet.'

'And is that the blue bag across her back? Is she the one who pats that wee dog?'

'It looks like it, ma'am. Her direct path home takes her close to this small wooded area, a large heavily leafed rhododendron and a few small trees. Very thick foliage there, dense shrubs, lovely thick blooms even at this time of year. Fortunei Discolor. They are an invasive species, ma'am, and they . . .'

'Do we see her beyond the wooded area? Where's the wee green van you were talking about?'

'It's not visible.'

'It's not there or not visible?'

'Not visible. It drives in and at 4.15 it drives out. We might see better on any phone footage that comes in. And that is Bethany. Lochran was sure. He knows the Shivonne girl and says she walks "like a navvie". His words.

'The specialists from Govan gave us a hand, they looked at all the footage overnight. They spotted this guy.' Craigo tapped the screen. 'This chap here is a person of interest. I think he's the road sweeper.'

'What's he doing?'

'Sweeping.'

'But he would have been there for a while,' said Caplan. 'She went into the park about half past three, broad daylight. What did he see?'

'You can ask him. He's in reception. That phone call was that he's arrived.'

'Do you want me to interview him now?' asked Caplan.

'Well, he's chatting to Stewart, having a cup of tea and a Hobnob.'

Craigo looked back at his pad. 'The helpline number has asked for all mobile-phone footage of anybody that was present.'

'This was a public park. Surely nobody can be snatched like that. The park is not huge,' said Caplan, then answered her own question. 'Not so long ago, a woman was killed in a big park in Glasgow. There were dog walkers everywhere, lots of people saw it, nobody realised what was going on. A couple sitting is a couple sitting. A scream is somebody larking about. A scuffle in the bushes is God knows what. The human brain doesn't suddenly jump to abduction. Anything from the search of the park?'

Nobody said anything.

Caplan coughed. 'We'll revisit the search results later. Let's go back to the film.'

They sat, paying close attention to the screen as the video advanced frame by frame, the little dog running towards the camera, his tongue out the corner of his mouth and his ears flapping. Then he disappeared into the rhododendron bush.

'Was that dog attracted by something in the bushes? Go through the statements again, see if anything was going on in there. From the feathers, it was probably an injured bird. We might think about doing a reconstruction tomorrow; ask everybody to be where they were the day she was taken. Do we know anything about that green van?'

'Nothing and it was . . .'

Stewart interrupted their train of thought, knocking on the door and telling Caplan that she was wanted in her office right now by DDC McEwan.

Caplan ignored him and handed Mackie a small, printed picture. 'Find Tiggerdean. Here's a tenner. Ask him if that's the bloke he saw.'

'DCI Caplan?' called Stewart, louder.

'Yes, I hear you.'

Mackie's eyes widened. 'Are you sure?'

'No, that's why I want you to ask Tiggerdean.'

'Maybe, ma'am, if we had a look at this? It's important.' Mackie pointed at the laptop showing a still from a video posted on Facebook of Shiv and Bethany at the seafront with a view of the road behind.

Caplan almost whispered. 'If that shows what I think it shows, then it goes no further than this room.' She turned to Stewart. 'Tell McEwan I'll call him back.'

'Zoom call, ma'am, and they want you now.'

'Tell him five minutes. Tell him it will be worth his while. And close the door behind you.' She waited until Stewart had slunk from the room.

'Can you run the video, Craigo? Whose Facebook page was it from?'

'Shivonne's. This was our second look at it.'

They stood round the single monitor and watched a few minutes of footage lifted from the social media account. Shiv and Bethany larking around. Shiv very alive, the prankster. Bethany the one being pulled along by the arm. The clip ended with the two of them on the beach, shoeless. Bethany's trousers were turned up neatly at the bottom, Shiv didn't seem to care if she got her clothes soaking wet as they went running into and out of the waves, laughing. Caplan asked for Craigo to put the sound up so she could hear their voices, hear who was holding the phone. Shiv pointed to the phone, and said something like *look behind you*.

'That sounds like Tiggerdean,' said Mackie, listening to the reply.

The phone spun round showing the beach, the row of houses, the sea wall and then landed on the face of a Newfoundland out on his walk. A disembodied hand appeared and ruffled the dog's forehead. A woman walked into view. There was a simple conversation about wet dogs and weather. But in the background was the road and a grey car parked there. A Skoda Octavia. They could see the rear of the car and an outline of somebody sitting in it. Caplan noticed the number plate was dirty. Deliberately so?

Craigo pressed pause and tapped the screen. 'It might be worth getting this back to Glasgow to see if their tech boys can clean it up. But if that's a grey Skoda, not silver, then look who is in the driver's seat. The passenger window is open.' Craigo gave another tap on the screen and the driver turned slightly. Even the profile within the car was recognisable as he leaned to look out of the passenger window. 'He's watching her.'

Mackie muttered, 'Shit and fireballs of hell.'

'Not a surprise to you, ma'am?' asked Craigo.

'No, but keep it quiet. That's an order. I'll tell you when we can go public. Social media on this can be a runaway train. We keep our mouths shut.'

DCC McEwan placed his hands on the desk, knife edge creases down his shirt sleeves, silver cufflinks on display.

While Linden leaned her elbow on her desk, Caplan sat with perfect dancer's posture, all her attention to the screen. She might need McEwan onside for McPhee's sake but she kept quiet; the DCC was angry. He ranted for a few minutes about the amount of work he had to do, and how his life was easier when Rory Ghillies wasn't on the phone complaining about the conduct of some members of the MIT.

Linden looked at her fingernails. 'To be precise, Rory Ghillies is up for an OBE. It's a bit weird that he initiates an investigation but when we ask him any questions about it, he comes running to you.'

'He went to Oban first. His contact wasn't there. So he got in touch with you, Christine.' McEwan rolled his eyes. 'Where's Bethany?'

'Funnily enough, we don't know!' said Linden, heavy on the sarcasm.

'Caplan?' asked McEwan. 'You do know who you're dealing with here?'

'Yes. I'm dealing with a twenty-one-year-old missing woman, a twenty-year-old missing woman who could be considered vulnerable, and another three, four, five bodies that could be linked.'

'I've heard this rumour, Christine. Nobody caused their deaths. There was no connection. End of.'

'Oh yes, there is,' whispered Linden, leaning forward so her face filled the screen. 'You need to be very careful here, Andrew.'

'Somebody was looking for Rory's DNA on the database. That could hit the papers tomorrow. I can't allow that to go unpunished.'

'Then I suggest you sack the person who committed that breach of confidence,' said Linden.

'DCI Caplan, did you do it?' McEwan fired the question at her.

'I did,' said Linden.

'What?' McEwan erupted.

'I didn't order his DNA. I enquired if it was still on the database. All service personnel have their DNA listed for exclusion purposes but Rory's retired. Did his DNA leave the database when he left the service? It's not unreasonable that his DNA could be found on Bethany's belongings because he was at her house on Friday night. Imagine we were celebrating to the media that we had a DNA sample from an unknown source, a stranger at the scene. Imagine the embarrassment when it turned out to be ex-DCC Ghillies. He has a distant relative still in the service, in Edinburgh. It would have tracked back to Rory eventually.'

'Have you found a DNA sample?'

'The bag we found at what we think is the abduction scene could yield something. We have a witness who I was about to interview before you called,' said Caplan.

McEwan sat back, then threw the pen down on the table, more in resignation than anything else. 'Okay, off the record, what's going on here?'

Linden remained quiet so Caplan spoke. 'Not sure yet, but there's something. And, well, it's starting to look like the top brass are stonewalling us. There needs to be complete and transparent cooperation. The bodies have been found in Dark Sky sites. Robertson, the misper's dad, has books in his house on that subject.'

'As do I.'

'Sir, if I can speak freely. We are connecting Bethany's disappearance with the rest of these incidents. It feels the same; vulnerable people taken from their place of support, then found months, weeks, later in a Dark Sky site, with similar injuries.'

'Bethany Robertson was *not* vulnerable,' argued McEwan.

'She was volunteering at the Revolve Centre.' Caplan held up her picture of Shiv, the Instagram image of the young woman with auburn hair. 'Look at her, look at Bethany. Would you know them apart from the back, from a distance? They had started dressing like each other. Shiv had dyed her hair red. Bethany was wearing a headscarf like Shiv's. Bethany's a lot more troubled than her father will have us believe. Robertson was spying on his daughter. He was scared for her. She keeps her boyfriend secret. Why? Dad wouldn't approve. The boyfriend, we think, drives a family car, an Octavia. You see where I might be going with that.'

'What does Rory drive these days?' asked McEwan.

'A Lexus,' answered Caplan honestly. 'Why did you ask, sir? Did Rory Ghillies jump to your mind? Does he have some kind of reputation that it might be useful for us to know about?'

For a moment their eyes locked over the ether.

'Am I missing something here?' asked Linden.

'There's an Octavia registered to Rachel Ghillies. I suspect it's still in the garage up on Cruitten Glen Heights. I think Mr Ghillies uses that car to pick up Bethany on a Wednesday morning and God knows at what other time. I'm asking you, Sir, if you think he's the kind of man who would be involved with a woman so many years his junior. Or is this an innocent, if clandestine, routine they have?'

'Fuck,' said Linden. 'Andrew, have you heard rumours?'

McEwan was quiet for a long time, tapping his forefinger against his chin.

'You're not jumping to his defence,' said Caplan.

'It's unsavoury but not a crime. They're both consenting adults. Any further allegation needs evidence. If you feel you have evidence then please, go ahead. Good work. You're thinking there's a connection between Dark Sky sites and the safe houses for the vulnerable. The volunteers are part of it and Rachel Ghillies had made the connection?' he asked rhetorically. 'Something that she was very clear she wanted kept from her husband.'

Caplan wished the meeting had been face to face. She dearly wanted to read Linden's expression. McEwan was telling them something without actually saying it.

'I presume linking the car registered to his wife as being used by him to meet our victim is reason enough to pull him in and interview him?' asked Caplan.

'I'd leave it, Chris,' said Linden. 'He's not going anywhere. You have a weapon there. And he'll talk his way out of it. She's not around to give her side of the story is she? I'd leave him to hang himself.'

Caplan looked at McEwan.

'I tend to agree with ACC Linden. For operational reasons, you keep that up your sleeve.' McEwan made a face that resembled a smirk.

'How many are on the list you are working on now, excluding Bethany Robertson and Shivonne McDougall?'

'Ardman, Pottie, Glen Douglas, Welsh maybe, Stratton.'

'Lisa Stratton? Up near Tyndrum? I recall that case. She wasn't vulnerable in any way.'

'She was helping out at a foodbank.'

'Didn't she work for a building firm? An accountant?'

'A PA. Fayer's Construction.'

'Well, ladies, the police service nowadays is all about transparency.' McEwan smiled, a curve forming in his tight lips. 'And how hard have you looked at Lisa Stratton? Where she worked, her life?' It was a question of encouragement.

'Her disappearance and the subsequent finding of her body was investigated at the time. She worked in an office which she left on the 6th January 2022. Her phone says she nearly got home then the phone stops dead. She disappeared into thin air. She was found in May of the same year. Rachel had already connected her with the rest of them, otherwise we would not have noticed her at all. The profile was wrong. It's still wrong,' Caplan said.

'Have you considered there might be two things going on here? Abduction and murder of service users. Then the abduction of two intelligent young women.'

'We don't have funding as yet to open up the former cases. I'm not stepping away from Robertson if we think he's involved,' said Caplan.

'Of course not. And don't step away from Ghillies if you think that he's involved either. Or as well. Linden, you are wanted upstairs. Best of luck with the funding. The decision won't take long.'

TWELVE

Bethany knew what the plastic sheeting on the floor meant; there was going to be blood and it was going to be hers. She felt the wound on her leg with her numb fingers, trying to concentrate on the association with her dad. Where had that been? That scent? She held onto that thought as she relived what had happened that morning, or was it last night? The pricking numbness at the side of her leg. A gloved hand had steadied her knee as the blade went in. She could both feel it and not feel it. What had her mum felt when she was on the treadmill, what blackness had fallen upon her when she'd been carried to the back of the belt, landing in a heap against that wall? Her mum's friend thought she had tripped.

And had laughed.

She'd told Bethany that at the funeral. She'd been laughing as she'd pressed the button to stop her own machine. It was when she went to help her friend up that she'd realised there was something very wrong. Bethany felt herself laughing as the knife went deeper, cutting its way down the outside of her leg. A searing pain and then nothing.

It had been bleeding on and off since then.

Dripping onto the plastic sheeting.

She heard the door. She dropped to her knees, pulling the hood over her head. They moved quickly this time, knocking the wind from her before she was pushed out into the frozen air.

Caplan was thinking of her next move with Ghillies. She was itching to see his face when she put the print of Rachel's Octavia in front of him. But patience caught the bigger fish, as her dad used to say.

'Is McPhee back at his flat?' asked Mackie, marching into the room.

'You can knock the door, you know,' Caplan said.

'Is Carrie-Louise in his flat?' Mackie was outraged.

'She's the one with a fractured cheekbone, Toni. Something happened. Let it all come to light.'

'Me? I'd rather stand up for my pal if that's okay with you ma'am. Can you speak to Angus McLeod.'

'Because?'

'Because I'm asking you to.'

He was a tall, large man who looked like he could stand up for himself in any company. He had a history of domestic abuse listed against his name, three times. Three times no prosecution had followed. Three times the complainant was his then girlfriend. Three times that woman had been Carrie-Louise.

He had come into the station easily enough, only because he was in the area. He lived down the coast and that's where he'd shared a flat with Carrie-Louise before they split up. Now he was penniless and living with his mother. He looked at Caplan, a look of resigned boredom on his face.

'Okay,' he asked, 'what's the bitch saying about me now?' His voice was surprisingly soft and educated. There was a faint Edinburgh accent in there somewhere. The resignation in his tone witnessed that this was not his first rodeo.

'And who would that be?' asked Caplan calmly.

'Carrie-Louise Miranda Hughes. I'm here for the paperwork. My cousin's a lawyer. She's dealt with Carrie every time she flings the shit my way. If she's accusing me of something then the whole process starts again. And you lot fall for it every time, every single bleeding time.'

Caplan took a deep breath. 'Well, the interesting thing about your situation is that a man like you, repeatedly accused of domestic abuse, is walking around.'

He rolled his eyes.

'Carrie-Louise has, in the past, made some very serious allegations about you,' said Caplan. 'But charges have never been pressed.'

'Because it's all a load of crap. Now that "no evidence found" works for official channels.' The voice became clipped. 'But the stories get around work, people look at you in a different way. You get ignored, gossiped about. Women you thought were friends leave the room when you walk in. It's like having the plague except you can cure the plague. With this crap, you can't stop it, you can't prove your innocence. If you say anything, well, "That's what men like you always say".'

Caplan was alarmed to see that he was on the verge of tears.

'Angus, I'm really interested in your situation.'

'What is this?' His voice croaked.

'On the 7th June 2019, Carrie-Louise said that you struck her, gave her a black eye, she had to have an x-ray and . . .'

He was already shaking his head. 'Here we go again.'

'Angus, I'm not accusing you, I'm trying to understand this. Do you remember what happened that night?'

'No, I don't.'

'Not at all?'

He leaned back in his chair. 'And don't look at me like that. I don't recall.'

'Why not?'

He shrugged.

'I find it odd that you don't. Were you suffering from anything else then?' Caplan looked to the ceiling as if she was plucking symptoms from the air. 'Bad sleeping pattern? Forgetfulness? Dizziness? Clumsiness? Going to the toilet a lot? Hair loss?'

'You been looking at my medical notes?'

'No, a good guess. Are you still in touch with her?'

'No, I've not set eyes on her since January last year.'

'Do you have friends in common?'

'She doesn't have friends. I had to get her evicted from my flat. You have no idea how much money and time that costs. She should come with a warning leaflet. Some poor guy will be swept along with the charm and the sex and won't even notice the control happening. The guy before me? His mother tried to tell me, but I didn't listen. What's this about?'

Caplan had no right to get involved with this. But then, duty of care and all that.

'Is this about the guy after me? Bet she told him she was in her early twenties. She's thirty-nine. And I'll further bet that she's tried to isolate him, take him away from here, his friends and colleagues.'

He nodded at her. 'Is that so?'

Caplan was very proud of her poker face. 'The law is there to protect us all, Angus.'

Back in her office, she phoned the Domestic Abuse Investigation Unit, making sure that they had taken bloods from McPhee as she had suggested. Then she called McPhee on his mobile where she left a message saying that he should go to his doctor and get another set of bloods done. She had the feeling he was there, listening, maybe too embarrassed to answer.

'Anyway, we look forward to seeing you back at work soon. Cheers, Callum.' She hung up, thinking what a dangerous world it was to grow up in nowadays.

Her phone rang almost immediately.

'They said no,' snapped Linden.

'I don't understand.'

'Well, I do.'

'Did they listen?'

'They listened to everything I said, but the victimology is wrong in one and the body at Glen Douglas died from complications of diabetes. I pointed out he'd been hit in the head with a baseball bat, so they agreed we could open that as a separate case.'

'He was hit multiple times on the head. His face was unrecognisable.'

'Could have done that falling off the rockface?'

Caplan wished she had followed the pathologist's advice and had somebody look up there so she could refute it. 'It would be good to have a budget to investigate whether I'm right or not. You said if we put it into the system and the system came out with an answer, then we could investigate. We've spent hours compiling that information.'

'You're right, I did say that. But what I meant was, if it spat out something of interest then I could take it upstairs and make a case for it to come to you at MIT. It did, I did, but they didn't bite.'

'But the system worked. It showed a series of planned abductions.'

'Did it? Or did it show that troubled young people are transient by nature? But, yes, if three university graduates from middle-class homes with parents who read *The Guardian* went missing it wouldn't matter that they were from London, Shetland or . . .' She shook her head.

'Calton?'

'I was going to say Outer Mongolia, but you're close enough. And I know you think that's down to class but it's not. It's ease and circumstances. You recall those kids who went missing in some loch last year. They stole a wee boat, took it out and it overturned. Two of the kids were what, five, six years old?' Linden took a sip of something. 'Their parents didn't know where they were. The rescue teams didn't know how many kids they were looking for, they couldn't trace the parents to ask. That search and rescue went on all night. Who the hell doesn't know where their six-year-old is?'

'Three of those kids weren't found at all.' Caplan sighed. 'I doubt they ever will be.'

'Yeah, and it was all laid at the door of the man who tied his rowing boat up with a rope when he took his motor boat out. But parents having no idea where their kids were? Nobody out looking for them when it got dark? Lack of responsibility. And guess what? It's somebody else's fault. Multiply that by a hundred when you are dealing with dispossessed individuals with substance abuse issues, no place of abode and no family who will miss them. They are invisible. They are difficult to track when it all goes wrong for them. Of course, the system churned out the similarities, because the similarities are there. Doesn't mean they are linked.'

'Makes them great victims.'

'Of course it does. What do you do now? Set up a crowdfunding project?'

'No, I want, I need, the notes Rachel made at the time. I want to know why she had included Stratton. McEwan was hinting at something. Rachel was an avid note keeper, she was a DC with MIT. She set us off on this case. She knows more. The notebooks are somewhere. Rory wasn't forthcoming.'

'That's the most interesting thing you've said about the case so far. You could ask Rachel.'

'I'm not keen to do that. You didn't see the state she was in. She's failing fast.'

'Oh, I guess that's par for the course.'

'Rory's very impressed with you. Seemingly.'

'Yeah, he feels that I owe him something for my career.'

'You're lucky, he doesn't think I have one.'

Linden was silent for a moment then said, 'It's a chalice with the malice situation. You don't have the budget to investigate what's going on, so you can prove what's going on so you can get the budget to investigate. You're stuck.'

Caplan knew the one way to get to Linden was to appeal to her professional vanity. 'Do you seriously think that these cases are not linked? The Dark Sky, one broken limb and the same tooth removed.'

'Variations on that theme, Christine.' Linden sighed. 'If it was up to me I'd give you some time. You, Lizzie, the crazy gang. But I can't fund what I don't have money for. If all these cases are linked then they'll make a mistake and take the wrong person. Then you'll be able to join the dots a bit better. And you'll be pre-prepared to track them down. How you do that with no budget up front is your concern, but I've bugger all for you.'

'And if Bethany Robertson is dumped naked in the middle of a forest and dies of hypothermia before I get there?'

'Then it will be the fault of whoever owns the woods for not putting a sign up saying, "Please don't enter this vast woodland without warm clothing on". Or "Please do not allow yourself to be abducted". Don't think I didn't raise that point earlier at the meeting. There was a comment about omelettes and breaking eggs.'

'Christ. What is wrong with these people?'

'They are not people, they are management. They aren't bothered by the bodies of young men, lying amongst the leaves, emaciated, teeth missing, brains eaten by maggots.'

'You saw Ardman's photos then?'

'Yes, and I showed them upstairs. Didn't even put them off their fruit scones.'

'Thanks for trying anyway.' Through the glass panel Caplan saw Craigo reach for the landline phone, then turn to look in her direction.

Then she heard Linden's desk phone ring. Her own mobile joined in.

Caplan heard Linden telling her to hold on as Craigo made his way towards the office door, then Linden's voice was back in her ear.

'You should be careful what you wish for, DCI Caplan. The body of a young redheaded woman has been found.'

Caplan felt her stomach twist. 'Deep in a wood?'

'In a Dark Sky site. Good luck, Chris.'

Mackie was trotting to keep up with Caplan as the two women walked through the wood to the track. Craigo was leaning over the bonnet of the all terrain Hilux looking closely at an Ordnance Survey map.

'What do we have? Is it Bethany?' asked Caplan.

Craigo was vague. 'They've found a body, ma'am. Young female, auburn hair, naked, in the middle of the forest, near the foot of a hill the locals call Ben Fillan – middle of bloody nowhere, ma'am.' He walked over to the map and pointed. 'Close to the deposition site of Lisa Stratton. Closest place would be Tyndrum.'

Caplan closed her eyes for a moment, thinking, concerned about Craigo's lack of movement. 'They haven't got a definite ID?'

Craigo shook his head. 'Don't know yet as they've not reached the body.'

It was Mackie who exploded. 'Oh, for fuck's sake, Finan, you said that they've found a body. Get a fucking grip.'

DS Finan Craigo ignored his third cousin, and cleared his throat. 'Yes, ma'am, sorry. Somebody found the body and described it. The person who found the body was lost. He'd to walk a long way out the woods to find a road, then get help. By then he'd lost his bearings. He has pictures on his phone. They'll be sent over once they've the situation under control. I said to bring in the tracker dogs. But the body is as I described to you.'

'A body deep in a Dark Sky forest. It sounds like Bethany,' said Caplan, with a sigh.

'Sounds as though it could be.'

'And who is in charge . . . ?'

'You, ma'am.'

'At the site, I mean.'

'In the hands of a specialist search person and mountain rescue, as they know the area. Between the two they will find her.' Craigo nodded.

'Who found the body? Did they just stumble over it?'

'A mountain biker. His dog ran away and after twenty minutes of following the dog he found the body. The guy dropped his bike in a panic, ran after the dog, and when he found the dog he couldn't find his way back to the body or his bike. He couldn't get a phone signal. It took him two hours to walk out. He came to a single-track road and followed that until he got a signal.'

'Get the mountain biker to do the same thing as he did this morning, then get the dog to do what the dog did. Bloody men.' Mackie was dancing around to keep warm.

'Tried that. The dog was too tired by then. The mountain biker tried to retrace his steps, and they all got hopelessly lost.'

'Craigo? Get somebody to go to the nearest house. See if they've noticed anything out of the ordinary recently. But we say nothing until we have a firm identification. I don't want any of this getting to Bill Robertson.'

'Might be too late for that, ma'am. I think the word got out.'
'Before I left I asked for media silence on this.'
'Like I said, too late.'

She was lying on her front, her body blackened, purple and swollen. The cover of the trees, the dense canopy above, had protected the body from the rage of the elements. Apart from the soft shuffle of the crime-scene personnel moving around there was very little noise. Her arms were tied behind her, knotted at the wrists. Some leaves from a nearby oak had fallen and partially covered her.

Some flies were feasting on wounds on her upper back. From what they could see, her face had been battered to oblivion. Caplan heard one of the younger officers mutter, 'Dear God.' Another was trying to gauge where the victim had come from and what had forced her to flee through the thick woods.

Caplan poked gently at the body with her sterile-gloved finger. The torso rocked like a stone, disturbing the flies. She looked closely at some marks round the shoulder blade, as if the skin there had been burned. She could see the black rope round her wrists, the fibres still tied.

Without taking her eyes off the hands of the deceased, she called Craigo over. 'Get your phone out and take a picture of that. You have shoe covers on, don't you?'

Her sergeant slipped in beside her, dipping his head down. 'Her wrists? That's an unusual knot, a falconer's knot.' He dipped his head down so low that the strands of hair that normally covered his bald spot fell to tickle the leaves. 'It's used by falconers,' he added, as if for clarification.

Caplan considered that for a moment. 'Bloody birds are all over this case.' She looked at the damage to the visible half of her face. Her attackers had been angry – as angry at her as they had been with the young man in Glen Douglas. She stood back, leaving the crime scene techs to their expertise and looked up at the sky, so very, very dark. Tyndrum's population of three hundred produced very little light pollution. From its situation at the junction of three glens, go five miles in any direction and it was wilderness. Where had the victim come from?

The sky, framed by the leaves, looked very far away. Another world.

'Feet.'

'Sorry?'

Her sergeant lifted his tablet, swiping the pictures with a gloved finger. 'The soles of her feet are dirty and bleeding, but she has bright-green polish on her toenails. Was Bethany a bright-green varnish kind of girl?'

In other circumstances Caplan would have been amused by what he was thinking; what did he think of woman with bright-green toenails? 'I don't know, Craigo, I really don't.'

'Well, her feet are cut and bruised by running over this rough terrain. On her left leg, there's a recent dark wound that doesn't look clean. It's not had the chance to form a scab. It's probably been broken. Like the others,' he added, needlessly.

She asked which pathologist was coming out.

'The one with the funny name.'

'Leonora Spyck?' She looked back at the path. 'Did you tell her how far she'd need to walk? She's eight months pregnant. Can you send somebody up to the road with a vehicle? And do it soon.'

'It's Bethany, isn't it?' said Craigo.

'No. This is Shiv.'

'It was on the news that they found another body.' Aklen got up and gave his wife a hug. 'Shit day at work, from what I heard. Do you want a cup of tea?'

Caplan shrugged her jacket off. 'No, I want to get the people who are doing this. How do I do that with no money?' She sat down on the swing seat, devoid of its cushions because of the rain, and sulked.

'Still no funding? I really don't understand how the police service works.'

'We have the goddaughter of a retired senior police officer still missing, four, maybe five, young people have been murdered and funding was refused.' She dropped her head into her hands. 'It's like I have no more cards to play. You know Rory Ghillies, don't you? Is that through Felix Vance and the Rotary? How about William Robertson?'

'Well, I know both Bill and Felix. Define know? If I met them in Sainsbury's, I'd stop and chat to them. But I wouldn't want him visiting me in hospital. I've worked with Bill a few times, didn't know his daughter's name. And Vance organises the Tinmen's Ball. I went to one. I went on my own. You were working, as usual.'

'He said something about it.'
'Long time ago.'
'His wife?'
'Pretty. Vacant?'
'Like the song? Any other female friends on the scene?'
'Are you interrogating me, DCI Caplan?' Aklen's eyes twinkled mischievously. Then he grew serious. 'Are you thinking one of them might be involved in this?'
'At the moment anybody connected with the case is of interest. But there's something here that I can't put my finger on. It's all too much. And at the same time, not enough. I bumped into Felix,' Caplan said, looking at the cloudy sky, no stars on show tonight. 'At the hospice. He had the dippy Wilma with him.'
Aklen smirked. 'Nobody accidently bumps into Felix Vance. He's always after money for one of his charitable endeavours.'
'He wants you to buy a table at the next ball.'
'Oh yes, that'll be for a donation of about eight hundred quid. That last one was at The Royal Hotel. The food was awful. Big Vern and The Shooters was the only good thing about the night. You were lucky to be held up at work. I drank rather more than I should have. Far, far too much actually. Wilma poured me into a taxi.'
Caplan tried to push away a memory of Aklen before the depression took hold as she listened to him talking, the rush and hush of the waves in the distance, the rustling of the trees behind them. Vance was a builder. Bill Robertson was an architect.
'What builders does Vance work for?'
'It would change every two years. He doesn't work for them, he owns them. He doesn't quite go bankrupt then he reopens under another directorship named after the dog – well, not quite but not far from it. Always legal but only just.'
She looked up into the clouds, and for a moment, felt that they were talking to her.

THIRTEEN

Bethany had been woken from a sleep so deep and disturbed she knew she had been drugged. They had pulled her to her feet. The hood was already over her face. She had actually tried to brush them away; she was tired, she needed to empty her bladder, could they just wait a moment?

The blow in the ribs knocked the wind out of her. She was sure her feet left the floor with the force of it, propelled sideways into the wall where her head hit the wall and she slumped down, stunned, dazed. The disorientation caused by the hood was absolute. She landed and was dragged across the floor by her feet. She realised, at some point through all this, her bladder had emptied.

Then there was calm. They rolled her on her side, bending her legs a little, as if she was going to sleep. Something soft, like a cushion, was placed between her knees. And that was okay. Then something that felt like a finger touched her on the outer part of her shin.

She heard somebody take a deep breath.

Then she felt the blow and heard the bone break, then another blow, another, and then she allowed herself to be swallowed by the darkness of the hood.

The press had risen early. By seven a.m. on Wednesday morning the police station was surrounded by reporters and two TV crews. A rumour was spreading fast that a body had been found. Everybody wanted to know whose body it was. They were after Caplan's blood but she was sticking to the 'until the family had been informed' official line. As she bounced the Duster into the car park, two uniformed officers closed a gate she didn't know existed behind her. She sat for a moment, checking her email. There was still no official confirmation of the identity of the body. That sounded like they were dragging their feet on a forgone conclusion and that in itself had started a tsunami of misinformation about Bethany Robertson.

During the night, she'd realised there was a real possibility that they would take the case off her. On her way into the station, she had driven up to the Lorn Hospice, to have a difficult conversation with a dying woman. *Is your husband the type to have a relationship with a woman thirty years younger?* It was Rachel who had started the ball rolling. Caplan suspected Rachel knew exactly the type of man she was married to.

She expected a difficult conversation. She wasn't expecting to be turned away. Only three named visitors were allowed in now.

The metaphorical door was closed, politely and firmly, in her face.

She walked into the station with a sense of dread, but Mackie was at reception, holding a cup of tea and looking out at the gathered press, her normal enthusiastic self.

'Did you get any sleep?'

'Yes, ma'am, I'm fine. I think we are in for a day of it.'

'Any news on McPhee?'

'He called Finan last night. He's back at the flat. He's not to go anywhere near her.'

Caplan nodded. 'To be expected. I wish he could come back here. That would keep them apart.'

'Is there nothing we can do, ma'am?'

'We have done enough without it looking like interfering. They'll get round to interviewing us. In the meantime, take the next thirty minutes to get up to speed and then we'll be manning the phones if we don't get any manpower.'

'ACC Linden has already called. Ten minutes ago. She wasn't happy you weren't here.'

'Bloody hell.'

As she called Linden she thought she heard Mackie mutter something about *still drunk* but she wasn't sure.

'The body?' Linden snapped straight away.

'Not Bethany, I'm sure of it. Awaiting confirmation from the DNA and the PM.'

'And when did you become a pathologist?'

'Bethany had an operation for a pilonidal sinus.'

'A what?'

'It leaves a scar, a bad scar. That body had no scar. Not Beth. I called last night to tell Bill Robertson that the body had no scar. He's not daft, he knew what I meant, but I think somebody had told him that it was Bethany already.' Caplan heard Linden tapping, as if drumming her nails on the desk. 'Ryce knows I want her to confirm it before we go public.'

She heard Linden sigh. The ACC had been prepared to be angry. 'The Brooke-Williams family. You've to go and speak to them. And be nice. On your phone you have the documentation on a DNA profile and a list of five surnames who were genetically linked to Mr Glen Douglas. There's a black sheep of a son who hasn't been around for a while – the youngest son with a few addiction issues. The age and broad description fits. The family think he's away being naughty. They have no idea about the fatality. Deal with it yourself. Don't take the wee monkey guy, don't take the fat one, don't take McPhee the wife beater.'

'DC McPhee is innocent.'

'Only because he's not married, but the bruises are the same. Don't underestimate what a family like the Brooke-Williams could do to the profile of this case.'

Caplan felt it was her turn to change the subject. 'Can we think about Rachel for a moment? She watched everything, noted everything. She saw something in this case, right at the start. What was it? We know it wasn't the body at Glen Douglas. It wasn't her own demise. One of those murders formed a connection in her mind. Addled with disease and drugs, she's still held onto that thought. Christ, after a bottle of wine you can't recall my name, but Rachel, with the chemo coursing through her veins, still held onto these victims.'

'We all have that one case that got away, the one that remains with you.'

'Rachel wasn't working on any of these cases so none of them could remain with her, could they?' Caplan said.

'If she's wrong then this could be career ending for you. It might already be career ending. Christine, I know you like to see patterns in things. And you think I spend my life in meetings about modern policing, diversity and the quality of the vegan soap in the toilets. But I did look into the cases that Rachel Ghillies worked on, I cross-referenced them.'

'No, you bloody didn't,' said Caplan quietly.

'Okay, I got one of the tech guys to do it because I've got no idea how to. As you say, Rachel had no connection with any of these cases, apart from a tangential link with Welsh. Nor did her hubby. He was too far up the tree by then.'

'But she did access them. What does that mean? No professional interest so a personal one? Could that personal interest about the perpetrator lead us to who killed Glen Douglas?'

'Last time I looked, you were a detective, so you figure that out. But get the Brooke-Williamses onside. Speak to the family. Bethany's the one you need to get home safe.'

In the end DCI Caplan drove to Kelbourne House alone to see the Brooke-Williamses. They had been told in advance of her visit. She presumed that the family might have some idea what it was about.

She enjoyed the solitude. The driveway up to the large house where the Brooke-Williamses lived was long and winding, through a large estate that started with smooth rolling fields filled with grazing highland cattle, whose coats shone auburn in the sun, before the road turned sharply into the woods, the daylight flickering through the canopy of leaves. She passed signs; bits of wood carved into arrows, saying 'To the log cabins', 'To the picnic area', 'The Selkie Walk' and 'The River Walk' in black lettering. These woods were not dense but there was the presence of silent isolation. She couldn't think of herself walking through these woods, through the trees, off the path, not under any circumstances. Why were they, the victims, taking the difficult way through the trees? Why not down the track? She pulled the car over and got out, enjoying the petrichor and the sweet humid smell of fallen leaves. The single track had been cleared of autumn detritus which was piled up to form a soft, brown, glistening border to the road.

She saw a lodge hidden by the trees, a single stream of woodsmoke curling from its chimney, as if drawn by the hand of a Disney artist. Looking around her, breathing in the damp, scented air, she tried to imagine herself running through here. Running away from something, escaping. She'd take the road. The victims had not done so. None of them had.

After standing and thinking for five minutes, ignoring the chill rising from the tarmac through her boots, she got back in the Duster.

Lady Brooke-Williams didn't ask why Caplan had asked for a meeting, so she presumed that they knew, or that they suspected something, even if they weren't going to volunteer it.

It was a delicate matter. The three of them in the room, the two parents and the older brother, a man in his mid to late twenties, although he could have been anything up to forty with early hair loss and a shiny face.

Caplan didn't need to ask. She saw the faces in front of her echoed in the paintings hanging above the fireplace and she knew. Even though the victim had had his face smashed in, she imagined she could see a resemblance in the build, the colouring. He bore some semblance to the sitter of one of the portraits, going back through the relative ages. It could have been his grandfather, maybe.

'You've found Xander, haven't you?' Delores Brooke-Williams offered her a seat.

Caplan braced herself. Sebastian, the elder son, rising through the layers of the banking world in London, had flown home. 'Please be frank,' he said, taking control, leaving Caplan to wonder what the script with the wiry, silent dad was. 'Have you found a body?'

'We have indeed. There was no DNA on record. We used a familial tracing method and that gave us the family name. We wouldn't say that the identification is firm. We need you to do that.' Caplan let the silence lie. Nobody was going to volunteer the family's dirty linen. 'As we're following a familial DNA as a line of investigation into the identity of the deceased, we need to know if you have anybody missing in your family, immediate or extended? Anybody estranged? Aged between twenty and thirty. About five feet nine.' She paused for a moment before she added, 'Diabetic? Would that be Xander?'

The answer was instant. 'Yes, my younger brother, Alexander. He was twenty-three.'

The silent father muttered something too quiet for her to hear, but his wife leaned forward to place an arm round him.

'When did you last see him?'

The son moved slightly. They had been asked an uncomfortable question and they were not sure how to answer it. The mother put a second arm round her husband, moving along on the sofa. A time for some hard truths.

'I got a few text messages from him in the summer of 2022 – 21st June in fact, the longest day,' the son said.

'And then?'

'Nothing.'

'Nothing at all. Any of you?'

'Are you judging us?' Delores asked.

'Not at all,' said Caplan, 'I'm establishing the facts. Children will live their own lives, they are free to roam, and boys in particular can be very bad about keeping in touch.'

'But not without money, DCI Caplan. No phone, no nothing. He had nothing. We tried to find out where he'd gone.'

'Did you report him missing?' asked Caplan, knowing that they had not.

Sebastian sat down and crossed one expensively trousered leg over the other. 'There was a young lady found last night.'

'Yes.'

'Was Xander found like that, in a forest somewhere?'

'Out in the wilds? Yes.'

'The police seem to think that her death was accidental, death by misadventure. The inquiry will probably say that Xander's was too.'

Caplan didn't want to correct him.

'You don't believe that though, do you?' asked Delores, peering at the police officer. 'I'm going to put the kettle on and get you a cup of tea, dear. Come into the kitchen.' She walked away so that Caplan wouldn't see the tears. They went down a short flight of stairs, bright brass runner rods holding the carpet in place. 'God, this is bad. My husband will find this very difficult to cope with. Thank you for not saying too much in front of him. What happened to Xander? Don't sugar-coat it, please.' She pulled her cardigan round her as they stepped into the barn of a kitchen. An old pulley hung overhead. The large oak table was spotless but the room was chilled. She placed an old kettle on the stove and lit the burner.

Caplan sat down, suddenly tired, too tired to lie to this woman. 'It could be,' she wiped non-existent dust from the table with her sleeve, 'that he was abducted, then killed later.'

'How much later?'

'Weeks, I think.'

'Weeks!'

'I think so. To be honest, I'm having trouble convincing people. Any toxicology test on their hair is clear for the weeks of most recent growth. This suggests to me they had no access to their . . . usual lifestyle.' She shook her head. 'But the police, like any organisation has its priorities.' She lifted her hand to her mouth. 'Sorry, I didn't mean . . .'

'If we, as parents, don't know our children are missing, then how can we expect others to prioritise them? Thank you for your honesty.'

Delores placed the palm of her hand on the kettle, seeming to get some comfort in the warmth. 'He would do anything for heroin. He sold his grandmother's engagement ring. Yes, I think I knew from the minute he went missing that something like this had happened to him. I waited for him to come back, or turn up. Time passed. I waited too long this time.' She turned and looked out the window; the strain, the relief, showed on her face. 'We asked around of course but Xander never had "our" friends, he never fitted this life. He was too good for us, too good for us all.' She looked back out the window, it was starting to rain in earnest. 'One young woman is still missing?'

'Yes. Her dad is beside himself. We think she's still alive, well . . . we hope.'

'I'd like to still have hope, but at least now we know.' She closed her eyes and Caplan thought there might be more tears. 'You were a dancer, weren't you?'

'Yes.'

'Sometimes we are what we are, sometimes we just cannot change.'

Back in the car, Caplan was refreshed by hot green tea and emboldened by a mother's determination to find out what had happened to her son. Only two, out of all the victims, had somebody concerned for them. She picked up her phone. Craigo and Linden had left voice mails. Caplan listened to Craigo's message. Linden could wait.

'Ma'am. The council didn't have any vehicles out in the park on that day, never mind at that time. It was a Saturday afternoon. We got Govan to clean up the logo on the green van. The logo is Heatherbank Raptor Rescue right enough. That fits with the feathers they found in the bushes and it fits in with the knot. But that van does not belong to Heatherbank. I checked all four wild bird rescue centres round here and nobody has a green van. Nobody had a call out. Like you said at the start, ma'am, there's something very organised behind all this. This isn't a him or a her, but a them, like your friend said. Oh, and there's reports that Ghillies has been burning stuff in his back garden. They don't like that up in the Glen. It's paperwork, apparently.'

* * *

Caplan stood once more at the red front door and wondered what secrets it kept. She knew her weapon – Ghillies wanted his OBE for services to policing, public order and for his charity work. And bad publicity about this could hurt him where it counted. She didn't consider herself vindictive, but Rachel had made connections between these deaths, young men and women had died of exposure or been battered to death in the middle of nowhere, and Caplan would use any leverage she could.

There was a smart Mercedes in the driveway. The plate read VAN 1275. It didn't take a lot of her detective skills to figure out who his guests might be.

Ghillies opened the door, looking stressed and upset, but his arms opened in a gesture of magnanimous welcome. Then he stood back, his hand out.

'Christine? I'm sorry, do come in. I'm just back from seeing Rachel. It was a terrible visit. Felix and Wilma are here.' He walked down the short hall, leaving Caplan to wonder what had been said.

Caplan said, her voice dry and reedy, 'I tried to see her yesterday. Wasn't allowed in.'

'Medical advice, something about infection.'

'Hello again, Christine,' Vance said, hand out. 'You have another body, not Bethany though. Wouldn't have your job for anything. Wilma's putting the kettle on.' He smiled at her, a slightly deflated smile.

Caplan could see how he and Rory would be friends. How he, Ghillies and Robertson would be friends. And that Aklen would not. They were professionals whose paths had crossed. Aklen didn't play golf and wasn't comfortable at the Rotary. Not part of the old boys' network.

'You know Bill well?'

'Oh yes, known him for years. I've known Bethany since before she was born. I was saying that Wilma and I bought her her first doll's house. Any news on her? That you can tell us, I mean. Bill told us that the body wasn't . . .' He regarded her almost imploringly.

'Felix, she can't say,' Ghillies protested. 'It's all to be confirmed.'

'But she told Bill that it wasn't Beth.'

Wilma came in, looking very stylish in a vintage light-yellow dress, sixties bouffant and slingback shoes, manoeuvring the tray through the narrow doorway. She turned round, seeing the new guest, her mouth wide as she smiled. 'Oh, I'll get another cup.'

They waited until she had left the room.

'If you want a word, we could use the dining room. I'm sure it won't take long,' said Ghillies, getting a nod of understanding from Vance.

Caplan got the feeling he was keeping Vance from her. Which was all right by her.

'Please go ahead,' Vance said.

'Yes, Mr Ghillies, let's have a chat,' said Caplan, going through the door and turning right into the dining room that she knew looked out onto the garden, complete with a patch of scorched grass and a wire-framed basket. The evidence of a bonfire.

'What are you burning, Rory?' she asked, as Ghillies closed the door behind them.

'Oh, that? A whole load of crap, to be perfectly honest.' He sat down on a dining room chair.

'Can you be more specific?' she asked, both of them comfortable on opposite sides of the table.

Rory Ghillies looked something like embarrassed, or guilty. He was a difficult man to read beyond the practised bonhomie. 'What has that got to do with anything? Your efforts should be focussed on Beth. What does Andrew think you are working on?'

Was the dropping of McEwan's name supposed to unnerve her?

'Well, I'll update him when I see him. What were you burning?'

He patted his hands on his thighs in irritation. 'Rubbish. Just rubbish.' Then he smiled slightly as if light had dawned on him. 'Nothing of importance. Rachel kept a whole load of nonsense round the house. She has two rooms upstairs full of junk. I've been going through lots of old paperwork, pension stuff, bank statements, insurance, going back years. She has cheque stubs from twenty years ago. I'm shredding and burning. Can't be too careful. I'm keeping myself busy. Wilma's going to go through the wardrobes, Rachel's summer stuff. Let's face it, she isn't going to be here next summer. Now, do you want to tell me what the hell that has to do with Beth?'

'Your wife was concerned about the disappearance of Nikolas Ardman, Lisa Stratton and a few others.'

'Oh, so it wasn't really a meeting of old friends?' Ghillies went pale. He looked upset for the first time. And something else that Caplan couldn't read. 'Like I've said, Rachel was obsessed over that Ardman thing.'

'I think they are all ingredients in the same soup, as my old DCI used to say. Give it a stir and see what floats to the surface.' Caplan sighed. 'That's what we intend to do. Rachel saw connections and she was right.' Caplan emphasised the last word. 'Sarah Linden has been very supportive.'

'Well, I'd listen to her. A bright woman, Sarah.'

'I've been trying to work out why your wife wanted us to know about Ardman. Why that case? Why him?'

Ghillies looked away.

'As I said at the time, if something was so important to me that I was thinking about it on my deathbed, I'd like to think that my husband would take it seriously,' said Caplan, studying the picture over the mantelpiece of Ghillies looking handsome in his kilt. What had the age gap been when he'd met Rachel? Time telescopes such disparity.

Was history repeating itself with Bethany?

'She was obsessing with that case. It got embarrassing. If she told you that she had a file, and that all the secrets she had discovered were in it, she was lying. She thought she'd uncovered intelligence that the entire might of Police Scotland had missed. Are you only here for her notebooks?'

Caplan gave a noise that was neither assent nor refusal.

'Well, they're not here. A bloody huge box it was. Gone. Remember she knew that this day was coming. All that took so much out of her. It was my wish that she might live a little longer, maybe give herself some peace. Instead, I think she tortured herself with it. Whatever *it* was.'

Caplan glanced out the window. 'Was there a purple Moleskin notebook?'

'Loads of them. The ones on the bonfire contained poetry and musings. Nothing. If I'd found any documentation that she shouldn't have been in possession of, I would have returned it. Embarrassing though that would be. Much of what she claims was going on, was only going on in her head. Why do you think she never got promotion? She got personally fixated on an idea and wouldn't let go. She'd talk about nothing else.' He patted his thighs with his hands again, emphasising each word. 'I do know my way around an investigation. Rachel was more of a conspiracy theorist. It didn't matter to her that an experienced team of investigators had ruled it as accidental death; she knew better. She was an embarrassment. And it's embarrassing that you're here going over all this when you should be out looking for these bastards who have Beth. They killed Shiv – that's the body you found?'

'Not yet confirmed... officially,' said Caplan, but nodded ruefully.

He sank his head into his hands. 'And Beth'll be next, so why the hell are you talking to me?'

'I'm talking to you because I want to see what cars you have in the double garage. A Lexus and an Octavia are both registered to this address.' She gave him her calm stare. 'Anything you want to say?'

'It's not what you think.'

'I believe it's exactly what I think.'

Suddenly his voice was chilling. 'And what do you think, DCI Caplan?'

'I think you've been having sex with your goddaughter. That's what I think.'

For a moment Ghillies's face froze. Caplan knew he was considering how to play this.

'What can I say? She found me attractive? I'm not proud of it but it happened. It's so trendy today to be offended when really all women want is a guy to show them a bit of attention. Bethany and I are very fond of each other.' He lifted his finger, warning her. 'And I was *not* in a position of trust.'

'I think her dad might see that differently. And you couldn't resist her charms?'

Ghillies shook his head. 'She started it. She was always keen.'

Caplan's stomach nearly emptied itself. 'If you had said she'd lost her mum, you were having a difficult time with Rachel, you grew close and that closeness grew into something else that you now regret, then I would have accepted that.' Her voice was razor sharp. 'Where were you when she disappeared?'

'Driving home from the golf club. Or at the hospice.' He smiled. 'Beth's disappearance makes it very awkward for me. It could make things awkward for you. You are not popular, DCI Caplan.'

'And you are a very nasty piece of work. I will send you to the worms where you belong.' She got up, walked to the door and then he was in the hall in front of her, his arm on the wall, blocking her exit.

'You have five seconds to move that or I will put you on the floor.'

The arm stayed in place.

There was stalemate for a slow count of five.
Then he hit the carpet.

Caplan was furious by the time she entered the interview room. The hospice had confirmed Ghillies had been there the afternoon Bethany had gone missing, and Robertson had called him. Ghillies had phoned back. But Caplan knew he was too clever to get his own hands dirty. He was a cop. He'd know not to leave a trail back to him.

DC Mackie, as if sensing her boss was not in good humour, pulled back the chair for Caplan. Colin Jacobs, the park-keeper, gave her a curt nod.

Caplan had flicked through the ever-growing file of witness statements from those who had been in the park between three and four on the Saturday afternoon, well, those that had come forward at least. But in her fury, she'd forgotten most of what she'd read.

Jacobs continued the chat that the DCI had interrupted. 'I don't know why you want to talk to me. I handed in the feathers I found in the bushes. It said on the radio, you know, if you saw anything, so I went back and looked. I thought a cat had got a bird. They were brown and white big feathers. I really don't know why you asked me in.'

Mackie was polite. 'Colin, tell us what you saw on that day.'

'It was a normal day, the park was busy.'

'Did you see this girl?' She held out the photo that Robertson had taken.

'Well, that's all over the papers that, isn't it? But no, I'm not saying she wasn't there. But I didn't clock her. I must've seen her before.'

'You must've been busy?'

'Sunny days, especially on the holidays, we've to keep on top of the dirty nappies, dog crap, half-eaten burgers, all the shit of the day. Literally.'

'And what day did you see the green van? You mentioned it to the desk sergeant when you handed in the feathers.'

'Saturday. I keep a note, time and date. These incidents can often turn abusive. I was there from half two to half three. I had my own lunch sitting on a bench, then I went up to the top end of the park. This green van had reversed into the bushes. Wildlife rescue. They were picking up a bird that had been hurt; somebody had phoned in. Nobody tells me anything. I thought they had the radio on too loud. I told them to turn it off. I didn't get close. Let me think; two blokes or two lassies in the bushes, wearing those baseball hats they wear at the birdy place. Later, when I heard what had happened, I got to thinking and I went back. Bloody feathers everywhere. I picked them up. I put them in a bag like they do on the telly and dropped them in here. That would be on the Sunday.' He thought for a moment. 'But that lassie's young and fit, she'd have screamed blue bloody murder, so no, I think you're wrong. I'd have heard her if she was there. It was Adele that was playing. From where I was, I could see they had a cat basket, and big gloves. They said sorry. The wee one turned the music off.'

'Was the van marked?'

He shook his head. 'Only the wee logo sticker on the door.'

'Two women you said? Can you describe them?'

He nodded. 'Aye, I'd say two women. A large one and a wee one. Baseball hats and sweatshirts. Green.'

'Hair colour? Skin colour?'

'Both white, Scottish accents. I think one had brown hair, the large one.' He looked at Mackie. 'I think. But maybe not.'

Caplan thanked him and told him they would be in touch.

Up in the incident room she grabbed Craigo. 'Get Jacobs traced through the park. Timewise they were very close. Get a good description of the two people. Anything of them on CCTV? Ask him for an E-fit. Any good visuals of them while driving? And have a good look at him. He was right there and . . .'

'Yes, ma'am, and there's somebody to see you outside. A Mrs Elliot? Come over from Fort William.' Craigo nodded like this was important.

'Who the hell is she? Does that Stewart not know what a desk sergeant is supposed to do?'

'It's about Pottie, I think. This old dear is his Granny, believe it or not.'

Caplan made to stand up. 'He had a Granny?'

'Well, she's very keen to talk to you.'

'Tell Mackie to put her in the nice interview room. I'll be there in five. Meanwhile, get hold of the security footage at the Lorn Hospice car park. Make sure Ghillies's Lexus didn't leave between two and five on Saturday.'

Craigo raised an eyebrow.

'I know he wasn't in the bushes in the park but I'd love something on the bastard. Where is the Granny?'

The old lady entered the interview room, grey hair spiked up with gel, several gold chains hanging round her neck and wrists, holding the arm of a younger woman. With the easy grace of a professional carer the younger woman helped Mrs Elliot to her seat. She smiled and they sat down. Mrs Elliot handed over a plastic bag with a jar of strawberry jam and a small Tupperware container.

'Thank you for finding Andrew.'

'You're his grandmother?'

'Yes, I am that.' The wizened hand came out and shook hers, holding on for a long time, looking deep into Caplan's eyes. 'I don't know much but I do know how to make a good scone. He was a good boy, our Andrew, when he wasn't being a wee shit. He always kept in touch. And now look where we are. But at least I know.'

'I'm sorry that it didn't turn out better for you.' She gave a grim smile.

'I had always believed that wherever he was, he was in pain. We know that he is at peace now.'

The eyes crinkled then with a bright intelligence. 'He would still be alive though if it wasn't for them. It might not have been much of a life, but it didn't allow them to take it from him.'

Caplan tried to stay calm. She smiled encouragingly.

'It was that bloody woman, you know. It was when she met him it all went tits up. Then he went away.' Her bony shoulders gave a shrug. 'He was a wee survivor. He'd not have come to any harm if he'd never met her.' The old lady nodded. Her hand reached out and patted the back of Caplan's. 'Enjoy the scones, pet.'

'Thank you. You've come a long way. Why don't you stay and have a cup of tea? I'll get Mackie to put the kettle on and you can tell her about your grandson and this lady he met.'

The old lady's hand gripped Caplan's wrist. 'She'd something to do with his disappearance, didn't she? I'm not thick. He was a right wee tosser. Why bother with him? But she did. He didn't have anything to offer, not even the brains he was born with, but she got him involved in something. It got him killed.'

'You seem very sure of that.'

'He was so . . . captivated. Would that be the right word? What she said, where she went, this woman.'

'How did they meet?'

'She was a volunteer. She did adult reading and stuff.'

'Her name? Did he mention that?'

She shook her head and her gold earrings jangled against each other. 'It was Maureen or Moira, he always just called her Mo. She talked a lot. Mo the Blow.'

'Did you ever meet her?'

Another shake of the head, another jingle of earrings.

'Can you describe her?'

'Better than that. I think I might have a picture on my phone.'

'Right, what do we have?' Caplan arrived in the incident room, her energy up. 'I've had to leave Mackie getting the life story of young Mr Pottie. Bloody tragic right enough but he was okay until he met That Woman, Mo The Blow. Who is That Woman? Mackie has a picture on her phone and that's being printed out right now. Mo is a big woman, she volunteered at the Loch Lomond Drop-in Centre from September to December 2019 then left, never came back. Pottie's last seen was what? The 29th December? Was she one of the ladies in the bushes when Bethany was abducted? We'll put the picture in front of Jacobs.' Caplan sighed. 'Then there was Mo at the Revolve, the ex-psych nurse, the one with the colourful dungarees. Mackie checked where she was on Saturday afternoon and guess what? She's AWOL as well now. This feeds into the level of organisation I suspect. God knows how many Moes we might find if we had the money to look properly.' She looked at the board. 'And I need to say something about Rory Ghillies. He's been in a relationship with Bethany Robertson for more than a year.'

She waited until that settled on the room.

'He knows as well as we do that it propels him to the top of the list. He's being watched. And he's banned everybody from seeing Rachel, except him and the Vances. Anything from the bird sanctuary place?'

Craigo flicked through some papers, talking before he found the right one. 'No call out for a raptor in trouble in any of the centres within a thirty-mile radius on Saturday.' He picked up his pencil. 'But the Heatherbank Raptor Rescue has a veterinary unit and reported that they've been having incidents of their drug supply, quote, "being manipulated".'

'Manipulated? What does that mean?' Caplan turned to the board.

'See if they recognise Pottie's Mo. If she's Raptor Mo in the bushes then we have a chain there. As the guy from the council said, a young fit woman doesn't get abducted in broad daylight without making a racket, even if they were playing Adele to cover the sound. But she would be quiet if she had a bumful of what? Diazepam? Any benzodiazepine?'

'Bupivacaine, benzocaine, midazolam and ketamine were the drugs Heatherbank mentioned. And, on the off chance, I asked who put the logos on their vans. They are just stickers, ma'am, they keep them in the office. Also, we've traced and got statements off the people who were out in the park when Bethany was. Some recall seeing her, one recalls the green van but thought it was the parkie's, nobody recalls a struggle, a cry, a shout. Nobody saw anything basically.'

'I think we might have discovered how the abductions can be so quiet. We have drugs, a falconer's knot, falcon feathers. Our abductor must have some commonality between Heatherbank and Revolve. Or Heatherbank and the Ashdown Community Unit where Nik was. Same with the Lomond Drop-in Centre. Maybe fling the net more historically and add Hand to Hand, Blueberry Centre and the Gretal Rooms . . .' Caplan stopped, looking at the board. 'The PUPSs? The pickup points. The place where they, let's call them the Moes, come into contact with their victims.' She sighed. 'But then what?'

FOURTEEN

As she went downstairs, Caplan got a phone call from McEwan, telling her that Ghillies was putting in a formal complaint for assault. She told McEwan to let him, and was aware of the DCC having a chuckle.

'It was obstruction of a police officer in the line of their duty.'

'That's not what Felix Vance witnessed.'

'Through a brick wall? Honestly.' She hung up, knowing it would go nowhere.

Who had the most to lose?

PC Stewart was ready with another handwritten message for her, the same number. Caplan took it, looked at it. 'Has she said what this is about?'

'Nope, and she refused to give her name.'

'Did you ask her?'

'Oh yes. She said that you'd know who it was and what it was about.'

'I've no idea,' Caplan said, adding mentally that she had enough to deal with.

On her way through the door, her phone flashed. It was Fergusson. Now she could give her friend an update on what Ghillies had said.

'Ghillies was a decent cop, if a terrible human being, but is he involved in this?'

Fergusson said, 'We did have a body last night.'

'And that's the worst of it. Now, somebody needs to put their hand up and fight our corner. Though I doubt it'll make any difference.'

'Well, the eyes of the media are on you now, your picture was in the papers. Don't forget the power of public opinion. Somebody will talk to the wrong person and that'll spur them into action. I don't see Bill Robertson going against Ghillies's advice and going public. I'd worry if they give you a designated liaison person. Those upstairs are nervous of the media.'

'We don't want to open that door,' warned Caplan, 'for personal reasons as much as anything.'

'God, I bloody knew you'd bring that up.'

'Me bringing it up isn't a problem. I'm saying that you never, ever want a journalist digging into your personal life.'

There was silence on the line. Caplan looked at Craigo through the window of the office. Her sergeant was looking happy, busy, looking at the list then looking at the wall, occasionally looking out the window, oblivious to the undercurrents in the office.

'Yeah?' Fergusson sighed. 'Actually the reason I called you was you have an appointment at four p.m. at the Crispy Bake House. Irene Kennedy had to come through me at Glasgow because you've not returned her calls to arrange a meeting.'

'Who is she?' Caplan looked at her watch.

'Irene Kennedy's maiden name was Irene Bellshaw. She's Rachel's sister and she's up here in the arse end of nowhere to meet us. I have driven up here and have been hovering around waiting. I figure she has something important to say. Hence why I'm on the handsfree talking to you.'

'Why did she not tell the main desk what she wanted like a normal human being?'

'One word. Rory.'

'You are Christine, aren't you?' The older lady bustled between them, hitching her leather tote bag up over her shoulder.

'Irene?' asked Caplan, aware of Fergusson sidestepping closer even though the coffee shop wasn't that crowded. The three women formed a cluster, as if sharing a secret.

'Yes, Irene Kennedy. I'm . . .'

'Rachel's sister.' Caplan noted the shape of the face, the dreamy blue eyes; take away a few years and Irene could have been Rachel as she was, back at police training college, back when they had known her. 'Would you like a coffee?'

'A latte please.'

'Green tea for me,' Caplan said to Fergusson.

They took a table in the corner, talking about the weather until the waitress had stopped wiping crumbs from the top.

'Thank you for going to see Rachel. I think it meant a lot to her. I gather that she hadn't seen either of you for a long time.'

'That's true.'

'Was it about the Ardman boy?' asked Kennedy. She leaned back as the green tea and lattes arrived, Fergusson throwing her friend a dirty look at being reduced to the role of waitress.

'Your sister seems unsettled by the way that case had turned out,' Caplan said non-committally.

Kennedy nodded and took a sip of her latte. Caplan waited. Fergusson watched them from under her blonde curly fringe.

'Did you go round to see Rory?'

'We did.'

Kennedy snorted. 'He screws around. He got between my sister and me. I didn't speak to her for years because of him, controlling tosser.'

Caplan nodded in agreement. 'Controlling to what extent?' She let the question lie.

'Looking back? The long sleeve blouse on a hot day. I saw deep bruises more than once, but there was always a reason.' She shrugged. 'And then she said he was "worse" when he didn't have a lady friend. I thought she meant mood not violence but now, I'm not so sure. And he's been sweetness itself in the last year, so he has another mistress on the go. Well, when Rachel goes, poor cow might find herself saddled with him.'

'Do you suspect that he's undermined her investigation, our investigation? Is he capable of that?'

Kennedy nodded with a jerk of her head, a tic shared by her sister. 'Of course he is. And I think she knew Ardman, whatever, would die with her, so she wanted to pass it on to – who? Three women she'd known for years? Three women who might push back against Rory. Three women not intimidated by him.'

'Why was it important to him, though? He had no professional respect for her.'

'It wasn't important to him. It was to her, and that was enough for him to belittle it, this thing about the Ardman bloke. She had notebooks, photographs and everything. I bet he didn't give you any of that documentation?' She raised the glass cup of latte. 'Am I wrong?'

'You aren't wrong.' Caplan sighed. 'We went to the house and asked him about her notebooks. They've gone. According to him.'

Kennedy nodded. 'No, I looked for the notebooks myself. Not there. There was once a box file jammed full of newspaper clippings, some stuff she'd printed off the internet. Gone.'

'I met the neighbour. He said that Rory had been burning stuff. Rachel's not even dead yet.' Kennedy looked at Caplan, directly. Caplan had thought the smudging of the eye colour was due to the illness, but it looked genetic. 'He has something to hide.'

Caplan was wary of being played. 'It could be as simple as the fact that Rachel was in possession of documentation that she had no right to possess. Awkward if she was sacked at this time for gross professional misconduct.'

'More likely to protect his reputation. But he was a womaniser. I bet that blonde cop, Linden, couldn't face seeing Rachel.' Kennedy nodded knowingly. 'What did Rachel say to you about this?' The cafe was suddenly noisy. Fergusson adjusted herself in the seat, holding her phone. 'Rachel only made it into the CID because she got there before they got married. She wasn't allowed to think for herself so she began to overthink her career.'

Caplan noticed Fergusson looking at her.

'A detective constable who was known to overthink things thought that there was more to the Ardman situation?' asked Caplan. 'You see my dilemma.'

Kennedy shrugged. 'When they hit the news she'd call me and tell me why she thought the most recent missing person was "one of hers or not".'

'One of hers?' Caplan frowned. 'But these were cases she never worked on. It does smack of a kind of arrogance, you must admit?'

Kennedy looked chastened. 'When we found out Rachel's condition was terminal, I got a phone call from somebody she knew at church. Rachel had given her something for safekeeping, for when she died. Rachel gave me something too. Rachel made us both promise to hand it over to you when she died, but I guess that time is now.

'I remember the tears the night after the senior detective had called her in and told her to cease. She was threatened with all sorts, even a mental health assessment. It was the week before Christmas. She went home in a terrible state, and Rory told her she was an embarrassment to him.' She mimicked her brother-in-law: '"That could damage my OBE for my charity work".'

Caplan's mind started to turn. 'Did she back off?'

'Of course not. It made her more determined. She was lucky that she went off on the sick when she did, otherwise they would have fired her. Rory would have been furious. But now all he does is talk to his old pals and get any movement on this case blocked. No money, no investigation.'

'Are you saying, Irene, that Rory was actively blocking the funding for this investigation?'

'Not in terms as definitive as that. More a discreditation of her opinions.' Kennedy looked at Caplan, eyebrow raised. 'Are they tripping over themselves to form a squad to investigate these bodies? No? Well, there's your answer.'

Caplan didn't look at her colleague but heard Fergusson let out a long slow whistle through her teeth.

'And what was it? The thing that she left you?'

'This. And this was the one she left to her friend.' Kennedy pulled a small bubble-wrapped packet from her handbag. 'There you go. I don't know what's on them. They're password protected. And don't look at me like that. You would've tried too. I need to get my train.' She stood up, straightening out the sleeves of her jacket. 'My sister had her heart invested in this. Rory's a bastard. She deserves some closure before she passes.'

Caplan said goodbye, regarding the two flash drives, one blue, one red, lying in their bubbled envelope, between the empty latte glass and the cup of green tea.

Fergusson waited until Irene Kennedy had gone out the door. 'I'll bet you a fiver you break that password within fifteen minutes.'

'I'll do it in five.'

In the end it took her ten minutes, but only because her phone rang as she was typing in her second guess. There were a lot of scanned newspaper cuttings and official documentation, neatly filed, some of which Rachel would not have had legitimate access to.

Caplan read on, tapping out the names and case numbers on the system. The flash drives were full of pages that looked like little cards where Rachel had written the name of a missing person, along with, sometimes, a number that closely resembled a case number but was altered to fit some code of her own. Caplan recognised some of them as ones that she herself had put together. Rachel had put crosses over some and ticks over others, working her way through, altering her little files. Some of the names turned up alive and well, others turned up in hospital, others turned up dead.

Then she read a letter from a mum whose son had died by drowning after being missing for a period of time. Caplan could imagine Rachel interviewing her and bonding with her. When the inquiry concluded that the boy had died by accidental drowning, the mum had written a touching and heartfelt letter to the supportive police officer.

And that would stick with Rachel, trapped in her unhappy, childless marriage.

Rachel had got a canonical four: Ardman, Stratton, Welsh, Pottie. The inclusion of Welsh and Stratton was only questionable with hindsight. And through access to material that Rachel didn't have.

Despite precise filing, Caplan was overwhelmed with snippets, Post-it notes, links to websites, the list of email addresses and scanned photographs. As far as the victims went, some were names she was familiar with, others she'd never heard of. Caplan started scribbling. There were sixteen names in all. She was sure most of them had turned up; dead by natural causes, dead by accidental death. But the amount of documentation Rachel had gathered was breathtaking. As Caplan scrolled through the document, she began to wonder, as Rory Ghillies had, if there was already some malignant process going on in her head, impeding her cognitive processes. Which is exactly what Rory would say.

Then she came across something highlighted in yellow. A printout of something from Companies House. She read it: Fayer Construction. Then Rachel's handwriting: *Owned by Albion Construction. Which owns Spire.*

Then a list of directors. Caplan saw the name Ghillies, R. It was Rachel, not Rory. Plus Vance, F and W.

Aklen had said something about opening and closing companies under different ownership. Sharp practice but not illegal.

She closed her eyes and leaned back in the chair, listening to her instincts. This put Lisa Stratton right in the mix. Rachel had noted the argument against Welsh – her mental health struggles and her close and concerned family – but not against Stratton, one of the two names Caplan thought didn't fit.

So what was Rachel thinking?

Did that mean it was personal?

Caplan felt a rush of excitement, seeing what Rachel had seen. Stratton's murder did fit, if it was about her murder, not about the victimology.

Just like Bethany.

'Oh Jesus.' She put her head in her hands.

'Are you okay, ma'am?' Craigo looked at his watch.

'Not really.' Caplan stood up and walked out her office into the incident room. 'I hate to do this to you guys but we've been handed some more information. At the moment, I'd be refused the cost of overtime, because it'll be seen as not having any bearing on the current case. So, unpaid, but I need help. I'll send out for fish and chips.'

'Throw in a wee Irn-Bru and I'll be right here, missus!' said Mackie.

'Me too,' said Craigo, sticking a pen behind his ear and rolling his sleeves up.

'Lizzie Fergusson and Sarah Linden will join in remotely,' Caplan said, wondering what carrot she'd need to dangle there.

'We could do with McPhee.' Mackie sounded wistful.

Caplan smiled, nodded, and gave Craigo her credit card before going through to try to explain to Aklen how late she was going to be.

Caplan put the phone down and rubbed her ear. Linden hit and did not miss. One of Caplan's team had leaked it to the press that the dead body was that of Bethany. They had been at Robertson's front door, wanting a statement. They wanted a statement from the senior investigating officer as well. She tried to call the FLO. Engaged. Robertson's landline was also engaged and his mobile was switched off.

Caplan put the phone down on Linden, refusing to take any more abuse. Then the phone rang.

It was Andrew McEwan. Was she available for a press conference because she was going to have to answer for the actions of her team? She told him they had just made an important break but wasn't going to tell him because HQ had a leak. Then she excused herself and hung up.

The phone went again.

Caplan swiped at it. 'Yes?'

'Can we have a word?' Ryce sounded worried, which wasn't like her. The pathologist was normally the epitome of fractious efficiency.

'Can it wait?' Caplan closed her eyes. 'Two minutes ago I was being berated by Linden because somebody on my team had leaked the identification on social media before she knew. Then Andrew McEwan decides it's my fault, so he phones and I'm now deaf in my left ear. Bill Robertson's neighbour saw on Twitter, X, that Bethany's body has been found. The helpful neighbour turns up at Robertson's to offer his condolences and to ask if there was anything he could do. And then postulated a few reasons why I might be lying to him.'

'Should the FLO not keep people away?' asked Ryce.

'The FLO thought it was another nice neighbour handing in some cake. Please tell me you have done the PM and I can release a fact to the world, or my superiors. Nobody is going to be happy until I'm lying on your table.'

'Can you get yourself to my office right now, before you talk to anybody else? Put your phone off and get here. Now.'

'You do know that I'm ninety minutes away?' Caplan looked at the clock, at Craigo and Mackie, heads down, working hard, following the life of Lisa Stratton.

'Don't worry, I'll wait.'

Caplan was wearing gloves and a scrub cap when she entered the post-mortem suite at the hospital. Ryce was already gowned, gloved and masked. She was looking at a piece of paper hanging on a clipboard, waiting.

'You took your time.'

'I jumped every red light, it was the best I could do. What's up?' She turned to look at the body lying on the table, covered now by a plastic sheet. The post-mortem hadn't even started. Shivonne's head was a mass of white, black and red. The initial incision hadn't been made.

Ryce said, 'You can see why I know the leak of identification hasn't been made from this office. She's been 'not Bethany' since you mentioned the pilonidal sinus. Some young journalist was watching the police, monitoring the calls, waiting for the body of a young woman to be found on a remote location and put two and two together. There's nothing we can do about that until stupid people find some sense of social responsibility.'

Caplan looked at the body again. Ryce was pawing at the clipboard then doing something with a plastic-covered file, something that would be much easier if she took her gloves off. Caplan waited. Ryce was deep in concentration. She'd never been guilty of Linden's silence power play.

The face of the victim was so disrupted, it was difficult to see the pretty young woman that she had been, mostly because there was no intact bone to give her face any contour; the forehead and the cheekbone were depressed and bloodied. The jaw had been pushed over to the left. She looked like a broken puppet. Caplan studied her. The battering had been more severe on one side. While one eye could have been sleeping, the other eye was a sunken pit, a black slit in the purple balloon of her socket. There were three piercings in one ear, four in the other.

Caplan showed Ryce the photo on her phone. The piercings and the holes matched.

Ryce walked over to the slab, her rubber-soled boots squeaking lightly on the light blue floor. 'We have here the body of a white female, probably early twenties. Dark reddish hair, dyed, natural colour dark brown evidenced by the body hair. Five feet six and eight-and-a-half stone.'

'Yes,' Caplan said. Ryce had her full attention now.

'It was noted that Bethany didn't have any tattoos. Shivonne did. Maybe Bethany did and her dad didn't know about them – they'd be mostly covered by clothes.' Ryce moved over to the body and deftly rotated the upper torso towards her, pulling down the plastic sheet. 'Whoever did this knew about the tattoos and removed the skin where the tattoo was, in an attempt to delay identification.' Ryce pulled a face. She pointed to a huge scab on the pale, white skin of the young woman's back. 'There. Can't tell you how painful that would be to remove. I doubt they would have given her any local analgesia. As we would expect, she's had her left canine tooth removed. And there's been an attempt . . .' Ryce shrugged. '. . . I have no idea of the level of insanity we are dealing with here, but the left fibula has been smashed with something, days before she died. The fracture line has indents above and below it, so somebody took a few attempts. I've seen that on a drowning victim who got their leg trapped between two boats in a high swell, but they had bruises to the inside of the leg. This lady does not.'

'Same injuries as the other victims?'

'Yes, enough to make a pattern.' Ryce laid the body back down on her back as carefully as if Shiv was able to feel the hard chill of the stainless-steel tray. 'Before you ask, the DNA is already away.'

'Wait.' Ryce rolled the body towards her again, this time holding it by the waist, then drawing the sheet back, pulling it down slightly so Caplan could see the lower back and the upper part of the buttocks. 'As you see, there's a few cuts. The purple patchwork's from how she was lying after her death. Bethany Robertson had a year out of uni on medical grounds for a pilonidal sinus. This lady has had no such operation, as you noticed. Even with all the skills we have nowadays the scar tends to be ugly, there's very little skin at the base of the spine to make it pretty. As far as the press are concerned . . .'

'"Identification has been confirmed but is not being released until members of the family have been informed",' quoted Caplan.

'I wanted to run something else past you. We looked back at the post-mortem pictures of who was hunted down, who got, let's say, chased. In particular, I've been looking at the X-rays that were taken at the time. And, well, I think we might've found another pattern. It's not clear, it might not even be accurate, but some of the victims have been subject to blunt-force trauma.'

'Did we not know that already? Shiv has had her face caved in. Xander's face was a mess. You plucked his expensive tooth out from his throat.' Caplan swivelled to the left on her seat, thinking, then swivelled back to the centre.

'Yes, what we found could be from previous trauma. It could be from a lot of things. But the final insults, those perimortem, are always, always longer than they are wide.'

'Hit with a stick, a tyre iron? A baseball bat but not a hammer?'

'Not a hammer. While alive, they are beaten to break ribs, arms, lower legs. It's a beating but never fatal. When they want it to be fatal, they go straight for the head.' She spread her hands, like a magician.

'There's a period of being beaten for torture, and then they're beaten to death by blows to the head to kill them? With a time gap in between?' Caplan let out a long breath.

'What if they are beaten to keep them compliant? Then killed with a beating to the head when they are no longer of use.

'I've enough here to request support to review your canonical five. And any others you wish. The blows are of different strengths which could mean many things, but it could suggest different people. Strong men. Weaker women. But over a period of time. And one more thing? Rod Taylor of the Rod-Todd situation, who'd been in a committed homosexual relationship for twenty years?'

'That's about it.'

'Well, he had sexual intercourse with a woman before he died.'

'Pardon?'

'You heard.'

'Are you sure?'

'I am.'

Caplan thought for a moment. 'The name Stevie? Male or female?'

'Stevie Wonder? Stevie Nicks? Can be either. Over to you now. I presume you are staying in town tonight. Hotel?'

'Sarah is putting me up. A huge pile of documentation to go through then a big bed, hot bath, ensuite, plush carpets, central heating. Don't know how I'll cope.' She shook her head, trying to shake out the Fleetwood Mac song that had floated in.

FIFTEEN

Bethany woke with the noise of wind through the trees and the chatter of crows. A murder of crows. It sounded so different from before. She was now out in the country somewhere.

They had moved her while she was asleep. She had dreamt that she had heard the rumble of the treadmill under her feet, and that she was running. The darkness outside was now in her room and in her head. She lifted her hand and stopped the treadmill before she went backwards and hit the wall. She ended up sitting on the stone slabs in the corner, right where she was now. Sitting on plastic, on stone, listening to the trees and the crows.

A different place. A different room. But still imprisoned.

Last time they came they had opened the door and a bright torch light had shone in her eyes, pinning her down. She never saw them. Him. Her. Whoever.

She knew there was one of them. There was one who stayed back, in the corner. Meanwhile, she concentrated on being Bethany.

She wondered how long she had.

What did they say? Three minutes without oxygen.

Three days without water. Three months without food.

Well, they were keeping her alive for some reason. So they could torture her, abuse her. Each time they visited, they took a little more of her.

It dawned on her that she was feeling stronger, her thought processes were clearer. They were preparing her for something. She tried to gauge the dimensions of the room, trying to think of a plan. That was all she needed. A plan.

Because Linden had decided to open two bottles of wine to celebrate Caplan decking Ghillies, they'd only managed five hours of sleep. But now up, after a breakfast of honey and porridge, a long shower and half an hour of stretching, Caplan called Craigo and told him that he was in charge. He was to assemble the team and tell them the body was suspected to be that of Shivonne MacDougall, former resident of the Revolve. He was to stand in front of the whiteboard and talk them through the operation as she saw it: a group of persons as yet unknown were taking young and vulnerable people. The clock was now ticking down for Bethany. He was to go through everything again, emphasising the where and the who. He was to go through the names Rachel had in her documentation. Mostly they matched what HOLMES3 had produced. Rachel had looked at many other victims. Her deductive thinking was in evidence. She had included Welsh, due to her lack of access to the woman's medical records. And she had included Lisa Stratton, detailing that victim's life in the extreme. She was the key.

Mackie suspected Rachel had done a lot of interviews, not saying that she was a cop, getting the detail of casual chit-chat, but more than that, the bigger concerns of the baiting as well. Who was researching what bait would work? Where were the victims being kept? Craigo told her they had traced a friend of Lisa Stratton, and she had agreed to talk in exchange for seeing where her friend had passed away.

'It's on your way home, ma'am, and she might have some information for us. She said that they didn't really listen to her the first time.'

Caplan made notes. 'Okay. How are we doing with the Moes and the PUPS? Start with the most recent, the Revolve, as whoever works there now will have known our baiter. I know it's hard with the time, sometimes years, that have passed with the others, but work backwards. I suspect you're looking for volunteers.

'Get somebody to look back at the social media of these organisations. Look for recurring faces. If you get nothing, throw the net a bit wider and further.'

Caplan scrolled through her contacts, not even looking up when Linden crawled into the kitchen. 'Sarah, can you do me a favour?'

'Probably not but I know you'll ask anyway.'

'Can you call the Lorn Hospice and ask for that nurse, Sadie? Lean on her a wee bit. Ask her if anybody had been interested in the time of our visit to Rachel.'

'Because?'

'Because I'm curious to know if Felix Vance was there for a reason.'

'Why should he be interested in you at the hospital? He'll have been visiting his friend's ill wife. But leave it with me.' She screwed up her eyes to look at her phone. 'I've had a text from McEwan. He wants to see us both ASAP. I bloody hope the shitshow that you carry around with you isn't going to land on my head. Again.'

Caplan cradled a cup of green tea as Linden slammed cupboard doors open and closed looking for the coffee and aspirin.

'By the kettle,' said Caplan, scrolling through her phone. Linden leaned on the counter.

'I'm going to meet Joanna Jones where Lisa Stratton died, on the opposite side of Chern Wood from where Shiv was found. Craigo's taking me in case we need the four wheel drive. I've never visited that scene – I think it might give me a sense of the type of woman Lisa was. I was thinking . . .'

'Chris, can you think quietly until I finish my coffee?'

Thirty minutes later Linden reappeared; sharp suit, hair up, make-up on. She pulled her professionalism on like a glove. Ninety minutes later they were walking along the corridor to McEwan's office.

Caplan felt sluggish. A lack of sleep preceded by a rich risotto was catching up with her. 'Any idea what this is about?'

'I doubt he's had a change of heart. You're probably in trouble for something. Decking Ghillies? Maybe you're being taken off the case. They'll parachute somebody in over your head. Either way you're fucked and you'll have no friends apart from your Neanderthal team. But he wouldn't have invited me to enjoy your distress, though . . . oh he might. Maybe I too am being seconded to police somewhere with three sheep and torrential rain.'

'I don't have time for his shit.'

'Is that file the results of last night's work?'

'Might be. Might be the ever-growing list of possible victims so I can make Andrew McEwan feel guilty. You know me so well.'

'I bloody taught you that trick.' Linden's face lit up as McEwan's door opened, the professional façade back in place.

He was smiling too. 'ACC Linden, DCI Caplan, please have a seat. We're under pressure here.'

'Yes, we are,' agreed Caplan dryly. 'You know the body we found was Shivonne McDougall?'

'I do. Who abducted her?'

'No idea. We're looking at her last seen. We have an update on Bethany. A van with a false logo. Maybe an injured bird of prey used as bait. Bethany had a fondness for raptors and a kind heart.

She might have climbed into the van quite happily or was drugged in some way.'

McEwan nodded. 'They knew her, then? And Alexander Brooke-Williams?'

Caplan was careful to respond. 'He fits a pattern recognised by HOLMES3. We think he's been living as Jimmy Williams. We're waiting on a sample of Jimmy's DNA to confirm he's Xander.'

'Good. His family were very impressed at the lengths we went to identify him.'

Caplan smirked at the 'we'. 'Actually, it was very easy. The difficult bit was getting the permission to use a genealogy database.'

McEwan bit his bottom lip. 'And now we're in an awkward position.'

'I don't think you are. We found the ID of that one man. Now we find who's doing this abduction, torture and murder. Because that's what we've been looking at all along.'

'Brooke-Williams was recent. Any fresh evidence?'

'Oh, for God's sake, they are far too clever to leave evidence,' said Linden coldly. 'Look at the way they left Brooke-Williams's body right under the nose of the MoD, between patrols. I mean, normal people think like normal people. Too scared to shove a dead body into the bed of a truck, cover it with a blanket and transport it or drug a live subject and stick them in the back of a van. That's what these people do with Bethany and with Shivonne. They are smart.'

'DCI Caplan, how confident are you that you can identify the perpetrator of these crimes?' asked McEwan.

'Plural. There's a team of them. I'm a hundred per cent sure. But I'm not sure it's possible to identify them with only three members of staff.'

'Well, quality rather than quantity, eh? You have seventy-two hours. Not a minute more. After that, you'd better have something to report back to me.'

'Do we have money allocated to us? We have many more cases to look at, this has been going on for years.'

Linden folded her arms. 'I think DCI Caplan knows what she needs to do and knows that it'll not be cheap. But then what price the cost of Shivonne's life compared to Bethany's or Nik Ardman's life compared to Alexander Brooke-Williams's? I know exactly what the *Daily Mail* will think of that. The general consensus of opinion, and the Police Scotland logic. You know what I am saying.'

'Do I, ACC Linden?'

'I hope you didn't agree to ask for funding again because the Brooke-Williams family asked you to?'

'Of course they didn't.'

'They've been in touch though, haven't they?' Linden gave a little snort. 'Same Lodge, same shooting party, same OBE list. All we want is money and time, Andrew. We need funds to do the job. And I'll repeat it to anybody who asks. Any journalist who asks.'

He raised an eyebrow in warning. 'I beg your pardon.'

'You can't turn away from this. Not now. DCI Caplan knows she and her team are unorthodox, but they could have been specifically gathered for a crime like this. Feral crime I'd call it. If you had put a MIT together, they'd need that skill set.'

'Really.' McEwan was unconvinced.

Linden showed him a photograph bound in plastic film. 'What do you see there?'

He looked at the hands, the knot. 'Bound hands of the deceased, I presume.'

'One of her team looked at that and immediately identified it as a falconer's knot.' Linden snapped her fingers. 'Just like that. They look back through the incident, the birds at Bethany's site, the van logo. Somebody who ties a knot like that is doing it so frequently, they do it without thinking. One of our abductors works with birds of prey. Can you see what a break that was?'

Caplan was sure McEwan was going to ask if it had got them anywhere so added,

'And we've linked Lisa Stratton to the case in the wider sense. That's all I'm saying.'

McEwan nodded. 'I'll take that to the meeting. You must have a perpetrator in mind.'

'As I've said, more than one. More than two. I'm not moving until I am sure. I don't want them to know how close we are.'

'And for that reason, I've closed down the chatter round the investigation. In case it puts any of our findings in jeopardy.' Linden was at her most authoritative.

'But we'll need to show progress to get funding.'

'No,' said Caplan and Linden in unison before Caplan continued, 'we don't want any of this getting to the ears of certain parties.'

McEwan opened his mouth. 'Oh. Okay. Hopefully Operation

Wandsworth can now commence if I get funding, but it will be for seventy-two hours. Are you going to tell me anything?'

The two women sat in silence.

'You actually want me to attend a meeting to request extra funding without saying what progress has been made so far.'

'Welcome to my world,' said Caplan. 'And it's Operation Dark Sky. I don't care what your bloody computer calls it.'

Shivonne MacDougall's body had been found in the same Dark Sky area as Lisa Stratton, but at the opposite side of Chern Wood. On the file, Lisa's next of kin was a friend called Joanna Jones. Caplan felt that Stratton had been killed by the same people but maybe for a different reason. Stratton had nothing in common with the rest of the victims except for some aspects of her death and the fact there was no family to miss her. Lisa, Bethany and Rhona were more visible. Were they targeting a more difficult victim, following some kind of sick progression? Or did they wait until a potential victim came on their radar? No doubt Stratton would have her PUP. All they needed to do was find it.

Stratton had been PA to the boss of a building firm, Fayer Construction, that had links to Ghillies and Vance. Ghillies was all over this. A police officer would know how to disrupt the investigation. And he had a lot to lose. Such thoughts rolled through Caplan's mind as she sat in the passenger seat of the Hilux, refreshing herself on Stratton's case as Craigo walked round, holding a compass and looking at the lie of the land, as if reimagining the hunt.

Lisa Stratton was abducted on her way home to the rented flat that she had moved into after selling her semi-detached in Drymen. Her friends thought she was looking for a life with her new man. Caplan thought she sounded like a woman who was searching for Mr Right in the wrong places.

Joanna Jones's Fiat was parked in the lay-by and she climbed out as they approached. Caplan wouldn't have recognised her from the photo in the file. Jones was older in the face, her hair greying. She was sensibly dressed in jeans and a long jumper and good walking boots. Standing still, in a circle of trees, looking up through the brown and coppery leaves to the blue sky above, Jones looked rooted in the landscape.

Caplan called her name. They shook hands.

'It's so tragic that she died here. Maybe it's best that we don't know how we're going to end up.' Jones stuck her hands deep into her pockets, looking around her. 'I still can't believe that she's gone. You know, I keep thinking that when my phone pings it might be her with her daft emojis.'

'Do you want to see where she was found?' Caplan began to walk.

Jones nodded.

'Did she have any family to speak of?'

'None.'

'Would you say that you were her closest friend?'

Her eyes welled up. 'I think so. I said to the police officer at the time that she had a man somewhere, but she never mentioned a name. I never asked. I presumed he was married. She'd come to our house at Christmas, sitting around, waiting for him to be finished with his family. You know how it is. She tended to see him during the day. I guess he was self-employed, maybe he'd retired young?' Her tone lifted into a question, fishing for information.

'Or was out of work?'

Jones shook her head. 'He definitely had money. He had the sort of job where he made his own timetable. Lisa and I were shopping one day and she looked at a calendar of Old Fart Sayings. She said it would suit him. I deduced he was a bit older.'

'But she never said who he was?' Caplan was tying them together. Ghillies and Stratton? Vance and Stratton? Robertson and Stratton?

'No.'

'Weird question but did she mention funny teeth or a bad limp, like he had a sore leg?'

'No, but he was important. She said I'd recognise his name so she could never mention it. She never did.'

'Never answered her phone and used his name?'

'Used a different phone. She'd go out the room to speak to him. I was nosey, but she never said, never let anything slip.'

Caplan stopped talking and listened to the wind whistling in the high branches.

'She wanted him to leave his wife. That was a bone of contention. But the situation changed – something "beyond their control", whatever that meant. Something, anyway, but she said it showed what a good guy he was really was.'

'Like his wife was terminally ill and he wanted to look after her? Or his wife died and he had a child to look after?'

Jones shrugged. 'Because he said it doesn't mean it was true.' She stopped and looked at Caplan. 'Do you think the boyfriend had something to do with Lisa's death?'

'He never came forward, did he? Both as a woman, and a cop, that makes me uneasy. She was found over there.' They stopped where a burn broke out from the undergrowth, creating watery veins over the stones before disappearing into marsh that bled back to the forest. 'She was lying there, by the bank of the burn. I'll leave you for a moment.'

Craigo was at the Hilux, leaning over the bonnet, studying his Ordnance Survey map again. Caplan watched him, while she stood on the grass verge of the forest beside the track that disappeared in both directions. Where had Stratton come from? Where did she think she was running to? Any direction would be the right direction if it was away from whatever was chasing her.

There was a case that had been nagging at Caplan's mind for a while. A woman, out jogging in the early hours, had been attacked by dogs, brought down, then abducted and imprisoned. It turned out she was one of many. Caplan tried to recall how many had survived. Two maybe? But they'd never been the same again. One of them hadn't been out of the house since.

Those women had been in the city, near houses. It was the time of day of the abductions, very early in the morning, that made the difference. And dogs, attacking. A woman lying bleeding, then a man comes along and offers help, gives them a hand up, maybe with a small friendly dog to explain why he was out. Yes, he'd help them up. *Can you walk okay? My car's just over here.* The isolation of the early hour. The victims ended up imprisoned in an underground network of tunnels left over from the Second World War, not so far away from where she stood now.

She looked up at the trees again, the upper branches swaying in the wind. Where were these victims being kept? They could have been close, but she doubted anyone would have heard their screaming.

A stack of box files, the paper files for all 'Rachel's Sixteen' victims, had been located in Central Records. Somebody had written Operation Wandsworth up on the board, the Wandsworth had been scored out and the words Dark Sky written over it.

'Leonora's in your office,' said Lizzie Fergusson, looking at the files. 'I had to sign for this. Is this all there is for those victims? I know we have what there is for our five.'

'I think most of them will have other causes of death but these perps chose their victims well. There's not that much to be known about them, so the documentation's as small as I expected for throwaways and runaways,' said Caplan. 'Thank God the cold case unit have given us gloves and masks so we can clean them before we start. They're filthy. Do they keep them in a dungeon over at CR?'

'Are you looking for a volunteer to clean it? Somebody who is used to getting crap jobs like this done?'

'Well volunteered, PC Fergusson,' Caplan said to her old friend. 'That was kind of you.'

Caplan threw a small map of the woods at Tyndrum, with the locations of McDougall's and Stratton's bodies clearly marked, on the desk in her office. Spyck was cradling a cup of the station's undrinkable coffee. 'Make yourself at home.'

'Where have you been? You have a hair out of place.'

'I was walking through the trees with Joanna Jones, Lisa's friend, like we were walking dogs. It's incongruous that Lisa was found there, and to know what she'd gone through before she died. It was very quiet, idyllic.'

'You don't need to tell me that. I knackered myself getting to Shiv's body.' Spyck adjusted her bump, making herself more comfortable. 'Anyway, that's me finished for a whole year.'

'You'll be back the week after the wee one starts screaming its head off, for the peace and quiet.' At that point Mackie got the punchline of a long joke Stewart had been telling her and screamed with laughter.

'You think?' said Spyck, rolling her eyes.

'They're a little hyper in the playpen today, you must excuse them. They've some new toys. Why are you here, Leonora? It's lovely to see you but you're going to give birth within the week. I'm sure you've better things to do.'

'Yes, I have. But still. Ryce and I went out for a pizza earlier this week and we were talking about that question you asked, you know, what's the point of all this? This game? What is the end point?'

'The end point?'

'Yes, what's the bloody point of it all? The leg? The tooth?' Spyck burped and apologised. 'I'm presuming these victims, your canonical four, five or six – I've no idea where you are – have got no state secrets, nothing worth torturing them for? The broken leg, but only a bone that's not necessary for weightbearing, it would only hamper movement . . .' Spyck's voice fell away as if waiting for Caplan to catch on.

'They are being hobbled. Then what? Followed? Chased?'

'Maybe by somebody who is themselves incapacitated by age or injury. The object of the game is the chase and the kill.'

Caplan thought of Rory Ghillies coming to the door, walking down the hall, shuffling like an old man, when he wasn't really. Was he carrying an injury?

'You're looking on these people as victims but they're young, they can run. Their pursuers are people of varying strength. The injury to the leg weakens the victims, then they are released and that's when they are hunted. Imagine being desperate to run but you can't and these mad people are closing in on you with baseball bats. It's like the worst anxiety dream ever.'

'Except they don't wake up.' Caplan swung in her seat. 'Is there a logical profile for any of this?'

Spyck shrugged. 'Somebody has a bad leg. Somebody has a snaggle tooth.' She tapped her upper left canine. 'That's what Sherlock Holmes would deduce.'

Caplan thought for a moment, her tongue tapping on her own left canine, then she pointed to the office through her window. 'These ones died. But we think Nik got away.'

'His skull had not been battered. Neither had Lisa Stratton's. I think you need to be careful when including her in all this.'

'Everybody keeps saying that. But Rachel was sure.'

'Rachel? Mrs Ghillies would that be?'

'Yes.'

'Don't know her, never met her, bit of non-starter I'd say. I've worked with a lot of DCIs and a lot of constables. You guys get promoted for a reason, you have the smarts.' She lifted her coat. 'But the answer to your original question was my in-laws are up here. I'm doing a fly past visit before the wee one comes.'

'Well, the best of luck.' Caplan gave her a hug and Spyck took a step towards the door. 'Why did Shiv get killed before she was . . . imprisoned for too long?'

Spyck sat back down again. 'Because she got away? Like Nik? Too young, too strong. Too streetwise. She outwitted the bastards.'

'She was a fighter. A biter in fact.'

Spyck smiled. 'Human bites are foul. I'll alert the hospitals. Such things are noted. Yeah, wee Shiv could have given you the break that you need.'

Caplan stepped over the box files. There seemed to be more paper about than could have been contained in them. Her team were having a coffee break. Due to the dust, the windows of the incident room were open. 'Right where are we on social media searches of 'Mo', PUPS, background? I may have a lead.' She turned to look at the board. 'Who put that picture up there?'

'Which one?' asked Craigo, looking at the single monochrome image.

'These three young women? That's Atkins, Van Houten and Krenwinkel, of the Manson Family. Who put that there?' Caplan unpinned the picture.

'No idea, ma'am, but it was a conversation between Stewart and Mackie – the power of a personality to make a group of normal people commit evil acts. Manson's name came up.'

'You took that picture down. Shame.' Mackie's eyes rested on the picture of Manson's women. 'It shocked people that young women from good homes could do that. Do you think they were bored? Why aren't women thought of as killers? I mean Black Widows and Angels of Death, all that crap. But look at these cases here. In each one it's a woman they've been pally with before they go missing.'

'Not the same female though,' said Craigo.

Caplan looked up.

Mackie was waving her pencil around. 'What if it's not the same female? All they do is dangle the bait to get the poor victim out of the shelter. They might not even know they're doing it.'

'Well, that might explain why there might have been two in the bush to abduct Bethany while Mo was still at the Revolve. That's three,' confirmed Craigo.

'Mackie, clear the board and let's get these women in order. Shiv might have bitten her captor so Spyck's looking at the hospitals. We have Revolve Mo; she's, slim, about five feet two, short blonde hair, wears colourful clothes. Whereas the Mo on Pottie's gran's phone looks tall, is big boned and has brown hair. Then we have two women in the bushes with the injured falcon according to the park-keeper, and I think he's right. It'd take more than one person to grab Beth, subdue her and get her in the vehicle before driving away. Did they get the bird, the logo and the drugs from Raptor Rescue? It's a working hypothesis so get some images and some descriptions up here. First person to trace one of these ladies to an address, a permanent address, gets a Tunnock's Caramel Wafer and my eternal gratitude.' Caplan's phone buzzed in her pocket. It was Linden, calling her back. 'Excuse me.'

She went back into her office.

'I quite enjoyed that. Bloody nurses. They do crumble quicker now that they don't have a uniform with epaulettes.'

'And?'

'Yes, the lovely Vance did ask. Yes, she texted him to say you'd be in that day, late morning. You were five minutes late, so it would seem they hung around to bump into you. I might be reading too much into it. Maybe they thought Rachel would be overtired. Vance fed the nurse a story about Rory not wanting Rachel to have too many visitors on the same day. Vance goes in one day a week to give Rory a day off. And, wait for it, he was there on the day you were because he's a consultant to a charity called the Lorn Support Centre.'

'As one of the Tinmen?'

'Indeed. They have four rooms for families of the terminally ill to stay in if they live too far away to visit or are from the islands. The words "squeaky" and "clean" come to mind. So probably as guilty as sin.'

'Too clean. Too much all over this; him and Ghillies, and Robertson.'

'Where is Bethany then? That's the question you need to answer.'

'Who are these Tinmen?'

'Bunch of old guys doing good works. Ask your lovely husband, I bet he'd know.'

Caplan sat down. The Vances had bought Bethany her first doll's house. That was suggestive of a close relationship. She'd set one of the team on a close look at all three of them. The initial pass had shown no red flags. Maybe it was time now to dig dirt.

She looked out the window to the board with the map and the island of Skone, letting another idea bubble and ferment. She had a question and knew somebody who might have the answer.

Caplan picked up her mobile and called her daughter. Emma answered, half laughing as she did so. 'Hello Mum, how are you?'

'I'm fine. Is Mags there? I'd like a word.'

'Is there something wrong with Dad?'

'No, not at all. I need to pick his brains about work.'

'Okay . . .' said Emma, drawing out the word in seeming disbelief. Then Caplan heard the phone being handed over and Emma whispering, 'Mum wants a word.'

'Hi Christine, what can I do for you?' The Magus spoke, his voice ever polite.

'You have property on your estate, don't you? The mainland estate? But you're on the island twenty-four/seven. How do you manage that? I presume you have people or a team in place to care for the property? How does that work?"

There was an ironic snort. 'That's a huge business nowadays with the increase in empty properties, holiday homes and investment purchases. Companies now move in and make the property look lived in, they put a name on it for council tax etc. It can be as legal or as borderline legal as they wish to make it. On our estate, we employ one person to factor it all, getting in services as needed. Some people use a centralised service, so I've heard. You know, all empty properties are maintained by somebody. Checked on, water turned off etc. Hang on, Emma's saying something.' Caplan heard low-level muttering. 'Oh yes, Emma's reminded me of one in the village on the mainland. There was a bit of delay on planning and somebody else moved in, a situation the owners knew nothing about.'

'Really? A caveman?'

The Magus was impressed. 'That was the word they used. I mean if I told folk Emma was my sister and she's living in that cottage there, folk would believe it. That kind of thing can go on for years.'

'Cavemen,' said Caplan. 'That's what we call them. Living in somebody else's house, inhabiting someone else's space.'

She was still thinking about it on the long drive home. When she pulled off the road Aklen was standing in the middle of the driveway, dressed in wellies, his hands deep in his pockets. He appeared to be staring at the house.

He hadn't heard her drive up behind him. She cut the engine and got out the car, quietly, not wanting to give him a fright. The cat, and then the kittens, ran out from under the caravan, causing

Caplan to look up to make sure that the falcon wasn't sitting on the top of the roof, watching. And waiting.

Aklen turned, tears rolling down his face, and put his arms round her.

Caplan had cradled her husband until he had calmed himself and she had warned him of the dangers of pushing to get better too soon and that doing too much would lead to a crash. An hour later he was back doing what he did best – not talking about it and changing the subject. 'Do you know I was listening to *Woman's Hour* today. They were talking about the Sit Spot. Somewhere to sit and think.' Aklen pointed to the swing seat and handed Caplan a glass of wine. The weather was still warm, it was getting dark and the very light rain was almost welcome.

'You know I'm close to closing this case. I can smell it but I can't see it.' Caplan closed her eyes, facing the rain.

'Rory Ghillies seems to have been doing a good job of stopping you getting what you want. Can you not arrest him and beat it out of him like you did in the old days?' Aklen sipped his wine.

'I took him down.' She swung backwards and forwards, smiling with satisfaction. 'Would you say that the Tinmen were a building company?'

'No, they're a charitable body who offer services to charities that have property. Not big stuff, not Oxfam, but the likes of the wee Salmon Centre. That building was reroofed by man hours and materials donated by the Tinmen.'

'Who organised that?'

'Well, I presume the committees of the charities go to the Tinmen and ask. Chris, I have no bloody idea. In a place as small as this I bet everywhere the Tinmen go, it's the same folk on the board.'

Caplan sat, swinging, thinking about the victims' injuries as she rubbed the side of her ankle. When it was really bad, mercifully few times, she limped, and it slowed her down.

She thought about the victims being injured so they couldn't run. They hadn't been found in the middle of nowhere, as she had thought, but within running distance from where they had been held captive. She thought about what Spyck had said about their injuries being not enough to kill them but enough to slow them up.

'The Tinmen, who are they?'

'Just bloody told you.'

'No, I mean why, why that name?'

'Something to do with the war. Was it the Clydebank Blitz that older tradesmen, those too old to fight or in restricted professions, went around covering roofs and fixing holes? They used tin, a rare commodity during the war. But they took it from places beyond repair and made do on a property that could be salvaged. Who're you investigating? A builder, roofer, an architect? After the war they became more to do with rural rebuilding, only on a very small level mind. They respond as time changes. I bet they advise on energy efficiency now.'

'Do you not get a lot of government grants for that?'

'Yes, but where do you start? Imagine running a place like Revolve, an old property, and the council slaps a notice on the place saying not only do you need new triple-glazed windows but you need them to be within planning regs as it's a seafront building. That's a nightmare if you're managing a charity. That's where the Tinmen would advise. Chris, it was a lot of old men in blazers.'

She lay back, causing the seat to swing, and looked at the cloudy sky.

'What are you thinking about?'

'You really want to know?'

'I did ask.'

'I'm thinking about the nature of evil.'

'I thought you're maybe hungry.'

'Do you believe in evil, real evil?'

'Is this this case you are working on?'

'People are being hunted down, for fun. It's evil.'

'There're no such thing as evil people. Just dangerous people. We are all products of our environment and our nature, the moral compass and all that.' Aklen nodded, as if he'd given this some thought. 'Tell you what, Chris, I'll go and put the kettle on.'

SIXTEEN

*S*he remembered the sensations, real or imagined. Her body had been moved then left on the stone floor. Her perception of time was totally distorted but maybe it had happened the day before, or the night before. There had been the sound of a car engine, maybe the smell of petrol; a sense of her being lifted and laid.

The last place had been silent but here she was very aware of trees, crows and the scent of fresh air.

No doubt there was a reason for the move.

They were ready to kill her now.

There was no panic. Not even a sense of fear.

There was always a plan. Feed her, starve her, move her, kill her.

But she had regained clarity of thought.

And she was letting herself get angry.

Early on Friday morning, Caplan pulled her car up outside the Robertson home, chasing down a lead that she thought might go somewhere, if she was right. Her phone went as she was getting it out from the compartment in the car door. Caplan swiped at the screen, checking her messages. The message was from Mackie claiming her caramel wafer. She'd sent a photograph of a female taken by a security camera, the image taken from above and to the left. The subject was middle-aged and carrying a little weight. Her hair, dark on the image, was cut in a style Caplan would have called a mullet. It definitely wasn't Mo from the Revolve, and on comparison with Pottie's gran's picture, there was only a slight likeness. It was not the same person. This woman had called into A&E on Monday 11th September, presenting with three bite wounds. She had identified herself as Morven Maitland, known as Mo. No Morven Maitland was known at the address the woman gave, though the NHS did have a Community Health Index number for one, with an appropriate address and date of birth. Mackie had found another two Morven Maitlands in Scotland and was still searching. CHI numbers were unique, but Caplan thought about the cavemen –

identities being accepted as easily as they were given. Mo Maitland. Caplan thought about that for a while then looked at the phone again. There were two pictures of the wounds sent on by Mackie. Shiv had bitten her hard. Human bites were a crime and photographed forensically – just in case. Craigo had sent the images to Ryce, but even Caplan could see the gap in the impression caused by a missing upper canine on the left.

Good on you, Shiv, thought Caplan, surprising herself by feeling a bit tearful, as she walked up the garden path, knowing that she'd seen a name like that somewhere. Mo Maitland in a list of names. She texted Mackie back, asking her to look back at the documentation of the Ardman case.

The front door opened. Bill Robertson had aged a hundred years.

The FLO Kathy Waddell was also looking stressed. 'Are you not supposed to warn me before you come for a visit?'

'You let the neighbour in easy enough,' said Caplan. 'Bill, tell me about the roof over the extension?'

He shrugged at the odd question then asked, 'What about it? It's glass.'

'I know that. What about the room at the top of the stairs, what's that?'

'Oh, my observatory.'

'Do you have a telescope in there?'

'Yes, the roof slides back so the telescope can look out.'

'And who did that roof work for you?'

'Oh, the building company who did the extension.'

Caplan raised her eyebrows in encouragement.

'Connell and McNair I think they were called. I designed it myself, of course.'

'How did you come to use those builders?'

'Well, they were recommended. Rory is on a charity board with them.'

Caplan quietly asked, 'And would that be the Tinmen?'

Robertson smiled. 'Yes, that's right.'

'Excuse me a moment.' Caplan walked out the door, and stood on the front step, pretending to be looking for a better signal. She dialled quickly. 'Craigo, look at the owners of Connell and McNair. Who is on the board?'

She was back inside, asking Waddell to make a cup of tea when her phone pinged. Four words: Technical Advisor Felix Vance.

Waddell was asking if she took milk and sugar when the phone pinged again. Another text to say that was from an old website but the address was the same as Fayer Construction. Then four words: Office Manager Lisa Stratton.

Lisa Stratton.

Caplan waited until Waddell was in the kitchen. 'Bill, keep this conversation between ourselves. I think Bethany's life might depend on it.'

He looked alarmed, took a deep breath, then said, 'Okay.'

'When you were getting the building work done, was Felix Vance ever in this house?'

'No, he was in America at the time but did the technical spec before he went. He's not been in the house since Rosemary's funeral, I think.'

'And Rory has been a huge support to you?'

'Oh yes.' Robertson nodded. 'A very good friend.'

'Anybody called Mo popping round to help support you?' she asked.

'Mo who?'

She showed him the image on the phone from the hospital security footage. 'Her?'

Robertson looked very carefully. 'No, sorry.'

'What about this lady? Or this one?' She showed him the photo of Mo from the Revolve and the other image, now known as Granny's Mo.

'Never seen them before. Why?'

'It was just an idea.'

Robertson paused for thought, settling himself slowly into the armchair. 'The only person who popped in was Wilma.'

Caplan took a deep breath. 'And when was that?'

'Erm, Monday, I think. All the days blend into each other now.'

The FLO came out of the kitchen and probably wished she hadn't.

Caplan turned to Waddell. 'You knew about this? The visit from Wilma Vance.'

'She's a family friend. She brought us some homemade cottage pie. It's in the log.'

Caplan swallowed her anger; not the time, not the place. 'Did she use the toilet?' she asked Robertson while glaring at the FLO.

'Yes.'

'The upstairs toilet?'

'Yes, I don't think she knew there was one down here.'

'I did say to her,' said Waddell, 'but I don't think she heard.'

Caplan rushed upstairs and went into Bethany's bedroom. She pulled open the drawer. The medication was gone.

Caplan pressed send on an email she had been composing to Lizzie Fergusson. Some things might be better being dealt with from Glasgow, like a background search on Felix Vance, and his lovely wife, Wilma. The timing of Wilma's visit to Robertson's house was early afternoon on Monday. Waddell had logged it and shared it with Mackie's electronic version but she hadn't flagged it, apparently not thinking it was important. But it could mean that the abductors had heard about Bethany needing medication on the local news, and realised they needed to get it, to avoid another Brooke-Williams. Caplan was only vaguely aware of Craigo hovering, until he coughed to get her full attention. She asked him to sit down and she told him quietly of her suspicions of Vance.

'Do you want me to write it up, ma'am?'

'I've checked the FLO's log. You have a look and see if you spot anything else. Wilma's visit was not innocent. And then we have Lisa Stratton working for the same company.'

Craigo pulled the odd expression that he considered a smile. 'We are getting closer, ma'am.' He nodded to himself.

'Anybody find any commonality that runs between these Pick Up Points? The PUPS.'

'There was a Mo Maitland at the Ashdown Centre, Ardman's place in 2014, another at the Revolve for the last three months, who now can't be traced. Mackie's tracking Hospital Mo, the Morven with the mullet who was bitten.'

'Right, so references, an address, a phone number, a picture on social media. Stick that image from the hospital under the nose of anybody you can trace. Do they recognise her? 2014, eh?' She looked at the stack of documentation. 'This feels right, it's been going on a long time.'

'And I'm on it, ma'am.' Craigo was enthused. He stood up ready to go.

'That'll be after we look at those maps you've been working away at. And after you tell me who were you getting close to at reception when I came in. You were being rather charming to her?'

'She's the wise woman.'

'All women are wise, Craigo, don't you know that?' She regretted saying it as, looking at him in his crumpled jerkin, he maybe lacked any life experience that would tell him if women were indeed wise.

'Spae-wife if you like.'

'A fortune teller – what? What was she doing? Telling you next week's lottery numbers?'

'No, ma'am, she's not a fortune teller. She has the ability to see beyond her own physical space if you like.' Craigo looked away in discomfort as if his thumbnail had become very interesting.

'But?' Caplan asked him to close the door. 'Was she here to tell you about Operation Dark Sky? Did you ask her for help? There's a tight lid on this operation.'

'I didn't go to her. She came to me.'

'Do you think the media will make a distinction? No, they won't, so don't have anything else to do with her until the investigation is over. The tabloids eat and breathe that sort of crap, so leave it.'

Craigo looked straight through her. 'Bethany's alive, she's near still water and there's a letter W nearby. But the clock is ticking.' With that Craigo got up and returned to the incident room, his manner making Caplan think that the spae-wife was probably another one of his relatives. But she felt weirdly calmer, hoping the wise woman was right about Bethany.

Craigo was behind his desk, the back of his hair spiked up like he had suffered a minor electric shock. His hands were clasped in front of his face and his jaw rested on his linked fingers. He looked deep in thought. Then he stood up and came back into Caplan's office.

'Do you understand it, ma'am?'

'Understand what? Psychics? Wise women? What?'

'You see, I think you always know what you're doing, ma'am.' Caplan was about to thank him for the compliment when he added, 'Eventually.' He stretched his neck, looking up at the lights. 'Makes you think about pretence?'

'Who're we talking about now?'

'The Rod and Todd situation, ma'am, I saw that note logged on the system. About Rod and the lady. There was no cancer, no perfect life. One went to work and one stayed at home. The one who stayed at home got bored. The one who went to work got jealous of that. It crumbled.'

'More like Rod was a prisoner in his own house. He'd made plans to get away. He didn't manage it.'

'And that's the most dangerous time isn't it, ma'am, when the worm turns, when the abused one tries to escape?'

'That's what the stats tell us. You think Rod was abused?' asked Caplan.

'I do. And what do the figures say about men suffering at the hands of women? Do you think they get reported enough?'

'I'd like to think that there'll come a time when nobody hits anybody. Are we any closer to finding Stevie? Who might be a Stephanie?'

'No. The IT boys are tracking it. She's well hidden.'

'If she's staying hidden even after his passing, then there's a reason, like she's married.'

Craigo dropped his gaze from the lights and regarded her with his beady little eyes. 'Pardon my French, ma'am, but people really are a bunch of bastards. Present company excepted.'

Craigo stood beside the largest map, one of the whole of Scotland, with areas of dense pins showing the forests of the Great Glen, the Borders, Argyll and Inverness. Each pin had a little flag and a number attached. Craigo held a clipboard and his specs were perched on the end of his nose, keen and ready.

'You have been very busy, DS Craigo,' said Caplan, taking a seat near McPhee's desk, her notebook at the ready.

'Thank you, ma'am.' He nodded and looked pleased. And remained standing there. 'It's geographical profiling, ma'am. And speaking to Stirling Council. I'm thinking about the victims. Where are they being kept? How many people are involved to keep something like that quiet? Somewhere out of the way, a farm, maybe, but a non-working farm, and an extended family who are on board with this kind of thing. Or was it this kind of thing that brought them together? Triangulation gets us nowhere. I've tried.'

'How many properties do we have?' prompted Caplan, thinking four or five, and costing putting a search team in each.

'Forty-six.'

Caplan nodded and held back her impatience. 'And how many do we have in Dark Sky sites?' She was ready with her pen.

'Forty-six,' repeated Craigo.

'Forty-six?' The surprise at the figure dropped on the room like a quiet bomb. Mackie leaned forward, peering at the map. 'How the hell can there be forty-six?'

'Well, I only put on here the ones that are in, or near, a Dark Sky site. Or are remote but near an area of interest to us. I used my initiative, ma'am.' He blinked slowly. 'Because that's what we're looking for.'

'Yes. Sorry, I was just surprised.' Caplan stood up and examined the maps more closely. 'Are they all unoccupied?'

'Sometimes.'

The site of each body discovery was marked with a black flag and a pair of initials, the date when they were last seen, if known, the month if the exact date was not known and the date their body was discovered. The work had left the top of Craigo's desk covered in coloured paper like a rainy day in play school.

'I spotted something rather interesting when looking at the properties within the Inverness Dark Sky site. Beauly forest. Where Ardman was. There was a house here. It's been lying derelict for a long time, years really, then somebody bought it and it was partially renovated.' He pursed his lips. 'And then the renovation stopped in Spring 2014, early spring, and it was restarted a year later.' He opened up a map he had hand-drawn.

'That fits with Nik's timeline.' Caplan's mind flooded with images of builders, architects, Pas. 'We have a site, remote, habitable.'

'So that got me thinking. Has the local council got any applications for planning and the building work might now be ongoing? I've a cousin in Building Control.'

'Of course you do,' sighed Caplan.

'He came back with a property in Chern Wood. Lochanview. I suggest a visit.'

'You're saying if the builders stop work for any reason . . .'

'Or are told to stop work, ma'am . . .'

'Then the perpetrators use the property to hold the victim. A wee clean-up after. Then they call the builders back in and get them to continue. Nobody'll question that. Another victim, another property. They had an eleven-month hiatus in work to utilise at that property in Beauly. All they needed was two or three months to keep Ardman.'

'Who owns it?'

'Ah, that's where it gets really interesting.'

'Please tell me it's Rory Ghillies. Fayer Construction?'

'No, it's a couple from Brighton who have holidayed up there since 2016, apart from during Covid. Rest of the time the place is empty.'

'The house is habitable but not occupied?'

'And I found a pattern. The victims are never in captivity over the summer or at Christmas.'

'When a holiday house might be used?' Caplan paused to think. 'It could be. Good work, Craigo. So we think houses in different areas. That explains the vast area covered, the different PUPS and kill sites. It explains how a human being is kept isolated, fed and watered for months.'

'Every flag is a different property that is unoccupied for some part of the year. Like now, autumn. As has been already pointed out, none of the victims are held over the summer. It suggests that the properties are unavailable, i.e. occupied by their rightful owners.'

'Okay.' Caplan nodded slowly, knowing that Mackie was paying close attention. Could this be right? Surely Craigo had gone wrong somewhere.

'The properties are of various types. The blue flags are properties at different stages of falling down and being built back up. All of them are being actively worked on because of the demand for second homes or the increase in people wanting to live off-grid. The purple flags are holiday homes which are not Airbnbs and where the owners are not close enough for weekend use.'

'It's a lot more than I thought.'

'We could cross-reference properties with builders and warrants and planning applications.'

'Craigo, a glacier moves quicker than the council. McEwan has us on a timer. We need to know about the here and now. Where's Bethany being held? Let's take away those within a mile of the periphery of the Dark Sky site.' Caplan stood up and looked at the map closely, thinking like an abductor. What did they need? What would they avoid? 'I'd also take away those that are semi-detached onto an occupied house, or those in a steading with others.'

Craigo said, 'Okay.'

'Toni, can you remove the flags so we know what we are left with?'

Slowly, they went through the list. The remaining thirty-two properties were those that were deep within the Dark Sky sites.

'There has to be access of some kind. What's near a forestry trail but still remote?'

'Near an unused logging trail, bike track, an unmarked single-track road,' suggested Mackie.

'Four of them – twelve, twenty-one, thirty-two and forty – are only accessible by canoe.'

'I'll take them out,' said Mackie.

'Take out complete wrecks. These houses must have a roof, they need to be secure.'

That took ten properties off the list, leaving eighteen.

'If there are four or five in each area,' Caplan sighed, 'that's coming into the realms of doable.'

'I have it all on a spreadsheet, ma'am,' said Craigo.

Caplan took a deep breath. The question was how to prioritise it further. 'Take out any not near still water?'

Craigo stared at her.

'Any of them near somewhere that starts with a W get some kind of priority.'

Mackie was staring at the map. 'Why?'

Craigo scratched his head. 'It was in my mind as I was going through them, and this one is near a system of pools and waterfalls, at the bottom of Ben Wheen. Before the Dark Sky accreditation, the pools were a tourist attraction in themselves. But if you drive a few miles further on this very narrow track, there's another small run of pools.' He tapped the map. 'There.'

Mackie went over to the map, pulled her glasses from the top of her head and peered at the map. 'He's right, ma'am.' She turned to look back at Caplan. 'So, we're going with what the spae-wife said then? I'm not saying that you're wrong . . . but?' Mackie shrugged.

'With that number of properties, it's better than any other idea that we have. And we need to review outbuildings, garages, farm buildings. Whatever each site has. People are difficult to hide and these victims have been imprisoned for a period of weeks, months in some cases.

'Can the presence of a basement go to the top of the list? Any reports of a car coming and going, a car with more than one person in it, an unknown car, with a couple of strangers.'

Caplan sighed. 'I'm getting a bit pissed off seeing dead bodies of young people on Ryce's slab. All thoughts welcome.'

'We don't need further thought. It's five properties. The nearest one is Lochanview,' said Craigo. 'Then there's Galloway Forest park – that's nearer to where Pottie's body was found.'

'Get on the phone about the other four, threaten Building Control with . . . ACC Linden. Tell them it's about the case in the news, just to put a bomb under them.'

There was a huge pile of papers on Caplan's desk. Fergusson had done a good job. The piles were wrapped in different coloured paper, one for each person of interest. She allowed herself a little daydream where Fergusson had found one person who had connections to all five locations of interest and that was Rory Ghillies, who was driving the car, being greeted by a lady matching Wilma Vance's description.

Caplan read her friend's notes. There was more than one man, or woman, behind this.

William Walter Robertson had been born in Edinburgh. He was a semi-retired architect, keen gardener, treasurer of the Pulpit Hill residents' association and treasurer of the local astronomical chapter. Not even a speeding ticket. But he had an alibi; he had answered his landline phone when Bethany had first gone missing and there had been an FLO with him every minute of the day. He could be involved without being physically active. But Caplan thought his distress was genuine.

As for Rory Ghillies, his career could be mapped out every step of the way. Born in Greenock but brought up in Port Bannatyne, he became a high-ranking police officer in Glasgow who then retired and moved north, his wife working as a constable and staying working. Linden knew him well. She'd had long conversations with a few of his colleagues and got the feeling they were keeping their distance. Female colleagues said he was a bit of a ladies' man. His profile didn't come near that of a sadistic psychopath. Yet despite his ambition to have an OBE, he was sleeping with his friend's daughter, almost thirty years his junior. Caplan wondered how that had developed. Ghillies was a second father figure to Bethany, giving her advice about university and her career. Much worse was the abuse of Bethany's trust and the betrayal of Robertson's friendship.

Felix Vance had led a very public life. Both he and his dad were pillars of the community in Glasgow. They were very close. He was an only child of upper middle-class parents. The father indulged his son in all kinds of activity: skydiving, formula three racing, underwater caving. Both father and son had many points on their licence for speeding.

Lizzie had attached a small paragraph and a wedding picture from a local paper celebrating Felix Vance, local businessman's, twenty-five-year marriage to Bute-born Wilma. The bride and groom looked very happy, standing with their best man and bridesmaid.

Mackie knocked on the door and came in, Craigo shuffling in behind her. Caplan stacked up the papers. 'Well, I've found the owner of that house, the one unoccupied but nearest to where Shivonne's body was found. Mr Casper Lyons. I get the feeling that money isn't a worry for them. They've always loved Scotland and their son is doing astronomy at university, hence the Dark Sky property. Not an easy thing with reference to planning restrictions, obviously, but you're allowed a telescope in the roof. There's a shutter that pulls across when it's not being used.'

'Has anybody got a key locally?'

'Not that I know yet. They have an au pair for the youngest two children and she comes up the week before them to open the place up, get shopping in and get the logs stacked.'

'Okay. Try to get a key from somewhere. Ask for consent for a walk round. Find out how they get in and out of the woods so we don't get lost.'

'And Lyons said there was a derelict property another mile along the same track for sale last year,' said Craigo. 'He read on Rightmove that it went for over £350K, ma'am. Are we going to have a look at that house?'

'We can have a look at the house after we've looked at the map. Come on.'

Mackie was already at her monitor. 'Listen to this.' She read from the screen. 'Mr Alexander Brooke-Williams, or Jimmy Williams, was arrested but released without charge in January 2023. He went to the Michael Bastion Centre, the Moonshine Hostel, on Commercial Road. He was good friends with the caretaker, Davie Silvers. He says Jimmy was friends with another older guy called Dougie Winshaw. Winshaw says Jimmy was friends with a volunteer called Mo Maitland. Mo worked on for another couple of days after Jimmy-Xander left or disappeared. Then she too left. She called in sick and never came back.'

'Because her job was done? I'm getting a bit pissed off with "Mo" not coming back to work. Description?'

'Five feet three or so, a bit overweight, shoulder-length, dark-brown hair. Slow was a word used. All her contact details are false. Her moby number is no longer in use. And they didn't recognise Hospital Mo.'

'Another Mo? And Mo gets pally with him, feeds him whatever line of bait works for him. He's taken, willingly, to a second location where unbeknownst to him, he was going to be kept prisoner. But they didn't know he was a diabetic, he didn't survive, so they had to dispose of him. Despite being dead, they battered him with a baseball bat, angry that he'd deprived them of their little bit of fun?'

'It was risky. They could've met a hiker.'

'A calculated risk. They'd leave somebody at the bottom of the glen and phone when the coast was clear. Or they might be upping the thrill of the game. Right under the nose of the MoD, in between their precisely timed patrols.'

'And they learned the hard way that a victim might need medication to survive. They didn't know what Bethany was on. The media release had said she needed her meds. It would spoil the fun if she died on them before they'd enjoyed themselves.'

Craigo didn't look convinced. 'How did they get Brooke-Williams to follow them in the first place? He didn't need money.'

'But he needed something. They'd hone in on what would work on him. Maybe he and this Mo became friends, simple as that.'

'And we have three, four, women all called Mo. Run me through them again?'

'Five gals called Mo!' cracked Mackie. 'This one, the Brooke-Williams one, is Slow Mo? The raptor centre, the Heatherbank one, was the one who got the bird to use as bait and got the drugs, the one who tied the knots. She's the one with the mullet who got bitten and turned up at the hospital. She's Hospital Mo. Revolve Mo is small but blonde, pleasant and chirpy. She's got Bethany and Shivonne and is there on the photomontage from the Revolve. I wonder if she flagged when the target left the building and put Operation Falcon into action. So, one Mo at the Revolve Centre. There'd need to be two Moes in the park.' Caplan scrolled through her screen as Mackie talked. 'Would that be Hospital Mo with the injured bird and Slow Mo?'

'And one of those Moes was in Inverness years before. Nik had a Mo, remember.'

'Yes, Glasgow accent, heavy, thickset, very short hair, spikey on top at her most recent. That sounds like Hospital Mo. Moonshine Hostel Mo, or Slow Mo, who befriended Brooke-Williams, fits the description of the lady in the bushes at Pulpit Hill Park.'

'So, leading from that I looked at Heatherbank, and found this

Facebook picture. A crowd of volunteers. But look at the back, walking across the shot, was this woman, not included in the set-up for the pic but accidently caught on the camera. God this is confusing,' said Mackie.

'And genius,' Caplan said. 'It's pure obfuscation. Get that image expanded and cleaned up, get it to all the locales. See if anybody recognises her. She looks very unhappy to be caught on camera so let's find out why.'

The DC appeared to be deep in concentration on her phone. Then she stood up and coughed. 'I'd like to claim the caramel wafer and the gold star. Hospital Mo, Morven, appears to have been brought up in Rothesay.'

'That's not illegal.'

'One of four girls.' Mackie raised her eyebrows.

'All called Maureen?'

'Morven, Morna, Morag and Moira. There might be a fifth. She might be Maureen. It's a bit like The Nolans, isn't it?'

'And did that clipping not say Wilma Vance was born in Bute?' Caplan rubbed her face. 'Four of them? Five? We need somebody good at logic puzzles. If the man at number 7 eats pizza, then who has the otter with vertigo.'

'Eh?'

'Just track them down. They will not be where they should be. They must gather to play their game, if I am right. For Bethany's sake, I'm hoping that I am wrong.'

The three of them stood, tired and weary, a still point in the day.

'Is Port Bannatyne not in Bute?'

'Rory? Yes it is. So find out where Ghillies is? Where Robertson is? Where Vance is? If you need manpower, call Linden. You might need Fergusson's skills. And for Moes, look at Facebook, TikTok, anywhere you might get a visual clue to exact identity.' The day was bright and sunny but bitterly cold. It was apposite that the mood in the room had become less fraught, with hot tea and the searching through files, seeing connections, stumbling across facts that made sense now they recognised them. Things were moving on, intelligence was being gathered. It would take time and couldn't be hurried.

She picked up the phone to call the Fiscal.

It rang before she could select the number. Followed by all the phones in the incident room.

* * *

The crows were noisier today, squawking and cawing as if unsettled. Bethany was lying on a narrow bed. She could see a wooden floor rather than stone slabs. She was in a different room. The wall facing her had been wallpapered once, in a cream and red Regency stripe, and there was a horizontal line of nicks and tears where a sideboard or a chest of drawers had been once. The ceiling had a central rose, with a single bulb swinging slightly on a webbed cord. A draught and a dull light were coming in from somewhere. The air was still fresh. She could still hear the chatter of the crows. So a different room in the same location? Her heart began to race. She closed her eyes again. Too much drug still in her system to make sense of it. But lying there, she screwed her eyes tightly shut and waited for the noise of her heart thumping to recede.

In the deadly quiet, the void of sound behind the birds, she could recognise the only voice that whispered in the distance. Wind. Wind through trees.

Was she going to take her last breath in here, between these four walls? She was going to rot away on this bed, undiscovered.

It would kill her dad.

What would happen then, if she was never found? Would they declare her dead without a body? Would her dad go insane thinking about what might or might not have happened to her? Lost. Never to be found. Nothing she thought of could be worse than what she was going through now.

Bethany tugged at the ties that bound her wrists together, not using her teeth or her fingers, too sore, too much blood, but then they slipped free. She looked at her hands, flexing her wrists, trying to quell the excitement.

She was going to make it. She was getting out of here.

Bending over, she got to work on her ankles. It wasn't as hard as she thought. They weren't tied as tight as they were before. Tears of relief blinded her as she eased her feet out of the bindings. It had been a tight fit.

Before, it had been impossible.

Bethany sat down and wiped her eyes with the heel of her hand, euphoria floating away, reality taking hold.

It was possible because they had made it possible.

Loose because they had left them loose. Soft Voice trying to help? They didn't make that kind of mistake. What did that mean? They were safe because there was no way out for her now? She looked down, then physically lifted her left leg over her right with her left hand. She couldn't get it to move on its own any more. Her foot was blue and swollen. The swelling below her knee was thicker than her knee itself. The pain was unbearable when she tried to stand on it.

Was this their plan? Had they disabled her too much to escape so they could safely give her a chance, knowing that she couldn't take it?

It would fit their sardonic sense of cruelty.

She collapsed back on top of the bed, her head on the hard pillow. She shook her hair from her face, looking at the wall, thinking where the fresh air was coming from. At the top was a long hopper of a window, six feet long.

A window to the world.

Could she slither through it? Bethany looked at it for a long time, considering the pain in her leg and her hand . . . the height of the window.

They didn't think that she'd be able to get out of there.

But she knew she was smart, she was a problem solver.

She let her eyes float upwards. She'd been in the dark for so long – the journey, her incarceration, the blindfolds – and her eyes now viewed this bright sky as painful. Up there, out in the world, darkness would fall. The moon would be out there soon along with plenty of trees; she was sure there were trees. She could make out the rustling of the leaves, the odd occasional creak of a branch and bursts of chatter from excited crows. She was sensing that the trees were close by.

She'd be safe in the woods.

Safe in the dark.

Slowly, she pulled herself to sit up. If she could find something in here, or break something to make a crutch, she might be able to walk, to get to the window. And then what? Climb up the wall? Think. Think. Maybe pull the bed over? She reached down, left-handed. The bloodied stub where they had pulled one fingernail out rendered her right hand useless. Trying to feel under the mattress, she worked her fingers along, feeling slats, wooden slats. It was a single bed. The length of the slats might make something that she could lean on.

Could she pull the bed over? Could she get to the window?

She felt dizzy, heady, but common sense told her that there was *still some analgesic over in her bloodstream. If she wanted to make this move, there would be this time, and there would be the last time. Bethany looked out, thinking that now she was sitting up, maybe she could see the sky, thinking that this being her last move might be the very point.*

Callum McPhee was lying behind the kitchen unit, curled into a ball, bleeding, the phone still in his hand.

Drury, a uniformed constable, was talking to Carrie-Louise, who was rubbing her arms, blood staining her face, a bruise reddening one eye. The young woman took a deep breath, risking a look over her shoulder to the kitchen area. She seemed wary of McPhee.

Caplan stepped to the side as the paramedics made their way through the hall of the small flat, moving past Carrie-Louise to the body lying behind the island.

Carrie-Louise's eyes followed them. Caplan whispered to Mackie to stay standing right where she was, blocking the young woman's view of her boyfriend.

Caplan introduced herself to the uniform.

'It's a bit awkward, ma'am.'

'Is it?' asked Caplan briskly.

'Well, this is proof of the domestic abuse that she's complained of. We're going to charge him and keep him in custody if he's breached the restraining agreement.'

Caplan agreed, her stomach sinking. 'You accompany him to the hospital. Make sure everything gets documented. All the bruises on both parties. Get another uniform to get Carrie-Louise to hospital then to Oban for a statement. You follow McPhee to the hospital. Don't let him out of your sight – handcuff him if you have to.'

'Are you really going for it, ma'am?' The uniform looked conflicted.

'He gets treated as every other suspect; she gets treated as every other abuse survivor. They both need medical attention and their injuries need to be recorded; you know, bruises of a different age, etc. And ask for more bloods on McPhee. Ask for a tox screen on his hair if they didn't take a sample before. And we'll make sure that we are nowhere near him, to keep things tidy. But he's the one bleeding out.'

The paramedic looked at the young policeman on the floor, at the knife, and said that they really needed to get going, as he placed an oxygen mask over the face that was fading, becoming whiter by the moment.

The constable's eyes were now on McPhee as his colleague was carried out on a stretcher, the blood stain a large red mushroom on his light-blue shirt. The creases he had ironed in that morning were still clear and neat down each sleeve.

Caplan felt that slow grip of terror that one of hers might not make it.

'Mackie? Stay with Carrie-Louise. She needs to know that she has somebody with her until support is put in place for her. Make sure her injuries are logged, forensically. Drury will stick with McPhee.' Caplan walked over to the far window looking down to where they were sliding McPhee into the back of the ambulance, his body rolling slightly under the blanket. A small crowd of neighbours had gathered. They had, no doubt, filled in any part of the narrative that they were missing. One dark-haired woman, still in her slippers, closed in on the ambulance doors as McPhee was half in and half out. She spat on the prostrate figure.

The paramedic turned on her. Caplan's ears picked up the obscenities going back and forth.

As Caplan left, Mackie was helping Carrie-Louise to her feet, making sure that she was steady before asking her where her coat was, and did she think she was okay to make it out to the car. Carrie-Louise gave Caplan a flash of her smile.

It didn't work this time.

SEVENTEEN

Slowly, painfully, she stood up and hopped round the bed, leaning on it as she went. It took time, but once at the other side, when she leaned on it, it moved easily under the pressure of her body weight. She had no idea how long it took her once it started inching across the floor. She kept it going, moving towards the wall, towards the window.

When there, she collapsed on top of it, exhausted. The pain pounding in her leg was so intense she had to count each one, each stab, each twist, each squeeze deep in the bone. They would be back – during the hours of darkness? Or would they dare to come in when the sunshine filled the room and they might need to show their faces?

Lying back, she looked up, noticing the two small curtains pulled neatly aside, their pleats forming little black squares at either end. If they fitted the window, and they were for blackout coverage, they would match the shape surely. Long. Thin. Could she make a rope out of them to get her out of the window?

She sat up on the bed, pulling her bad leg over and pushing away the pain, not daring to hope. Standing on her right leg on the bed, both hands on the wall, she slowly made her way up, bloodied fingertip by bloodied fingertip.

At the window ledge, above her head, her fingers reached over and curled round the edge of the sill, finding the metal frame. Then the long handle with holes, the swan neck. She pulled herself a little closer, searching for the clasp with her fingers, lifting the bar and feeling it spring open. Petrichor. Woodland. Fir trees. Fresh air so strong she almost passed out.

She slid back down, collapsing into the small gap between the wall and the bed.

At least she had something now, something that she'd not had before.

She had hope.

She decided to agree with herself on that one thing. If her life was going to be in this much pain then it was better not having it.

She closed her eyes, staring at the ceiling, and thought about dying. She found herself humming 'The Lord's My Shepherd' to herself, the tune then the words. Walking in death's dark vale, she would fear no ill.

Yes, that was it, feel the fear then do it anyway.

Ignoring the pain in her leg, the aching in her arms, she was buoyed up by her elation. They had finally made a mistake and left a window unlocked that she could get through. If she could climb up, lift herself over the ledge and to the other side, into the cover of the trees to hide, she could be guided by the stars in the clear sky. She gave a wry smile to herself; she was going to be where she needed to be.

She could taste freedom.

Looking at her broken fingers and persuading herself that they'd still work, she hooked them over the ledge, placed her good foot on the wall, then pulled herself up. There was a sickening pain in her leg as she went up and over the window frame, the metal digging into her stomach, then she let go, getting one hand down over her head as she went through the other side, slithering down the wall. Still trying to hold on to the lower frame of the window, she dropped gently, collapsing on the rough ground. There she stopped for a moment, retracting her arms and legs, trying to disappear into the wall, making sure that nobody had heard. She nursed her wounds for a moment, feeling the burning pain where she had scraped her hands on the bricks, and the ever-present pain in her left leg. She looked out at the world; the dancing trees in the gentle wind, the blue sky – there was a myriad of invisible stars up there. She envied them.

But the air was fresh.

Her ears searched round for any noise not of nature. Even the crows were silent, high in the trees watching her with their black eyes.

Nothing. But she stayed where she was. Waiting.

Then, something in the woods – something.

Breathing?

She imagined the wind was holding its breath.

Then letting go.

'Are you sure we are doing the right thing, ma'am?'

'Quite frankly, Craigo, I have no bloody idea. But it was your list, I agreed with you when you were compiling it and we should be acting on it. Rod, Todd, Callum McPhee? They are where they are, but with Bethany we can change what's going to happen to her. Take a right here. Lochanview is the closest house. If she's not there then we keep going.'

'And if we don't find her?'

'We keep going until we do.'

They drove along the single-track road, Caplan following on the map as the satnav had lost its signal three miles before. They were starting to get a feel for the places; full of overgrown trees, nothing that the Forestry Commission would come checking on every three weeks. A few single-track roads criss-crossed the area. It was easy to think of the most direct route in and out, but maybe for other purposes the tracks formed a hidden network that allowed covert but slow movement across a lot of country.

Lochanview was such a house. Semi off-grid, there would be nobody at home at this time of year. It was deep in a Dark Sky zone in Strathfillan and built on a slight lift in the landscape. Like the house Caplan was renovating, the living area was upstairs and a huge glass window ran the full length. The house was three stories at the front with a workshop and garage underneath. It was built in the late 1960s.

The owners had friends who had a key, and had given consent for Caplan to enter from their flat in the south of France where the family had relocated for a four-year work contract.

Craigo pulled up outside.

A murder of crows took to the sky.

'There's hundreds of them.'

'Mass murder of crows?' Craigo was deadpan.

'Well, it scores high on the serial-killer checklist,' said Caplan. She lifted the envelope from her rucksack and took the key out.

A path ran from the track over a wild garden of heathers and moss to the front door. They climbed the three wooden steps, free of leaves as if they had been swept recently.

She opened the door, the key sliding in the lock easily. A smell of slight dampness and something like cooking oil floated towards them. The hall was carpeted with the same green and purple tones of the landscape outside. An open-plan staircase went up to the right and to the left were two rooms, with doors closed. The kitchen and diner lay ahead.

'Is there a door to the basement from within?' asked Craigo.

'Why are you whispering?' whispered Caplan. 'There's nobody here. On the plan there's a way down to the garage through the utility room.'

They walked, their feet making no noise on the thick carpeted floor. The door on the far side of the kitchen opened to reveal another small hallway, three steps down. Caplan put her hand on Craigo's shoulder. Stop.

She pointed to the door at the bottom of the three steps, to a turn of the stairs and another door which she was sure had closed in front of them.

Craigo put his hand up and stepped to the side of the stairs. He went down, one step at a time, Caplan behind him, noticing the change in smell; washing powder, a sign of recent activity in a house that was supposed to be empty. Craigo stood to one side as Caplan pushed the door and let it swing open fully.

A bank of white appliances stood under a white worktop. On the far side the window showed the view of the trees, nothing but trees. Caplan sensed rather than heard something behind the door, trapped now that it was opened fully, hidden until one of them entered the room and it closed behind them.

'Just the laundry,' said Caplan, and let the door close again. She slipped into the shadows as Craigo noisily made his way downstairs to the basement. They waited and waited.

Then the laundry door opened by an inch. Somebody was checking the stairs, not seeing Caplan pressed against the wall, beside the door. There was an audible sigh of relief, the door opened and a middle-aged woman stepped onto the landing, pulling her anorak on and stepping forward to creep up the stairs and get back to the kitchen.

'Can I help you?' said Caplan quietly.

She thought the woman's feet left the ground as she jumped in fright.

She was a chubby woman in her late forties, with her anorak unzipped, her house keys in her hand. She had slippers on her feet, but her thick woollen socks told their own story. There would be hill-walking boots somewhere. That explained the lack of car.

She made a strange mewling noise, her hand over her chest. 'Oh my Jesus Christ, you gave me a fright. I didn't hear the front door. I thought I heard somebody walking around in here.' She smiled and gave a little laugh. 'I thought you were here to rob the place. You two must be lost. Nobody ever comes here. Can I help you?'

It was a good act. Her expression was one of genuine shock. She was very softly spoken.

'Who are you?' asked Caplan as Craigo approached the woman from the stairs below.

Her eyes grew a little suspicious. She looked over their heads to the trees visible through the stairwell window.

Caplan held up her warrant card. 'There's nothing to worry about.' They introduced themselves. The woman took a long time looking at their identification as she walked back up to the hall, looking out at the Hilux. The sight of that reassured her.

'What's your name?'

'Maureen. Maureen Maitland.'

Caplan couldn't look at Craigo.

Maitland chattered on, innocently. 'I work for Spire properties. Is there an issue? Is it the septic tank again? I've all the paperwork back in the office.'

'How often do you visit here?'

'As often as I think I need. After storms or severe winds. Once a month to keep it shipshape.'

'Has this property lain empty at any time in the last five or six years? For a couple of months or more?'

Maitland leaned against the front door slightly, as if thinking. 'Well, yes, the owners bought it, well, end of 2019, then we had the whole Covid thing and it was empty and uninhabitable. Builders were working on it on and off for the next two years, then I think Spire took it on. I'm sorry, I can't be more precise without looking it up but is there something wrong, has somebody complained? Like I say, the septic tank? Well, it was all sorted out in the . . .'

'Do you have any outbuildings?'

'No. There's a basement.' Then she appeared to think. She was a pretty woman, older than Caplan had first thought, in her mid-fifties maybe. The gentle blonde had thick streaks of white and her blue eyes were framed by a concertina of wrinkles. 'Well, actually, there's two rooms and a wee toilet.'

Again, Caplan didn't look at Craigo's face. 'Can we have a look, please? We have permission from the owner to make sure that the property is secure.'

'Oh, come on down then. You've no idea what we sometimes find in properties that have been lying empty for a while.'

They followed her, Craigo making small talk as Caplan pointed at her own mouth. They had both spotted that Maureen Maitland had a snaggle tooth, her canine, on the left.

Caplan stood well back as Craigo followed Maitland into the basement. This room had a sink and a small tick-over heater.

Craigo opened each of the two doors that faced him. He did a cursory glance around, then looked around the room he was standing in, a blueprint of the living room above. 'Were you ever round when the work was going on down here?'

'I was in and out.' Maitland looked at Craigo.

Caplan excused herself and said she was going out to get a phone signal, glad to get some fresh air. Maitland didn't come across as a guilty party caught. And that made Caplan nervous. Was this just the dupe who had access to the property information? She walked around a little, appearing to be strolling up and down, killing time, while texting back to the station. She confirmed where they were and asked for a status check in ten minutes if she wasn't back in touch with them. Then she returned to the house, to the top of the stairs and looked down.

She froze, some instinct of self-preservation kicking in. The door of the basement had swung closed, or it had been closed.

Caplan retreated out to the Hilux, looking into the rear passenger seats. There had to be something there to defend herself. Against what?

Looking around, she saw plenty of logs of all sizes, some free of the moss and growth that would render them slippy, things she could use as a weapon. Gently, phone in pocket, she flexed her fingers, ready. Slowly, she walked back into the hall and down the stairs towards the door again. There was no noise coming from inside. Of course, Maitland with the snaggle tooth could have a syringe down there filled with ketamine, or God knows what.

She placed the palm of her hand on the knob, her ear to the door listening.

Silence except for her own heartbeat.

She was considering her next move when the jerk of the door being pulled open made her jump. Craigo emerged into the daylight of the hall adjusting his glasses.

She didn't have time to get the words 'Are you all right?' out her mouth when he started.

'Ma'am? Maureen here recalls one of the plastic dust sheets being a bit stained. She thinks it was on a Wednesday after a bank holiday weekend, and one of the builders said it was blood, thinking that somebody must have hurt themselves and it hadn't been put in the accident book.' He raised his eyebrows as if that was the most significant detail of all.

'And?'

'The plastic sheeting is still there, folded up in a box with rollers, paint and God knows what. It looks like blood to me, ma'am.'

Caplan whispered, 'And how's Maureen feeling?'

'She's very nervous, very nervous indeed.' Craigo looked at her, with his weird sepia eyes. 'You've less than seventy-two hours, ma'am. That's what McEwan gave you to get something solid on his desk.'

'And how long does Bethany have?' Caplan wiped her face with her hands.

Caplan didn't ask for a whole forensic team, but they got permission to close the house up then take a tearful Maureen Maitland back to the station with instructions that Mackie had to be nice to her.

As Caplan explained what they were looking for, Maitland stood outside the door, watching them, her hands deep in her pockets, alternating between deep breathing and crying. If she knew anything, she was a good actress. Still, Caplan thought, she could just be pissed off at getting caught.

'Mo Maitland' was sitting in the interview room in Cronchie. She had her jacket pulled round her as if she was cold, though the autumn sun that floated in through the window had warmed the air. The aroma of coffee filled the air but the cup sat in front of her untouched.

She had looked up when Caplan and Craigo had entered the room. A wary look appeared in her eyes before peace settled on her features.

Caplan introduced herself and Craigo again and placed the file of photographs in front of her but didn't open them.

'Are you being looked after?'

'Oh yes, quite happy, thank you.'

'Do you know this man?' Caplan turned over a picture of William Robertson.

'Yes, I do.' She took her glasses off and looked more closely at the picture. 'That's the dad of that lassie who has gone missing.' She looked back at Caplan, staring at her.

'Is there something you want to tell me?'

She shrugged. And sighed.

'You volunteered the dirty floor sheets. You know.'

'I'm very glad I did. You were police. I'd been thinking about the blood. If that property has been used for . . .' She tapped the desk. '. . . For this kind of thing then that's awful. It has to be stopped.'

'Yes, no normal person would disagree with you there.'

Caplan placed the photograph of Lisa Stratton on the table. 'Do you know her?'

'No, I don't.' She looked away.

'This one is worse, this young man.' A picture of Brooke-Williams. 'What about him?'

'Look, it's been all over the news. Is that the body found in Glen Douglas?'

'You're bright, Maureen, if that's your name. You see,' Caplan leaned back in the plastic seat, 'you are a Maureen, and, I suspect, a Mo. You are part of a collection of interchangeable women, sisters, all called Mo. I have four kittens at home: Eeny, Meeny, Miny and Moe. It's a picking game. Which Mo are you? Mo with the raptors? Hospital Mo? Mo at the Revolve? Slow Mo up in the bushes? Mo the Blow? Inverness Mo? Are you any of the above?' Caplan looked round the room, appearing bored. 'But, the removal of the tooth is interesting, the same upper left canine. The location of a snaggle tooth, which can be hereditary? Are you Moes all related? Or does the mastermind of it all have a snaggle tooth?'

Maureen stayed silent, but the look in her eyes had altered to something that Caplan could only read as fear. But she didn't seem scared of anything Caplan had said.

'Nothing to do with the five Maitland sisters brought up in Bute? Near where Wilma Johnstone grew up? No? Near Port Bannatyne?'

Again, something, close to nothing, but a slight glimmer of fear.

Maitland held her hand up. 'Yes and no. We were separated as children. The records will tell you that. I use my real name but apart from that I have nothing to do with my siblings.'

'Is that a fact?' Caplan placed the picture from the newspaper in front of Maitland. 'There's Felix Vance and Wilma Johnstone on their wedding day. The caption says they're with with best man Kevin McCall, and bridesmaid Maureen Maitland.'

Maitland stared at the picture for a long time but said nothing. Her face was unreadable.

'Are you scared of them?' Caplan let that question lie. 'How well do you know Wilma Vance now? Or maybe, how well do your sisters know her?'

'I wasn't brought up with my sisters, I've just said that. And Wilma used to be a friend of mine.' She bit her lip, watching Caplan, then Craigo. 'Why am I here?'

'Yes, why are you? Why you? Why not Morag or Morven or whoever? Why you? It took us a long time to piece together what kind of location these poor victims were being kept in. Yet you told us about the floor covering.'

'Because you were looking at the floor. Up to then, I hadn't really thought about it. I was expecting somebody from the health and safety. There was a lot of blood and nothing in the accident book. That was all.' She leaned forward on her hands, showing stress, and took a long, slow breath out. 'And then there were two detectives, not police but detectives of a high rank standing on the doorstep. I've seen that about those two women missing, then one's found dead in the Chern Wood, then you turn up on the doorstep. There was a picture of you in the paper.' She nodded at Caplan. 'What the hell was I supposed to think? I thought I was being helpful. Because your colleague was looking at the floor.'

'Okay, good thinking.'

'Who are the builders?'

'Oh, you'd need to ask Spire. They keep all kinds of records. They do project management, all trades from different places.'

'Why would you stand by and watch that?' Caplan tapped Xander's head. 'Why wouldn't you help her?' Caplan tapped Shiv's bruised and battered face. 'I can't understand that. To do such a horrible thing to a human being, hunting them down.' She banged the six pictures on the table, fanning them out in front of her. 'So, Craigo, she's brave enough to do that? But not brave enough to look at them now, not brave enough to stand up and confess to us that she did that.'

'But why would any human being do it? Pull out their teeth and break their legs. Why?' said Craigo.

Maitland slowly blinked, her pale-blue eyes filled with tears that swum and rolled their way down the creases of skin. She looked at Craigo and then looked at Caplan.

'Ma'am, maybe we could let her go and then let them go after her, and then we could watch over her and hope we got there in time?' suggested Craigo.

It was that serious, slightly offbeat thing that Craigo did so well.

'You know, Craigo, we might just do that if she doesn't tell us where Bethany Robertson is.'

Maitland blinked slowly, then looked down at the photograph of Shiv. This time she seemed unable to tear her eyes away. Then she was violently sick.

Caplan and Craigo remained seated at the table. Caplan handed her some paper tissues.

'Well, Maureen, I think that if I knew the person who was capable of doing that . . .' She slid the picture of the remains of Nik Ardman's face under her nose. 'I think I'd be worried sick as well. We can put you down to the cells for now, for your safekeeping.'

'I don't know where Bethany is. I don't.' Maitland was staring at the pictures, wiping her hands, her mouth, her jumper. She looked at the picture of Lisa Stratton. There was a slight shake of the head. A look of puzzlement passed her features.

Then she seemed to deflate in front of them.

'She wasn't in the game. I've never seen that woman before.'

Caplan was calm as she spoke. 'But you did do that to the others?'

'No. Yes. Not like them. Please, I didn't ever do what they did.'

'Why did you do any of it?' asked Caplan.

'Because if I didn't, it would be done to me.'

'Ma'am?'

'Yes, Mackie. I thought I told you to keep talking to Maitland. She's our key to the rest of them and it's not as if she's going anywhere, is it?'

'We got her a solicitor in case we need to use her statement. Here's a cup of tea. I've sent Stewart out for some sandwiches. And Lucozade.'

'Why?'

'For the journey down to Dumfries and Galloway. Well, Maitland was right about the folded dust sheets. It's proved positive human blood on a presumptive test.'

'Who's out there?'

'Purdey. You don't know him. He says he has a good sample from an inner fold, right on the crease, where it'll have been protected from the elements. Hopefully the sample will not have degenerated. And Maureen Maitland has no criminal record. Nothing at all,' said Mackie.

'So what do we do, ma'am? A full Scene of Crime team at Lochanview which is half an hour down the road? Do we need search teams for each property? Or do we head down to Galloway ourselves?' Craigo said.

'Do we wait?' asked Mackie.

'How can we? Bethany's still out there.'

Craigo looked at his watch. 'It's been eight days, ma'am.'

Caplan felt the skin on her face tighten as the stress bit. He was looking at her, expecting a decision. 'Is this your best guess, Craigo?'

'Down at Dumfries and Galloway there's a forest park. There are two properties, both under stalled renovation. They tick the most boxes. It's only a hundred and eighty miles, ma'am. We can do them both ourselves. If we are wrong then I'll have another look at the map, divide it up, flag the properties and get ourselves in position so that we can move.'

'What's the alternative?'

Craigo shrugged.

They climbed into the Hilux, jackets on, boots on, sandwiches and three bottles of Lucozade – Mackie's idea of an energy diet. Caplan's phones had eleven missed calls. Two from the Fiscal's office. Another two from Bill Robertson. Three from Pordini and the last one was from Rory Ghillies. The other three were from McEwan. Everywhere she went in this investigation she thought Ghillies was either two steps in front or one step behind, watching every move she made.

All the calls were from mobile numbers. The only one to leave a voicemail was Pordini. He sounded stressed.

She put it onto speaker-phone so Craigo could hear while driving.

Pordini had found the items taken from the Rod-Todd house at the lab, in a long queue for processing. 'So I find the Smoo Cave picture from Amazon, thought it might be relevant after reading about that 'Stevie.' And the note that Todd had put through Mrs Gains's letterbox was there in an evidence bag. I mean, was he not supposed to have great italic penmanship? The neighbour said that in her statement. The note in the bag was written in panic, I'll bet my last Rolo on it.'

'He's good that Pordini bloke, isn't he?' said Craigo.

'Confident if he's giving away chocolate.'

The voice continued. Caplan could hear the eagerness of the young DC. 'The Smoo Cave image was in portrait, not landscape. I mean, who does that? The glass had smears in two distinct places, thumb prints, left, right, as if it had been held that way, often. So I opened the back and found nothing but the Smoo Cave picture. But it had another picture on the back, stuck with double-sided tape. And guess what? A middle-aged woman. Kinda looks like Stevie Nicks. Got that blonde witchy thing going on. And the tape looks like it was hauled off. So one person, Rod maybe, opened the picture with care on Monday night. Then Todd finds it, rips it open and goes a bit mental? Or Todd comes home, finds Rod with her, kills him, then opens the picture at a later date? Remorse? Hangs himself? Have I to write this up? Not sure what happened to be honest. Cheers, sir, sorry, ma'am.'

The interior of the Hilux fell quiet.

'I'd like to see him when he does know what happened,' said Caplan, hanging up on the voicemail. She wanted to think.

There was nothing wrong with Rod, except that he was kept in that house by Peter Todd. Or was he? Rod was at home, looking at holidays. Todd was out earning the money, happy because he loved his partner, the kept man being the one exerting the control, holding all the cards. It was the same dangerous game that Carrie Louise had been playing.

Then Rod met Stevie online. They would spend hours online together when Todd was at work. Then they chanced a weekly visit in person. That would have been some kind of betrayal. Did Todd plan the anniversary dinner on the second as one last chance? Then the box from Amazon arrived, intercepted by Mrs Gains, who gave it innocently to Todd. Who examined it later. And was not fooled.

That was the final straw for Todd. He could've thrown Rod out. Rod could've walked out at any time. But they didn't. They should have separated earlier. Rod had already checked out of that relationship. How easy was it to mention an illness, something that nobody liked to talk about, to keep the ever-watchful Mrs Gains from the door. Was that possible? Of course, it was possible. Aklen had hardly gone out of the house in seven years. Todd must have gone along with that, laughing at the old woman and her concern.

The visitor was no more a therapist than Caplan was the Maid Of The Loch.

Then, had Todd come in, put on the kettle, had a biscuit, sat down, started to watch Countdown.

Deceitful.

And maybe he realised the enormity of what he had done, the thought of the body upstairs. Or was it the thought of life without Rod?

A psychologist had once told Caplan that suicides happen in a moment; a perfect storm of circumstances. Another day, another week, different weather, different medications and it would never have happened. But for the unfortunate few.

Caplan let out a long slow breath. Like Pordini, she had no idea if her proposed chain of events was correct. She needed Ryce's help on that.

As he often did, Craigo honed in on her thoughts. 'It's just a sad business all round.'

'It truly is.' Caplan went back to looking at the map and the floor-plans of the two houses they were going to, memorising them as well as the surrounding area.

Four messages came through in quick succession.

Fergusson, under a DI whose name Caplan didn't catch, was trying to set up an informal chat with Felix Vance and his lovely wife Wilma but was finding it difficult to track them down.

Ghillies was not answering his landline or his mobile and Mackie couldn't locate him. Robertson, unusually, was not in the house. Waddell said he'd gone for a short walk but had been away some time.

The rats were gathering.

It wasn't a surprise.

EIGHTEEN

Caplan woke with the bumping of the vehicle along a rough track. Craigo was driving quicker than she thought was safe.

'Did you tell Dumfries that we were coming?'

'Yes, they noted our presence in their jurisdiction and we've to call in any assistance required.'

'They think we're on a wild goose chase, don't they? Can't say I blame them. They know that if we were confident we'd have called in operational support.' Caplan sighed. 'Doon Alba. Stupid name for a house. But it's the next best match for our criteria, and we weren't wrong last time.'

There were two houses identified by Craigo in the Glen Trool area of Galloway Forest Park that were unoccupied, undergoing building work or were considered uninhabitable. There were many such properties being unearthed by people wishing to escape from the cities and willing to pay high prices for a 'project' or a property that needed a lot of work.

This house, Doon Alba, was bigger than the previous property. It was deep in the forest, and the seven-mile single track was rough enough to deter any casual explorers. At two points it turned ninety degrees; the path of the track after the turn was almost indistinguishable.

They were running into nothing. The track was petering out in front of them. Caplan was glad of the Hilux, bouncing around, sometimes on the verge rather than on the track. Twice it had to climb over fallen tree trunks, the engine roaring like a lion. When they stopped and looked at the destination house, all Caplan could think of was how quiet it was now darkness was falling. How silent and secluded it was. A dream. A serial killer's dream.

She recalled a line from a film: 'In space no one could hear you scream.' They had little chance out here either.

They checked the map. The track they had been following kissed the land at the back of the house, then it swung out a little away from the house, going deeper into the forest.

And they didn't have a key, but being a mother of one sensible child, Emma, and Kenny, the forgetful self-styled genius, Caplan stood back and had a look around, finding the spare key at the third time of trying.

She pulled the key out the box and it slipped easily into the lock. The house smelled vaguely of dampness; an older, deeper dampness, not that of being without heating for a month or two. There was a square hall and a narrow staircase that would have been added at some later date to get access to the old roof space which had been converted into a usable area. The front room had originally been small, with wooden shutters up at the windows. An old wood-burning stove was disconnected, standing isolated on bare floorboards. Across the space a wall had been taken down. Small lumps of rubble and brick lay dotted around like islands on a wooden sea.

She heard Craigo shout from the hall. A door that led out of that room under the staircase went to the back of the house and opened to a set of steps going to a cellar.

'Did anybody say anything about a basement?' asked Craigo, waiting for Caplan.

Crouched on the steps, their torches picked up a single damp space. Two cans of Irn-Bru and a crushed paper bag evidenced some activity – by builders in Caplan's experience. But down here, there was room to keep somebody prisoner.

Caplan crept upstairs to the upper floor, her footsteps creaking underneath her as she made her way to the attic space. Peering out the window, she saw the chain of little waterfalls, visible from here, not so from the shuttered living room windows. The owners lived in Spain. They had no intention of coming back until the following summer. Caplan knew, if they dug deep enough, there would be a trail back to the Tinmen, building regulations and the Land Registry. It would all come out in time. She looked up at the ceiling. It was complete; no loft hatches, no way into the small roof space that must be above her. There were no doors in the low sides of the rooms that might take her into the eaves. She walked across the narrow hallway into the second bedroom. It smelled differently. There was a slight mustiness in the air, a tang of something that reminded her of dried fruit. She saw the loft hatch at once and, on the far side, the dark line of unpainted wood showing where it hadn't been closed properly. Something unusual in a house like this, and it was the unusual they were looking for. She glanced round at the plasterboard, the rolls of insulation and bits of four-by-two lying against the wall.

This bedroom didn't have as high a ceiling. It wouldn't be difficult to get up there with a ladder. She turned and walked around looking for one, or something that she could stand on.

Nothing. She shouted to Craigo who joined her in the room.

'There's no way they were keeping anybody up there, they'd get out,' Caplan said.

'You'd hope.'

'Unless they escaped and they'd have fun finding them, then dragging them out into the woods to start all over again.'

'Sick, ma'am.' Craigo nodded. 'Do you think you should go up and have a look?'

'Why do you think I called you?'

'Because I could go out and find something for you to stand on, ma'am?'

'Or?'

'Or I could give you a punt up. Wouldn't be the first time.' He cradled his hands together, bending slightly. 'And you're as light as a feather, ma'am. I've seen you nearly carried away in a strong wind.'

She placed her foot on his cradled fingers and stepped up, her balance perfect. She reached above her and punched the hatch up, hearing it slide above.

'You okay?' she asked Craigo.

'Yip.'

She lifted herself on top of the ledge of the hatch with a surprisingly strong boost from Craigo, and asked for her torch to be handed up to her.

'There's a small stepladder here right enough. Hello, is there anybody here? We are the police; you are safe.' Then she added, 'Bethany? Bethany, are you here?' She prayed to any God that might be listening that there would be an answer.

She shone the torch around and saw the new water pipes – narrow plastic pipes that led somewhere – netting full of fluffy insulation and a cardboard roll of green wire.

It was all very quiet and dark except for the beam of the torch making its way methodically over the walls of the space and the interior of the roof.

She listened. No noise. Not a sound. And she waited long enough for somebody who was holding their breath to exhale.

Then there was rustling; a mouse or a rat disturbed. Caplan

shivered, retreating slightly towards the hatch, so she didn't have to lean on her outstretched arm which might be lying on top of who knew what. She pointed the beam up to the skylight which had been tiled over with the new roof. Then she pointed the beam out to the four corners, first at ceiling height, then at floor level.

When she got to the fourth corner, the one the furthest away from the hatch, her subconscious registered a shape.

She was moving the beam too fast but it had flickered over something recognisable.

She retraced its path, her heart pounding. In her mind she'd seen the eyes of a rat; pale, beady, sharp little eyes like Craigo's. Something smooth and round, then a tuft of hair and the eyes, grey and dull, looking back at her, definitely human.

Caplan recoiled instantly, rattling her back against the corner of the hatch, knocking over Craigo as she tumbled down. Her sergeant softened her landing but the suddenness of it took them by surprise and they both landed badly.

Craigo jumped to his feet, peering up into the hatch, ready. 'Who's up there?'

'Nobody that's coming down here. You can relax.' Caplan slowly got to her feet, rubbing her elbow. Craigo started to flex his spine back and forth, wincing, but still keeping a wary eye on the opening to the loft. Just in case.

'Sorry about that. You okay?'

'Tweaked my back, ma'am. What did you see?'

'Well, I've no idea who they are, but they are not Bethany. They're mummified.'

'Mummified?' Craigo shook his head. 'Bloody hell. Insulated space, hot weather? I don't know.'

'Neither do I. I don't think he or she cares. What scared them so much they'd stay up there and die rather than . . .?' Caplan swore to herself, walking slowly out of the house and looking back at the fairytale cottage from this angle with the grassy road leading up to it and the vastness of the surrounding wood. She took a few deep breaths. Then she got onto Newton Stewart Police station and found out it didn't open outside office hours, so she texted Mackie to deal with it. Just a squad car whenever they could; it wasn't time critical. The next house might be.

'Ma'am, I know this is a shock, you've a sore elbow and I've hurt my back, but we're on the right track. We predicted this. We hoped it would be Bethany. It wasn't. The next one might be.'

Caplan smiled through her fatigue. 'Blame your spae-wife. We had a W and still water.'

'Yes, ma'am, but the W was the waterfall and where's there's waterfalls the water is not still, is it?'

'DS Craigo, I've fallen out a loft and I'm very tired. I think I've fractured my elbow. I'm about to have the first huge failure of my career . . .'

'Second, surely, ma'am.'

Caplan thought she was going to cry but decided to laugh instead, because it would confuse Craigo. She rubbed the skin of her forehead, closing her eyes for a moment.

The moment lasted some time.

'Ma'am? Bethany? Not finding her would be a career disaster. We have one more property.'

Caplan looked at the crumpled little Post-it arrow on the folded map. It was dark and the night air was turning cold. She needed a toilet. And she wanted a cup of tea. They still had to find Bethany.

'There's a pond right in front of it. Still water.'

'Is that why we are going, Craigo?'

'One of the reasons, ma'am. Nobody is living there now. From the plans, it sits on a slope. The basement is above ground.'

'Where is it?'

'About twenty miles.'

Caplan closed her eyes.

'I have a tank full of gas as the Americans would say.' Craigo went, limping slightly, towards the Hilux, forcing Caplan to move along with him.

'One more haystack to check.'

The trees were taller here. Sparse. The roof canopy was very high up. While on the main road Caplan switched her phone on to text Aklen to say that something had come up – she'd be in touch when she could but she was about to be out of signal for a while and he wasn't to worry. Then she turned her phone off again. Even in that little interval of time, pings of messages cascaded through. Those going to Craigo's phone were persistent and with increasing frequency until he too turned his notifications off.

Google maps showed that Cloverhouse was a modern house with a sloping flat roof with water channels and solar panels. At the far end of the roof was an odd structure, like a circular dormer. To Caplan's untrained eye it could have been for a telescope. Her heart began to beat a little faster. She looked at the 'unnamed road' that ran close to the back of the house then deep into the forest again before stopping abruptly on her phone screen. Again it was way off the beaten track but Craigo stopped the Hilux a fair distance away. Then he parked it off the track, sending the crows fluttering in panic.

'What are you doing?'

'Trying to hide the vehicle, ma'am.'

'From whom? There's nobody here.' She looked around her. There could be a thousand hidden eyes staring at them. 'Nobody.'

'If we're right, we don't know who we'll run into. They will know now that we have one Mo. They'll be on a damage limitation exercise.'

They walked the final three hundred yards or so without torches, in silence, with night, in the gentle darkness of autumn. As they walked, the darkness grew denser. Caplan stopped to look at the broken stems of the shrubs that had grown over where an old track used to be; the smaller twigs of the trees at waist level had been snapped.

Silently they approached the house, woods in every direction. Some of the tallest trees had fallen, too tall and thin to be strong, sacrificing themselves in the race to get to the sunlight first.

They walked up to the side of the house built on the slope, positioned so there was room at the back for a door and an above-ground basement. A wide pane of glass, ten inches in height, lay open.

Caplan looked at the growth underneath the window, scanning it with her torch. 'Has someone trampled these?'

'By climbing out the window. Which way would somebody go?'

They stood and looked at the view from the front of the cottage. There was the kidney-shaped pond. Craigo was looking at the two fallen trees, one to the left, one to the right. The fullness of branch, twig and foliage had caused them to catch on their neighbours.

'Let's check the house. I'll kick the door in if I have to.'

'Not with your back, you won't. If we find any evidence of her being here, we'll call in the dogs and get the whole forest searched.'

Craigo jemmied the door open with confidence and expertise that, once again, made Caplan wonder.

This house felt more lived in. A thick, piled carpet ran through the entire ground floor. Dust sheets lay on top of the carpet, slightly crumpled in places. Caplan looked round. The cream-coloured sheets were flat ahead and to the left and right, but going up the stairs they showed signs of disturbance. Not as clear as footprints but, still, somebody had walked over this floor.

Up these stairs.

At the top of the stairs, the dust sheets stopped.

She looked overhead. No loft.

Two bedrooms to the left, two to the right.

Caplan walked into a Wedgewood themed room. Blue and white wallpaper, pristine light-blue carpet. The woodwork was the brilliant white of fresh gloss paint. Deep into the eaves were two doors, one at each side to give storage space. Caplan opened the clasp and carefully looked in. It was dark. No noise. But she could smell the presence of human life. She had smelled it before. Human fear. She shouted for Craigo, turning in time to see a blade come towards her, lashing wildly.

Caplan, kneeling through the small door, couldn't get out the way.

'Police,' she said breathlessly. 'We're the police, you're safe. You are safe.'

'Is it Bethany?' whispered Craigo from behind her.

The Stanley knife stayed in mid-air, pointing, the top wavering. Caplan could see the tiny, childlike fingers grasping the handle as if her life depended on it. For a moment she thought the bleeding hands were too small to belong to a woman in her twenties.

The voice was a growl. 'Get away from me.'

Female.

'Bethany? I can't see you. It's too dark. We're the police. I'm Christine.' The blade came at her again. She felt it on her upper arm, slashing the sleeve of her jacket. The power of the edge when it reached her skin was a sharp, stinging pain.

'Please stop doing that. Is it Bethany? If not, then tell me who you are?'

Craigo held out the torch. Caplan leaned back on her haunches, drawing herself out of reach of the knife. 'We're here to save you. We're going to put the light on now. I need to know who you are and get you out of here.'

The blade jabbed again. The effort of holding it was hard going for the scrawny arm.

Craigo held the torch over Caplan's head and illuminated the tiny space. How a human being could be in here and not be obvious to the eye was unbelievable. Finally, Caplan could make out a fold of black material and the hand that clasped the knife. Pulled back into what could be a collar was a small, pinched face, eyes red and sunken, and teeth that looked too big for the rest of her. One side of her face was so swollen and bloodied her eye was closed. She was terrified.

But she had freckles and the dank unwashed hair still had highlights of auburn.

'Bethany? Are you Bethany?'

The knife came up again.

'Please, I know you are terrified but we don't want anybody else getting hurt. What can I say that will convince you that we're the police?'

Craigo's voice echoed from behind her. 'With all due respect, ma'am, but they might have told her they were the police so you saying the same thing isn't going to cut the mustard, is it?'

Caplan pulled back, relief overwhelming. Bethany was alive. 'Ta, Craigo.'

'Poor kid is terrified out her wits.'

'We'll get your dad. Bill. It'll take time but we can get him.'

There was a tiny flicker of response. Maybe her captors had used that line as well. Different ones with different stories watching her joy at the thought of release then clamping down before she got anywhere. Bethany had seen it all, and she wasn't going to be fooled again.

'I'm going to leave the door open but I'm climbing out as I'm too old to be hunched up like this. We'll be waiting outside in the bedroom.'

That got a response; a cough, a snort.

'You wait until your dad comes. Though I guess you're not going anywhere, are you? We'll be outside the door.' There was another wee flicker; a movement that might have been a nod. She wasn't yet allowing herself to dare to believe.

Caplan slid out of the cupboard and told Craigo to keep watch. She allowed herself a few tears, of tiredness, of relief. She didn't know why. She dug around in her pocket for a fresh tissue and wiped her face. God, she was tired.

She hoped that they weren't about to alert the wrong father.

'Who are you?' the voice hissed, thin and raspy. Bethany's gaunt face was looking round the corner, the bloodied fingers of her right hand against the upright of the door. Her left eye was almost closed with swelling and a mass of dried blood and tissue distorted her jaw.

'I'm Christine, DCI . . .'

Bethany flicked her sight from her to Craigo. Caplan noticed that only one eye moved. She knew that was a dangerous sign.

'He's Finan Craigo and . . .'

'Voice. I need to hear his voice again.' She looked feral, glaring at him.

'I'm Finan Craigo, DS from Cronchie. Do you want my jacket?'

The eyelids fell, relief eased the strain in her face. She had not recognised their voices as those of her captors. The thin hand, the first finger bent at a ridiculous angle, came out. Caplan took Craigo's jacket and held it up, encouraging Bethany to leave her sanctuary. It was then Caplan noticed how injured she was. Movement was difficult for the girl. Caplan placed her arm gently round the thin waist, the naked skin feeling cold and clammy, and held her until she was fully out of the cupboard. Craigo had gone to the window, looking out to give her some privacy, as Caplan slipped Bethany's arms in the sleeves, trying to move her limbs as little as possible. Once on, she kneeled to zip it up for her – memories of Kenny and Emma when they were small. Bethany looked so fragile. She couldn't stand on her left leg for any length of time. It was black, blue and very swollen. She steadied herself on Caplan's shoulder.

Caplan removed her own jacket. 'Here. Sit on that. You are going to collapse anyway.' She helped the girl down and looked at the wound on the left leg. 'Craigo, there was some paper roll out near the paint thinners. Can we put a dressing on this? Some kind of support?'

'Gaffer tape, ma'am, it's very good.' And off he went, one hand holding his back.

Bethany rolled her eyes against a wave of pain, her pupils pinpoint small.

They heard him rummaging.

'He's a man, he won't be able to find anything,' said Caplan, getting the smallest of smiles. Bethany smelled terrible; stale urine, dried faeces, sweat and a sweeter smell that clouded the body. Infection brewing somewhere.

'If they find us, they'll kill us.'

'If,' replied Caplan, smiling back, subtly pulling her phone from her pocket. As she suspected, no signal.

Craigo limped back into the room, armed with two blue rolls of paper, a thin stick of wood, half of it covered in white paint and masking tape.

'That could be a splint. That leg is broken.' He pulled an unopened packet of polythene dust sheets from under his arm. He got to work, the polythene binding the leg, then the splint behind the fracture, then more polythene, then rings of tape.

Caplan watched as he worked. He had done this before, many times on animals no doubt. His podgy fingers moved swiftly as he talked to Bethany, not loud or distinct enough for her to make out the words but the singsong tone, the flow, had the right effect on the young woman, who leaned back and closed her eyes, trying not to wince.

'I have a first aid kit in the car. I'll go and get it.'

A bloodied claw of a hand gripped Craigo's wrist. 'No, don't go.'

'Well, let's see if we can get you on your feet, then get to the door? Let's try that, eh?' said Caplan.

The next minute was spent slowly easing Bethany to her feet, gingerly testing her weight on her bad leg. She said it was fine, when it obviously wasn't, but with one arm round Caplan's waist, the two women managed to hobble to the top of the stairs. And stopped.

'Just take a deep breath, Bethany,' said Craigo, taking one himself, and he picked the woman up on his shoulder in a fireman's lift, his face contorting with the effort.

At the bottom Caplan took the weight of the girl and sat her against the wall. Her face was ashen. Craigo rubbed his back and winced.

Then they heard it. A noise coming from outside. Then another.

'Backup?' Caplan said, trying not to make it sound like a question, but she was moving Bethany over to the wall behind the door. Caplan left her there and picked up her jacket.

Craigo looked out of the gap between the blind and the side of the wall, then looked at Caplan. No lights in the dark. Something about her colleague's stillness told her that no backup was coming.

'Who is it?' asked Bethany, her voice breaking. She had picked up on their concern.

'It's okay, we have help coming,' said Craigo.
'But that's not them, is it?'
'Not yet.'

Caplan gripped Bethany tighter by the elbow, holding her up against the wall, out of sight. Bethany pulled Craigo's anorak round her, her eyes widening at another unexpected sound. Somebody's laughter. A conversation. Female voices.

'I'll check. You two stay here.'

Instinctively Caplan backed onto the wall behind the door and closed it with her foot as Craigo walked out into the night. She could hear nothing once the door was closed. She crept to the far side of the window of the front room and pulled the blind back slightly, just as Craigo had done. Her heart missed a beat. Craigo was standing at the end of the cultivated garden, his arms out in supplication, talking, but she couldn't see who he was talking to.

Then four figures, barely visible in the darkness, walked towards him. Balaclavas covered their faces. Each of them held a baseball bat, two of them tapping the bat against the side of their legs, the other two holding them across their bodies, spinning the bats in a show of impatience and confidence. Craigo took a step towards them, then another, still talking. He stumbled as if his lower back gave him an unexpected jab of pain.

Then they started walking as one unit, a slow advance. In the darkness she couldn't be sure but the smaller, broader figure was male. The one with the thin legs was female. The other two were slightly behind but advancing with a determination that was alarming.

Her police training told her not to go out. Two against one at least? They were armed. And Craigo had started to back up. He wasn't coming back to take refuge in the house?

She checked her phone, but the display still showed no bars.

'What's happening?' said Bethany, still full of panic. 'They're here aren't they?'

'Nothing we can't deal with.' Caplan watched Craigo, her face pressed against the side of the window, viewing the scene unseen, seeing it all through one eye. She heard a noise behind her. Bethany was coming slowly to the window, as if trying to see what she could see.

'They're here,' she repeated, her voice a little more than a whimper.

Caplan raised a finger to her lips, keeping Craigo in sight, then rested her hand on Bethany's shoulder. Craigo was walking away, limping like the other victims. And they were moving after him, not hurrying. Why did he not outrun them? But where would he go?

The terrain was hard for both hunter and hunted. They knew which way they were sending him – away from the house, away from her and Bethany, away from the Hilux. Or was he leading them that way? She pressed her way further to the wall, trying to increase the angle. She saw Craigo stumble in a really awkward way. His right hand touched the ground, the left circled in the air. Then again, a strange stumble, and the left arm raised again, like he was bowling a cricket ball.

Out of the dark, a figure dashed up to him and held the baseball bat high, bringing it down with force on the back of his knee before withdrawing back to the pack. There seemed more of them now.

Involuntarily, Caplan shrieked quietly, willing Craigo to get back on his feet and keep moving.

'What's happening?' asked Bethany. Caplan had never heard a voice so devoid of hope.

She forced herself to stop panicking and to think strategically. They had passed the house now and were heading into the forest. None of the others had survived but Craigo had her, Bethany and the Hilux.

What was he doing? Buying them time. The Hilux was at the back, three hundred yards away. She tried to recall the map. The track went behind the house and then veered away.

'Chris?' She jumped at Bethany's voice. The girl was still leaning against the wall. But on the small finger, rising out of Craigo's anorak pocket, were the keys to the Hilux.

Caplan nodded. 'Okay. Good.' Caplan looked round at the wallpaper, the unbuilt prepacked units, the paint, the thinners, looking for anything to defend herself with.

Bethany was tearful but there was a resolve about her; her fingers were round the knife again.

Caplan said, 'We need to get to the car, quickly. Or do you want to stay? You can hide. I'll come back for you.'

'No! I'm coming.'

'You need to move. Your leg will take your weight. They are careful about the bones they break, believe me.'

They made their way out the front door, closing the door behind them, leaving it unlocked. Bethany leaned heavily on Caplan.

Then Bethany's nerve seemed to fail. She froze. 'They'll come after us.'

'They'll come after us anyway. We need to get to safety. You can still go back into the house. Last chance. It's not a decision I can make for you.'

Bethany was sobbing now. 'I'm coming. It's so sore.'

Caplan looked at her bare feet and the way the bone jutted out at an angle. In the quiet, she thought she could hear the ends snapping against each other.

She'd never make it.

'Can you get to the trees? Come on.' Caplan half carried her, Bethany hopped on her good leg, making weird noises that Caplan realised was laughing.

But they got to the nearest tree. Bethany hugged the broad trunk. 'You stay here, behind this. When you see a red 4x4 coming, check behind you then get across the path and climb in.'

'How long will you be?'

'Slow count of fifty, I'll be back.'

'If they come, they will kill me.' The left hand clasped round Caplan's torn jacket.

'They will, but they'll have to find you first. And, they've no idea where you are. So, stay here until you see the car. But they won't come after you. They are hunting other prey.' She took two steps then turned back. 'I've done this before.'

Bethany gave her a weak smile. Caplan crossed her fingers.

Running at speed on the path, in the darkness Caplan overshot the Hilux, having to turn back to reach it. She was moving cautiously now, being careful where she put her feet. Moss tuffets, dead branches. She stepped high over those that jutted up, the sharp ends of them digging into her shins. Then she heard it, a snap in the darkness to her right.

She looked up.

A figure stood there, watching her, almost invisible in the dark.

Caplan couldn't help but focus on the baseball bat being spun slowly in one hand. She took in the lie of the land. She was closer to the Hilux, but her terrain was rough. Her hunter had an easy, flatter run. Caplan was younger. The hunter was carrying a baseball bat. Her hunter was heavier. Caplan was more agile. If she got close enough, the baseball bat could do her no damage. In her youth she'd broken up mob riots at Old Firm matches with her standard-issue baton. She could cope with a mad woman with a baseball bat.

A mad woman who broke other people's legs for fun.

Caplan stood tall, assessing the other as the other assessed her.

They must have stood there for a very long minute, Caplan wanting to draw the hunter onto the rough ground. If they wanted her, they'd have to chase her.

Then the hunter raised a hand and walked away.

Caplan wasted no time. She opened the door of the Hilux then noticed that the tyres were flat, all four slashed. Caplan had no idea what that meant for her ability to steer the vehicle but she guessed she was about to find out.

The engine started, roaring through the silence of the forest. She turned the Hilux, the lack of traction making it swing wide, but she headed towards the tree where she'd left Bethany. Before, she'd been confident of going cross country, but now she had to stick to the track and even then it rocked and rolled, the steering fighting her. The noise from the rubber of the tyres being shredded against the soft earth was deafening. Once she got up to ten miles an hour, she was hanging onto the steering wheel for dear life. She saw Bethany moving in front of her and tried to slow down. The back of the vehicle swung out again.

Then Bethany was gone from her sight. For a moment she thought she'd run her over.

With the Hilux bucking and sliding from the left to the right, she looked around, then checked the rearview mirror. She could feel panic rising in her chest – images of Bill Robertson, sitting at the big table on his own, Caplan explaining it to him. They got her out alive . . . but . . .

Then she saw movement at the rear window, the door swung open and a hand reached up to hoist herself in. There was a flash of white – Bethany's face appeared over the back of the seat. 'Go.' Then she fell onto the seat as the vehicle rocked violently.

Caplan almost cried with relief, then concentrated on getting after Craigo, pulling hard on the steering, the roaring and battering coming from the tyres getting louder. She drove as fast as she dared, still painfully slowly, following the dirt track, mentally calculating the speed that Craigo, and the others, were walking at. They were moving in the same general direction that they were going now but on a constantly divergent path. Caplan knew she was fit. She'd leave Bethany lying in the back, then run across, maybe leave the engine running – they'd hear it anyway. She could attract Craigo's attention. A run back to the vehicle, they'd have a head start, and once they were in, they'd be away. Where was the gang's vehicle? She hoped like hell it was a long way back; it'd be somewhere their victims couldn't reach it. Or was it parked amongst the trees, with somebody in it, lying in wait for them to try to get past on their way out to the main road?

The solitary one was too far behind now, and if she came near the Hilux, Bethany would have her by the throat; she was as spirited as her friend Shivonne. And as angry.

Then the track came to an abrupt halt.

Caplan swore loudly and profusely, then hauled on the steering as hard as she could to perform a ten-point turn. She told Bethany to stay hidden under Craigo's jacket if that were possible. In fact, when Caplan climbed out and looked back, she couldn't see her at all. Good girl.

Caplan zipped up her anorak, making sure there was nothing light visible that might attract attention. Her suit was navy blue, her jacket black. She started moving, through the trees, her eyes scanning in front of her, looking for any movement ahead.

She came across them too soon. She was behind them, in fact. It was, she whispered the word, Slow Mo keeping up the rear. She pulled back and heard Mo call to those ahead.

A weird banshee screech responded, like demented wolves calling to each other across the tundra.

Knowing now she had her line of sight she looked ahead and could see the one she thought was male. The build, something about the way he moved, the slight limp, the roll of the shoulders; she'd seen that before. From this perspective, he seemed to be closing in on Craigo, who was still moving away but not fast enough. They were gaining on him.

Then the man shouted, letting go with a Viking warrior cry.

'Felix Vance,' she whispered, resisting the urge to shout.

She pulled back as far as she could, keeping them in sight. They were focused on looking ahead and not to their left. Caplan ran quickly. The trees were close together. She wound her way through the trunks, like an ancient dance. She moved ahead of Vance then ahead of Craigo, then crouched down, speaking low but calling his name as quietly as possible. She gave a low branch of a tree a good tug, hoping the movement would catch his eye.

Then she lost sight of him. Had he fallen? Gone a different way? She looked through the trees but could see no movement. If she tried to get closer she risked being spotted by somebody hell bent on battering her to death.

She moved forward, keeping a parallel with them, but slightly ahead. Still no sight of Craigo. Had she missed something?

Had they caught him and now they were after her?

She slipped behind a tree, carefully looking ahead, scanning the trees, looking for any sign, ignoring the little voice inside her head that said they had him. He was gone and now the best thing to do was go back to Bethany. Every step this way was a step away from her.

She leaned against the soft bark, getting her own breath, hearing fractious breathing that was not her own. Turning to look round the tree trunk she saw Craigo bending over for breath but looking in her direction.

She whispered his name, then called as loudly as she dared. He didn't hear her.

He looked over his shoulder and whatever he saw behind him, frightened him.

So Caplan threw a stick at him. It hit the ground but the movement made Craigo glance over, a tense look on his face that Caplan had never seen before. He didn't need to be told. He suddenly made a dash towards her.

A shout from the hunters filled the air, followed by a cacophony of yells and shrieks, as they knew immediately that something had happened. Caplan ran, Craigo limped after her, as fast as he could. She reached the Hilux first. The passenger door was open, the passenger seat empty. In the driver's seat was a slight figure dwarfed by a bulky jacket.

The Hilux was revving up.

Caplan jumped in. She felt, heard or sensed movement behind her and somebody shouted.

And Bethany put her foot down, holding onto the wheel with straight arms, her broken finger sticking out. Caplan looked out of her window, looking for Craigo. She hadn't seen him. He hadn't got into the rear seats.

She screamed at Bethany over the screeching and thudding noise of the bare rims on the track. 'Craigo?'

'In the back.'

She checked the back seat over her left shoulder, then her right. He wasn't there.

Then she saw his face through the rear window, swinging on the roll bar; he'd got into the flatbed and was holding on the best he could.

Caplan, feeling strangely joyous, leaned over, hands on the wheel, helping Bethany to steer. They didn't get far before Bethany slammed on the brakes. There was a dull thud and a cry of pain from the back of the Hilux.

The figures in black had cut across the forest to intercept them. All their ideas discussed in the team chats of victims being driven in a certain direction, deliberately pushing them deeper into the forest, further away from any help, suddenly made sense.

Figures stood in front of them, blocking the track. Vance and a slimmer figure that could be Wilma, stood straight-legged, hitting their hands with their baseball bats in a slow, sadistic rhythm. The other two were further back but closing in. Caplan couldn't see the others amongst the trees and the darkness.

It felt eerily quiet now the tyres had stopped their thumping and screeching. The wind gave a little song and dance to the leaves, but everything else was still.

Stand off.

They hadn't reckoned on how angry Bethany was.

She put her foot down, gunned the engine.

The Hilux jerked sideways, sparks flying from somewhere underneath. Caplan was rammed into the back of the seat.

She closed her eyes.

She expected a baseball bat to come through the window. She shielded her face, ready to help Bethany steer once they were through the human roadblock.

But whatever, whoever, hit the windscreen and splattered it with blood. Then the seat was spinning under her. There was a loud bang. The Hilux jerked to a halt.

At first all Caplan could see was blood, blood over her hands. She got out, unsteadily.

Slow Mo still lay off the track, her limbs distorted, blood gushing out the corner of her mouth.

There was steam hissing from somewhere.

The engine was still going.

She sensed movement behind her. Slow footsteps on the forest floor. She took down Ghillies, she could take down this creep. It was all about balance.

She spun round.

It was Craigo. 'Will I drive now, ma'am? You're bleeding from the head.'

'Should we stop?' she asked. 'They could still be alive.'

'We'll phone for assistance when we get a signal. The rest of them vanished into the trees but they could be back. We need to go. Now.'

They climbed in, Caplan easing Bethany's fingers from the steering wheel before moving her across into the passenger seat.

Craigo put the Hilux into gear. It ground slowly forward, driving out of the big sky.

They didn't say a word. Bethany had gone into some kind of catatonic state; eyes wide open, staring ahead.

Caplan turned around, looking behind them, fearful that somebody might be following and not knowing what to do if they were. She looked back at the track, narrowing into the near distance, and saw two trees that had outgrown their roots and toppled, getting caught in their neighbours, forming a perfect W.

NINETEEN

Caplan was sitting on the swing seat, a blanket wrapped round her to ward off the chill of an autumnal night. She was supposed to be reading notes, trying to compose the report she had to construct tomorrow about Felix Vance, but the beauty and stillness of the sky was a distraction.

While she was sitting, Kenny was annoying Pas De Chat, Pavlova and the kittens with a stick. The cats were getting the better of him.

Her mobile rang, loud in the still night air.

'What it is, Sarah?'

'Good news. Bethany's out of surgery. She's got more metal in her now than the Forth Road Bridge. How's McPhee?'

'He's doing okay. As expected, they found benzodiazepine, probably midazolam, in his system. She was poisoning him, all because he wouldn't put her name on the deeds of his flat. He thought he loved her, but he knew – maybe sensed is a better word – that something was wrong.'

'Did you doubt him for a moment?'

'No. I know him too well. She was pressurising him to go for promotion, to get more money, to move to Glasgow, isolating him from family and friends. And she lied about her age. He's convinced that Carrie-Louise has something wrong with her, and he's right. She's a violent, manipulative little gaslighter.'

'Say what you mean, why don't you. If his head's that messed up, get the wee monkey to talk to him. Wee Craig.'

'Craigo.'

'He'll sort him out, man to monkey, homespun truths and all that fireplace chit-chat about home baking over a fine whisky. Any more of this crap and I might go and talk to him myself. Rachel has taken a turn for the worse. Rory Ghillies wants to know what you're up to. The hunt for Felix Vance is all over the wire and Rory is furious.'

'Furious with me more than upset about Rachel?'

'Oh yes. Whatever you are doing, you keep doing it.'

'I'm after Felix Vance. And Rory Mr OBE Ghillies.'

'Vance is too clever. He was only playing the game until somebody rumbled him. He always had his escape planned. I think he threw the others under the bus, or under the Hilux in your case. Good luck, but you're wasting your time.'

'I've one question for you. Did Rory know? Did he hint to his friend that he might like to get rid of Bethany? She was getting clingy. Rachel wouldn't last long. I think their ideas of the future might have been divergent.'

'I've thought of that. I really don't know. It's possible.'

'The close relationship is Vance/Ghillies, not Ghillies/Robertson, and . . .'

'I want to meet you tomorrow. I have something for you.'

Linden rang off.

Caplan dropped her phone on the cushion beside her, smiling as Moe the kitten sank his teeth into Kenny's leg.

She'd spent a fruitful hour with a forensic psychologist who had been impressed with the picture of Manson's female followers now back up on the wall. It showed the team had some understanding of the mindset they were dealing with. Vance and his crew.

Caplan decided to agree.

From what they had put together, Felix Vance had made a lot of money living in London, then decided he'd have a better quality of life back home. By a malevolent turn of fate, or by design, Vance rekindled the relationship with the Maitlands, a family he and Wilma knew growing up. Back in the day they had formed a posse; Felix, Wilma and the five Maitland girls. Four of them grew up in difficult circumstances. Morag, Morna, Morven and Moira, while Maureen, the youngest, was brought up by an aunt and lived a relatively easier life.

While there was no 'Mo', they were all Mo. Interchangeable Mo. Two were dead. One was hit by the Hilux and killed instantly. The other was fatally injured by a glancing blow from the vehicle that threw her body wide, impaling her on a broken branch. Caplan neither knew or cared who lived and who died. All that mattered was Maureen was being kept at a secure location and was being very helpful. Or very manipulative.

The psychologist suggested that they had invented a game. How did that start? Kicking a homeless person? Picking up a homeless person then dumping them in the woods? Then the game got nasty, and organised, each egging the other on, each taking their part. Vance sent the women out to volunteer in charity institutions, using each other's paperwork, in some cases, their ID backed up by a reference from Vance, the pillar of the community, or a senior police officer. Then, from the vulnerable people, they picked a subject. The subject would disappear. They'd be held against their will, tortured, weakened and then set free in the middle of nowhere. Then chased down and killed.

Vance lived a life on the verge of being bored. There was nothing he couldn't do in business. In his own way, keeping one hand on the helm of the business, he developed an addiction to the thrill of dangerous sports like skydiving and Formula 3. His insurance for that became problematic after he hit forty, and the injury to his left leg started to bother him. His thrill seeking took on a darker edge. Caplan couldn't imagine how that conversation would start; she found it all hard to accept. The psychologist asked her to think about Charles Manson. People who aren't susceptible to that kind of charm don't see it, but Vance's Moes, in their own way, were full of love and devotion for him. They lived in houses that Vance rented to them. Vance gave them jobs, looked after them, and kept the sisters together. 'Optimism bias' pulls them in; *my life is rubbish, Felix makes it better so I'm sticking with Felix*. They'd see him as inspired. He was the one who transformed their lives. They believed they owed him everything. 'Don't mock them, Christine, just be glad you don't have that mindset,' the psychologist said.

They started with easy targets, those who wouldn't be missed, those who couldn't fight back. Those that might prove too much of a challenge would be left alone.

Until they upped the ante.

The psychologist, sensing Caplan's cynicism, tried again to explain the bond that existed between them, a friendship that had lasted forty years or more, and was still holding strong. Vance owned the Maitlands and they, in turn, both hid under his protection and were too scared to escape.

This feast had been a long time cooking.

The gang – all in their fifties or older – were physically compromised before they started, so they compromised their prey as well. Drugged, weakened by hunger, unable to move fast because of that telltale injury to the left leg which echoed closely the injury that had curbed Vance's own hobby as a skydiver. With each one they upped the game again, ending in taking a young woman who was loved and would be missed, then performing, like Jack the Ripper, a double event. Taking one in a busy park in broad daylight, the other from a town centre at night. They were on familiar ground with Bethany apart from the fact that she would be missed, but only by her father. The gang bit off more than they could chew with Shiv, who didn't go down without a vicious fight. Her bite to Morna's arm had really closed the case for them. Caplan wasn't sure how much Ghillies knew. But he wasn't a stupid man, and both his girlfriends had been abducted.

That power Vance had over Ghillies, and vice versa. Or was it a mutual back-slapping? Ghillies had gained by the convenient death of his previous mistress, Lisa Stratton.

Ghillies in the middle of it all. Robertson pressing him for help for Bethany, Ghillies thinking that if he brought it to the attention of his old colleagues, he might retain some control. The troublesome mistress was gone. The troublesome goddaughter was gone. His embarrassing wife was going. Her tragic passing might even hasten his OBE.

To Vance, Ghillies and Robertson were a means to an end, nothing more.

Meanwhile the Moes would be out in the field. Working for Spire, for Fayer, for Albion, keeping an eye out for ideal properties. Volunteering in places, looking for victims.

Caplan wasn't sure where the Dark Sky thing came in; maybe it upped the ante to let their victims run free under a clear sky. Or maybe the properties were there in the first place due to the Dark Sky designation. How did anybody make sense of any of it?

The protocol was clear now though. The victim was lured by their own personal bait. From there on in, they were unwittingly playing a game they wouldn't survive. They'd be allowed to escape, not knowing that their captors were probably ten feet away armed with baseball bats, ready for the slow chase.

Did they have some kind of wager on how long it would take them to catch up with their prey? And Craigo had pointed out that they could be guided to run in a certain direction, as border collies would drive sheep. The prey were never allowed to run along the smooth path, they were forced into the deep wood. Moving through that would sap the energy of the fittest.

Two of the victims had taken the chance to double back to the property, where one had died 'peacefully' and the other had survived.

Even the exit plan showed control. The Mo they had abandoned,

Maureen, was the one who was most terrified of talking. Caplan had called in some of the best interviewers she knew but still the woman was saying nothing. Such was the power and control of Vance.

And where was Vance now? Where was the lovely Wilma? The two remaining Maitland sisters? Nobody knew.

Still, the world was a small place.

Caplan looked at the notebook lying open on the cushion, still a blank page.

How the hell was she supposed to write this up?

Kenny bent down to pick up the feral Pavlova and got a handful of scratches for his trouble. The cat came trotting back to Caplan and hid under the chair.

How much pleasure had Vance taken in controlling the amount of distress and emotional pain that Robertson was in?

Aklen joined her on the seat and looked at the notebook. He picked it up and flung it over the back of the chair.

'Tell them your team did an excellent job. These victims were difficult to track with their chaotic lifestyles and vulnerability. I've heard you say it a hundred times.' Aklen was looking out over the ebony water, blending into the sable sky. Bright stars, more than Caplan had ever seen, twinkled above. A wide arc of stars, as fine as snow, was visible near the horizon; the Milky Way.

So many stars.

She hoped there was one up there for Shivonne, a young woman who had never had the chance to shine. There was Kenny, at the water's edge, staring out to the darkness, lost in his own thoughts.

Caplan felt tearful. For some reason she was thinking about what Rod Taylor had thought when that pillow was put over his face, when he'd felt the compression on his chest. Betrayed, by the person who he had loved. Why could they not sit down and talk about the issues they were having?

'You've heard me say it a hundred times. I thought you never listened to anything I said,' said Caplan.

'I do, sometimes. Occasionally.' He pulled her to him and kissed her on the forehead.

Sarah Linden got out of her car and walked towards Caplan who was already waiting, sitting on the sea wall.

'So here we are. Having called me to a remote location for a rendezvous, I presume you are auditioning for a spy thriller? Are you not supposed to sidle up to me and say something like the swans fly north in the winter?' asked Caplan.

Linden lit up a cigarette. 'The mummified body at Doon Alba is Troy Adamson. He still has scars of fistulas in both groins, so a substance abuser, probably heroin. He did what Bethany did. He escaped in daylight and used his burglary skills to break into the house he'd just escaped from. He crawled in there and slid into the eternal night as they say. The blood on the sheeting was a DNA match for a Jamie Wilkes, last seen in April 2019. His body has never been found. Ryce actually patted me on my shoulder, but I'll take my jam where I can. We stopped God knows how many more.'

Caplan winced at the word 'we' and stepped out of the cloud of her friend's cigarette smoke. 'Were they on Rachel's list?'

'They were. Ryce says she's not the only pathologist who is waking up in the middle of the night with a faint, probably incorrect, memory of an unidentified body with a bad leg and a missing tooth they thought was lost in a fight.'

'Operation Wandsworth is going ahead – all the bells and whistles they could want.' Caplan sighed. 'Sixteen cases altogether. Folk are now coming out the woodwork claiming that missing relatives have not been investigated with due diligence. Lizzie texted me yesterday with a winky face emoji, asking me how fucking unpopular did I want to be.'

'Well, I felt like shit. I was thinking how great it was for our Misper clearance rate. I could've got a promotion out of this.' Linden chuckled. 'Pottie's funeral had a free bar. Four people were arrested. His grandmother's going to keep his ashes on her mantlepiece, to be scattered with her when the time comes. At least she'll know where the wee bastard is.'

'I heard Stevie turned up at Rod's funeral.'

'Her husband has thrown her out. If he had thrown her out before Todd found out, two people might still be alive. And as for Rod and Todd, their respective distant families have started fighting over who gets what already.'

'Parasites. Why are we here?'

'Here's an envelope – it arrived for you at HQ. Be careful how you open it.'

Caplan took it. 'Feels like a card. Do you mean gloves type of be careful or blow up in my face type of be careful.'

'Just open it.'

It was a card indeed. On the front was a black and white still from *The Wizard of Oz*; Dorothy and the Tinman. Inside was written, in large loopy lettering, *Until we meet again! Felix.*

Caplan pursed her lips. 'I'll get that logged.'

They watched the waves for a moment, Caplan thinking of the blood on the windscreen of the Hilux, the chilling thud of flesh on metal.

Linden was quiet.

'Did you come all this way to play postie?'

'I'm not really sure what to say to be honest. Can I trust you, Christine? I need your advice. If you'd rather not know what I'm about to tell you then say so and I'll get in my car and drive away.'

'Will anybody die?'

'No.'

'Will I be chased by psychos through a dark wood?'

'No.'

'Let's have a conversation as friends then. What's the worst that can happen? But let me go first. Do you think Rory knew? How much did he know?'

'I think he must have known but could have convinced himself he didn't. He was very good at compartmentalising his life.'

'We have no direct evidence linking him with Bethany's disappearance. That worries me.'

Linden took a deep breath of sea air. 'Don't let it. Lisa Stratton?'

'One of the two victims that didn't fit. Her and Bethany. And Maitland claims Stratton wasn't part of The Game. Was somebody else responsible?'

'Maitland didn't recognise Stratton. With opening the cases up again, some of the evidence is being examined – forensically re-examined.'

'It should have been forensically examined in the first place,' muttered Caplan.

'There's talk of that investigation being subject to gentle pressure. But there was a DNA sample on her necklace. It's now been tested fully and McEwan was very keen to show me that the sample showed a close match to a PC in Edinburgh, Mylo Reynolds. He hadn't been at the scene. Reynolds is the son of Terry and Joanna Reynolds. Joanna Reynolds's maiden name is Ghillies. She's the younger sister of Rory Ghillies. Rory's DNA is no longer on the system, because he's no longer a serving police officer, and he for most of his career would not have been near a crime scene. Even then, he requested that his DNA was removed. He did that three months before Stratton went missing.'

Caplan couldn't look at Linden. She kept staring out to sea, thinking that she had seen a dolphin's dorsal fin arc through the water, then another and another, then nothing but the grey waves. 'What are you saying? Rory Ghillies was at the deposition site.'

'No, more that he had handled the necklace at some point. Do you have another reason for his DNA being there?'

'Do you think Lisa was murdered when she was because there was a new young lady on the horizon? Bethany?'

Linden snorted. 'And by who? My money's on Rory. He's desperate to find out what I know. You could ask Rachel for clarification. She's the one who told you about Lisa.'

'And now I know why.' Caplan smiled bitterly. 'Why don't you ask her yourself? Because you were involved with Rory?'

Linden pulled a face. 'We were involved before.'

'Oh,' said Caplan. 'He's an old flame?'

'More damp squib.'

Caplan thought, then said, 'Does Rachel think that Rory had Lisa murdered?'

'Maybe.'

'I don't mean, go out and murder her. I mean *she's a nuisance* and there's an inbuilt murder protocol, so they followed it.'

'Then Rory gets involved with Bethany. It would look bad for the OBE if he was having an affair while his wife was dying.'

'Murdering his bit on the side might have put a bit of a damper on it as well.'

'As would shagging his goddaughter.'

The hospital car park was quiet. Caplan sat in her car for a moment and texted Bill Robertson, asking if he was at the hospital and where they could meet. He was already at the door when Caplan got there. He looked as if he had aged ten years. And he was close to tears.

'She's not awake,' he said, by way of apology.

'Sleep is the best medicine there is.'

He updated her on Bethany's progress as they climbed the stairs to the ward. She was healing fine; the fibula fracture had been set properly. She'd probably recover without a limp. Her bloods were normal; things were looking good.

She was lying in the bed, a thin duvet over her. The fluffy owl from her bedroom at home was perched on the headboard. The smaller one, still squashed from being in the evidence bag, was sitting on the bedside unit, nestled in a box of tissues. Beside them was another fluffy bird, this one brand new. Bethany herself looked much thinner, and childlike.

'Does she know about Shivonne?'

Bill shook his head. 'Have you caught the bastards that did this?'

'Their house of cards is tumbling. Don't you worry about that.'

Robertson was surprised by the anger in her voice. 'More power to you.'

'You'll have your hands full here. Her mental recovery will be a long haul.'

Robertson took a few steps back from the bed, indicating that Caplan should follow.

'You might not be able to answer this but, Rory?'

'Not the friend you thought, Mr Robertson. But you don't need to worry about him or Vance. That's my job. You have a lovely daughter; you look after her.'

'Somebody thinks so. The big owl was a present from somebody called Lochran.'

Caplan smiled. 'I hear he's a nice guy.'

'Will she have to see them in court? I don't think she could go through that.'

'The legal system can be very sympathetic. The one thing I would like her to do is listen to some recordings when the time comes. They kept their faces covered but she knows their voices. She recognised Vance by his aftershave. And, from her behaviour when she was driving, she'll be happy to help nail them. She's a strong-minded lady.'

'Takes after her mother.'

She patted the man on the shoulder. He went to sit at the bedside with his only child and his thoughts.

The hospice was dark, with low level cream light falling over the blue floor like an early dawn over a calm sea. There was nobody at the desk. The two nurses were in with a patient. Caplan could see them through a large glass pane, moving around the room, slowly and silently, then one leaned over the bed, holding the patient's hand. The other nurse cupped her hand to the patient's forehead; a delicate touch, a humane gesture. Caplan couldn't help but notice how young the patient looked. Early thirties maybe? Far too young. The nurse adjusted the drip with a flicking of the forefinger. One of them looked up and caught Caplan's eye. Caplan raised her warrant card, receiving a small smile and a gesture that resembled a nod of approval. As the nurse turned away, she was back lit, her hair on top of her head shining like a halo.

Looking like a ghost in the light, Caplan walked along the short corridor, passed the mural of flowers, to the room where Rachel was lying. The thinnest of duvets was folded halfway down the bed, lying across her waist. Caplan didn't think it would have been possible for Rachel to lose any more weight, but she had. Any light in the room came from the gentle daylight lamp, sitting on the floor, used as a night light. Much of the equipment had been removed. There was, she thought, the faint noise of some classical music floating down from somewhere. With her fingers on the door handle, she paused, listening. 'The Dying Swan.'

She had danced that once. More than once. The slow descent onto the stage and then one final flutter before closing up and falling for the final time. It had been hard, but she had danced well. Or so she liked to think.

The Dying Swan. How apposite was that?

Waiting. Was Rachel waiting for her to come along and pass on her news? If her prognosis was accurate, then Rachel was staying alive for something. Maybe this was it.

She entered the room as quietly as possible. The music was a little louder in here. She could smell something scented. There was a bottle of Chanel No 9 on the side table, a tub of moisturiser, a lip stick and a hairbrush.

Rachel herself was little more than a skeleton lying on the bed, cheeks sunken, almost bald, her mouth open, gaping, lips drawn back over her teeth.

She felt her old colleague was waiting to hear what she had to say, and the hearing was the last sense to go. Caplan walked round the bed, pulled a chair over and sat down beside the small bedside unit. She leaned forward, both elbows on the bed, her fingers folded together, as if in prayer.

She leaned close to the side of the bony face, the curve of her cheek, the ear that looked too large to belong to her elfin face. It was almost amusing.

'I hope you can hear me, Rachel. You need to know that we got them, we got them all.' She lied. 'You were right. Felix Vance, Wilma, who you had the measure of from the start. And the Maitlands. I'm not sure who was brainwashing who. Quite frankly, I am past caring. We nailed the bastards. You suspected Rory, didn't you? You knew about Lisa Stratton. Rory thought nobody was going to touch him for that while he had friends in high places. They are bringing him in for questioning tomorrow. I expect him to be arrested. I thought that you'd like to know.'

She looked at the slow rise and fall of the light-blue blanket, the gap between the fall and the rise was starting to lengthen, Rachel's breath was lingering.

For a moment, Caplan thought her old colleague had slipped away. Then she saw the mouth move, gathering her strength for one word. It was a long time coming.

'Thanks.'

'No problem.'

The breathing continued, each breath slightly more laboured than the last.

'Rachel? Do you want me to get somebody?'

'Stay.'

So she did.

Caplan sat for a while, listening to the music; it had always calmed her. This must be what Rachel had asked for; something that was precious to them both, but they had never shared it. Would they have been friends if they had known each other better?

Who knew? It was too late now.

Caplan kept hold of the warm bundle of bones in her hand. The cannula had gone, the wedding ring had gone. Each absence had its own significance. She looked around the room, thinking about this woman, this woman's life. It was a privilege to be here at this time. She'd been in circumstances similar to this before, four times. In an emergency, she knew what to do; keep talking, keep reassuring them, let them know that she was there, that they were not alone. She'd thought she was good at that.

The room was very warm. Reaching to get a bottle of water from her handbag, she saw lying upright, tucked into the shelf, a purple Moleskin notebook.

'Read.'

Caplan looked up to see Rachel's eyes had opened. A weak smile floated over her face. 'For your eyes only.' The lips closed then fluttered a little, then said, 'Bond Girl.'

'Nobody's called me that in a long time. I took your husband down though. He deserved it,' Caplan whispered, sliding the notebook out, seeing the lottery ticket, and a picture taken from a distance but clear enough to see Rory with his arm round Bethany. Their faces were turned towards each other. It wasn't godfather and goddaughter; it was much more than that.

Caplan looked at Rachel, her eyes open now, looking right back at her. 'You knew?'

Rachel nodded, pursing her lips, gearing up for something. 'He has to know I knew.' She closed her eyes. 'Hold my hand and read. He has to know, I knew.'

Caplan took the hand again, tighter this time, and placed the notebook open on the bed. Rachel's fingers crawled across the duvet cover, reaching out for it, feeling the pages. Caplan started to read the handwritten words; a flowing script written by a fountain pen.

The Grim Reaper never shouts.

He whispers as he taps you on the shoulder.

I still smile at the irony of thinking that I've been blessed, as I have time; time to think, time to plan. It's something not given to many of us, a few moments of reflection, to put right a few wrongs, to say my goodbyes.

The dying is definitely for the now.

And it is for me.

It's all going, slowing slipping, and I am focusing on one thing: the clock. Don't wait too long as you never know how long you have.

There's more to life than life.

There's always love.

And revenge.